Sailor and librarian, navigator and researcher, teacher and trainer, and—always—a traveller: Chris Armstrong has had three careers, working as a merchant seaman, a farmhand on the farm where he still lives, and as an information scientist before retiring to become a poet and writer. He has one collection of poems in print, *Mostly Welsh* (Y Lolfa, 2019). Although initially entirely focussed on poetry, his writing has branched into short stories and works of fiction including this volume, *The Dark Trilogy*. He has published elsewhere: in *Storgy, Agenda* and *London Grip New Poetry* for example. Although born in Sussex, he has lived in a cottage in the mountains of Mid Wales most of his life.

To my good friends, Ray Lonsdale, Ioan Williams and Margaret Williams who read so many drafts and yet still encouraged me.

Chris Armstrong

THE DARK TRILOGY

AUSTIN MACAULEY PUBLISHERS™

LONDON * CAMBRIDGE * NEW YORK * SHARJAH

A CIP catalogue record for this title is available from the British Library.

ISBN 9781398434066 (Paperback)
ISBN 9781398434073 (ePub e-book)

www.austinmacauley.com

First Published 2022
Austin Macauley Publishers Ltd®
1 Canada Square
Canary Wharf
London
E14 5AA

Table of Contents

Agon

So, a beginning. The agon, that conflict of my personae, that conflict of my characters. Today, the wind has been blowing from the west and the rain, which has kept me from the little garden surrounding my cottage for the past week, continues on and off: then it was sunny…

As I drove slowly along the country roads towards home, through the leafy shades, between the high hedges and patches of sunlight, past hamlets and villages, my mind ran back to the many times I had passed this way before. Times almost half a century ago when we were new to both the country and the countryside, when we drove to explore and expand our territory, sometimes trying some smaller lanes or alternative routes, but always inevitably heading inland and south, away from the sea—she would always, instinctively, draw me away from the sea, the sea that had been the first, or perhaps, after him, the second, to lay claim to my spirit—towards the cottage. Drawn to it—an ironic spin—as if it were some gentle maelstrom sucking us in and we were no more able to escape its pull than pieces of driftwood in the ocean. Its Bardic mysticism as strange to us then as the language.

Of course, I saw his darker Gnostic soul was drawn to that—he told me later that both systems stress the fluidity of personal spiritual growth (the Druids would say the *awen*) over any fixed set of beliefs. And he was never one for those! Tempting his soul, and so maybe mine too… his influence was strong even then so that perhaps I had already begun to feel or imagine that I felt the need for some sort of further release from conformity. And it did not matter, I thought, if it came from book learning or old teachings—both of them would teach me.

I can hear his deep voice now as he quoted Plato: 'The only one true reality is spiritual; because unlike physical reality, it is eternal and unchanging.' Hers, more musically, quoting a Lowry poem: "He reads and reads, this poet to be…

He reads and reads, but does not understand / Set at a tangent even in his own land." I make no response. I have no response. Yet.

In my mind, we all seem to have been together forever and the magnetism is becoming ever stronger so naturally, I see us as some sort of an existential congeries or *élan vital* intermingling our life forces as fate deems necessary. I loved them both dearly. Intensely. We were a sacred trinity that seemed the very centre of existence as my world spun on its fateful course, and there were times when we could not tell ourselves apart. Although, strangely, we were rarely all in one place—I think I remember only one gathering together of the three of us. Perhaps two.

In those days, the cars had been older, less reliable; sometimes smaller, and once—in the very early days—the cockpit was often open to the skies. Now I cruise in air-conditioned comfort along the same roads through a countryside that has changed little over the years. It is strange to think how many times these same trees have shaded my passing, how many times I had passed over the little stream in the village before relishing the last minutes of approach to the little cottage that has been my home since the country embraced us. So many years, so many years!

This time, today, I stopped in the little parking spot to the north of the bridge and leaving the car walked down to the bridge over the rill that is almost a stream and gazed down at the trickle of water as it rippled and splashed over the stones behind the public house flowing into its own moist future. Mesmerised by both my own and its past, I dreamed my way home with the wind in my hair and the car's canvas top down—through the village and past the little school before the road dipped into a little valley and rose past some outlying houses to bend into an avenue of old beech trees—the younger of two such avenues around the farm, the trees in the other bounding an old farm track on the far side of the cottage were decades older—before straightening out just at the point where I would turn up the little lane to reach the cottage.

We didn't often stop here by the road bridge over the stream, but in my mind's eye, the spot a little further upstream into its bubbling past where we sometimes picnicked is crystal clear. I can see her paddling from the little beach with the breeze blowing her lovely auburn hair, one hand to her ear holding strands out of her eyes and the other outstretched towards some primroses on the bank. I see the fresh green of new ferns and the dapple of sunlight through some oak saplings and a young rowan; long grasses dipping into the stream's flow under the bank: I hear her happy laugh at the cold water and am so many years younger!

How often did I have company as I drove these roads? In truth, I can say that it was always, for if it was not physical, their spirit drove with me… or perhaps I should say drove me. Once I came to know companionship and love, his first and then hers, there was no escape. And indeed there was no wish to escape—I was in thrall, and happily so, and led through life. He led me to my manhood and she led me away from my sea to her books, to their books, to learning and enlightenment. I remember every moment of our times together: all of our actions are come together in my mind.

I remember once driving back from the little university town in a winter's night that was white with a sudden heavy snowstorm—the roads treacherous and slippery as we climbed into the hills. My whole focus was on the road—on the driving—to the extent that I became almost unaware of the dark figure in the seat beside me. We had been talking, as we left town, about words, about their play, about their careful and precise use to conjure feeling (I was returning from a performance at the theatre) and inevitably, thoughts moved on to my early poems—I think about their shortcomings, particularly their narrow, self-serving—how I recoiled from that word—focus, which perhaps detracted from their possible strength as a collection.

And then, with most of the journey done, breasting one shallow hill, we came upon cars stopped in the road failing in their traction on the slope ahead and all literary thoughts fled before the need to navigate on the icy surface.

Other journeys were more pleasant, less sombrely dark and cold, and the head beside me shone auburn in the sun, laughing at my sincerity and care. Then, I was not writing and had no dark shade at my shoulder. The talk was of love, of the future we imagined lay ahead of us, and I think we were happy. How could we not have been? The spectres—daemons—of the past had been conquered, we were in love and the world was ours. Little did I know how short a time we had. And in that short sentence, I am plunged once more into those dark months that took us to eternity.

They began with so many medics in so many clinics; there was a period when we visited herbalists and other kinds of quackery. All to no avail. The evil that was in her would have its way. I see her pale face on the pillows, the pain so briefly lost to her as she slept, or propped up when someone visited desperately trying to hide her struggles. I would lie beside her trying to bring her warmth, to lend strength, and my mind would wander as she slept so that I would remember the good times we had shared when even so slight an embrace would have led to passion and that deepest of joys when two souls meet in harmony. I must have moved because she groaned and came back to her pain. He was not there to see her distress—I do not think he could have borne it and he stayed away, a subliminal presence that only I acknowledged.

Of course, not all of our driving was in the countryside—even in the country—that surrounded our little cottage. Some journeys led back into a wider world, into the past, visiting friends and relatives from former lives—staying with them and enjoying their company until—I think—our complete and untrammelled self-sufficiency and introversion began to wear on them and, fleeing their companionship, I returned us to our little home. I remember one winter journey back, crossing the mountains near the cottage in thick fog when it was necessary to peer out of the open car doors to see the edges of the road and save the car from dropping over the edge into the valley. Another time—snow again—my little car failed and we made most of the journey on the back of a rescue truck! But these were only little adventures and my companion was one with me in enjoying their slightly darker frisson of destiny.

But now, as I come back in the present to bring my memories together in this little narrative, and begin again the hunt though my notebooks and diaries, to explore all those old images, the past does not seem so remote. In many ways, it is almost more real than the present, more in my mind. I am more *of* my mind and less about my surroundings. So what of that past? What peculiar aspect makes it so special? In one sense the answer is simple: it is love.

In another, it passes all understanding—it is so deeply incomprehensible that it has almost robbed me of reason, has sometimes left me locked into a reclusive spiritual world that is often unaware of the friends surrounding me, buried in my books and the papers at my desk, writing and writing. Thanks be to all of the gods that it has not often robbed me of my lucidity.

He will be waiting for me in the cottage—my editorial alter-ego, and of course, she will be there too. How could they not be? They are my past and my future. They are what balanced my life and allowed in some sanity! They are my unconquerable nemeses for I have learned that I can never defeat my past. Never forget. Why would I want to? This whole project—this *writing*—is one more, the final, turn of the wheel, one more balancing act of reason. A final resolution in my psyche, a resolution of my voice. And so I turn up the lane once more, crest the little hill at the exact point the old Roman Road—the Sarn Helen—crosses the lane and slip downhill past the ugly new farm house and the entrance to the top yard, still unsurfaced after all these years, to turn right into the lower yard just before the lane makes its sharp bend to the left by the entrance to the new sheds.

The cottage—the old farmhouse—lies out of sight from the lane behind the sheds, making the third side of an older farm yard, the fourth, easterly side being open to the fields and an old farm track—the track that passes under the ancient beech trees. Of course, we were entranced by this little home with its own garden walled with those strange pointed stones from some demolished mansion. Of course we were! It was to be our first home and we explored it joyfully! Its kitchen with its possibly defunct Rayburn, its lounge with a Welsh dresser and unmatched armchairs, its three little bedrooms up a winding stair hidden behind a door.

And at the rattle and drag of the old gate—long fallen on its hinges—they come out to meet me, these ghosts of my past and my present, these pneumata. So here we all are at last: the lovers and loved, the leaders and the led, the teachers and the taught. Once more—for perhaps only the third time—brought together to pray over our past… or to prey on a past that brought us here to the hills of the Bards. And what has it all taught me? This long introspection. He would say that as we become ever more immersed in my writing and poetry I have grown spiritually, at least to the extent that—in his Gnostic terms—I am no longer merely sarkic!

A perhaps surprising acknowledgement that I have risen above worldly and ignorant, instinctive thinking: that iniquity of the flesh. It is true I am—have always been—oriented toward growth in knowledge, and I think in my writing I do explore new ideas, I would have to say, as well as the past. I do not think my lovely muse would agree, I am sure she sees in my verse an unhealthy dwelling on our past. Perhaps she means, the past that might have been. I hope the Bards—and she—will at least acknowledge a growth towards destiny in my awen. I like to imagine that I have become a man at peace with his life. His lives.

And so, we come to the crux of the matter. The labour has been slow and painful, and not a little messy as my demons were exorcised, but now that I have successfully followed the trail through my personal Gehenna, and emerged with a tale to tell—I hope you will forgive this agonised cry, my last words, and we may begin

Book I
Dark Ashes

Some would argue that no genre is more fictitious than a biography.

—Carlos Ruiz Zafon

Foreword

I first came across Vladimir Nabokov in the late sixties or early seventies when I read, and immensely enjoyed, *Ada*. The pleasure came not so much from the story itself but from the beautiful use of language—something that has stayed with me ever since. Even when writing my dry academic reports and articles, the need to use the 'right' word for a perfect emphasis or cadence was never far away! It was my good friend, Trystan Lewis—both the subject and instigator of this work—who once wrote of his own use of language, "I think it is the colour of the words… or not so much their colour as those subtle hints of luminescence that surround them, lighting up the passage to show dimensions that would otherwise be lost to the reader, that attracts me." [1] But, back to Nabokov!

The infamous *Lolita*—by no means his best work, I came across much later and after I had read several other titles, including *The Gift*, *Despair* and *Pale Fire*. There was no plan or structure to my reading of Nabokov—these were the days of browsing second-hand bookshops, and while they all always had copies of Charles Lamb's *Tales from Shakespeare*, Nabokov was a rarer find! Always to be devoured on the day of purchase. I know that Trystan Lewis, also read his work with a similar enjoyment—one of the many loves we have shared over the years, although I suspect he bought them new and unsullied on the day that they arrived in the shops from the publisher.

Apparently, my copy of *Pale Fire* was given to Len by Doris for Christmas in 1973, so it must have been a while after that it fell into my hands, some ten years after it was first published. *Pale Fire* is unusual in that it is a 30 page poem in four cantos, some nine hundred and ninety-nine lines, said in the Foreword to be written by a dear friend, John Shade. This is followed by a commentary of notes apparently by Shade's editor and friend, Charles Kinbote, that is some six times longer than the poem itself and which readers are advised to read before

---

[1] Private correspondence: Letter from Trystan Lewis to Chris Armstrong, August 2018

the poem. In it, their author does not so much explain the lines in the poem but expands on them in prose, sometimes taking a single word or phrase as a starting point.

Line 130—I never bounced a ball or swung a bat—gives rise to over fourteen pages which elide by way of a note about four verses discarded in the Fair Copy and a reported request in a Dulwich park from Shade, "Tell me more," he would say as he knocked his pipe empty against a beech trunk, to a parallel story of Zemblan royalty ("Zembla, my dear country," notes Kinbote elsewhere) with a story of a King held captive in a "South West Tower" during a revolution, and a description—a mischievous memory's glimpse of a time past triggered by nothing more than a bedside light gleaming on the gilt key in a closet door—of an adventure some three decades earlier when as a 'dark strong lad of thirteen', he played with Oleg, the handsome twelve-year-old Duke of Rahl!

While the poem here published does not pretend to the excellence and power of *Pale Fire*, nor its poet to approach the fame and stature of Vladimir Nabokov, I am privileged to have been asked by him to act as editor and explicator to this edition. Having written that rather negative sounding first sentence, I should add that Trystan Lewis is a poet of some repute, well-known internationally as a man of letters and a bon viveur of the literary world, constantly in demand at literary festivals and conferences. I might call him a socialite—he certainly has mixed in society's better circles—but that would be to downplay his real strength as a speaker, writer and poet with a truly extraordinary knowledge of world literature. That a birth led him to mix with a society that included rulers and royalty is of no immediate consequence here. That he educated himself some years after he had left school, is!

Lewis has written some 450 poems—mostly shorter than this one and mostly requiring little or no explanation, and some of which I am lucky enough to have acquired in my collection; but his longer poems are more abstruse—he would have been the first to admit—and I shall be worked hard by this one, although I have known it since before it was first published and he had discussed some parts with me as they were being written! Even without reference to my commentary, it will be clear to the reader that the poem is some sort of an autobiography of at least a part of the poet's life—Lewis was an intensely private man so even the *idea* of this poem is in itself surprising and I know it would have been a difficult project for him, which may well explain why he feels the poem will now benefit from some elaboration.

I know that Lewis had read all of Durrell's works early in his life—I remember him quoting some lines from early in the first book of *The Avignon Quintet* to me once in Italy: "Reality is too old-fashioned nowadays for the writer's uses. We must count upon art to revive it and bring it up to date." [2] Strangely, in all our talks, we never discussed his reasons for producing such a work but I think that I probably understood that it was cathartic, or perhaps like any autobiography, such writings simply offer their authors—if I may borrow Carlos Ruiz Zafon's words, albeit from his description of a literary cafe—"the chance to look at themselves in the mirror of memory and for a moment believe they'll live forever." [3]

More prosaically and perhaps rather more negatively, Evelyn Waugh wrote, "Only when one has lost all curiosity about the future has one reached the age to write an autobiography" [4], but I cannot see Lewis as incurious. In his note to me, Lewis wrote, "Christo"—he used the old schoolboy nickname he had coined all those years ago—"Christo, having known me for most of my life, I know that you will be able to unravel the often difficult themes and thinking lying behind the lines of the work I am now calling 'Dark Ashes'—but I leave to you the decisions on how you may explain my mind, or indeed my life."

I trust his faith is not misplaced, but can think of no one better able to undertake the task: my intimate friendship and knowledge of his life can only add value to the necessary scholarship that I can offer [5]. His letter went on, "It seems appropriate at the same time to ask you to take on the role of my literary executor and archivist after my death—a task I do not envisage troubling you for

---

[2] Lawrence Durrell (1974) *Monsieur, The Avignon Quintet.* London Faber & Faber, 1992. p.7 (Spoken by his character, the writer, Rob Sutcliffe.) Now, I am unsure whether he was talking of his art or mine.

[3] Carlos Ruiz Zafon (2018) *The Labyrinth of the Spirit* (Volume 4 of The Cemetery of Forgotten Books). Translated by Lucia Graves. Weidenfeld & Nicolson.

[4] Evelyn Waugh (1990) *A Little Learning: An Autobiography* (volume 1). Penguin Modern Classics.

[5] A slightly heretical thought, but I had to wonder if, like T S Eliot's 'The Waste Lands', Lewis' poem had not turned out "inconveniently short" for stand-alone publication so that in the same way that Eliot had expanded his "notes, in order to provide a few more pages of printed matter, with the result that they became the remarkable exposition of bogus scholarship that is still on view today" (as noted in his *The Frontiers of Criticism*), Lewis had sought my scholarship to extend his own notes—knowing, of course, that he would not suffer from *bogus* scholarship.

some time to come! But I know that I can trust you to properly value and preserve my papers." The importance, the immensity of the role that those archives played in this story—particularly the tempting little taste that he sent to me as I approached the end of this work—will be seen when you reach my notes to the final lines (lines 319-326) of 'Dark Ashes'.

After all we had shared over the years, this was not a request that I could, or would ever want to turn down. Even as children we had been inseparable, and I could not forget how even then we worked together on composing and perfecting stories and fables. Lewis was the creative yang to my quieter, controlling yin: the bright, shining, positive and ultimately more successful force—and perhaps too I may admit here without detracting from the work that all those months ago, I might have seen in the task he had asked of me an opportunity for my own advancement, to balance the yin-yang equation and have some of his success rub off on me!

The poem here, originally published as 'Retrospective' is reprinted—unchanged and un-edited—under the poet's new title, 'Dark Ashes', which is both appropriate to the lines and, perhaps can be seen as, a light-hearted nod to Nabokov's more extraordinary exegesis. 'Dark Ashes' is a poem of six short cantos and is written by, and most obviously follows the life and love (as Frank Harris almost wrote) of Lewis for all the years of his life with K. It would be misleading to talk of an original manuscript as Lewis worked on a computer and all versions of the poem exist only digitally, and perhaps as a result of this there is only one earlier version extant.

Most of the marginalia—or whatever the digital equivalents are—became footnotes to 'Retrospective'; only in a very few instances do they show a correction, an emendation or a clear path to an additional line—or indeed, a rejected line. As a poet, Lewis frequently listed, after a space and a diagonal stroke at the end of a line, alternative words that he was considering in his draft writings. This device is almost entirely absent from the first version; indeed, there is very little evidence remaining of re-drafting.

The poem was originally published with a series of very brief footnotes added as an afterthought, mostly explaining literary, mythological or folkloric references; these have been removed in this edition, expanded and combined with my own commentary below. This is the only change I have made to the text of my dear friend. I feel the need to emphasise that point as some literary critics will know, and others will discover, that Lewis and I were living together near

Rome at the time the poem was written and some or other of them may choose to suggest they can see my hand in some of the lines. Would that it were so!

Many times during those idyllic months in Italy as he tried out his lines on me did I suggest different approaches or the more specific inclusion of his earlier life, but Lewis was very clear—adamant even—that every word, phrase and indent should be his and his alone. And, while I may have known and admired K. from afar, and although I was so much more to her lover, I could have no real part of, or in, his narration of their story. The poet, Andrew Motion, wrote recently of his 1993 award-winning biography of Philip Larkin that he did not describe his friendship with the poet as "I was present everywhere in the book anyway" [6].

In the same way and for much the same reason, I have written little of my relationship with Trystan Lewis. I have also tried in my text simply to tell the story; I have not brought my considerable literary scholarship to bear in an attempt at some form of literary criticism or analysis of the work: Lewis only asked for a commentary.

'Retrospective' was an extraordinary poem even as it emerged—a stream of consciousness in both the Buddhist 'mind stream' or *Citta-saṃtāna* and the narrative senses that flowed directly and with little hindrance from the writer's digital pen. If I use the phrase 'stream of consciousness' I do so not in reference to a literary *device* (that is, a conscious approach designed to give an impression) but meaning that the words flowed more-or-less *without* conscious design from the poet's mind. There was one point when the flow was blocked for a while but when he was writing, the words, the story even, emerged almost in its final form. Subsequent editing by the poet merely served to improve the lexicology or tidy up the structure.

'Retrospective' is also remarkable for the use—even within that mind stream, during and intrinsic to the flow of words—of a strong sense of individuality, the individual identity, of everything mentioned. Phrases like "day's depthless deep unbounded sea" or "the distant blue the faint horizon round" and perhaps even "where umbral time is released by light" bring to mind the ideas of inscape and instress, even if we are more familiar with them in

---

[6] Andrew Motion (2018) My friend Philip Larkin. *The Week* 1192 (8 September 2018): 52-53. [*Philip Larkin: A Writer's Life* (2nd ed). London: Faber & Faber.]

longer, denser expressions of uniqueness [7]. Perhaps the best example of Lewis' use of inscape can be found in another of his poems, 'Hope' [8]:

Yesterday, the sun shone black upon my soul
Depth's depth deep beneath my heart.
Lumined ne'er by hope
Thoughts sank weighted low

Charles Kinbote wrote that Shade's poem was a "sudden flourish of magic" and it will be evident from the above that I feel similarly about the poem of *my* friend. Like Kinbote, I might suggest that the commentary should be read first as well as during a reading of the poem as a reference (and I would emphasise the importance of the many footnotes I have added to help readers understand the text of the commentary), but unlike Kinbote, I will not add that without my notes the text is unapproachable. He says:

Let me state that without my notes Shade's text simply has no human reality at all since the human reality of such a poem as his (being too skittish and reticent for an autobiographical work), with the omission of many pithy lines carelessly rejected by him…

---

[7] Inscape and instress are complementary concepts about individuality and uniqueness derived by Gerard Manley Hopkins, who "felt that everything in the universe was characterised by what he called *inscape*, the distinctive design that constitutes individual identity. This identity is not static but dynamic. Each being in the universe 'selves,' that is, enacts its identity. And the human being, the most highly selved, the most individually distinctive being in the universe, recognises the inscape of other beings in an act that Hopkins calls instress, the apprehension of an object in an intense thrust of energy toward it that enables one to realise specific distinctiveness." (Stephen Greenblatt *et al.* (eds) (2006) "Gerard Manley Hopkins." *The Norton Anthology of English Literature*, 8th ed., Vol. 2. New York: W. W. Norton & Company, p. 2159.)

[8] 'Hope'. Published in *Mostly Welsh* (2019). Talybont: Y Lolfa

…but I would suggest, like Kinbote, that there is some deeper truth or actuality, a…

…reality of its author and his surroundings, attachments and so forth, a reality that only my notes can provide.

And so, as editor, I tread a narrow path, delicately poised between explication and extension. Because of that extraordinary love that Lewis held for K., I see that narrow path—the path along which the story I shall unfold will bring my readers—as always having at its source a tiny gold cross, a wonderful symbol of eternal love. But let it never be said of my work:

"Who is the Potter, pray, and who the Pot?" [9]

As T. S. Eliot wrote in his 'Note of Introduction' to David Jones' *In Parenthesis*: "A work of literary art which uses language in a new way or for a new purpose, does not call for many words from the introducer. All that one can say amounts only to pointing towards the book, and affirming its importance and permanence as a work of art. The aim of the introducer should be to arouse the curiosity…" [10]

I think that if Lewis had selected a single poem from his writings to stand as introduction to this commentary, he would almost certainly have selected:

Ashes in a Wilderness
To you, readers, I say
I am no writer—
these words
placed themselves
on my page
to tell a story

---

[9] *Rubáiyát of Omar Khayyám*, translated by Edward Fitzgerald. London: Zodiac Books (1950) LX. iv.

[10] T S Eliot (1937) 'A Note of Introduction' in David Jones: *In Parenthesis.*

To you, writers, I cry
I am no chronicler—
these tales
spun their web
through my mind
to make a memory

To you, poets, I sing
I am no rhymer—
these lines
etched their pattern
on my paper
to form a psalm

To you, who come, I whisper
I am no voice—
these sounds
lift their hymn
from the book
to sing your future [11]

I hope that this whispered affirmation may be what I achieve, and that—to
some extent, at least—I am able to satisfy that continuing curiosity aroused by
the poem itself. Lewis is clearly writing an autobiographical poem, and there are
places where his lives float over the lines almost invisibly, indeed, maybe there
are places where more detail could have been forthcoming, but—as a friend who
has often shared with him a late night drink while discussing one or other of his
works—I know that his decisions as to what should and what should not be
specific would all have been the result of careful and probably lengthy
consideration after a line or a stanza had been first written. That he has now
offered—through me—a deeper insight into his life, his life with K. and thus also
a life with Yseult is almost astonishing for such a private man, although as Swift
noted "there is in most people a reluctance and unwillingness to be forgotten…

---

[11] Unpublished. A poem found in Lewis' archive.

[and] if it be founded in our nature, as an incitement to virtue, it ought not to be ridiculed" [12] . I am both humbled and privileged to offer my notes as a last word.

Chris Armstrong, The Cottage, Tregaron, 29 September

---

[12] Quoted in Charles Peake (1971). *The Coherence of Gulliver's Travels*. In Claude Rawson (ed.) *Swift*. London: Sphere Books, 175.

Peake comments on this passage that "love of fame was a human passion to which writers and orators had always appealed, and in doing so, it is implied here, they were not addressing themselves to man's lower self but to an instinct providentially designed as an 'incitement to virtue'." More recently than Swift, George Orwell noted that "*Sheer egoism.* Desire to seem clever, to be talked about, to be remembered after death" is one reason that people write.

In his article (George Orwell: 'Why I Write', *Gangrel* 4 (Summer 1946).), he also mentioned aesthetic enthusiasm, historical impulse and political purpose. I could never see any politics in Lewis and his historical impulse was obviously well sublimated (or even hidden), but as I (and he) have already suggested he had an enthusiasm for the aesthetic—a "Pleasure in the impact of one sound on another, in the firmness of good prose or the rhythm of a good story."

Introduction

When Trystan Lewis died—in the latter days of my work on this volume—his small funeral was marked by eulogies from one or two contemporary writers and poets in addition to the usual homilies from the family. I could have added much myself, but it was warming to hear my friend categorised as "perhaps the last great poet of the age" and—offering praise by association—"Thy days are done, thy fame begun"[13]. It is always nice to hear great poetry read in praise of a great poet!

If Lewis can indeed be regarded as a great poet—and I would be the first to argue his corner—I would suggest that it is his epic poems such as 'Retrospective'/'Dark Ashes' which raise his status from run-of-the-mill poet to great poet. Which is not to say that his short works are unworthy, simply that the longer poems give or have more stature, more gravitas. Many of his short poems are exceptional in their use of language and structure and are deservedly anthologised.

I think particularly of 'I, Fynnon Di-rewi of Mynydd Bach', 'The Land of a Giant', 'Forvie, March 2017' and the 'Druid Lane' poems as major poems of place and of 'Suicide's Beck'[14] and 'Role Reversal'—which was a sideswipe at the nonsense that was Brexit—as triumphs amongst his other poems. Of course, many of his poems—like 'Dark Ashes'—deal with the one great love of his life

---

[13] Lord Byron, 'Thy Days are Done'.

[14] I know Lewis was deeply touched and saddened by the sudden death of a friend and a colleague who had worked with him on several occasions. Particularly, he was upset that he had not understood the depth of his friend's depression and had been unable to help at an earlier date when they had talked about the inadequacies he felt. Also, by chance, he had very nearly travelled past the place of his death at the moment he died, but a whim had made him take another road. Lewis always felt guilty!

and nearly all of these are succinct, passionate works of art exhibiting a very fine hand with the brush. All of which begs a question.

We may ask, what makes a great poet? To quote Gerard Manley Hopkins, "Every true poet, I thought, must be original and originality a condition of poetic genius" [15]. So originality—of idea, of structure, of lexicology, of form may be seen as one condition. Lexicology. "In the beginning there was the word" [16] although Goethe's Faust wonders whether *that* word was 'deed', like Francis Bacon [17], suggesting that words—the written word—express things imperfectly: "In short, language does not impart to the mind a true or accurate picture of material reality, but fills it with more or less fantastic ideas of nature." [18]

D H Lawrence picks up this notion and mocks the old adage, that poetry is simply 'a matter of words'—"Poetry is a stringing together of words into a ripple and jingle and a run of colours. Poetry is an interplay of images. Poetry is the iridescent suggestion of an idea... But poetry is still another thing. The essential quality of poetry is that it makes a new effort of attention and 'discovers' a new world within the known world." [19] I do not think that you can define poetry so easily any more, still less define 'great poetry' but I am struck by the final words quoted from Lawrence, that poetry hides worlds within worlds.

That is a very apposite notion for 'Dark Ashes', as we shall see. I am particularly attached to Umberto Eco's ideas on the 'open' text. In 1962 he

---

[15] G M Hopkins (1938) *Further Letters of Gerard Manley Hopkins, including his correspondence with Coventry Patmore*, p. 222.

[16] The Bible, Book of John 1:1 (King James Version)

[17] And many others. Perhaps the most beautiful quotation demonstrating this point comes from *The Zohar* (a mystical commentary on the Torah) which says that "in any word shine a thousand lights".

[18] Frances Bacon. Quoted in Richard Foster Jones (1965) *Ancients and moderns: a study of the rise of the scientific movement in seventeenth-century England* (2nd ed) Berkeley: University of California Press. p.48.

Professor Andrew Large notes in *The Artificial Language Movement* that "although both Descartes and Leibniz gave considerable thought to the construction of a philosophical language, neither succeeded in constructing a complete structure of grammar and vocabulary which could express graphically or orally human thoughts." p.184.

[19] D H Lawrence (1928) Introduction to *Chariot of the Sun* by Harry Crosby. Published as 'Chaos in Poetry' in *Exchanges*, December 1929.

published *Opera aperta* [20]. In it, he argued that literary texts are fields of meaning—perhaps a similar idea to Lawrence's 'iridescent suggestion'—rather than one dimensional strings of meaning; that is, they are open, dynamic and psychologically engaging. He suggests that literature which limits one's potential understanding to a single, fixed line (or story) is less rewarding.

As Schiller wrote: "Language puts everything in terms of reason, but the poet is supposed to put everything in terms of the imagination; poetry calls for vision, language supplies only concepts. This means that the word robs the object it is meant to represent of its sensual and individual nature and thrusts a property of its own upon it, a generalness that is foreign to the original object" [21].

In a world where false news and social news are forever coming under the spotlight—as O'Hara has suggested, "[p]olitically, there is obviously a great deal of interest in engaging with people on the [Inter]net, and its anarchistic, countercultural ethos has encouraged hacking and informational vandalism" [22]—and facts have come to be seen as paramount, it may seem odd to be quoting Matthew Arnold decrying the limitations of 'fact' in favour of 'ideas'.

He wrote: "in poetry, where it is worthy of its high destinies, our race, as time goes on, will find an ever surer and surer stay. There is not a creed which is not shaken, not an accredited dogma which is not shown to be questionable, not a received tradition which does not threaten to dissolve. Our religion has materialised itself in the fact, in the supposed fact; it has attached its emotion to the fact, and now the fact is failing it. But for poetry the idea is everything; the rest is a world of illusion, of divine illusion. Poetry attaches its emotion to the idea; the idea is the fact. ... Without poetry, our science will appear incomplete; and most of what now passes with us for religion and philosophy will be replaced by poetry." [23]

---

[20] Umberto Eco (1962) *Opera aperta* (1962, rev. 1976—English translation: *The Open Work* (1989)). Eco also wrote, "I would define the poetic effect as the capacity that a text displays for continuing to generate different readings, without ever being completely consumed" and again: "The unlimitedness of the sense of a text is due to the free combinations of its signifiers, which in that text are linked together as they are only accidentally."

[21] Friedrich Schiller. Quoted in Ernst Fischer (1959) *The Necessity of Art: A Marxist Approach.* Penguin Books, 1963. p.27.

[22] Kieron O'Hara (2004) *Trust: From Socrates to Spin.* Duxford: Icon Books. p.98.

[23] Matthew Arnold. 'General Introduction'—Ward's *English Poets.*

Maybe Lewis was not so far wide of the mark when he wrote "Books make visible the writer's soul" [24]. Perhaps more pertinent are the words Arnold wrote in an essay on the poet, Maurice de Guérin [25]: "Poetry interprets in two ways: it interprets by expressing with magical felicity the physiognomy and movement of the outer world, and it interprets by expressing, with inspired conviction the ideas and laws of the inward world of man's moral and spiritual nature. In other words, poetry is interpretative both by having natural magic in it, and by having moral profundity." [26] If poems can be said to have both magic and morality, and I think those of Trystan Lewis possess exactly those qualities as they guide us through the poet's mystical and half-glimpsed visions in search of his life's truth, they are surely great. As I have noted later, great poetry, or 'good' poetry, is a force.

And there is a secondary question: how may the reader respond to the poem? Particularly when that reader's referential system of images, symbols and tokens comes from an age that is remote from both the poet and the poem. And if there is a schism between the *rhyme* and the *time* can any poem—no matter how great—ever be more than a 'matter of words'? I believe that it can if the reader is willing to allow it. Add to this that Roland Barthes [27] argues that conventions inform both language and style so that neither is purely creative. Instead, form, or what he calls 'writing' (the specific way an individual chooses to use these conventions of style for a desired effect), is the unique and creative act. But a writer's form is vulnerable once it has been made available to the public, something Lewis realised only too well—he once wrote a poem which explored that idea.[28]

---

[24] The first line of the 2018 poem 'The Interface', now in the editor's collection.

[25] French poet. His works were said to be imbued with a passion for nature whose intensity reached almost to worship and was enriched by pagan elements—something we also find in some of Lewis' works, for example, 'Llyfnant'.

[26] Matthew Arnold. Quoted by William Sharp in 'Introduction'. *The Strayed Reveller, Empedocles on Etna, and Other Poems, by Matthew Arnold.* London: Walter Scott Publishing, c. 1900.

[27] Roland Barthes (1953) Le degré zéro de l'écriture (English translation: Writing Degree Zero (1968), Hill and Wang: New York).

[28] Unpublished poem, 'Process', written by Lewis in 2018 and now in the editor's collection.

Process

what spills onto the page
falls from   my mind:
it tells of   what is there
it tastes of   my thoughts
so they are   spread here   with care
                                as verse

the page   becomes
my mind   bared
what is there   visible
my thoughts   naked
spread here   exposed   read
                            ravaged

this thing   that was me
this thing   here
this thing   printed
this poem   read
this poem   is now
               in you
               is now
               yours   forever
               in
your thoughts   occupying
your thoughts   surrounding
               your mind

On the surface, the reader may be only dealing with words, but delve beneath the surface and the poet's art, his 'writing' will be discovered. I think 'delve' is the wrong word as it is indicative of an active, participative ambition in the reader, something perhaps that only a scholar may claim, but more generally it would be better to say, perhaps, let the words—the content—flow over the reader and the poem's depths—the poem's worlds—will become apparent. The German poet, author and philosopher known as Novalis once wrote "The world must be romanticised... Thus the original meaning is discovered again... The fact that we cannot see ourselves in a faery world is due only to the weakness of our physical organs of perception" and the "poems merely melodious" [29]—the 'faery world'—behind the real one can only be approached unconsciously. Which is not to say that the reader need not concentrate!

W H Gardner rephrased sentences from Gerard Manley Hopkins' essay, 'Poetic Diction' as "...verse both necessitates and engenders a difference in diction and in thought" since "verse alone does not add a beauty to thought, because prose thought is actually made worse by metrical expression." Reading poetry requires concentration—by which, we are told Hopkins "means not merely terseness, definiteness, emphasis, but rather *vividness of ideas*" [30]. So understanding poetry is difficult!

And understanding 'modern' poetry may be seen as more difficult than understanding 'conventional' verse—as Aldous Huxley once wrote, "It is a grammatical apocalypse. A whole world of ideas is miraculously concentrated by means of syntax into what is almost a point" [31]. And perhaps if that aphorism was true of Mallarmé, it—or at least some variant of it—is certainly true of Lewis. Perhaps we might say: it is a logistical apocalypse. Two worlds of ideas are miraculously concentrated by means of syntax and structure into what is almost a narrative!

So the reader may (or may not!) freely interpret, explore the *fields of meaning*, mine the *iridescent suggestions* of ideas, perhaps feeling that the prose thought made worse by verse hides what the poet is seeking to express. And he or she may or may not negotiate successfully all those hidden fields of meaning. Throughout the ages scholars have sought to codify or clarify literary works so that they may better be understood... and nowhere is this more necessary than in a poem such as this, where what is written is so *vulnerable once it has been made available to the public*—especially so as the poem's words offer a very personal account.

Dennis Taylor wrote, "We live in an age of critical discourses that are expert in discussing the dimensions of class, gender, textuality, and historical context.

---

[29] Georg Philipp Friedrich Freiherr von Hardenberg (Novalis) (1772-1801). Quoted in Ernst Fischer (1959) *The Necessity of Art: A Marxist Approach*. Penguin Books, 1963. p.60.

[30] W H Gardner (1944) *Gerard Manley Hopkins: A Study of Poetic Idiosyncrasy in Relation to Poetic Tradition*, Volume 1. Chapter IV, 'Diction and Syntax'.

[31] Aldous Huxley. Comment on Mallarmé's 'O si chère de loin et proche et blanche, si...' in his anthology, *Texts and Pretexts*.

Yet an important part of the literature we read goes untouched by our discourses, or is deconstructed, historicized, sexualized, or made symptomatic of covert power relationships. The negative hermeneutic of such reductive discourse has been thorough and successful. Attempts at a more positive non-reductive hermeneutic tend to be soft discourses, appealing to general unexamined values…" [32]

So there is a need, as Derrida would have it, for scholars "to decipher, dream of deciphering, a truth or an origin which is free from freeplay and from the order of the sign" [33]. T S Eliot wrote of James Joyce's *Finnegans Wake* that it was a "vast prose poem" that required some sort of "dissection for its enjoyment and understanding." He goes on to suggest that "one can explain a poem by investigating what it is made of and the causes that brought it about; and explanation may be a necessary preparation for understanding. But to understand a poem it is also necessary, and I should say in most instances still more necessary, that we should endeavour to grasp what the poetry is aiming to be" [34]. Where a work is vulnerable to some kind of lack of understanding, scholars can help by way of a commentary.

I believe that G K Chesterton once suggested that literary scholars "merely paraphrase the literary work"—I suppose he meant rather than the negative hermeneutics of a reductive explanation of the work or a grasping for what it is trying to be. As Eliot suggests a good commentary should explain the work [35]

---

[32] Dennis Taylor (1997) The Need for a Religious Literary Criticism. *Religion and the Arts* 1 (1).

[33] Jacques Derrida (1966) "Structure, Sign and Play in the Discourse of the Human Sciences". A lecture presented at Johns Hopkins University on 21 October 1966, subsequently published in 1967 in *Writing and Difference* (Chap 10).

[34] T S Eliot (1956) The Frontiers of Criticism. *The Sewanee Review* 64 (4): 525-543.

[35] As an aside, I would note that such commentaries do not necessarily need to be third-party commentaries—Charles Peake quoted Humphry House's opening remarks on Kubla Khan in his Clark Lectures on Coleridge: "If Coleridge had never published his Preface, who would have thought of Kubla Khan as a fragment? Who would have guessed at a dream? …Who would have thought it nothing but a 'psychological curiosity'? Who, later, would have dared to talk of its 'patchwork brilliance'?"—a preface of unmatched absurdity, the most implausible account of the composition of a poem that has ever been offered to the public, says Peake (Charles Peake (1970) The Quest for Crabtree). Perhaps we might think that third-party commentaries are the more worthy.

and what brought it about, and I hope that I have done so here. He wrote of Harold Munro's later poems: these were the work of a man whose interest is centred "never in the visible world at all, but in the spectres and bad dreams that live inside the skull, in the ceaseless question and answer of the tortured mind..." [36].

So, in the commentary it is my task—indeed, it is the reason for the commentary—to make clear those narratives, those worlds, and make visible the memories buried in, and the workings of, Lewis' mind. A mind which poured "natural magic" and "moral profundity" onto the page; a mind which, consequently, produced great poetry.

At the publisher's suggestion, following the unexpected death of my dear friend while I was working on this commentary, I have added a short Introduction to this volume. In it, it is not my intention to cover ground dealt with by the poem itself, but rather to provide some biographical background to it: to set 'Dark Ashes' in the context of the poet's life, as it were. So before my Commentary on 'Dark Ashes', I offer a short biographical study. I started with Frances Bacon so let me also end with him. If as Bacon would have it, "The winning of Honour is but the revealing / of a man's virtue and worth without disadvantage" [37], may I be—to use his phrase—that man's *pater patriae*!

i. Origins

Trystan Lewis—Trystan Guy Lewis to give him his full name—was born in Hove in Sussex shortly after the Second World War to the daughter of an auctioneer and to a banker. One month short of four years later they presented him with a sister. The family was neither rich nor poor although his mother's parents owned a large house and entertained lavishly, enabling his own parents to socialise occasionally—particularly through the Freemasons' Ladies' Night dances—with the area's wealthy faux-bourgeoisie. Trystan often spoke of his grandparent's house—he never understood why his memories of it were so vivid but I suspect that it was because it was so different from their own small post-war 'semi'. The first verse of Lewis' poem 'Rooms' describes its lounge (and, incidentally, his grandfather!):

---

[36] T S Eliot, *Critical Note*. Collected Poems of Harold Munro, p.xv.
[37] Frances Bacon, 'Of Honour and Reputation' *in Essays or Councils, Civil and Moral of Frances Bacon*. London: The Folio Society, 2002. p.189.

Netted windows with fawn roller blinds
lowered a little by their macramé tassels for his forty winks
Shush! Be quiet, he's having his nap, don't make a din—
or completely, when at night
he shovelled the last coal from the bin
concealed in its wooden cabinet
and lowered the heavy lid on the fire to keep it in [38]

Unlike his own, their house smelled of furniture polish on the heavy oak and antique furniture and was replete with old china, glass and pewter (his grandfather's specialty): tankards of all shapes and sizes, jugs, plates, a communion set, a vast carving dish with runnels to drain the blood and juices, and space underneath for hot water to keep the roast meat warm, and—his particular favourite—a pepper pot in the shape of a boy crying, presumably as the pepper touched his eyes!

It was a magical place—remembered in several of his poems, particularly 'Lunch with my Grandmother' where he remembers the starched linen table cloth on his bare knees, the cut-glass water tumblers, and the plate and pewter on the dresser. Their own house was in a newish estate on the edge of town and he remembers it—probably unfairly—as being cold and Spartan. Although he did not know it at the time it was most remarkable for the neighbour at the end of their garden whose second daughter was to become his wife!

There was a small kitchen with a blue-grey enamelled gas cooker and outside it, under the stairs where the perambulator was also kept, a small square refrigerator—also enamelled in speckled blue—a box on spindly legs. The lounge or 'front room' was not often used so life centred on his bedroom, on the dining room and the kitchen—as well as the long garden which ran uphill from the house, up some steps past a small greenhouse and some grass to a path through some fruit bushes to the chain-link fence at the top. The little girl with pigtails—there was a photograph, I remember, of the two of them sitting together in an upturned wheelbarrow—living beyond the fence was to become his life-long friend, but it was her younger sister that he married!

His father had seemed to him—I suppose, because when Lewis was about, he was always out at work—a rather distant figure, although not so distant that he was afraid to run up the street to meet him from work. On one occasion when

---

[38] 'Rooms' Published in *Mostly Welsh* (2019). Talybont: Y Lolfa.

he did so without permission, he remembered tripping on some steps—he thought of them, even now, as *high* steps—and cutting his lip only to be carried home in tears by his father ("You should do what you are told," his mother had said when she saw him again)! But his mother always seemed clever, pretty and loving!

Like her own father, she had a flair for drawing and painting and Trystan always remembered that the bottom drawer in their sideboard was heavy with her inks, pens, paintbrushes and paints… and also with a large roll of paper on which she had in her teenage years set out her family tree—all the way back to 1703 and a Lieutenant who had gone down with a man-of-war, the Stirling Castle, on the Goodwin Sands during a great storm. Both parents were also keen tennis players, his mother being particularly good having played throughout her early years with her brother, who briefly played for Sussex.

That brother—Guy, for whom Lewis was named—had a tragically short life, so this uncle—of whom the young Lewis was very fond—featured only in the first few years of his life. Like Lewis, he had left school for the Merchant Navy but ill health had forced him to leave after a year. After a few months he had found work with an insurance company and subsequently been moved to Nairobi by the company to run their office there, contracting polio and dying without ever returning home.

Although it was largely hidden from the young Trystan, his sudden death had a devastating effect on Guy's parents and his mother had dressed only in greys and black for many years. Trystan told me that his letters spoke of a time in Africa that had been a mixture of the usual colonial excitement—visits to game parks, driving on unmade roads that often involved ropes and help to get his little car out of the deep ruts, tennis at the Club, dancing in night clubs, meeting the young Princess Elizabeth on her visit—and angst, as he had been forced to leave the love of his life behind in Hove, thus much of his energy had been devoted to persuading, or trying to persuade—by post—both his own parents and those of the lady he loved that a short engagement and an early marriage were both acceptable and desirable. Some of his letters could have been better phrased, but there is no doubting his love:

You will be pleased to know I think that G. and I are going to get engaged. I am sure it will come as no surprise to you as you know we are both very fond of each other and I know you both like her. I have hopes of flying back for

37

three weeks in the summer to get married but I gather that [her parents] won't commit themselves yet till they hear what you think about it. Apparently [her father] seems to think it is an unfair burden for me till I have been out here longer. This would not be so because a wife is as much a necessity as a car out here and I certainly don't want to stay in hotels for any longer than need be. [39]

Her mother also thought that that her daughter needed longer at home with her in order to learn how to run a home—to which Guy replied that she would have no need as everything was done for them in Africa! Even his engagement had been directed by post from his room at the Club to arrange for his father to take his future wife out to buy a ring! Re-reading some of his letters now we can see both frustration and anger at the delays imposed by both sets of parents: he simply could not understand it and wrote to his sister asking her to "PLEASE see if you can do something about it". Sometime after his death, his fiancé went on to become a Greenham Common protestor so it is doubtful that the colonial life would have agreed with her!

Early holidays—with one exception—were taken in Bexhill, staying in a bed and breakfast establishment, between the sea front and the outdoor swimming baths in the park, run by the wonderfully named widow, Mrs Ida Rippingale. Lewis told me he always assumed that the waste land of rough grass and buddleia behind the house, across which they passed to get to the stony and usually windy beach, was a bomb site—probably because it dipped down in the central area—but much later in life discovered to his considerable amusement that it was just land that had never been built over—probably for the very reason of that central depression!

Neither the cold water of the open-air swimming baths in the park nor the instructor who dangled him in the water at the end of a pole persuaded him to swim—that came much later. The one exceptional holiday was to Norway—sleeper train to Newcastle upon Tyne and the SS Venus to Bergen—to stay with his grandmother's one-time maid, who had come to England to learn English just before the war.

Afterwards, the holiday was chiefly remembered by him for the scare he caused his parents as, disobediently running ahead across a snow-covered field,

---

[39] From a letter in Lewis' archive of papers, written in early 1952, a few months before Guy's death.

he had suddenly vanished from sight as he plunged through the snow into a cave hollowed out by a stream, now fortunately more or less dried up! He was rescued and admonished (again)!

Shortly after his sister was born, they moved to Worcester. And his life-long love of and passion for the countryside began. His father had travelled to, and worked in, Worcester for some weeks—months, probably—before the family moved and had procured for them a timbered house with a huge garden in the suburban village of Claines. The garden—which Trystan remembers almost better than the house itself was notable for a huge rectangular lawn surrounded by apple trees and, nearer the house, a huge damson tree which gave them around a hundred pounds of fruit each year and under which, against the garage wall, the children had a cage with two guinea pigs.

He remembers learning to cycle on that lawn, learning the rudiments of tennis from something called a 'ComeBack'—a tall wooden frame with a tennis ball on an elastic, and an old rusty and squeaky swing on which it seemed he was forever destined to push his sister! And the children had a playroom of their own at the back of the house, remembered as a large and usually cold room with linoleum on the floor and without much furniture.

Trystan had a small wind-up gramophone there (78 rpm records: his own Davy Crockett "man of the wild frontier" and Robin Hood, "riding through the glen" as well as some that had once been Guy's including the Broadway Melody and April Showers!) and there was a large black cupboard for their toys, the pride of which for Lewis was a clockwork train set, although after he saw and was allowed to play with the large electric train set belonging to one of his Worcester school friends, it somehow seemed less marvellous.

Life was—or at least is remembered as—idyllic: a childhood without cares—a time of sunny summers in the garden, country lanes, and tennis to be watched in the club which was just a little further down their lane. Perhaps his memory of the time was influenced by two books that their neighbour had lent him—*A Romany in the Country* and *Romany on the Farm*—which described what seemed to him at the time a wonderful existence travelling the countryside without a care in the world in a Romany caravan pulled by a piebald horse! [40]

And just as the family had settled to life by the River Seven (along which he walked to school, although not in winter when the path was slippery and

---

[40] Both books are from a series by Romany (George Bramwell Evens). London: Epworth Press, 1932-53.

dangerous), Trystan's father was moved again and life in Wales began. At the age of nine he moved with his family to Swansea and a modern house on a new estate. It took a little getting used to! But as another summer began the magic of Gower beaches, easily accessible by the number 64 bus—they had no car— became apparent and a new passion supplanted, at least for the time being, his love of the countryside: swimming and surfing. His parents believed in private education so he was sent first to a preparatory and then to a grammar school run by a Church Missionary Society within walking distance of their home. Looking back on his education from the dizzy height of adulthood—an adulthood during which he read voraciously and widely—he often said that for him the school had been a poor educator. Certainly, he was not pushed to excel and only gained a handful of mediocre 'O' Level passes. His time there is summed up succinctly in a later poem:

I was taught in Wales
In Swansea's English Grammar
But little learned of little taught
And left in search of glamour [41]

and perhaps more tellingly:

The School Room
Of course there were old desks and huge radiators
and a blackboard that rolled up its wisdom
endlessly [42]

I remember once reading an essay in which Lawrence wrote: "The Jesuits say: Give me a child till he is seven, and I will answer for him for the rest of his life—Well, school-mistresses are not as clever as Jesuits, and certainly not as clear as to what they are about, but … They make the little boy into an incipient man" [43]. Lawrence is railing against the female teacher as an appropriate educator of boys but I am only suggesting that the education system of the day did not do

---

[41] 'Mostly Welsh' Published in *Mostly Welsh* (2019). Talybont: Y Lolfa.

[42] 'Rooms' Published in *Mostly Welsh* (2019). Talybont: Y Lolfa.

[43] D H Lawrence (1929) 'Enslaved by Civilisation'. *Vanity Fair* (September 1929).

well at producing an almost-man by the age of fifteen, the age at which Lewis went out into the world.

Perhaps the nuns did better for his sister as, in due course, The Convent School took her all the way through to A-Levels and Durham University! It was during his time at that school that I met Lewis, and we instantly became firm friends and soul mates. I think there was a natural affinity or connection between us—shared passions, shared likes, shared trials, shared loves, shared interests—certainly to the extent that we both ended up amongst the literati, but much more beside. We spent so much time together—evenings, weekends—in each other's houses, how could we not have become so close?

I remember that, after school on Fridays, we both went to work in the school's little printing press, where we learned how to set lead type by hand and use the printing presses; all under the watchful eye of a kindly old man known to everyone behind his back as 'Tosh' due to his small moustache. We used to have tea during the two and a half hours working at the press—Lewis always remembered the rhubarb and ginger jam he had never had before and I remember Tosh cleaning his teeth—false teeth I presume—after tea with a powder meant for cleaning the sinks!

I do not think at that stage, at the age of ten or eleven, either of us would have guessed at the depth and longevity of our friendship; all we knew was that at school, during the weekends, and throughout the school holidays we wanted to be together! We talked incessantly and I am sure it was my imagination that fuelled much of our lives; in the early days of our relationship, in preparatory school, I remember a series of extended stories set in an imaginary world that I began—even in my early years I saw myself as a story teller although in the end it was Lewis, and not I, who controlled the plot and went on to write from the imagination—which continued on and off for some years, while we both added strands to the tales.

Most of it was never captured on paper and it gradually became immensely complex, although it began with the simple need to rescue a lovely girl from a castle—we probably both had the same classmate in mind—and as the fiction grew the adventures wove their way across continents and, it seemed to me owing to Lewis' confusion over historic time, across centuries. I was a great reader even at that age and ached to see my story published as a book (with the cover: "RESCUE! by Chris Armstrong") and sitting on my shelf. But it was Lewis who often set the direction that the plot would take: one weekend he might suggest taking the story south to the palaces of Ottoman sultans (of course, it was left to me to add historical detail!); later in the week a note would be slipped into my desk, "Christo, we sail south!"

When Lewis became famous, I always expected, hoped even, that my stories would surface in his writing! Ironically, I was also, at least in part, responsible for re-enforcing the one interest we did not share: ships and the sea. My father was a Lloyd's surveyor and hearing of the family's connection with the sea—the Uncle who, following in the footsteps of his father, had become a Master Mariner and Commodore of a shipping company, his Nairobi Uncle who had spent a couple of trips with the same company before ill-health forced him to change careers and the father who had served in the Royal Navy during the war—he often took Lewis with him to inspect ships, taking him down into the depths of the dry docks to walk under the huge hulls, on one occasion up onto the bridge, and often into the noisy and greasy, hot engine rooms! If I did not accompany them, it was probably because I was reading!

So Lewis' childhood in Swansea comprised school, beaches, fishing from the pier, tennis (he never achieved his parent's skills and only ever entered one tournament, preferring in later life another sport to which his father introduced him, badminton) and a Saturday job at a local plant nurseries which, I think, confirmed his love of nature and gardening. I remember that on hot summer Saturdays when the tide was right, I would meet him from the nursery and we would swim.

The bay wasn't ideal as the tide went out over acres of muddy sand (where sometimes we dug for bait) but at high tide there was one spot beside a breakwater where there was a small pool deep enough for swimming and we would rush there, strip off and swim. It was never easy getting our wet bodies back into our clothes without our nakedness being seen from the tram, which in those days rattled and clanked its way around the bay just behind the beach— timing was everything! I wonder if he ever took girls there, or was it something that only he and I—his handsome Duke of Rahl—shared. Now, the breakwaters and—sadly—the trams are gone and the sea has changed the beach forever.

It was a childhood which had been largely unfocussed—Lewis, and I think I also, to some extent, only lived for the day—it was only in his last year of school that his parents suggested, and he accepted the idea of, a career in the merchant navy. So while I remained for another two years' study and headed for an English Tripos, Lewis joined a cadet ship and sailed the seven seas! These were no easy times for him as he was unused to independence: everything had always been done for him or, at the very least, he had been guided in everything—he was not used to making even small decisions on a day-by-day basis. I think it would be fair to say that he was late to mature, but I loved him none-the-less and missed him badly.

Perhaps we were both late to mature as, at that time, neither of us had any experience of the fair sex, other than to admire them in some vague and unrealised way from afar—from the other side of the classroom or from the boys' playground—at school: I remember that we both used to try to walk some of our way home from preparatory school with the lovely Jan although she turned off our route almost as soon as we reached the end of the school grounds and I know he told me of the dark-haired (and much older) Marilyn who used the same bus stop from school in Worcester; and then there were two beauties, always together in the grammar school—Wendy with her twinkling eyes and curly black hair and Pam who had a perm… but we never plucked up the courage to speak to them! Later he wrote of himself—and readers should note the theme of innocence recurs in 'Dark Ashes':

Callow, green, innocent!
   So you could describe him
   as he was delivered
   by his parents
     – fresh faced and newly uniformed to his ship. [44]

ii. Adulthood

I remember well him telling me after his first voyage how lost he had felt in those first days and weeks on the ship, in an unknown world for which he had gained no real preparation amongst a mass of people who all seemed to know what to do and where to be! Even the nine other cadets who joined at the same time as he did had been to a 'pre-sea' school and came prepared for the small challenges of life on board. He had been braver in his letters, or at least those to his parents and to his sister—for he wrote to me as much as to his family, and he was a serial correspondent—and also in his diary.

---

[44] 'The Voyage' Published in *Mostly Welsh* (2019) Talybont: Y Lolfa.

But his first two letters (I have included these and some of his other letters as an appendix as they illustrate his feelings so well) shocked me as they showed how unsettling this time was for him. He had always been—perhaps it was the beginning of his writing career—an inveterate diarist, recording in some detail his day-by-day work. I know he felt, even in those early days, dissatisfied with his diaries, seeing them as mundane lists of tasks, meals, places, with few deeper insights and almost no record of his thoughts and feelings.

In a strange way, too, he felt that his script should be neater and more rounded in his diaries—perhaps he felt that a more flowing hand would produce a better flow of thought. I think somehow he knew they lacked any literary merit and were probably a boring read! I now have in my possession all of Lewis' diaries and those from the earlier days are indeed very factual accounts, often detailing every aspect of a meal! Later diaries—from the times when he was writing articles or poems—are far more interesting.

And so Lewis went to sea [45]. His first voyage was long—they had spent unusually long on the New Zealand coast—but he returned to a whole month of summer leave while the ship was in dry dock in Falmouth and we enjoyed our time together on the beaches and at a few school friends' parties. Lewis—perhaps strangely given his time in so many ports around the world—remained quite shy with girls and did not seem to make friends—particularly female friends—easily. I think he was still very much under his parents' influence.

As a child, he had been brought up to go to church regularly and although he was not overtly religious, religion, along with the need for parental approval, probably governed his behaviour, at least when he was in Wales. Several trips later when his leave partly coincided with his parents being away, he did ask a girl out—at first only for a walk around the bay as he walked the family dog—but his behaviour towards her was so old-fashioned that I am not sure they even kissed!

After a few years, Lewis had grown up to be more sure of himself! He had money and a car—a blue-grey MG Midget with a detachable hard top which he loved—while I was penniless at University. We remained firm friends,

---

[45] A poem, the first lines of which are offered above, documents the difficulties experienced during the first half of his first trip—his inadequacies, his ignorance of what was expected, his feeling of inferiority as everyone else seemed to know what to do and when to do it and, perhaps most tellingly, the lack of information passed down to new cadets. I do not think 'Health and Safety' was an accepted term in those days!

companions when I was home at the same time, and regular correspondents, but I saw no evidence of—and we certainly never talked about—his girlfriends. There was what I took at the time to be a very strange letter about some previous existence—although, of course, it all makes sense now, and I remember once he suggested coming to visit me because he missed my company when he was on leave and wanted to see me, so there were even times when I almost felt that he saw me as a substitute girlfriend (the two letters from Swansea are in the appendix)!

My studies had progressed well and a First was being talked about by my tutors, while Lewis was just beginning to study himself as, after three years as sea, he joined a Technical College in Cardiff to prepare for his first Board of Trade examination in things like seamanship, ship stability, navigation, and signals—something of a bête noir for Lewis whose Morse code was always poor! But beyond his maritime studies, his time at sea had allowed Lewis to acquire a wider education—he had become an avid reader of both the great novels and, to a lesser extent, poetry and we began to have lengthy discussions about literature—although his penchant for Russian authors such as Sholokhov, Tolstoy, Pushkin and Dostoevsky gave him a different slant to my own. My degree allowed me to direct him, to introduce him to literary criticism as well as the primary sources, and it would not be an exaggeration to suggest that this greatly enhanced both his reading and his literary skills.

iii. The Dark Ashes Days

It was not long after this time that he met K. At the time I was in London working at a publishing house and living in a small flat in east London, which was fortunate as it enabled me to perform one very important service for Lewis as he was about to set sail from the docks in Tilbury. K. had decided to surprise him and had arrived at his ship—as it turned out, while he was on duty and only hours from sailing: she—they—had to be rescued! I remember this particularly as it was the first time I met her, and as my old car drew up below the huge bulk of the ship and Lewis hustled K.—a sad and chastened K.—down the gangway, I could only open the passenger door for her and grasp Lewis in my arms to assure him all would be well.

I was struck at once both by her diminutive stature and her beauty, and had trouble keeping my mind on my driving as I returned her to her Aunt's house in Forest Hill. She remained silent for most of the drive fiddling nervously with a ring Lewis had given her—rolling it up and down her finger, while I attempted to sooth her with amusing tales of my life in publishing and accounts of how much Lewis loved her—how he was always writing and talking about her—and how difficult was his position as duty officer with a girlfriend in his cabin! I think I managed to cheer her up a little! And it was I who had moist eyes as I drove back to my lonely bachelor flat—Yllka, the love of *my* life, having been recalled to the Ottoman Empire by her father to marry her childhood sweetheart!

Her father was something in the Albanian communist government and I suppose he could not be seen to allow the betrothal to founder. I felt betrayed—so innocent was I of the ways of the world—and often wondered how else our story might have played out!

From then on, while I was both publisher, and a writer of increasing importance, lecturing on my own work, Lewis' career and life continued, spiralling around that passionate love affair between him and K. As 'Dark Ashes' makes clear this was his first love and first relationship which may be why it so completely took over his life. I remember he told me, "When I was dating V. [the girl with whom he walked the dog in Swansea], I never once woke up thinking 'I love you' but now—every day dawns with that explosion of light. Almost a fanfare and town crier moment. An overwhelming, dominating, all embracing joyous shout!"

But I am at risk of treading on ground covered by the poem, and thus by my subsequent Commentary. Lewis and I remained friends throughout the period—indeed, I was his best man at the little wedding in Beddingham near Lewes. St Andrew's is a beautiful Norman country church with a nave dating from 1066 set in trees on a mound just off the road, and the service was simple and soon over. The bride looked beautiful and Lewis was not the only man in the church who thought so! Once the obligatory photographs had been taken, all present retired to a reception at the bride's home in Brighton.

It was a curious mix of people: grandparents, and aunts and uncles from both sides of the family mingled with hippies from university and merchant navy officers! There were no, or almost no, speeches and all too soon K. had changed from her bridal dress and Lewis had whisked her away.

I will not dwell here on their life together at sea and in mid-Wales, on their three sons, on the farm on which they lived until K. died of cancer or on their life together, except to say that I have never known a couple who throughout their time together remained as passionately in love as when they had first met!

46

I visited them together only a few times in their little cottage but was always struck both by their complete domesticity and adaption to farm life, and by the peace of the spot. For such a small cottage, the library was impressive—books filled every spare shelf and were even stacked on the little staircase.

Lewis continued to educate himself and had even gained a degree—he was still immersed in literature and on one of my last visits was reading Anglo-Welsh poets such as R S Thomas and Idris Davies and learning about the Bardic tradition of Wales. The place was a little treasure house—I can see why Lewis never wanted to leave there even after K. passed away. Shortly before her death, I had moved to a small town just outside Rome for the first of several summer lecturing jobs and so was unable to attend the funeral, but when I next visited, Lewis was immersed in his writing and his reputation as a informatics scholar, a thinker and a poet was secure. His connections in academia and society had served him well and he was often asked to speak at conferences and literary festivals. He had just returned from a major conference tour in Croatia—a country, he told me, with which he felt a strange but close affinity.

This old farm cottage of mine
keeps all my years safe
for it knows my secret ways
and remembers

There are shadows in the shadows
but in some rooms
my sons have hidden smiles
to lead me in

There is solitude left indoors
but here and there
she has retained a past caress
to warm me [46]

---

[46] Verses from an unpublished poem, 'Hen dŷ', written by Lewis in 2017 and now in the editor's collection.

iv. The later years

There were undoubtedly times when Lewis had difficulty writing—not something I had ever experienced myself—but there were days, even weeks at a time, when some sort of 'writer's block' held back his hand—or more accurately his mind—and not a word was typed. These were times when his hideaway in the hills of Ceredigion came into its own: he would pull on an old coat and boots and walk the lanes and the hills, lost to the world. I suppose he was working somewhere in his mind but he said that he emptied his mind of anything to do with his latest book or poem and just waited.

There was one particular period when he was working on the poem then called 'Retrospective' which lasted longer than any he had experienced before. Happily, it also coincided with a visit when I was home from another semester in Italy—although he had written to me putting off the visit and begging my forgiveness as he was under the weather and unable to write, I decided that he needed to be rescued! He was very unsure at first—although he welcomed me with open arms when I arrived—he was not convinced that he wanted company and still less convinced that my invitation was either wise or welcome.

Of course, we spent days walking and long nights over a bottle talking and gradually I was able to lift him out of his depression—if that is what it was—and get him talking about his latest project. He was clearly excited by it but had hit some sort of dead end, unable to see how the tales would unfold, and I told him firmly that he needed a holiday! He should come to Italy with me when I returned in a week or two.

I had a small apartment in the little town of Frascati in the foothills on the outskirts of Rome and there was a spare bedroom that was quite large enough to accommodate a desk. It would be his and he could work undisturbed for as many hours each day as he wished—for the rest he could walk the narrow street and the hills, sit in my favourite cafe in a small square and drink coffee or wine in the sun, or—when I was home—just talk. It would be a wonderful reunion and a break from the ordinary for both of us!

Frascati is a small wine-growing town at the end of a valley and a railway line from Rome, which, a mere thirty minutes away, is where sits the university at which I was currently lecturing for the summer. The apartment is quiet—apart from the early morning buzz of scooters heading for the station, it is in a quiet street in a quiet town and Lewis would be uninterrupted—or as uninterrupted as he wanted to be! I have no idea why he took so much persuading!

He spent some months with me in Italy and I am happy to say that he began working, began writing again. Sufficiently so, that he felt able to write to his publishers with an update on progress—this final short letter is also in the appendix. It was an halcyon period in the late summer and we spent many an hour on the little balcony putting the world—the literary world—to rights! Eventually, Lewis asked me to read his work—I am sure he had just reached the end of the third canto—and I was able to make some useful suggestions, which— if they did not find their way into the poem certainly triggered the train of thoughts that generated the words that did! There were also my suggestions to extend the story which were left high and dry! Probably, he just wanted my ear!

I think he used me as a kind of literary canary to test the air within his writing to see if it was pure … an atmosphere that would allow the readers to flourish as they mined the depths of his text. But it was as if he did not want to hear my ideas—did not want anything to bring down our idyll. I think we discussed the epic poem every day.

I remember one time I reminded him that although Sisyphus was known as a proud king and a navigator, he was also known for the deceit and trickery which led to his eternal punishment. Tipping the last of the bottle of local wine into his glass, he had sat back in his chair and signalled me to tell him more. And as the sun was lost in the low evening clouds at the end of our little street and my pile of marking remained untouched on the balcony table, I was happy to do so. Zeus, I told him, had abducted Aegina but Sisyphus revealed her whereabouts to her father, the River-god Asopus, in return for a perennial spring in Corinth. It became known as Peirene and was apparently where Bellerophon took Pegasus to drink.

Infuriated, Zeus ordered his brother Hades to take Sisyphus down to Tartarus—the deep abyss that is used as a place of suffering for the wicked — but such was his cunning that Sisyphus tricked Hades into demonstrating how the fetters would work, locked them, and escaped. He remained free for a while by dint of further trickery, but eventually Theseus brought an end to his freedom and the Judges of the Dead showed Sisyphus a block of stone identical in size to the one that had served as a disguise for Zeus when he was fleeing from Asopus, and ordered him to roll it to the top of a hill and send it down the further side.

But he is always forced back by the weight of the stone before reaching the summit and the stone rolls back to the base of the hill where Sisyphus must begin the task again [47]. I thought it was an important tale as the story has to do with a hidden daughter and I was wondering where Lewis would take his own narrative. I do not think Lewis understood, or perhaps even recognised, the point I was making.

Eventually, as the summer came to an end, Lewis had to return to Wales and our idyll was over. I had a few weeks more work—essays in Italian English to mark—before I would leave for my London flat. Although we had once again become close during that time in Italy, it was followed by a hiatus in our regular correspondence. I assumed that Lewis was lost to the world as he worked feverishly on completing the mammoth poem in his little Welsh cottage. For my part, I had other speaking engagements and writing deadlines to meet. I think it was less than a year later, perhaps sometime in the summer, that I received a package from Lewis.

I had seen the poem, 'Retrospective', published to some acclaim and had sent him a card to congratulate him but had not heard very much from him. Most critics had been kind but a few had—mistakenly, in my view—found it disjointed and without any apparent focus, and it was probably those few unkind comments which persuaded me to take on this editorial task when Lewis asked me. Particularly the comment in *The Times* that the poem was self-indulgent and had no poetic integrity [48]! Another critic wrote:

> It is a shame that a poem that promises so much ultimately fails to deliver anything more than words. It is obvious that the poet is writing from life but, while the shape and rhythm of the lines carry the reader forward, the underlying story is obscured, often incomprehensible. Clearly the poem speaks of a great love with great sincerity, but the hints of a second voice singing a second passion in some Baroque counterpoint never really work. A sad epitaph for a once great rhymester.

I could not but help think of John Shade's comment on critics, "when I hear a critic speaking of an author's sincerity I know that either the critic or the author

---

[47] I confirmed this story during editing from Robert Graves' *The Greek Myths*. Penguin Books 1955.

[48] Clearly, a critic who did not know his Swift! (See my Note 12.)

is a fool" [49]—and there was no doubt in my mind which! Some of these so-called literary critics can have read no more than nursery rhymes before they were employed!

But if there was any agreement amongst Lewis detractors, it was that the autobiographical elements were disjointed and not easily understood and, even as I penned my card of congratulations following its publication, my mind was running over the many conversations we had stretched into the Italian night and I was wondering what more could be said—what details added—to make the poetic narrative work better as an autobiography. I think my mind had already begun working as Lewis' editor before the telephone call came a few days later which asked me to act as editor to the poem and add a commentary for a second publication under the title 'Dark Ashes'.

A letter followed to finalise the arrangement. Although there passed between us a few more or less desultory letters in the next six or eight months, none of them suggested that he was working on anything further—in fact in one he sounded almost depressed—and although he asked incessantly about progress with 'Dark Ashes', he did not seem particularly interested in my other comings and goings... or at least he never commented on them! So the package came as a surprise. Beside a letter and a small folder of papers there was a manila envelope sealed in a typically old-fashioned way with sealing wax.

On the envelope was simply a Chrismon—the pictogram Lewis had allocated to me when as lads we had abbreviated our names—he had felt that the symbol perfectly matched the name, Christo, that he had given me, and notes from him were often simply addressed to me with a crude representation of that cross. I put it aside for later—perhaps a little impatiently—and read his note.

The letter was brief, very brief, and I was saddened to hear that Lewis was ailing and, feeling unable to maintain his home in Wales, had retreated to the ancestral home in Lewes to be nearer to one of his sons. He made light of his illness—"old age, I suppose, or what accompanies it"—and quoted the last lines of one of his old favourite reads:

---

[49] Vladimir Nabokov (1973) *Pale Fire*. Notes on line 172. Harmondsworth: Penguin. p.126.

This was all life had left him, all that for a little longer gave him kinship with the earth and with the spacious world which lay glittering under the chilly sun. [50]

A sombre thought, and I shuddered at the idea of him being on this earth for only a little longer. But I was comforted by the rest of his letter which sounded more like the Lewis I knew and loved, although it suggested that writing was now more akin to work than pleasure. That said, he enclosed for my comments a long lyrical drama—I think only the second in that style that he has ever produced—called 'Prometheus Redux'. The very title, with its redolence of such a famous and great poem [51], worried me, but once I had realised that the first two lines were not addressed to me (or perhaps they were):

O Thou that watches over all
And marks the good in man [52]

I got down to work! It was a quite remarkable poem—very much an echo—a short echo—of Shelley's great work (although neither he nor I would pretend any equal merit!). While Shelley's poem seeks to create in Prometheus a perfect revolutionary in an ideal, abstract sense, Lewis's revolutionary fights against the self-aggrandisement and rich pomposity of most formal religions which dictate the impossibility of worship without their support. A theme that we had often discussed between us as evenings wore on. It speaks of

Glorious spires and towers ring with the clamour of pealing tongues
Carved granite and bright stone raise high the Saints while gargoyles spout;

---

[50] Mikhail Sholokhov (1940) *The Don Flows Home to the Sea*. The final volume of *Tikhi Don*. Translated by Stephen Garry. London: Penguin Books, 1970.

[51] Percy Bysshe Shelley (1820) 'Prometheus Unbound' and the Prometheus Bound of Æschylus.

[52] 'Prometheus Redux'. From the unpublished poem now in the editor's collection. He had at one time been a great fan of John Updike and I think the idea for the title came from his *Rabbit Redux*, as—slightly incongruously—he mentions "the burrowing rabbit" in the poem.

while:
> priests must magnify their gods
> The mullahs and the cardinals require their own eminence

and asks:
> When will that deep crypt wherein Prometheus is held bond
>> His belief in his god shrouded by his rejection of the
>> panoply which surrounds
>> That earthen manifestation and governance of his god.
>> And bounds his very prison
> Be opened that he may once again join that lesser pantheon

These are large themes and I felt—despite our previous exchanges on the topic—quite unable to do them justice in a letter! It took me some while to read Shelley's longer work and then some while to work my way through 'Redux' making many notes as I went—but always it was putting my work on 'Dark Ashes' further back. My plan that early Autumn was to work my way through my notes and turn them into a critique that was meaningful and useful to Lewis. But it never got written. Lewis must have been more severely ill than either he knew or was willing to let on and he passed away before I could begin the work in November. That he passed away while writing to me touched me immensely.

Of course, there was a funeral in Sussex attended by the great and good of the literary world. I had prepared what I thought were a few salient but touching remarks—the usual sort of thing, with quotations from a couple or so of his poems—but in the event I was not asked to speak in the church and was left to read my favourite poem—relevant to the moment, I felt—during the reception afterwards—an act to which, for some reason, his son took exception.

Time
It is so many years
since I felt some part of me wane:
all those thousands of days
since we spoke of nothing—
could find no words;
and even many more
since there were whispers
as we lay naked in the night

or in the cottage garden
beneath the harvest sun

It is so many years
that I have known that dark void:
deep within my very soul
and in all those long days
not one has passed,
scarce a moment,
when I do not rejoice
at all each had of each—
every moment that we knew
in the sun, before these years [53]

[53] From the unpublished poem, 'Time', now in the editor's collection.

The Poem

Dark Ashes

i
Innocent
   he met a force
Untried
      it held him

… and wonder drained the world of substance
   re-arranged the pages of his book to give more radiant
                         a reading.

                                     10

The light of new possibilities
pressed down on time.
The girl sang to him "You can hear the boats go by". He
learned her mystery
   and destiny understood his loss.
She read "Man is condemned to be free". And he
knew his responsibilities
   but flew with her wings

                                   20

Newborn
… he spoke of peace and joy; saw the wonder
      of his destiny
      and dreamed.

                        The Daemons frowned on them
                        and, remembering meaning,
                        sought to divide
… wiser, she saw another future; tasted their bitter gall
            but soared   30
            and vanquished all.

Time…
Peace came with distance. Fal smiled on them.
A lull
        when senses knew only a single silent bell
        He remembered
        "Worship is transcendent wonder"   40
and as they rose above the surf
        the gulls, and time itself, stilled: mute and 'mazed at
                the clear karma of their love.
He devoured her mind; she drank his soul.
        The river becomes the sea
                the tide welcomes its waters,
                and it is content.

She drank at his well; was intoxicated by his spirit
        her gaze danced to his will   50
        his future was written in her eyes.
Later, the dark sands kept their secret:

        she wrote her love on his soul
                he read her script and was lost
The night sea whispered

When you see such passion in her eyes
it's time to leave port
        the old sailor said

                                                                         60

ii

Then

he became the high candle around which she flew

the tabernacle in which she dwelt:

    she was the centre of his being

    and all that he knew. The cedars whispered,

    the unicorns knelt and bowed their heads

    and Albina—she of the dawn, protector of ill-fated lovers—

    watched over them.   70

"Your body travels with me; your blood flows in my veins"

For the sway of his calling held him

    and on many days small partings disturbed them;

    briefly.

He did not leave her: only his body was absent awhile.

    She held his mind in thrall to her love

Life spun:

to the west the profane skills of the sea held him;

at each easting his very being was uplifted by her: 80

    she was his guru

    his sun.

It was as if eternity was theirs among the southern cedars

But even heaven knows a world beyond.

He knew.

He could only guess

    at her strength.

    For Llŷr called from the West, Eingana beckoned   90

        He was a thing of the sea and parting was ordained:

            he must forever navigate old horizons

      She—for all her vision—could not see beyond the shore

He knows

the possibility of an orbit

    where umbral time is released by light

    long days on that higher plane eclipse longer darker time

in earthly solitude
her body calls out for understanding
    and cries out…   100

He is torn
    but his odyssey is decreed:
    His ship awaits—the very seas wait to welcome him back.
    His earthly gods demand their due.   105

                The ghost of blind Teiresias prophesied, "…you ask
                about your sweet homecoming, but the god will make
                it a bitter journey. I think you will not escape
                Poseidon, the Earth Shaker, who is angered at heart
                against you… Even so, though you shall suffer, you
                and your friends may yet reach home… when you
                have escaped the dark blue sea…think only of your
                homeward course."

But Teiresias—for all his vision—could not see beyond the shore
or divine the suffering visited on this mortal man's Penelope.

iii
The night that has passed can never return: 120
    the sea quenches all.
Cruel parting after such passion
O woman left behind!

O ship
    Of steel, rivets: deck, bridge, hull and keel:
    Fore and aft, moored tight to her
    Cargo holds: soon filled
    Cabins! One cabin she knows so well!
Bearing him away   130

O man
    Of charts and night watches
    Scanning horizons: navigating so many seas

Do you dream of her? Pine?
     Touch her in your dreams?

O woman left behind
  You can only pray…
  and wait: 140
     It is easier to sail away than be left home!

She could not hear his voice
Time stands still while his letters speak only from the past:
  write to the future and read of the past
  how do you talk when every penned sentence and its answer
  must crawl so far?
                          you in me in you
                          they wrote
Memories!   150
Time is dammed in its hourglass: the stubborn sand
will not fall
she sees him drifting never nearer: a world away
  but she sees nothing!

  she cannot touch his body
  she cannot feel his soul
  she cannot sense his mind

On long southern seas beside the slow gliding albatross,   160
  it seems he too is burdened to drift these cold waters eternally;
time passes, but in passing still leaves its stubborn sands behind.
  Home has never seemed so far.
Without
  he sees her face in everything, at every turn
  her voice whispers
Calls.

Time passes.
And—because it is so ordained—once again   170

the great ship slides gently up her river
    the lovers are joined and… again… the cedars bow over them.

But then, but then
Must he, a sea-bound Sisyphus for ever reach with her the height
- so brief a crest—again to drift down in the spume
    to sea to crest sea's surge again, again; nor
    back to the pebbled shore
    beneath the pier?
Can either he or she withstand the tide's eternal wash?   180

iv
As to the watch a distant mast glint in the empty sea
As on the empty horizon an island speck appears
As in the night a breath touches his skin
So he became aware.
    the waves stretched out towards her and cirrus painted the way
    in his mind he held her   190
        her arms enfolded his being, her body welcomed and
        his late compass calmed their seas:
Their union had always been inevitable

And as again the land held him, she shared his joy…
the very land—each simplest sight: meadow, grove and stream
seemed dressed in brighter light
the flinty shore, the chalky downs sang with them
Old Ælle rejoiced
Time and the world was theirs alone.   200
            The Daemons still frowned:
            sensing a different division,
            their power diminishing

Lace dressed she came to him
The waxy blooms she held seemed eternal
Her body is the ocean and every wave returns
    an echo of the vow. The churchyard trees hold the sound

and the wind carries it forever:
on its breath their love will always sing   210

They are alone!
    So short a time is left,
    her arms held him her body rejoiced she blessed his body
    his arms warmed her his eyes wept for her love
    he held her like a raft she held them afloat

So few days joined and they—who might then have then been rent
apart—saw a further heaven ope:
his lonely watch, her desolate vigil conjoined   220
to cross the seas companioned
    his lonely cabin cell now lighted, soul lifted
    his time now speeds—the sands not held

Above day's depthless deep unbounded sea
    and under many a star at night
she sees the distant blue the faint horizon round
the dolphin cleft wave at the bow the still albatross on station
sea-changing fog and mighty storms, Eingana's distant shores
    and understands their siren call   230

Tasting the sea brine, knowing the ship's noise
Swept by passing airs, dampened by blind fog
she travels
Stranger to the southern stars, guest of warmer seas
Lost to all she has known, hull cloistered
she travels
    By day, by night he keeps his watch
    and marks their time
    else, he wonders at their bounty, revels in their bliss   240
    embraces their time

But now his ship has voyaged too soon (would he had restrained its
                   course): one long year is ended

three departures and three homecomings mark the time
all things pass, her seat of learning calls
He cannot bear to leave

He knows she will struggle to write. Alone, he sees her weep
she yearns for his arms; her books no longer talk to her—   250
he is her text she reads his body repeatedly but
finds no sense. Alone, bereft,
she knows no shore

Where both had sailed, he sails alone. Adrift, his mind can only see
the currents of her sea: her body is his ocean
her mind his distant shore. He plots his course on her flesh
navigates his watch on her skin. He
is lost

        260

When will he—pilot of the seas; helmsman of his destiny—return
his heart to homely Hestia's domain?
    cross limen: see parlour, range and crib again?
    oceans crossed, is he securely docked within the cove, or
    can tide's ebb drag him hence?

Only the Moirai know

        270

v

  He will remember his summer homecoming:
  The joy, the uncharted waters of surprise
  The warm sun on the door, the bees in the honeysuckle.
  She held him close and at arm's length, examined his smile
  Understood his passion:
    he would never leave; the sea had let him go.

        280

  And now their life was compassed by a closer horizon
  Hid from the old world, the larch watched over them.

Behind cattle sheds lost to sight
Walled with borrowed summer stone
    bounded by alder, beech and thorn
Their new haven held their hearts
    at ease:
no pilot would ease a seaward passage from this land
    this Elysian field where life is good to man

                                        290

Ceredig's land became their home…
Arianrhod seemed to smile on them:
    And the home became fruitful
    Their time was blessed

Their home, the cottage, the old farm
surrounded them
    by day its land fed them
    at night its old roof creaked and rustled
        as if the mice were busy too   300

vi
Through tens of years their roots sank deep
Seasons passed…

Winter's bitter winds and Summer's softer edge
Strengthened their kinship with the land
The peace of its earth and space held them
its embrace enclosed them   310
    the only place they wished to know
But in that Spring
some tree, a field seemed somehow less
the hint of something passing
She read "It is not now as it hath been of yore"
and he learned a new mystery
    and the Moirai knew his loss.

From that first love, that light which overcame the shades

is left the warmth of memory   320
      These lines are legacy of
that heat which seared his mind and etched his soul
that love's dominion which held him
            worshiping

In the ashes of the fire there is a memory of the flame.   326

Commentary

Canto i

The poem begins with an almost abrupt and emphatic declaration of change: of movement from one state to another. Clearly, from what follows, the poet is talking about the almost seismic change wrought on his life by the sudden, overdue and very welcome arrival of female company but, as editor and as one who has read and re-read the poem so many times over the years, already in those first few lines I have glimpsed my gilt key and my reading alerts me to the fact that, hidden under the early lines—behind his memory's closet door, as it were—are also references which speak to Lewis' sense of temporal dissonance, or at least to the fluidity of time. In his early letters to me from abroad—long before he began writing poetry—he often spoke of his sense of having travelled that path before.

By which he was not suggesting simply a recognition of place or the simple sense of déjà vu that we all experience from time to time, but of a deeper and almost mystic sense of a parallel or—more accurately—a previous existence. He once wrote these words, spoken by a priest in his short dramatic poem, 'Water' [54].

All my words are water
Flowing
You have lived the way
Flowing
Your lives are water
Flowing
On our land

---

[54] 'Water' Published in *Mostly Welsh* (2019). Talybont: Y Lolfa.

I think it is clear that he was hinting there at the continuity of life: at the idea that life is an endless cycle—like water that, flowing down the river, reaches the sea, is turned into rain to fall on the mountains and return to and down the river to the sea forever. Certainly, his reading in his early life would have introduced him to the Hindu, Sikh and Buddhist belief in karma and rebirth and he was always very conscious of the spiritual idea of cause and effect wherein an individual's intent and actions influence their futures. I believe that he believed that with such a spiritual understanding comes, at least a subliminal, recognition or knowledge of previous lives [55]. And those lives cannot be subtracted from the life now lived. Or indeed from any account of that life.

They are, as Shelley wrote, "episodes of that cyclic poem written by Time upon the memories of men." [56] [57] That much of the story is set on a sea within a sea, an island within an island, is no coincidence and clearly underlines the idea

---

[55] Transmigration or reincarnation—the idea that some part of a living being—be it the soul or mind or consciousness—starts a new life in a different physical body or form after each death is central to Jainism, Hinduism, Buddhism and Sikhism and is also found in many societies around the world (Ceridwen was the Celtic goddess or rebirth) as well as in Orthodox Judaism.

Essentially, this cyclic *Saṃsāra* continues for ever unless a person gains spiritual insights leading to that ultimate spiritual goal, liberation. Kabbalistic reincarnation says that humans reincarnate only to humans and to the same sex. One Buddhist theory suggest that reincarnation occurs through consciousness. But perhaps it is Hinduism that most clearly suggests the possibility of memories of a former life: Ātman is a Sanskrit word for the inner self or soul that is described in the Bhagavad Gita as meaning unborn, eternal, omnipresent, constant, and immovable: "Just as in the body childhood, adulthood and old age happen to an embodied being. So also the embodied being acquires another body. The wise one is not deluded about this."

Interestingly, Greek mythology suggests that the dead who drink from the River Lethe would lose all memory of their past existence and Plato (*The Republic,* Book X) even notes that the souls of the dead *must* [my emphasis] drink from the "river of Unmindfulness" before they can be reborn—thus no memory of a past incarnation is possible. So much for mythology…or perhaps the Lethe has lost some of its potency over the centuries.

[56] Percy Bysshe Shelley (1821) *A Defence of Poetry.*

[57] This seems to be a rich seam for some future doctoral research: "Poets' Lives—Death, rebirth and reincarnation: An investigation into…" As a further example, Robert Browning wrote, "For I believe we do not wholly die," and again, "I think the soul can never / Taste death" (*Paracelcus*. Part IV).

of a story within a story. Equally, it is no coincidence that as we approach the end of the poem, Lewis references Arianrhod, the Celtic Goddess of fertility, and thus also reminds us again of rebirth, and the weaving of cosmic time—something usually associated with her name [58].

No one would argue other than that a surface reading of the poem offers an autobiographical, current-day love story. However, a little careful analysis reveals the message at the poem's start: that there is a second layer hidden beneath the first. Even the draft title under which the poem was originally published—'Retrospective'—suggests that it is dealing with a review—a re-telling—of past events. I believe that when Lewis changed the title as he started me on this course, he did not entirely lose this idea (ashes speaking of past fires) while at the same time both producing poetical precision by referencing the ending in the title and also, perhaps, suggesting editorial circumspection by obliquely referencing a previous editor and his work.

The first four short lines clearly speak of the force of destiny and its ability to effect events over long periods of time. (We will, of course, deal with the more apparent, narrative readings shortly.) The following two lines—particularly the second—also suggest quite clearly the idea of two readings—rearranging the content to give "more radiant a reading". The case is almost made! But the final argument for two narratives held apart only by time certainly becomes clear in the next two lines:

The light of new possibilities
pressed down on time.

As Lawrence wrote, "we struggle mechanically, unformed, unbegotten, unborn, repeating some old process of life, unable to become ourselves, unable to produce anything new" [59]—and that struggle is confused by our memories. Bertrand Russell suggests that a memory image is only separated from an image of the present by being accompanied by a feeling of familiarity [60]. And in August 1999, Leonard Cohen—of whom, more later—wrote:

[58] Canto v: Line 292.

[59] D H Lawrence (1914) *Study of Thomas Hardy*. Chapter v.

[60] Bertrand Russell (1921) *The Analysis of Mind*. Lecture ix.

All he knows
is that this has happened before—
this moment, next moment, last moment.
It is playing a second time,
maybe a third.
Yes, a third time.
He remembers remembering it. [61]

So Lewis' memories: his life narratives run through 'Dark Ashes' with barely anything to separate them, with barely distinguished identities: the more obvious present day and the almost subliminal historic accounts woven into a single cloth. As any weaver will tell you—and I look to one of my mother's samplers, hanging over the back of a chair in the lounge of my cottage, for confirmation—the same threads, the same warp and weft, create different patterns on either side of the finished fabric, and it is only by folding the cloth—as Lewis has done—that both can be seen at once. 'Dark Ashes' is that fold in the fabric of time.

I have always known the front of the cloth intimately of course, but over the years I think that I may have glimpsed its back occasionally when Lewis has lifted its selvedge—almost a nervous tic, rarely exhibited—during conversation; so a considerable amount of historical and literary research was needed to piece together his earlier 'adventures'. But I am confident that I have teased out correctly the underlying account so cleverly threaded through by the poet. I feel that I have earned my editorial stripes! And indeed, as an ironic aside, the new possibilities—as I suggested in the Foreword—did 'press down' on my time too.

Students who read my commentary in conjunction with the poem may wonder at the breadth of detail I have supplied, often triggered by only a word or phrase from Lewis. It is the work of scholars to determine the underlying meaning and to place it in the context of the writer's society and history, and my research has been painstaking and I am confident of my analysis. Observant readers will note that some of the poetry apparently read by Yseult was actually published long after she lived—where it was impossible to determine the words she read, I have taken the liberty of using more modern lines to express both what were clearly her feelings at the time and to reinforce for the reader her acknowledged love of poetry.

---

[61] Leonard Cohen (August 1999) "All He Knows". *The Flame.* Robert Faggan and Alexandra Pleshoyano (eds.) Edinburgh: Canongate, 2018. p. 78.

Lines 1-9:
Innocent
    he met a force
Untried
      it held him

As I suggested above, the poem begins with an almost abrupt and emphatic declaration of change: of movement from one state to another. Clearly from what follows, the poet is talking about the metamorphic change wrought on his life by the sudden and welcome arrival of female company. And such a change. We can only begin to imagine what this sudden transformation in his life might have been and how it would hold him, although perhaps there is some clue in the use of the word 'innocent' applied as it is to a grown man. We can imagine him at this stage: the first lines presage an almost shocking transformation.

The lone sailor from Zeta [62] had almost reached his home port, but returning from a long voyage, he landed on the North East coast of the nearby island of Mljet to replenish his supply of water. Hardly necessary given how close he was to home but perhaps he felt the need to pause and collect his thoughts, or perhaps he was drawn there by some whispered song of the wind. There on the shore, as he walked back from the spring with a container of its pure and sweet-tasting water, he was met on the beach by a beautiful young girl and was immediately spellbound by her loveliness: her long auburn-gold honey-coloured hair and amber eyes were remarkable in themselves but they only served to illuminate a face at once wilful and strong, and softly beautiful.

Already, Tristram was entranced. She was robed in a simple white kaftan belted at the waist by woven cord which did little to hide her perfect figure. Tristram felt powerless against the almost magnetic pull of her beauty and was suddenly unable to continue with his task—in the moment, he had almost forgotten the need to take water on board his ship, *Bäckahästen* (he had named her for a mythological horse of Scandinavian folklore [63]), and his urgent need to continue his voyage, and he was lured away from the beach and the jetty and further onto the island. It seemed his mind could only consider, could only see

---

[62] As well as being the sixth letter in the Greek alphabet, Zeta was a part of the medieval Serbian state, roughly equivalent to part of present-day Croatia/Montenegro.

[63] *Bäckahästen* translates literally as 'Brook Horse' but Tristram had apparently understood it as Water- or Sea-Horse.

the girl he later learned to call Yseult, and nothing else seemed to matter. He later told her that it was as if she had cast a spell on him—its effect on him could have been no stronger than was his first sight of her.

He had been away a long time as his father's, the King's emissary visiting his outlying lands to secure their continuing agreement to trade and to their tythes, and had been returning to the Zetan capital to report to the palace. He knew that, once he had delivered his report, his return south was crucial if a breakup of their union was to be averted. He also knew that if no agreement could be reached, Zeta would certainly be the poorer as the trade agreements would break down, and—although it was ill-understood by the majority of their ministers—the southern colony's future prosperity would be in doubt.

He feared for their people. But his responsibilities and his report on his time away, long expected by his father, seemed to mean nothing now in the light of this transfiguration, his almost transubstantiation from base mortal to heavenly suppliant: courtier to courter! His further travels were temporarily forgotten, his only destiny had become Yseult.

Leaving his *qārib* [64] tied to the jetty—although he did glance up at the sky, out to sea and at *Bäckahästen* to make sure her sails were adequately stowed and it was safe to leave her, Tristram followed behind Yseult across the yellow sands and through pine and cedar woods to a large lake where she was waiting for him by a small rowing boat. In a moment when he remembered his father and his duties to him, Tristram pleaded with her to come back with him but she seemed determined that it was not to be and she pushed the little craft from the shore. Tristram could not bear to lose her and so felt he had no choice but to leap aboard as she began to scull away from the beach with a single oar over the stern.

In all this time, Yseult had not uttered a single word although there was no doubt that she wanted Tristram to follow her. Even as she propelled the little boat forward while Tristram cried out his newfound love for her, she remained silent. Only when the prow bumped against a little jetty did she speak a single word, "Come!" she said.

As they had approached, Yseult had taken the boat around to what proved to be the far side of a small island in the lake, but all of the time as they approached close to the shore and under the threatening bulwarks of a castle Tristram did not see any other sign of life—no guards, no servants or indeed inhabitants of any

---

[64] *Qārib*: a small caravel-style sailing ship.

kind seemed to live in the silent castle. Yseult beckoned him forward and almost ran along the short jetty, up a grassy slope and through a hidden gap in the walls.

Almost stumbling in his fear of losing her, Tristram hurried after her, just in time to see her disappear through a door at the foot of the South West Tower on the far side of a wide courtyard. Becoming ever more fearful of the outcome and wondering if he would ever get to see—let alone report to—his father again, Tristram followed—through the door and up an old spiral stairway.

It seems extraordinary that the young sailor—some twenty years old when the poem begins—can have been entirely innocent, but that is certainly how our hero would have described himself. Looking at his story, we can see his strictly religious upbringing in which although love, let alone sex, was never discussed he was somehow aware that—should anything physical erupt before marriage—it would constitute a dreadful and unforgiveable sin. His father's awkward parting words (unexplained) to him as he boarded his ship, "If you can't be good, be careful" did little to help.

So, while in his early time at sea opportunity must have presented itself, he was shy of women and did not find it easy to form even innocent friendships with girls, the more so as he knew that his peers would have assumed—and probably loudly applauded the fact—that such friendships were entirely intended to satisfy a carnal urge he did not have!

In the early days, as a young cadet, when formal dances were organised, he drifted around the edge of them, awkward and lonely. When he was on leave, most of his former friends would be away at some academy or university and he knew only the court of his parents.

Now, arriving at the doorway of what was obviously Yseult's chamber, no such awkwardness remained. Through the door could be seen elaborate hangings and draperies, a large chair covered in fine silks, a small desk and table with a candelabra, and the floor covered in woven rugs and the pelt of a brown bear. Books filled a large alcove near the desk and two volumes of poems were on a table by the bed. On the wall behind a bed hung a fine and beautiful rug woven in silken threads of many colours. The light from the small, high window to the right of the doorway in which he stood fell on Yseult and showed her in all her beauty facing him with a silver chalice from which almost without thought or pause he drank deeply. Again she offered it and again he took his fill—it seemed the chalice was never emptied nor his thirst satisfied.

Time passed, and Tristram learned that Yseult had lived in the castle all her life and, since the death of her old friend and tutor, only ever seeing a few servants when they brought food and supplies. Although she was able to leave the small island in the lake, she had never been able to leave the island of Mljet. This she had been told was only possible if she was invited to do so. She had wanted for nothing and had been almost entirely happy in her life until she had seen Tristram arrive, when her eyes were opened to a new radiance and the beauty of an outside world to which she had been blind before, and words she had once read but, she said, not really understood, were blazoned again before her eyes—"How beauteous mankind is! O brave new world, That has such people in't!" [65] Almost frightened by this new shape of nature and scarcely daring to hope that this wonderful creature would not vanish before her eyes she had brought him to the one place that was truly hers and where she felt safe. She remembered Iolanta's awakening to the light and her words:

o čego spasti,
bezropotno mogu ya vsyo snesti.
On dorog mne, on pervïy mne otkrïl
čto značit svet, i serdce mne sogrel.
Teper' ya veryu, znayu, čto svet est'!

oh, to save him,
I can endure everything without a murmur.
He is dear to me, he made known to me
what light means, and warmed my heart.
Now I believe I know what light is! [66]

She gave him a gold torque which, she said, must bind him to her forever and Tristram was more than happy with the exchange. As night darkened the room, they fell asleep in each other's arms but even as he dreamed of the riches

---

[65] William Shakespeare, *The Tempest* Act 5 Sc.1. Miranda's speech to which Prospero replies, "'Tis new to thee!"

[66] Pyotr Ilyich Tchaikovsky (1892) *Iolanta: A Lyric Opera in One Act.* Libretto by Modest Ilyich Tchaikovsky. Iolanta's words and the translation by Jane Iles taken from sleeve notes (eds. Manuela Amadei, Eva Reisinger): 479-3969 Deutsche Grammophon, 2015.

ready to drop on him, Tristram's sleep was troubled with thoughts of his father the King and the reports that he was still to make.

In the morning light, there was fruit and drink on the table and, while they broke their fast, Tristram begged Yseult to accompany him to his father's palace where he was sure she would be made welcome and that their marriage could be celebrated in short order. Tristram had explained his mission and the heavy responsibilities surrounding its success; had told her of Zeta and his heritage; and had explained his urgent need to return. Yseult, newly aware of the greater world and freed from her curse, could only agree, and she did so joyously! She was rescued from her castle tower by a real prince! Gathering the few things she needed, it was her turn to follow Tristram as he led her back to the jetty and onto his boat. Where before Tristram's journey had been arduous and lonely, now he sailed with a light heart and hope for the future: even the wind remained favourable!

Arriving in Zeta's fortress harbour, Tristram summoned the King's guards and was brought fresh clothes. Together with Yseult he was escorted to the palace and they came before the King. Hearing and seeing the reason for the delay in receiving the important news carried by his son he flew into a rage and banished Yseult from Zeta. Nothing that his son said could change the sentence once handed down. It seemed as if Yseult was seen as a scheming witch—even a Siren [67]—who had tempted his honest and loyal son from his duties by her songs of love. Yseult was now terrified of this new world to which her eyes had been opened and fled back to her castle on the island within an island. And, of course, Tristram could only follow and, in that moment, seemed lost to Zeta.

Soon after I met Trystan Lewis, when we were still at school, Lewis, though not I, used to work in a local nursery—mostly outside with the men digging or tending to the tomato greenhouses and to the shrubs they sold, or loading the lorry with decorative plants to place around the concert stage at the Brangwyn Hall, where he marvelled at the painted murals as he brought in the plants. The irony of decorating the Hall with foliage far less exuberant than what was already present in the Empire Panels—themselves "far too exuberant for [the]

---

[67] The first of many references to the *Argonautica* and Odysseus/Ulysses: the slightly contrived connection seems intended to elevate the poem to a higher level. As Dr Johnson says (*The Rambler* 121), "The wars of Troy and the travels of Ulysses have furnished almost all succeeding poets with incidents, characters and sentiments!"

conventional and restrained surroundings" [68] of the Royal Gallery, but somehow deemed perfect for the new Guildhall in Swansea—was not entirely lost on him! But sometimes, too, he would work in the flower room helping the girls to prepare blooms for wreaths and bridal bouquets.

And so it was that at the age of nineteen on leave from the sea, he was able to rekindle a friendship with one of the girls, asking her nervously over the telephone in his parent's hallway, whether she would like to stroll along the shore with him as he had to walk the dog. That she accepted, amazed him! But what followed did nothing to end his age of innocence and although they went out together several times to see films at the cinema and even for an occasional meal, it was clear that she had a real boyfriend and that while he was welcome to put his arm round her shoulders as they watched the film, nothing further was on offer! Lewis probably kept the relationship going out of desperation. On leave from the navy, he was lonely.

And his parents retained a strong grip on his life at home. On one occasion when an old school friend invited him to a party—a party which did not start until late in the evening and would continue into the small hours, so "expect me when you see me" he told his parents, his mother telephoned the friend's house at five minutes past one in the morning to see where he was! It was the last party he ever went to from home.

And so, for Trystan, life went on. He bought a sports car and enjoyed the open road but did not often venture far from home, using it chiefly to get to the beaches and to facilitate a summer spent at a nearby nautical college which allowed him to return to sea as an officer. This meant that his three or four months away travelling to New Zealand or Australia was now as a young officer responsible for the navigation and the cargo; time interspersed with weeks at home where time moved slowly towards the next departure.

So much for background and innocence. We know that the poem begins as he arrived back in the Royal Albert Docks in London and prepared to return home on leave. He knew that, unusually, his father and sister were to meet him from the ship and he was planning to show them around before leaving. From his cabin overlooking the foredeck he could see—between the cargo nets of frozen lamb and the pallets of butter being lifted from the forward hatches and swung out over the dockside to drop down amongst the workers for dispatch to who knows where—the approaches, and so was able to be at the gangway to

---

[68] The Fine Art Commission (20 February 1930).

greet them. He was surprised to see a third person on the dock—short, pretty and dressed in a mini-skirted frock that—to his considerable embarrassment—was already causing some whistling and comment from the nearby crew members. It stopped when it became evident that the guests were his!

He must have learned in short order that this was the daughter of a family friend who was on her way to holiday with his sister and that this unusual but welcome lift home had been occasioned by the possibility of collecting her at the same time. His private diary records the impression she made on him and notes that by the end of the five-hour journey the first stirrings of love—or at least, of interest—had begun. And he eventually wrote excitedly to me about her (there is a letter to me from Cardiff in the appendix). The girl, K., was lovely and she was neither shy nor put off by his evident awkwardness with her.

On board when he had been in his element, he had been confident and sure, talking about his work on the ship and about the cargo that was being unloaded. In the days that followed, as the sea ran out of his veins, and home life resumed, K. noticed that Trystan was quieter. Only when he began talking about his ships and the sea did he seem invigorated… and she encouraged him to tell her of— her phrase—his adventures. Inevitably the two girls and Trystan went out together—Lewis was the one with a car after all—but the two of them also spent much of the following two weeks on beaches or sightseeing alone.

But the effects on Lewis were both evident and intense. And I know from a conversation with his sister some years ago that she was also affected and felt awkward: very much the odd one out—and often left out—of outings. She, possibly parentally influenced, felt at the time that K. was the driving force in the budding relationship and that her brother was being sucked in or taken in, although she could probably not have expressed it in those terms. Lewis was blind to this as, in quiet moments, the first stumblings—at least on his part—into a physical relationship took place.

Lewis would be the first to admit that much of the early impetus came from K. He was not only shy with girls, he *knew* he was both shy and inexperienced and had rationalised this into the feeling that it was 'polite'—perhaps 'appropriate' is a better word—not to force himself on someone—as if he ever could have done so—but to allow them to accept him! And to demonstrate such acceptance. So the first touches and kisses were nothing if not magical: now his life knew nothing but his newfound love and he was blind to almost everything else: the story of his life had changed.

Lines 12-19:
The light of new possibilities

These lines seem to set the pattern of at least one aspect of the new relationship. K. may have been in awe of Lewis's apparent worldliness but she was in most senses the more worldly of the two! Not only was she better read at that time but her knowledge of life: languages, music, history—as well as literature—far surpassed his. Her musical tastes included Woody Guthrie, Joan Baez and, by far the most important, Leonard Cohen, while her reading included Sartre, Zola, Camus and Herman Hesse—most of whom were unknown to Lewis. Ironically, given that K.'s language skills included Russian, he was reading Mikhail Sholokhov (although he had not discovered Solzhenitsyn—or indeed, Nabokov—at that time).

So, from almost the beginning, she set out not so much to educate him as to make him her equal. Lewis was acutely aware that he had left school and gone to sea while K.—like many of his own school friends—had stayed on in the sixth form: he was in awe of learning and erudition and he would have been unable to quote from either Leonard Cohen or Sartre!

So, from the lofty heights of the present, Lewis reaches out to his former self, remembering the intimacy hinted at by Leonard Cohen in 'Suzanne'—which at the time was an intimacy far beyond if not his wildest dreams, then beyond life in his parental home—and the way it seemed to link with his nautical life: "Suzanne takes you down to her place near the river / You can hear the boats go by / You can spend the night beside her". He knew that in some almost mysterious way that visiting K.—and this was something they had already imagined—would occasion a break with his present life because it was already apparent that it, in the personage of his parents, was not about to be accepting of her entrée into the family, either now or in the future.

Sartre wrote—although I doubt in fact that K. read it to him at the time—"Man is condemned to be free; because once thrown into the world, he is responsible for everything he does" [69] and he had begun to understand that he was already 'of the wider world' rather than being simply a part of—an extension of—his childhood home. It was an idea that had not perhaps occurred to him before—or at least, not so forcefully—suddenly he was a man in his own right!

---

[69] Jean-Paul Sartre: (1943) *L'être et le néant* (*Being and Nothingness*).

At the same time he knew that he had familial responsibilities—a debt of allegiance, if you like—but understood, too, his new responsibilities to life.

However Lewis saw himself in this life, the influence of his parents and of his upbringing remained strong and he could not quite shake off the view that physical love should only be within the context of marriage—not that there was much opportunity beyond the occasional fumble as they lay together on the beach. That he ached to hold her and that K. was more than willing for him to do so cannot be doubted, but he was held back by—or held himself back because of—the heavy, dominating, censorial and unforgiving presence of his parents.

Despite a number of tortured conversations and telephone calls with Lewis, I cannot know all that passed between him and K. ... or indeed between him and his parents at this time. Life was on the one hand wonderful and the sun shone both literally and figuratively on their time together; but in the background there were dark clouds and a clear tension developing as his parents sought to stop what they saw as a silly flirtation becoming a love affair. Following her holiday, K. was due to catch a train to join her family on holiday in Cornwall so a time apart seemed inevitable and it was clearly expected that this enforced separation would bring an end to this nonsense. The lovers—we can call them that although their physicality went no further than a hidden kiss or a fondle—had other ideas.

Lines 22-31:
Newborn…

This was a new world for Lewis and he existed in a dream only grounded when the outside world interrupted his euphoria. And disruption from the outside world was parent shaped. He felt as if his life to this point had been nothing: simply preparation or groundwork for what was to come in the future, but an imperfect and incomplete training which left him unsure of how to behave and of what could reasonably be expected of him.

We are in the sixties: on the one hand there was free love, peace, flower power and the sexual promiscuity which surrounded both his time at sea and—seemingly—everyone else, and on the other, an upright, chaste and moral background—confusion was inevitable! He was torn—torn between the habit of obedience and loyalty to his family and the remarkably strong, new feeling of love which he had never experienced before and which seemed to promise him everything. Of course Bob Dylan's lyrics can never have been far from his mind as he struggled to come to terms with the expectations of his parents and those of K.:

> Come mothers and fathers
> Throughout the land
> And don't criticize
> What you can't understand
> Your sons and your daughters
> Are beyond your command [70]

He was probably not in the best place to make rational decisions and later, he acknowledged that his strategy of confronting everyone on the morning of K.'s departure with their plan was wrong headed and foolish, but perhaps it stemmed in part from his knowledge that this would be a difficult conversation and so it was put off. After breakfast he announced that they had—he and K. whom he had come to love—an idea. Simply, it would save the train fare and the need for his father to take K. to the station—he would drive K. to Falmouth!

The eruption of anger at their silliness—such a plan was absurd, his parents stood *in loco parentis* and could not allow it, he had nowhere to stay in Falmouth and so on—shocked him. That his father almost forced K. into his car against her will angered him beyond rational thought and stopping only to grab a bag of clothes and without a further word to anyone, he leapt into his own car and left! He stopped at a telephone booth and with his AA book and some difficulty managed to find a hotel that had a room left and headed for Cornwall.

Meanwhile, K.—having little choice—accepted her fate in the certain knowledge that this was not the end game: the fates would bring them together again. Little could she have known how soon! K. was banished!

The word daemon or daimon goes back to a Proto-Indo-European root and came to signify a deity who provides or divides (fortunes or destinies), but although referencing the *da-* (for divide) root, here Lewis has used it in the ancient Greek sense where rather than referring to a specific class of divine beings, daimon references a peculiar mode of activity: a power that drives someone forward or—as in the case of his parents' forceful efforts—acts against them. That, all these years later, Lewis should make such a forceful and bitter declaration, with all the implied arcane, demonic references can only show the

---

[70] Bob Dylan (1963) *The Times They are a-Changin'*.

strength of his feelings at the time [71]. His long drive south gave him ample time to reflect righteously on the evil done to them by "the sad weight of parental love" [72].

I remember suggesting to him that he could make so much more of these lines and of the allusion within them. I thought it was too oblique, too subtle for the reader to understand what was being referenced. But I had been an external observer of these events and knew that my actions would have been very different; Lewis—although his parents may not have thought so at the time—remained dutiful to his father and mother and, even at this remove, would not write anything that could have hurt them.

The King and his Lady had long awaited news from the distant corners of their world and of course they looked forward to seeing their son again, not only to hear his news but to welcome him home with all the celebrations due to a traveller and adventurer before he returned to the southern colonies. They knew that he had weathered storms and travelled far—in fact, they thought almost as far as it was thought possible to venture, and probably saw him as some epic hero lashed to a mast exhorting the crew to greater things so that his ship and the precious cargo it carried would reach port [73]. In addition to waiting on his news, the King had invited guests to hear of his adventures and these were expected in court soon, having been put off several times as his son's ship had not been sighted. Perhaps, too, the King and his wife had worried at his continued absence.

Whatever the cause, Tristram arrived in a Court that was more concerned with the Siren who accompanied him than with the news for which they had been long waiting, for word had travelled from the port with the guards. So, when Tristram—without much, or perhaps any, of the ceremony and manners that he

---

[71] Lewis once told me that, even then when he was most upset and angry, he did not consider his parents as acting malevolently—they were clearly acting in what they thought were his best interests, and to protect K. for whom they were temporarily responsible. That they thought they knew better, could control his life and dictate to him seemed at the time to stem only from the rather selfish thought that K. was not good enough for their son. This came mostly when he telephoned me in the hope that I could cheer him up but he also wrote a second letter to me in London from Cardiff.

[72] A phrase taken from an unpublished poem written by Lewis in 2018 and now in the editor's collection. The title 'Who breaks a butterfly upon a wheel?' comes from a line in Alexander Pope's 1735 'Epistle to Dr Arbuthnot'.

[73] This oblique reference to Homer's *Odyssey* is not entirely out of place: Lewis' poem is also a marine epic in which the gods test valour and love.

had learned as a young courtier—announced (in his haste he did not even consider a more appropriate course of action would be to request permission) his intention to marry, the King and Queen were momentarily nonplussed before the King, calling on as much dignity as he could muster, shamed as he had just been by his son, silenced him with a gesture. And made the awful pronouncement.

As we shall see, there can be little doubt that he lived to regret the action that was forced on him; indeed, even as he spoke and the hush fell on the gathered court he must have felt the enormity and the dreadful possibilities of his decision, but Kings do not falter. In his pain it is as if this visitation is from a scheming, vengeful sister of the Erinyes [74]—she must leave the court forthwith, be given a boat and supplies, and escorted out of the harbour. He did not even enquire whether she could sail a boat!

Tristram fell back as if he had suffered a blow in battle, stumbling briefly to one knee while Yseult, horrified at this cruel new world with its semblance of social graces but flourish of real power, stood proud and met the King's eye. Pointing a finger directly at him, she seemed to speak—but none heard the words above the anguished cry from Tristram. As Kafka has suggested, "Sirens have a still more fatal weapon than their song, namely their silence" [75]. Only the King knew the significance of what had transpired and, although he remained proudly erect in front of his throne—where he had stood to pass judgment—he paled and, as if momentarily undecided, glanced at his wife who seemed not to have noticed what had passed. By the time he had regained his composure and looked up again, Yseult had fled. Moments later as the ladies and gentlemen of the court withdrew in deference to their monarch, Tristram was gone too. The King understood then that it was unlikely that he could ever escape her silence—his heir was gone and his goods and the country's future seemed forfeit.

Lines 35-43:
Time…

---

[74] In Greek mythology, the Erinyes, also known as the Furies, were female chthonic (from the Greek *khthónios*—meaning the underworld) deities of vengeance.

[75] Franz Kafka (1931) *Das Schweigen der Sirenen* (*The Silence of the Sirens*): "…it is conceivable that someone might possibly have escaped from their singing; but from their silence certainly never."

Reunions can be magically wonderful but before the dizzy heights of transcendent pleasure there has to be a slough of despond [76]. As the little ketch in which she had been placed skimmed over the calm seas towards Mljet, Yseult barely troubled to trim sail or adjust her course—she simply slumped over the tiller in the stern and wept bitter tears of despair. Had she stood for a moment and looked astern she might have made out a larger vessel on the same course as hers—but, being larger, it was not as fast and fell ever further astern until—as she approached her island—it was no longer in sight.

Although she had sailed boats nearly all her life and could reasonably have been considered a skilful sailor, her arrival at the jetty was ill made and she scraped along the side with sail still set, only leaping ashore with a rope as the boat began to ground in the shallows at the landward end of the pier. Leaving the sails flapping in the light wind she leapt down onto the golden sands of the beach and collapsed sobbing.

Which was where some forty minutes later Tristram found her after securing his boat unnoticed—and somewhat more carefully—behind hers. The late afternoon sun lit rivers of fire in her hair and, even slumped on the sand as she was, accentuated her beauty—Tristram, knowing he could never leave her, knelt beside her and embraced her, pressing a braided ring of royal gold with a green jade stone onto her finger. For her part, Yseult could barely believe the turn in her fortunes—in less than seconds she gone from a condemned and banished 'Siren' to a Princess. The calm peace of her island home "dropping slow"—like the sound of the lake's lapping waves—to her "deep heart's core" restored her and the only thought she had, the only thing she knew, was their love [77].

Hand in hand, they walked through the woods towards the great lake— Veliko Jezero—with its island, a sea within a sea; an island within an island— their two-fold mystic release from Saṃsāra [78], and the castle and the church,

---

[76] On re-reading this, I have to recognise that my original footnote was probably an inappropriate allusion—the pilgrim in John Bunyan's *Pilgrim's Progress* sinks into the slough under the weight of his sins and guilt. If Tristram felt guilt at his hasty departure from his father's court, it is not apparent in the poem.

[77] Lewis cannot but have made the connection to another lake island (although Tristram was far from living in clay and wattles). I am sure William Butler Yeats' poem, 'The Lake Isle of Innisfree', would have been in his mind throughout.

[78] Sanskrit word that means "wandering" or the "world" and which also refers to the idea of rebirth to a new life.

Crkva Sv Marije, where perhaps in the future their union could be blessed. What greater sanctuary could they have than this worldly Moksha [79]? Outsiders could never attain such liberation from the world or reach the heart of their love.

After the troubled times in South Wales, the reunion in Cornwall was wonderful for both Trystan and K. She had had no idea that he would be there and had spent the long hours on the train in a near suicidal mood cursing Trystan's parents for their cruel intransigence and—to a lesser extent—Trystan himself for his failure to stand up to them. Although, she acknowledged, there had been little chance for him to do so. She was met from the train by her father who was unable to understand why she was so unhappy. Explanations did not really come until Trystan knocked on the door of their holiday cottage later that evening. And then she knew peace.

The hell of the last week was far away, the soft Cornish air whispered peace. They had respite. After Trystan left for his hotel that evening, K. told her parents something of what had happened in his home—how they had been condemned for their love, how it was made clear that she was not good enough for Trystan, and how she had been treated at the end.

Trystan had suffered two lines from a recently-learned song playing through his mind for almost the entire journey from Wales, probably triggered by an innate guilt at his abrupt departure:

Yes you who must leave everything that you cannot control.
It begins with your family, but soon it comes around to your soul;[80]

but now the guilt he had felt was overcome by the other sensation which had been temporarily driven to the back of his mind: love! Driving back to his turret room in the hotel he had found—probably the last room available in Cornwall, Trystan could only see one thing, and it shone out of the darkness with a clarity his vision had never known before: it was as if a heavenly light sang in his ear at the same time that it fell on is eye—it consumed and overwhelmed his senses so that all he knew was the light of his love for K.—anything outside or beyond that was a bleak and silent darkness void of any sensory stimulation, void even of air to breath!

---

[79] From the Sanskrit: a term in Hinduism which refers to various forms of emancipation or liberation: freedom from the ignorance of the world, freedom from the world.
[80] Leonard Cohen. *Sisters of Mercy.*

He was astonished at the power of his feeling and knew that—come what may—their futures were forever conjoined. He had read somewhere "Worship is transcendent wonder; wonder for which there is now no limit or measure; that is worship" [81] and he knew that this described perfectly his state of being at this moment. Perhaps also, he had in mind:

In that I loved you, Love, I worshipped you. [82]

As an editorial aside, I have no idea where in his past Lewis finds these quotations nor indeed why he sprinkles them throughout his own lines so freely, but there are some eight or nine points in his 326 lines where Lewis borrows the erudition or perfect phrasing of another to enhance or strengthen his own words. Of course it is not unusual—it is even expected—in 'scholarly' or editorial writing, indeed only a few lines back I referenced Kafka! But perhaps Lewis felt some weaknesses in his poem—places where it needed some borrowed authority—and fell back on my habits of an academic lifetime.

Our own conversations about the text while it was in preparation certainly hinted at some uncertainty and insecurity, but I had taken this to stem only from his concerns about exposing aspects of his past, his life—and the lives of those around him—in such a way. Now I think that while that was the literal truth, Lewis was unable to recognise or express it as such—even to himself—and used scholarship, sometimes *my* scholarship, to disguise and strengthen his own elegant words, while—perhaps unconsciously—softening what he was exposing by the use of universal truisms. If actually that is the case then this commentary may, I suppose, undo some of his good work... but I refer the reader to Lewis' advice in his letter to me.

Line 38:
when senses knew only a single silent bell

It is quite possible to read that line as redolent of a present wonder—a perfect chime of happiness—particularly in the light of the lines that follow. However, a silent bell—as Lewis knew only too well from his family's love of

---

[81] Thomas Carlyle: Lecture: 'The Hero as Divinity'.
[82] Wilfred Owen. 'Eros' *The Collected Poems of Wilfred Owen*. London: Chatto & Windus, 1963. p100.

campanology—is a bell waiting to sound, standing, finely balanced, waiting to toll at the tug of its sally. So there is a sense of something impending, a threat of a tumbling, crashing noise that would destroy their peaceful heaven. Trystan doubted that his parents would try to intervene further but as Lewis has—so subtly—suggested, it was always there at the edge of his consciousness.

Many years later, he wrote:

Wonderful was that time in summer [83]

In the days that followed, it felt as if—whether they were alone or on a beach with her parents—the world stood back in wonder at their love. Maybe all young lovers experience a similar selfish self-centred radiance when each feels that nothing is in focus except the other and time moves slowly around them, when their love is so clear and perfect that it can only lead to a perfect future, but Trystan and K. were not concerned with what others felt.

Lines 44-51:
He devoured her mind…

If these lines express anything, it is love—intoxicating, all embracing young love! "she drank his soul"—Lewis would have undoubtedly remembered Tennyson's lines:

O Love, O fire! once he drew
With one long kiss, my whole soul thro'
My lips, as sunlight drinketh dew. [84]

Each of the young lovers was entranced by the other and each gave, and each took as much as the other. There is an innocence in the language and an obvious joy in the giving of one to the other with complete abandonment to the consequences. Perhaps, too, there is a hint of the beginnings of sexual gratification. Given the maritime background—both of the coast and beaches, and of our hero—the symbolism used is unsurprising. If he is the sea, then she,

---

[83] From an unpublished poem—'The Summer of Love'— written by Lewis in 2018 and now in the editor's collection.
[84] Alfred Lord Tennyson (1833) 'Fatima'. Possibly inspired by Sappho.

the river, becomes—and I am certain that this is meant in both the sense enhancing or making more attractive, and of adding to or turning into—the sea, and the sea is pleased to receive her! It is a theme that surfaces in a number of his other poems, particularly in 'Ocean' and the dramatic work, 'Water'.

In these lines, too, we can also detect the differences between hero and heroine. He may be the stronger and more capable of the two, but she has the learning and a strength of will that will see them through whatever the outside world may throw at them!

When Tristram had first seen Yseult's chamber he had been struck by the library of books near her desk but had thought little of it. He was to learn that this was, in fact, only a small part of the castle's old library and that, left alone and lonely on her isle since her parents had been killed—apparently in a hunting accident, Yseult had read, in fact had devoured much of what was archived there. Her particular passion was for poetry, and many of the books by her bed were by local poets.

The prince had been well educated in Zeta but his conventional tutoring was no match for the breadth of what had been consumed by Yseult. While Tristram's mind was newly assaulted by a thousand new philosophies and ideas, by the power of poetry, Yseult loved and revelled in his tales of the wider world and his love of the oceans—it was, she felt, the very life force that empowered him.

Together they walked around their little island and together they sailed around Veliko Jezero, picnicking in its little coves shaded by the dapples of the tall eucalyptus or shaded by cedar trees. To his surprise, Tristram discovered the water was salty and that at the far end of the lake there was a channel to the sea. They did not venture through in the little lake dingy but on other days they swapped the small sea for the larger, and sailed around Mljet in Tristram's boat. All the while Yseult recounted her life's story to him or Tristram, perhaps remembering his neglected responsibilities, rather shame-facedly told her of his father's palaces and lands. But the first day when Yseult showed him around the castle with its great banqueting hall, its library and schoolroom, the walls and towers and the myriad of lesser rooms Tristram understood her love of her home and, too, thought that he understood his future.

Yseult had been born far away in the Ottoman south but, for reasons never explained, the family had suddenly fled north and found a home on this isolated island. She was just four when her father, accompanied by her mother and a retinue of staff, had sailed to the mainland to hunt wild boar. They had never returned but her father's chief aide—her Uncle Iski, İskender Çelebi, a disgraced lord who had fled to the island many years earlier—had brought most of the staff back and when she was older, with great sadness told her the story of the death of her father and mother at the hands of a band of marauders from the southern lands beyond the mountains where he and they had been born; killed because they would not reveal their homeland.

The old man had pledged to guard and educate Yseult and had been her faithful confidant and advisor until his own death some eighteen months ago. It was his wisdom that had both brought Yseult to the library and ensured her education there. Yseult had loved the old man dearly and it still grieved her to think she would never hear his voice again. The more so as she had never understood the last thing he had whispered, something which had sounded like: "Promise to sell..."—that was all she heard before his breath had failed him.

But if their past memories held sway, so too did present happiness. The little island seemed to hold everything they needed and, although they rarely saw anyone else, all their needs were cared for. Life could have been idyllic, indeed for Yseult, it was, although she knew shadows behind the future that she saw writ large in the eyes of her love. Tristram knowing his father well and with the weight of his responsibilities to the colonies in the south weighing on him, could not believe that they would be left untroubled so close to the home waters of Zeta.

In the furthest reaches of his mind—kept their by sheer force of will—he saw a troubling future in which he was captured, their castle destroyed or Yseult killed by raiding parties... and he knew he could do little to prevent it should his father take such a course. He hoped that, just possibly, his father was in ignorance of Yseult's home or even of Mljet itself, but this was a remote—there's the word, he though bitterly—possibility.

Perhaps K., as she listened to Trystan, also heard an echo of her past or the lighter chime of her future. It is certain that she revelled in his life at sea—the adventures, the storms, the distant lands and ports—and the authority with which he recounted them. For Trystan had seen his future and had no intention of letting it slip away.

Lines 52-55:
Later, the dark sands kept their secret...

The road back home to the holiday cottage crossed the headlands of a small beach and they stopped there a while. In the total darkness of a moonless summer night, they slipped out onto the sands keeping to the Western edge of the bay until they could hear the gentle sea-wave susurration and rested against a rock. Almost as if she thought it unclear until now K. swore her eternal love for Trystan in terms that left no doubt that—for her—their union was as close to eternal as it was possible to be. Trystan, taken back by the force with which she held him and the strength of her passion, still had no trouble in echoing her promise of life. That they stayed in each other's arms by the rock in the dark longer than it took to exchange vows is not surprising—it was almost the first completely private moment they had shared! The magic of the moment in that warm, dark night with the rippling waves breaking gently nearby, and the feel of the other's body pressed close was total.

I suspect that K. would—had they been more certain in the pitch black night that the lapping waves were not about to swamp them—almost certainly have given herself to him there on the beach, but Trystan, for all his love and the passion of the moment, could not but help succumb to the influence of his upbringing, and that moment—although not the pledge—was lost. Like 'Fatima', a poem K. had probably not studied at the time, K. was single minded in her love—even if the sky was dark rather than sultry:

> My whole soul waiting silently,
> All naked in a sultry sky,
> Droops blinded with his shining eye:
> I *will* possess him or will die.
> I will grow round him in his place,
> Grow, live, die looking on his face,
> Die, dying clasp'd in his embrace. [85]

Lines 57-59:
When you see such passion…

One evening, the lovers stopped for a drink in a tavern by the harbour—it was crowded and noisy and they decided not to stay long, although one drink turned to two before they left. As he led her out Trystan was suddenly conscious

---

[85] Alfred Lord Tennyson (1833) 'Fatima'. Final verse.

that the white-bearded old man in a skipper's cap—did he have a wooden leg and a parrot?—at a table they were passing was speaking to him, "She's got you lad! When they have that look in their eyes, it's time to leave port!" Embarrassed that his lover may have heard, he muttered something about his luck that she had, and fled!

In fact, his diary suggests that this scene in the tavern happened just before rather than after their sandy tryst.

Canto ii
Lines 63-76:
Then he became…

The second canto begins by reprising the power of love: the reciprocal pull which held them close. Again the language is powerful with images of a beautiful butterfly—or perhaps less likely, a helpless moth—drawn to a candle flame and—following the earlier theme of love as worship—the man as a place of worship in which love might live. At the same time, she was the very centre of his universe—"all that he knew" and all that he needed.

For Tristram, this was literally true, and as they walked together in the cedar woods it was marvellous to see that the wild animals seemed to regard Yseult with the same awe and wonder as he did. On one occasion a pair of unicorns[86] knelt before them and bowed their heads and—even with his limited reading— the symbolism was not lost on Tristram. As Auden wrote [87]:

O Unicorn among the cedars,
To whom no magic charm can lead us,
White childhood moving like a sigh
Through the green woods unharmed in thy
Sophisticated innocence,
To call thy true love to the dance,

Auden's use of the unicorn as Christian symbolism may seem unusual at first but the King James Bible uses that translation for re'em/reëm in several places,

---

[86] I suspect that these were, in fact, white stags and Lewis has used the idea of unicorns to heighten the servile/religious connotations—where white stags that "pause not for love nor sorrow" (Ezra Pound: 'The White Stag') would not have suited.
[87] W. H. Auden *New Year Letter (January 1, 1940) To Elizabeth Mayer. Part Three.*

including Deuteronomy (33:17), in two of the Psalms (22 and 29) and in Job (39:9): "Will the unicorn be willing to serve thee, or abide by thy crib?"—so these pure white beasts have always been symbols of purity and grace. Their subservient posture before the pair seemed clearly to acknowledge something less numinous and more worldly: that the couple's relationship could move to another plane. That Albina [88] was called on to watch over them at this time is surely significant.

We can only guess what Lewis saw in this unusually unattributed quotation: "Your body travels with me; your blood flows in my veins" [89] but it seems to signify both a consummation and times when the lovers might be parted. Tristram spent time maintaining and repairing his *qārib*, which after his long voyaging was desperately in need of a shipyard and the care of shipwrights and sail-makers as well as a ropery to repair his sheets and halyards. Perhaps his frequent absences from the castle may have given Yseult pause for thought but she knew the power of their love and felt that in reality, Tristram could and would never have considered leaving her for even a short voyage. She assumed that his attention to his vessel was an automatic response to its long spells moored, unmoving at the Mljet jetty.

Less happily, the lengthy holiday period over, K. was forced to return with her family to Sussex, separated from Trystan who had to travel to Wales, where he must rekindle his ties to the sea. Fortunately, not by joining a ship, but through a period of study which will further his career and move him along the way to becoming a ship's captain. But he does not return home, other than briefly, and any time he has away from college is spent in Sussex with K. Each time he leaves her it is more difficult, both for Trystan as he leaves his very heart and soul behind, and for K., this Daughter of Albion who weeps; "a trembling lamentation" [90] although, in another guise, Albina is caring for the lovers.

---

[88] There were three Saint Albina—one in each of the second, third and fourth centuries, but in this context it refers to Albina, "the White Goddess", the Etruscan goddess of the dawn and protector of ill-fated lovers. Perhaps significantly (nothing is there by chance in a poem by Lewis), there are said to be similarities to Ceridwen—the Celtic goddess of rebirth.

[89] Lewis often called on me to verify his quotations but not in this case. If it is a quotation, I am unable to trace it! It is possible that Lewis used the quotation marks to indicate the spoken word, something Tristram said to Yseult.

[90] William Blake (1793) 'Visions of the Daughters of Albion'.

Interestingly, given our lovers' circumstances, Blake's poem is a critique of the Christian values of marriage… but that is an editorial comment from the future!

Elsewhere, Lewis has written powerfully of his physical love for K. as a form of worship; up to this point in 'Dark Ashes' we see only the cerebral; although there is just the faintest hint that a more primal pleasure has become acceptable—or possible—as that symbol of purity, the unicorns, kneel and bow their heads. By the time they are established under the Sussex cedars the possible had become fact. Absent, in his mind Trystan saw K. beside him—as he drove, as he studied, as he slept—if only he could have held her!

Their love had stripped away every pretence, every barrier, and spiritually they were together even when they were physically apart. K. may have wept at his parting, and certainly she begged him to stay each time although she knew he would only be absent for days at a time, but she knew the power she wielded—that she held his mind captive. In his poems Lewis often confesses the all-embracing power of, and the sheer physical force within, his love, perhaps nowhere more strongly than here, "lost to your soul, / I bared my heart"—"I bared my breast… / For you to enslave and own." The complete poem is as follows [91]:

Ah! I loved you!

Lost to your soul,
    I bared my heart

Within your mind
    I held my heart…

        as if all hearts sang with mine
          as if all lips knew

I felt your blood pulse
    and heat my soul
    as your hair scourged my body
        (Ah! I loved your hair!)

---

[91] 'K.' Published in *Mostly Welsh* (2019). Talybont: Y Lolfa.

Mirrored in your eyes
　　I felt my skin tremble

Feeling your touch
　　I bared my breast...

　　for you to enslave and own
　　　　as if all flesh cleansed

I felt your dominion
　　and withdrew from the world—
　　as worshiping drained my soul.

Poetry is a force, and in lines as nakedly passionate as these it is a force that can only make the readers examine their own hearts and souls; if having read it, or even when reading it, it speaks to their own passions, they can never be the same again for it will have called forth something deeply and powerfully spiritual from within. Maybe, even, some poems have a healing power.

And this power—as John Keats has hinted—is more important than precise, accurate reportage or documentation [92]:

　　　　When old age shall this generation waste,
　　　　Thou shalt remain, in midst of other woe
　　　　Than ours, a friend to man, to whom thou say'st,
　　　　"Beauty is truth, truth beauty,—that is all
　　　　Ye know on earth, and all ye need to know."

And so, Lewis' short passionate poem to K. speaks of his first love from a point in time as he looked back on his life, and almost as a consequence of this schism in time, jumbles the precise chronology, bringing together their first physical passion with the end of her life (the tense at least suggests that) and—somewhere in the middle—his withdrawal from his profession to be with K. Or, I have to wonder, perhaps, as an editor with too intimate a knowledge of both his works and their lives, I am imposing something on the poem that Lewis did not

---

[92] John Keats (1819) 'Ode on a Grecian Urn'—ironically an ode that is itself something of a celebration of the unsaid (final lines).

intend: the withdrawal could equally refer to his cloistered retreat after the death of K. Poems are about feelings and passion; they are not precise historical documentation.

Lines 78-89:
Life spun…

And so, as the sun rose and set, and rose and set again, Tristram would set off to the West, across the lake and through the pine and cedar woods to the little jetty where his craft was moored. With few tools and little supply of sail cloth, cordage or cut timber, work was slow and difficult but most days he spared a few hours to work on *Bäckahästen,* returning to the castle to join Yseult for their simple midday meal. And with each return his spirits lifted.

Rested, they would set out to explore the island that was their mainland, the island of Mljet. At the nearest point to the castle-island was a small village of simple farmers and a few fishermen who would either fish in the lake or venture out through the canal at its southern end into the wider sea. It was this village that kept the castle supplied with fruit and vegetables, milk, bread, honey—Tristram was intrigued to spot the two straw skeps or hives in one garden and spent some time with their owner learning the ways of bees—and fish. Like the villagers—her father's people—the couple's needs were simple and they wanted for nothing.

And always, they talked! Yseult became his guide and mentor: it seemed to him as if her wisdom knew no limits—and Tristram was an eager and willing pupil. Sometimes, returning from their walks, they would enter the library and explore its shelves. The original bookshelves stretching all around the long room were some six feet high, but sometime in the past a second tier had been added so that the walls of books stretched up into the gloom some ten feet, well above Tristram's head.

In a couple of places, old ladders leaned against the shelves. The shelves were dusty and the higher levels had been populated by an army of spiders so that in many places the old volumes were festooned with their webs. As he looked around, Tristram could see leather spines with gold lettering as well as many more ordinary volumes. It seemed to him that the whole world's knowledge must reside there: somewhere among the shelves, Tristram thought, must be hidden the stories of his lives.

At some point in the distant past, a monk had been employed to bring order to the thousands of volumes and had indexed them into a kind of roster so that it was now possible to find books on almost any subject without hunting along the shelves title by title: it seemed almost magical to Tristram! Within minutes after their return from the village, he had discovered the 1677 work by John Gedde: *A new discovery of an excellent method of bee-houses, and colonies : which frees the owners from the great charge and trouble that attends the swarming of bees, and delivers the bees from the evil reward of ruine, for the benefit they brought their masters; advantaging their owners many-fold, above whatever any method heretofore practised doth. Experienced seven years by John Gedde gent. inventor; and approved by the Royal Society at Gresham College; A short treatise of the excellency of bees, honey, mead, and metheglin : with their singular and approved virtues* by T. R. Med Dr published in 1681; and another by Samuel Purchas (Master of arts, and pastor at Sutton in Essex) and the excellent *A theatre of political flying-insects : Wherein especially the nature, the worth, the work, the wonder, and the manner of right-ordering of the bee, is discovered and described. Together with discourses, historical, and observations physical concerning them. And in a second part are annexed meditations, and observations theological and moral, in three centuries upon that subject,* as well as Storch's *Die Flugloch* [93]—he was entranced!

It was as if an eternal summer smiled on them in a world that had no evil! As if they were in a private heaven! A heaven that was renewed by each and every kiss or touch. But Tristram knew his responsibilities and could neither forget the troubles that his long absence may be visiting on Zeta nor rid himself of the worry that something bad was necessarily bound to happen to destroy their little world.

The failure to broker an agreement with the south would spell disaster for both the Zetan union and for the south itself. It would be sad for Zeta after such a vote in the south, the King had made no secret of it: their vote would cut off one of his wings, as it were. But we would still be flying, thought Tristram. But for the country cut off from the riches of the north, alienating itself from many years of more or less harmonious trade and travel between the two countries, the consequences would be much worse. And he knew that they were not prepared for such radical change—indeed when he was last there many ministers had told him that it would never happen, saying that they knew of no government in any

---

[93] *The Hive Entrance.*

country that had enacted a policy that would make both its country and its people poorer. It would be a grand folly.

The move he had heard for a 'ZetaSplit' could only be a huge disaster for them! So he felt that it was inconceivable that his father would not seek to bring him home and, as this could not happen through discussion and diplomacy, Tristram expected every day to spot a fleet of ships heading their way. In part, it was why he spent so long at the port—not only did he need his ship ready to sail but the port, and the hill above it, offered the best vantage point to see vessels sailing from Zeta. He tried to keep his concerns from Yseult but, as with his frequent absences on *Bäckahästen,* she sensed a darkness: there were storm clouds gathering on their horizon and even she was powerless to hold them back.

When he tried to explain, she held her finger to his lips to silence him but he only kissed its tip and took it into his mouth to taste her beauty before he continued. But it was as if she did not want to hear—did not want anything to bring down their idyll. She could only see to it that their fortress was a place of light and joy. And that—to the best of their abilities—her people maintained its defences. Timber was felled and huge new gates, a door and a portcullis created. It was painfully slow work for her few old retainers but eventually they were in place and she believed that they were nearly as strong as the huge stone walls. To Tristram, she explained it as an ongoing maintenance project she had started long before he had seen the island.

> There is no meaning
> and no sense
> only clarity [94]

Weekly—and perhaps, also, weakly—Trystan travels West to his professional, nautical life to brush up on the very worldly skills of navigation, seamanship and ship handling, and ship stability. For a few days, he almost focuses and then, as the week drew to a close, he headed back East to the real focus of his life—the very centre of his universe. In vain, his father demanded, and his mother pleaded—guiltily, he wondered if his mother was suffering his loss in almost the same way that her own mother had mourned the loss of his Uncle Guy—with him to come home, to apologise, to discuss what was happening, to see sense, to remember his career... the very tenor of the almost

---

[94] 'Love' Published in *Mostly Welsh* (2019). Talybont: Y Lolfa.

one-sided conversation was, for Trystan, instructive, and also destructive. It certainly did not suggest a resolution that would satisfy him, let alone K.—who, he knew, wished to have nothing to do with his parents again. Ever. So, when the week's work ended, he returned—with both haste and happiness—to his lover in her parent's mansion beneath the Sussex cedars.

It seemed as if the sun always shone in the land of Albion [95] and the top was rarely up on his little sports car. In the short time they had, they visited her friends—there was probably an element of showing him off—or simply toured the county enjoying the simple pleasure of doing things together. Often too, they visited the many second hand bookshops and increased their growing library, although Trystan's taste's did not always coincide with hers. K.—in the guise of a tutor—strove to educate and bring his tastes into some conformity with hers. Trystan was happy to be guided and, as an avid reader, consumed anything that was put in front of him. Ironically, the one area that he failed to inhabit at the time was poetry.

Sussex weekends used a different area of his brain to the weekdays, where learning was much more mundane and factual—it was, in fact, just that: 'learning' as opposed to expanding his mind using the more Socratic or maieutic and discursive study to which K. introduced him as she put book after book in front of him to present literature and philosophy... which he rather enjoyed, although he would have been the first to admit, it did not come to him readily nor was he particularly good at it to begin with! K. suggested that he was too used to being told what was right—both in work and at home!

If the days were filled with exploration—both intellectual and geographical—the evenings were given over to a more hedonistic life style. They were either out with friends, in which case they would be close together, travelling home in the small cockpit of his car or together in her parents' lounge! I remember a conversation with Lewis from that time when he recounted a stop on the way home one night. They had parked off the road somewhere in a dark car park with a view over the town and been considerably frustrated by the lack of space in his little car! Even so, heaven was under Albina's care for the while and the lovers held fast to each other for every minute that was given to them.

For his part, Trystan knew that his time ashore was finite. Eventually, he would pass his examination and then would come a seriously testing time. He

---

[95] According to the Welsh monk, Nennius, Britain gains its earliest name, Albion, from Albina, the White Goddess, the eldest of the fifty daughters of Danaus.

knew, or he thought he knew, what it might be like to be left behind; he also knew that K. had probably not understood what was in store for her. He had no idea whether she would be able endure a parting of some months—it was difficult enough returning to Wales for a few days! At this stage it was not something they discussed.

Innocent of what the near future might bring, K. was nevertheless building strong walls to hold her lover safe. Everything she did, cemented their relationship—her parents had accepted and liked Trystan and he had been accepted happily into her circle of friends. With almost every word or action she drew him closer; quietly, too, she sowed—or at least, watered—the seeds of his discontent with his parents. She may not have considered what it would be like to be parted for the months that he sailed the seas, but she did consider where and to whom he would return! She built bridges! And Trystan had no quarrel with that!

> There were those moments
> pressed
> against a Cornish rock
>> in beach blackness
>> with the shush of the rippling waves
>> nearby in the night
> lying
> in a Sussex garden
>> with the hot sun
>> dappling our backs
> parked
> on a Ditchling hill
>> with town lights
>> spread below
>
> that I remember now [96]

Lines 90-92:
For Llŷr called from the west and Eingana…

---

[96] From an unpublished poem—'Lovers'— written by Lewis in 2018 and now in the editor's collection.

And as the summer passed, the inevitability of his return to the sea became more and more pressing [97]. The sea gods and those of the land to which he travels were calling him. In his dreams, Llŷr [98], his most immediate link to the sea called to him to return to her arms, while that 'Dreamtime Snake,' Eingana [99]—the snake that calls to him nightly from across the sea—coils around his mind. He had been too often in Australia where she is said to have the power of life over each of her children, and Trystan could feel the pull of the sinew which attached him to her. He knew that Aboriginal legend suggests that should she let that sinew go, he would perish. As dawn breaks the gods leave him alone but he knows that his parting is coming closer.

His contract—that connection that cannot be let go—means that he must join a ship as soon as his examination is passed... and he is running out of money! Soon he will once again navigate his way—as he has so many times before—from London around the Cape of Good Hope to Australia. There he will stay a while before bringing his ship safely back. All those old horizons seen with such pleasure before...

Line 93:
She—for all her vision...

Yseult may have had a sense of foreboding—a darkness at the edge of her field of vision—but she had no way of understanding it. She had no real knowledge—book learning, but no experience—of lands other than her own. Her only time away from Mljet had been the doomed visit to Tristram's land, to his father's court in Zeta. It had been unpleasant and humiliating but too brief for her to gain any real understanding of how the wider world worked. And Tristram had not shared with her what was troubling him, what possible disasters his dereliction of princely duty might bring down on Zeta. And Yseult had begun to sense a grey shade—an unseen spectre hovering—a disquiet within their love making. One day when he returned from his ship, he was more than usually

---

[97] While the references in the first line relate geographically only to his current life, it is clear that the two following lines cleverly weave both stories together. This is where Lewis is at his best. "Parting was ordained".

[98] Llŷr is a Welsh god of the sea and father to Brânwen of *Mabinogi* fame.

[99] Eingana is an Australian aboriginal snake goddess who is the mother of every human and thus also the goddess having control of their deaths: each of her children is attached to her by a sinew and when she lets them go, they die.

sombre and when they had eaten, Yseult pleaded with him to tell her what was wrong.

In Albion's charge, K. watched the late summer pass with increasing unease. Trystan, when he is with her, seems on edge and worried and one weekend, briefly, she wonders if he has found another muse in Wales but his evident love for her, his continued passion, pushes that silly thought away. He had bought her a silver ring made up of three triplets of interlocking rings that rolled pleasingly up and down her finger—not exactly an engagement ring he joked, but perhaps the three rings might symbolise three children! But she senses his concern for her, which heightens dramatically when he hears that he has passed his Mate's Ticket. K. knows what this must mean, but cannot see beyond a tearful parting. She has no experience of being alone—wondering alone, dreaming alone, waiting alone and does not know if she is strong enough.

Lines 94-100:
He knows…

While K. had little or no understanding of what was to come, Trystan had some small understanding of how it might affect him—he had seen fellow officers silent and morose on their first days from port before they settle into the routine of watches and work. Like prisoners in sunless cells, they mark off the days towards their release back in their home port—when girlfriends, fiancés, wives and children stand laughing on the quay to greet them. The endless dark days: time of lonely work and even lonelier nights always cycle round to high-summer happiness.

Of course, he has never seen or experienced the pain of being left behind, and can only guess at the difficulties—the constant worry that something might happen, be it swamping wave or some foreign passion, that drain days of light and happiness. Trystan has heard also how wives throw themselves into the close organisation of their lives so that each day, each hour and minute is carefully filled and their lives run smoothly. The return of their spouse becomes at once a time of immense pleasure and joy and a time of frustration as their careful lives are thrown into disorder by the 'intruder'.

So, Trystan worries for his lover and, about to be plunged into his first personal monastic retreat, he also wonders how his new life will affect his ability to cope with shipboard life. K. looks to him for help but there is little that he can offer beyond the assurances of eternal love, the promises to return soon... K. cries out in agony.

Tristram is no stranger to navigation and the movement of the sun and planets; he understands how that movement brings the sun by day and the stars by night and has watched from his lonely deck as the moon changes its face night by night. All of this brings a wider understanding of the rhythms of time and the eternal drift from one state to another... and the necessary balanced pull that returns day after night, light after dark, good to follow on from the abominable, happiness from sadness. And so he rationalised his need to honour those responsibilities hanging over him—it would not take long, the pain could be borne, he would return! Happiness would return!

But while he knew that he would be so busy that the time would pass—pass painfully slowly, but pass—and that he would always have Yseult on Mljet as his evening star, he knew too, that Yseult would suffer. And so he had put off telling her of his plan. Confronted with her tears as he answered her questions he was nearly unmanned... nearly persuaded that another course could serve as well. But he had been over this so many times as he had worked on *Bäckahästen* that he knew this was the only way. Yseult pleads with him and cannot understand his need; afraid that she will lose him, she cries out in agony.

Lines 102-114:
He is torn...

As the time of departure approaches, Trystan knows that his company, which has paid for his time ashore, expect him; his ship—he already knows which ship he is joining—expects him; even the port, its river and the seas seem to be waiting for him! Time rushes towards his departure. And, even before he leaves, he is concerned for his homecoming, trying to pin his employers to a time although he knows there can be no guarantees. In his use of the Odyssey [100] as a parallel for Trystan's voyage, Lewis is both raising his hero to godlike status and emphasising the perils of travelling the seas.

---

[100] Homer: *The Odyssey*. Book XI: 90-149. Odysseus tells his tale: The Ghost of Teiresias. Translated by A S Kline. Available at: http://www.poetryintranslation.com/PITBR/Greek/Odyssey11.htm. Lewis' use of the mythic to ennoble both himself and his voyage is perhaps a little risible, but we have to acknowledge the power of such allusions.

His masters may well not have drunk blood in order answer him, but their response must have echoed Teiresias! You *will* come home but, of course, you must be prepared for storms and other unknown delays! Trystan knew that even the vision of a blind Teiresias could not foretell how K. would fare when they were parted but, for his part, he feared for her. And too, the warning to control his crew's greed—to keep them, as it were, on the straight and narrow course—could not but worry him, for all his confidence in his own skills:

... if only you can control your own and your comrades' greed... you may yet reach [home... Otherwise], then I foresee shipwreck for you and your friends, and even if you yourself escape, you will come unlooked-for to your home, in sore distress, losing all comrades, in another's vessel, to find great trouble in your house, insolent men who destroy your goods, who court your wife and offer gifts of courtship. [100]

Not something he needed to be reminded of as for the first time in their relationship, he and K. were parted.

With the ever present worry that the King and his Zetan navy will attack their island and the knowledge that it is within his power to resolve the trade issues with the south and prevent a war which would engulf Mljet as well as Zeta, Tristram can see no way forward other than to once again set sail. In preparation, he has careened his little ship with some difficulty in order to clear off the barnacles and weed growing on the lower part of her hull, he has made good all the timber work and spars, repaired the cordage, and patched a sail. *Bäckahästen* is as near seaworthy as he can make her and with her newly cleaned hull he is confident of a fast voyage, so long as the winds remain in the right quarter.

He is certain that the gods will look favourably on his venture, given that he seeks to do no evil, but rather right the wrong he has caused: Poseidon, mighty ruler of the waves, may give him a rough passage by way of punishment but he knows that the auguries from the flights of birds passing overhead presage success. What neither the gods nor any other omen could tell was how his lovely Yseult will fare in his absence. He knows that her people will care for her, but cannot judge her fortitude—the strength of mind she will need to conquer her fears. He can only pray to the gods to give her strength, and he knows that he will spend every waking hour of his voyage communing with all of his gods in an effort to strengthen her resolve.

Canto iii
Lines 120-141:
Cruel parting after such passion

Lewis begins this canto by quoting in full from one of his earlier poems, 'Cruel Parting after Such Passion' [101]—a poem which shows an unusual sensitivity to his lover's situation: he clearly understands that it is easier for the sailor to up and leave than it is for his lady, left behind at home!

The night that has passed can never return:
    the sea quenches all.
Cruel parting after such passion
O woman left behind!

O ship
    Of steel, rivets: deck, bridge, hull and keel:
    Fore and aft, moored tight to her
    Cargo holds: soon filled
    Cabins! One cabin she knows so well!
Bearing him away

O man
    Of charts and night watches
    Scanning horizons: navigating so many seas
    Do you dream of her? Pine?
        Touch her in your dreams?
O woman left behind
    You can only pray…
    and wait:
        It is easier to sail away than be left home!

In the event, he did not find it at all easy either! He was collecting a new ship from the shipyard and bringing her to London to load before beginning the long voyage to Australia, so more than ever, this was a step into the unknown. The

---

[101] 'Cruel Parting after Such Passion' Published in *Mostly Welsh* (2019). Talybont: Y Lolfa.

ship was larger than any he had been on before and carried its load differently—the bridge from which he would keep watch was aft of all the holds and, once loaded, nearly as much of the cargo would be carried on deck as below the enormous hatches. So, even as he arrived at the dockside and boarded his new ship up the steep gangway—she was riding high in the water with no cargo on board—a time that would normally have been filled with a thrill of the unknown and of adventure, he was almost scared of what the future might bring.

Although, he reminded himself, this was the 'Jervis Bay'—a name already a part of his family history as, famously during the second world war, her namesake had sacrificed herself to save an Atlantic convoy in which his mother's uncle was master of a passenger ship—and his voyage could not possibly be so terrible. He remembered the letter he had seen describing the event:

Here is an account of the attack on the convoy by the German battleship [the Admiral Scheer] of the same type as the one sunk in the River Plate—Graf Spee—on 4.00 pm on Nov 5th, an unidentified ship was sighted hull down on the port beam gradually closing steering at right angles from the Northward. At about 4.45 pm she was seen to be a warship of heavy calibre, though there was evidently no suspicion by the escort H.M.S. Jervis Bay that she was an enemy vessel and the convoy continued doing the fast and furious speed of 9 knots which was as much as some of the ships could do.

At 5.15 pm, the enemy suddenly opened fire with her forward [gun] at an estimated range of 14000 to 15000 yards, the target being either the "Jervis Bay" or [my ship] "Rangitiki" as we were the largest ships and had two funnels. At the same time the convoy turned to starboard (right) and dispersed and luckily did not run into each other whilst doing so. Whilst these operations were going on by the convoy, the enemy had turned on a parallel course to the convoy and opened fire on the "Jervis Bay".

This ship when the convoy had turned to starboard steamed towards the enemy and opened fire on her but it appeared that all her salvoes fell short. The enemy after the first ranging shot which went over the "Jervis Bay" fired a salvo which fell short. The second salvo struck her amidships on the port side, evidently putting her engines out of action as she lost way immediately. The third salvo struck her just before the bridge and the fourth aft setting her on fire. The enemy now concentrated his fire on this ship, the first salvo fell on the port quarter some 400 yards short, the second salvo straddled the ship amidships, the third straddled the ship just forward of the bridge. The shell that went over was about 50 yards away or less from the ship smothering the bridge in spray, shell fragments striking the ship forward but not doing any appreciable damage.

The enemy were also apparently firing their secondary armament as small pieces of shell have been found all over the ship. While all this was going on from the firing of the first shot all the ships of the convoy were using their smoke floats and as there was only a light wind from the South East, the retreating ships were being gradually hidden by the smoke, which coupled with the gallant action of the H.M.S. Jervis Bay enabled such a large number of ships to escape.

Luckily, there was only a quarter moon which was hidden from time to time by heavy clouds which also helped our escape. All this time we could see the flashes of the enemy guns even through the smoke screen and as our gun was out of range during all of the attack and the flashes from our gun would have given our position away which would have been disastrous as we were gradually increasing our distance away from the enemy.

As we got further away, we could see the German using star shells to enable him to see some unfortunate ship to shell. It was five hours from onset until we saw the last of the gun flashes, they were then below the horizon. We continued on our course until 8am on the 6th when we estimated that if the enemy had returned the same way as he had come—North—he would not loiter but return at full speed and if he had gone South would have been well out of the way. [102]

He marvelled at the resolve of Captain Fegen—the Jervis Bay's master posthumously awarded the Victoria Cross—who had steamed towards the enemy battleship in order to save his convoy. If he was worried about his own resolve, he was also worried that in her abject loneliness and distress K. might succumb to those 'insolent men'—old friends—for comfort. And even as that possibility flashed across his mind for the first time, Trystan knew it was unworthy of him, was both appalled and ashamed at his lack of trust—of, faith even—and also knew that the thought was irrevocably lodged in his mind to travel with him forever.

---

[102] Lewis had once told me the story, but I was able to quote from the letter itself as the original was located in the Lewes family archive to which I was given access.

That he was travelling from the Clyde to London—almost back to K.—did not immediately strike him as either ironic or relevant. The break between each leave and each voyage was absolute for him and there would be no chance for extra days away from the ship. Once in London he would have responsibility for ensuring the safe loading and stowage of cargo—a doubly difficult job as every aspect of it was new to him on this ship. He was now—at least as far as his mind would allow—'a thing of the sea' and the almost tenuous links to the other world existed only in the thin strip of blue leather that K. had woven around his wrist to bind him to her—her torque, he had suggested—and the single telephone placed on board as they docked in London!

How well I remember receiving—in my little London flat—that late-night call! There, suddenly, was Trystan's voice, the voice of a man I had assumed to be in the middle of Biscay by now, asking me rather nervously to do him a huge favour: to collect K. from the docks and take her to her aunt's home in Forest Hill. His ship was due to sail with the morning's tide and, as he later explained, K. had arrived in the early evening while he was on duty watching the last of the cargo come aboard. He had known nothing of it until he saw her at the foot of the gangway and had been in a difficult position as an officer receiving an illicit guest while he was on duty—K. had been so sure that her arrival would be a wonderful and welcome surprise and obviously had not known that they were due to sail so soon. I think they managed a little while alone in his cabin between his times on deck!

And so, it came to be that half an hour or so later, I presented myself in the middle of the night at the dock gate with a request—rather nervously presented—to be allowed in to collect a friend's wife from the Jervis Bay before she sailed! K. was smuggled ashore and Trystan, grasping my hand and arm, thanked me repeatedly and profusely for what I was doing. There was a break in his voice I had never heard before. Of course, I knew K. slightly from his letters but was shocked by how slight and frail she looked, weeping and clinging to Trystan in the harsh light. Between us we got her into the car, a final kiss and we were away while poor Trystan hurried back aboard, presumably hoping we had not been seen!

No! It was not easy for Trystan!

On the island, Yseult has had the difficulties that Tristram faces explained to her. She knows what the documents he carried would have told the King—that further assurances were needed—and that, by a second visit to the colonies, a trade war or, more particularly, a war over trade should be averted, and that perhaps more importantly, knowing his part in the negotiations, it may be that the King will leave them in peace. She understands, but cannot find herself at ease with the plan. Tristram might have wished to slip away one dawn with as little fuss as possible but there was little possibility that Yseult would allow that and she accompanied him as he provisioned his vessel, and—on the day of his departure—personally rowed him across their inland sea and escorted him through the woods that they both loved to the jetty.

As he boarded *Bäckahästen* she could not help but cling to him despite her vows to be strong. It meant much to Tristram that it was Yseult who untied his ropes from the jetty—a symbolic act of acceptance, he felt—but as he drifted away from her side and raised a sail to catch the first breaths of early-morning wind—he saw her collapse on the wooden jetty weeping.

No! It was not easy for Tristram!

Lines 142-149:
She could not hear his voice…

Time stands still and yet as it passes, his voice somehow fades from her mind. Those softly whispered words of love, the promises, the stories about their future all drift further away and she can no longer hear his voice. All that is present is the past! Not only is every minute of every hour of every day taking him further from her, but there is no real means of communication. If a letter could be delivered to him it would be from the past, yet read in the future. It would be meaningless! Every word, every sentence she might write would trail behind her man as he worked his boat—she imagined a long pennant of love trailing from the top of his mast reaching all the way back to her!

At the same time that his voice faded in her mind, the remembered feeling of his body against hers gave her strength. She remembered some words she had found in the library—she almost remembers the page more than the words, with its winged angels flying close to a harvest moon and stars, but she had read:

I am in you, and you in Me, mutual in Love Divine
Fibres of love from man to man thro' Albion's pleasant land [103]

---

[103] William Blake. *Jerusalem The Emanation of The Giant Albion.* Chapter 1 (written and etched 1804-20).

Although she thought it was probably a misunderstanding of the text, it seemed to perfectly describe the balance of their love, the tenuous strand—the pennant she had imagined—that holds them together while they were apart. She did not understand what was meant by 'man to man' but was happy to simply remember the words that seemed most relevant.

Lines 150-159:
Memories!

All that was left were memories! For Yseult on her island within an island, Tristram seemed so far removed from her castle she could scarcely believe he had existed—only the pain of his absence made the dream real! He had given her some idea of how long the sea voyage would take and suggested that he may need at least a week ashore in discussions with the Elders, but time did not seem to pass at all and his return seemed no closer one day than it had a few days before. In her mind he is forever sailing further away—she tries to visualise him at the tiller or tending to the canvas but it is all abstraction—she knows that these are just ideas, almost fantasies, and that what she is thinking probably bears no resemblance to what is happening at sea. She yearns to touch him, or just to see him. But she cannot. She feels that he is so far away that she can no longer sense his thoughts or feel his soul next to hers. She begins to wonder whether she ever did!

The old hourglass in the schoolroom drips sand so tantalisingly slowly that she cannot see that there will ever be a need to reverse it! And that thought, that word, captures, traps, enraptures her mind and she imagines time running backwards—as if in some kind of rushing wind—until once again she and Tristram are in this room together pouring over her old atlas and discussing his need to leave her for a while. And then, more joyously, back further, until they are simply together and in each other's arms. She dreams.

Memories seem to offer little to K. Of course, she remembers every moment of every little thing that they did together and, to begin with, can almost feel Trystan beside her, but as the days pass all that she is aware of is the ever increasing distance between them: the fact that he is purposefully sailing away, ever further away, from her. The logical part of her mind knows that this is ridiculous sophism—she liked that word—but she cannot rationalise his absence any better. Having little knowledge of life on board large cargo ships, it is difficult for her to imagine how he spends his time—she can only hold, desperately hold, onto the images she has of his cabin from her last far too fleeting time with him. She remembers the pale wood desk, the bookshelves— full of all the books she had given him, and the large cupboards; the private bathroom; the turquoise blue couch and arm chair, the coffee table and the bed. The bed, yes, she remembered the bed with the windows over it from which they had watched the car draw up to take her away! Beyond that, she can feel nothing!

Her life of study goes on but does not hold her and she struggles to focus on anything other than her loss. Friends, her parents, her sisters comfort her and try to help but nothing can take away her empty feeling of loss. Weeks pass, and in passing rob K. of even the tiny pleasures she gained from imagining Trystan— Trystan standing, Trystan talking, or laughing, Trystan eating! But, always, Trystan beside her. She can no longer sense his spirit or his mind—even his soul seems to have drifted out of reach.

Lines 160-167:
On the long southern seas…

Although Lewis has added no footnote to these lines it is clear that he had Coleridge's poem, 'The Rime of the Ancient Mariner', in his mind as he describes Trystan's voyage. The wandering albatross often follows ships in the southern seas—perhaps simply to pick at their leavings but more likely in order to take advantage of thermals and wind drift. Lewis once told me of an albatross that spent an entire four-hour watch drifting slowly towards the bow and then back to the bridge where an updraft from the cargo deck lifted him so that he would suddenly appear in front of the officer of the watch as he stood on the bridge wing—and in all that time he never flapped his wings once. He just glided quietly and with a dip of one wing turned and glided again until the updraft caught him. "I'll swear he grinned as the officer of the watch jumped at his sudden appearance; he was certainly enjoying the sport as the ship's passage carried him every further East," Lewis had said.

> And a good south wind sprung up behind;
> The Albatross did follow,
> And every day, for food or play,

Came to the mariner's hollo! [104]

Coleridge describes a near eternal voyage destined, it seemed, to last forever although the ancient mariner—the 'grey-beard loon'—who caused the terrible catastrophes that overtook the ship by shooting the albatross with his crossbow in the first place—did eventually return home to his own country and narrate the story. Trystan also feels that he is burdened to sail these seas forever. He is almost at the opposite extremity of the globe now and home—or at least what he chooses to call home now: K's home—has never seemed so remote. Or am I remote from home, he wonders? And in that thought, he knows the truth: in every sense of the word, he is remote, estranged from K.

At night on watch as he stares at the empty horizon, he sees her face reflected in the bridge-front windows; by day she is never far away from his thoughts and he wonders if the other officers are finding him poor company. They have travelled from London down the channel, across the Bay of Biscay and ever south around the bulge of Africa until, off Cape Town they slow down while the pilot boat runs alongside and they swap sacks of mail—theirs he thinks must be heavier than usual with all his letters to K.! Rounding the Cape, they are now heading across the southern extremes of the Indian Ocean towards Fremantle, which they should reach in about five days.

The seas are grey and they have the beginnings of storm waves breaking around them; the horizon is always empty. He is alone in a vast and windy universe with only a large bird for company! He has read—devoured—the several unhappy love letters so many times that the thin airmail paper is beginning to tear where it has been creased. He loves to read and re-read the many forceful declaration of love and longing that K. has penned but hates the sadder parts where she tells him how she is missing him (good!) and that she cannot live without him there, by her side (bad!). He can see that she is trying to be positive for his sake and knows that underneath or behind every word there is lonely desperation. Like his own letters, she has ended with what has become their mantra: "you in me in you" they write. Longingly.

There is a sad poem from long after K's death in Trystan Lewis' *Mostly Welsh* collection that refers to these letters:

---

[104] Samuel Taylor Coleridge (1834) 'The Rime of the Ancient Mariner'. Another rather obvious literary allusion for Lewis to employ in an effort raise the stature of his voyage to match early voyages of discovery!

Letters

Those love letters from the seventies
I could not bear to read again
and could not bear to throw

Those airmail forms
those tortured lonely twelve page laments
that I read and read so many times
in my cabin off Cape Town,
in Melbourne and Sydney:
So many words
So much love

But in the end
They were just ash
And I scattered them
Ashes to her ashes [105]

More so than ever, Trystan hears her voice at every turn—on deck checking the cargo lashings, on watch, in the officers' lounge, alone in his cabin. A cabin he can at least see with her eyes now—he can write of his lonely life in that cabin knowing that she will recognise it, so he reminds her that she sat on his bed wearing his cap and that she ran her fingers over his books, sat at his desk to write the little message that she hid in a drawer for him to find later. Too, he can imagine her with him at sea after they are married, but he does not, cannot, really know whether the future will be so kind to him!

While K. finds that the only reality in her life is his absence, Trystan's imagination is so vivid and his image of K. so real that he almost feels her presence with him on this trip. He wonders if he is going mad! And this is only the first stage of the voyage—he still has to endure the passages between, and time in, ports while cargo is unloaded and loaded and then the return journey—not even one-third of the time between seeing K. and seeing K. again has passed. Even as he, prisoner-like, ticks off the days on the company wall calendar in his room and in his diary, he enjoys adding a note, "3 weeks since I held K." simply for the pleasure of writing her name. Perhaps, too, for the pleasure of that

---

[105] 'Letters'. Published in *Mostly Welsh* (2019). Talybont: Y Lolfa.

remembered hug… kiss… caress—his mind spirals into a dream from which delusional madness he is woken by the telephone calling him to the bridge!

But Tristram has no time for dreams or madness! He is very literally alone with a sea bird in his vast and windy universe. His are the only hands to change sail, to alter course or bail water from the bilge. When the wind rises, although it speeds him on his course, he dreads every surging gust which may be too much even for his shortened sail and he starves as he has no way to leave the helm. He is not afraid of Poseidon's anger—welcomes it, in fact, for the fact that it keeps him too busy to pine for Yseult—but, as a seasoned sailor, he has a healthy respect for the power of the wind and waves.

Bäckahästen is seaworthy and sails well in both light winds and storm, but she demands some skill of her sailor. Tristram glances astern—as he has done repeatedly since rounding the northern tip of Mljet and beginning his southerly passage—but only sees, again, the giant bird that glides silently over his bubbling wake, never closer and never farther away, gliding just astern keeping watch with him.

He needs to keep a little east of south to reach his destination, staying away from the coast to avoid marauding pirates until working his way east he recognises a lush green peninsula before picking up the peak of Mount Çika on his port bow and knows he is nearing his destination. Another day at sea—if the favourable winds continue—and he should see the hilltop Kalaja e Lëkurësit or Lëkurësi Castle which stands over and protects the small town of Saranda. The castle walls are over two metres thick and there are two large square towers on the Western or sea-facing wall, but Tristram has no intention of attacking—his mission is all about diplomacy. And it is to the son of the Kanunî Sultan Suleiman (Kanunî meaning 'The Lawgiver') who built this castle that he travels on his difficult mission. The son, Selim, had continued his father's rule and tradition of law but has not inherited his father's love of poetry. His father had once written to his wife and the mother of Selim—who had once been his favourite in the Harem:

My woman of the beautiful hair, my love of the slanted brow, my love of
      eyes full of misery …
I'll sing your praises always

and Tristram cannot but help be reminded of his own woman of the beautiful hair, of his own tormented heart.

Throughout the voyage, whenever time can be spared from keeping his ship on course, Tristram has pined for his auburn-haired beauty. He cannot believe that he has left her so far away and as he gazes at the horizon, judges the wind and the waves, watches the sun and keeps his course, he sees Yseult in everything. Every noise—the chuckle of waves under the counter, the rush of air over the sails, even a creak from a mast—seems to be Yseult speaking to him. He turns his ear the better to hear her whispered protestations of love and finds himself looking into the steely unblinking orange eye of the bird. Tristram sails on.

Selim is passionate about following the will of his people, many of whom have taken up the rallying calls 'ZetaSplit' and 'Veto Zeto', and also, of course, about protecting his own rule, but he also knows that the long-standing ties with Zeta cannot be ignored. That he has kept them at arm's length for so long he attributes to luck and the inexperience of the previous Zetan negotiators rather than to his own power. Now, he has to come up with a proposal that will be acceptable to both his people and to the north, and he is finding it difficult— there are so many things that must be arranged anew if they break with Zeta and he does not have the ministerial support to make it happen.

There are powerful arguments being made against the continued union with Zeta. It had begun with the crowds and their hatred of foreign interference in their country's governance and trade; they hated the fact that Zetan people could come and go as they pleased in their streets and could set up stalls in their markets. The fact that they had to pay Zeta an annual tax incensed them! But it was the hard core of Selim's ministers who had backed the 'split' that was causing the trouble—it was easy for them to call for ZetaSplit, but none of them seemed capable of coming up with a plan to manage the break.

Time and again, Selim had listed the hurdles to be overcome and the planning that was needed—he had even appointed a minister to bring the plans to fruition—but no new laws, no treasury plans, no negotiating stance had been

---

[106] The final lines of a poem written by Sultan Suleiman under his pen name, Muhibbi, meaning "lover" or "sweetheart".

forthcoming. War had to be avoided at all costs so Selim had to find some way of appeasing Zeta at the same time as he persuaded them to accept his country's independence—now, more than at any other time he needed a wise Kanunî!

Zeta had countered his initial calls for a negotiated split with request after request for his terms, his government's negotiating position, and it was clear that they felt that they had the ruling hand—in effect the ability to accept or reject his terms. In the end they had sent the King's son, Prince Tristram, with their own 'suggestions' and the clear message that this had to be settled soon.

Rounding the final headland, Tristram hears the trumpeters announcing his presence and runs up the Zetan flag. He adjusts the sails and changes course to the north with the huge fort towering over him on the starboard quarter and comes up to the stone jetty. Ropes are thrown and secured, he lowers his final sail and secures it, and sits to wait the inevitable escort.

In the early afternoon, he arrives at Kalaja e Lëkurësit and is escorted into the Court of Elders presided over by Selim. And so the negotiations begin. Each night Tristram is escorted back to his ship and each morning as the sun rises he is collected and returned to the castle. Food and wine are brought and consumed but Tristram scarcely notices. He has no further papers with his father's seal attached so can only refer to those he had brought on the previous visit, and this arouses some suspicions among the viziers. But he is nothing if not earnest and can be very persuasive with such terrible outcomes threatened by his failure. And all the time, the image of Yseult hovers before him—she is his advisor and his mentor, and he remembers the wisdom in the books from her library, he sees everything there might be lost if he fails.

An idea from one of the books he had read, a translation of the *Arthaśāstra*, an ancient Indian work on statecraft, originally in Sanskrit, came to mind. The *Arthaśāstra* suggests that taxes should be convenient, easy to calculate and administer, equitable so as not to inhibit local growth. Fair taxes it states build popular support for a king.

> "As one plucks one ripe fruit after another from a garden, so should the king from his kingdom. Out of fear for his own destruction, he should avoid unripe ones, which give rise to revolts." [107]

---

[107] *Arthaśāstra* 5.2.70.

He thought that he saw a way forward that would avoid the inevitable split if no deal is reached, and suggested to Selim and his viziers that a new formula should be used that would be less difficult to pass on to the ministers, local chiefs and their people. It would also be easier for the court to oversee. He offers some overseas help for the poor people in their country and a new system of trading which, although it would result in a smaller income for Zeta and the loss of some lucrative market trading, would be better for Selim's people. He did not want to close the land border, but limiting the free passage of goods seemed a good compromise. And of course there would be the huge savings to both countries from the continued peaceful union.

Was Tristram betraying his King? In this case, I do not think so; he had originally been sent to negotiate peace, albeit with a fixed position that he was to present, had been forced to return, and was now taking the initiative to resolve a dispute that had been in the making for much of his life. Selim withdrew with his Elders to discuss the sudden change of approach that had been offered, but it did not take long before they returned. Tristram asked for the services of a trusted member of the court and told the young man:

"Go to my father's court with this talisman and tell him he is at peace with the South, that a settlement has been reached, the Union remains. In my name, tell him to rejoice!"

He still had much work to do in preparation for the official North-South treaty, but the end was in sight. He ached to share his news with Yseult... and to tell her of the part she had played! That evening there were celebrations and a banquet to mark the settlement; musicians played and the wine flowed. Soon the return voyage would begin. At one point during the evening Selim, perhaps inspired by the wine he had drunk, confided in Tristram that now peace was assured he will be able to claim his bride and marry. Quoting from his father's poem—My woman of the beautiful hair—he says that she too, like his mother, is said to have long red hair.

Lines 169-172:
Time passes

There were times—many times—when it did not seem possible, but the sands of time did move inexorably onwards. The slow journey back passed, much of it again under the watchful bird's eye, and soon the ship was passing through the narrow channel and nearing its new home port. He ached to hold his love again and could imagine rushing ashore as soon as the boat had come alongside to meet her. He ached with desire.

Of course, it was impossible for her to know the time of his arrival; of course it was impossible she would be on the quay; of course, he would have to square things away before he could disembark; of course there would be further delay. He could not stand it! But he is home! His ship has slipped into her berth! The lovers are reunited and the cedars bow over them in their passion. Once again, days pass in which quiet contemplation of their future is only interrupted by their pleasure in the present.

When Lewis first showed me a draft of this section of 'Retrospective', I suggested further lines that he could have used here to great effect, to strengthen both the composition and to balance the heightened passion of his return, of their reunion. I think I had some quiet and oblique reference to Lao Tzu [108] in mind but, if they were ever even pencilled in (gone are the days of index cards so, again, whatever the digital equivalent is!) they did not survive to the final draft.

After his leave, instead of sailing for Australia, he had been placed in charge of one of the company's ships which was in dry dock in Hamburg and had spent several weeks stuck in a hotel near the Reeperbahn while spending every other night on board—K. told him he might as well be in Australia but then hatched a plan to join him for his last week there. (The letter in the appendix that I received from Hamburg was sent before K. arrived.) Although he didn't dare take her on board, it was a lovely summer interlude in which he showed her the city he had already explored. He had told me that he was much taken with the huge Stadt park around the planetarium in which both squirrels and birds would feed from the hand and he enjoyed showing K. how the squirrels would run up his leg if

---

[108] I was probably thinking of the line which can most easily be translated as "Being deeply loved by someone gives you strength, while loving someone deeply gives you courage", which seemed to me to encapsulate rather well the situation in which the lovers had found themselves. I always found it strange that while Lewis was more than happy to ask for advice, or an opinion, on his text, where his text might go next or how it might link up to the next section, he rarely accepted my ideas.
The arrogance of the author, I suppose, coupled with the idea that he would always have to acknowledge my help and would not be able to claim that the book was all his own work! Such is the ignominy of friends and editors! I rather think he simply wanted me to read it and praise it! *(Publisher's note: this footnote was added at the last minute and without being seen by Trystan Lewis.)*

they thought there was food to be had! They had to return to England separately—he tried, but the office would not allow anyone but wives on board, much to K.'s fury—and she went home, as she had arrived, alone, by ferry.

Lines 174-180:
But then, but then…

It must have been depressing for Tristram so soon after his return to realise the need for a further voyage; or perhaps we have to assume that he had always known that it was inevitable and had hidden it both from himself and Yseult in those first days of joy following his return. The scant message sent to his father from the south contained no details of what should go into the new treaty and, in reality, there would have to be discussions between his father and the southern Court to work out the fine detail of his promise to Selim. And his father could not negotiate without a detailed knowledge of what had been agreed by his son! But it must have seemed as if he was eternally doomed to be dragged from the happiness of his life with Yseult and plunged into the mundane world beyond their shores!

Lewis' use of Sisyphus [109] in the second of these lines is no casual reference! Sisyphus was also the son of a king and was also a navigator, but I believe that Lewis was also referencing Tristram's sense of pride in what he thought he had achieved in both love and—through his work with Selim—in diplomacy. Lewis would also have been worried by another fact: Sisyphus betrayed his lord by revealing the whereabouts of a daughter.

And of course, he was concerned for his lovely Yseult, knowing that he would have to break the news to her that he was to leave again, albeit for the much shorter journey to his homeland.

Can either he or she withstand the tide's eternal wash?

---

[109] As we have seen, Sisyphus is a figure from Greek mythology—a king who was punished for pride and dishonesty by being forced to roll a huge boulder up a hill only for it to roll down when he almost reaches the top, and to repeat this action for eternity. He could have used the Danaids rather than Sisyphus: they too represent the futility of repetitive tasks as their father, Danaus, ordered his daughters on their wedding night to kill the husbands that had been forced on them—thus they are condemned to spend eternity carrying water to fill a bath with no bottom.

In Sussex, Trystan and K. both know that he will continue time after time to leave her. That their times together will always be all too brief—shorter by far than his time away—and both seek to come to terms with it. Sometimes— often—Trystan is the stronger but his words of comfort seem to help little. And many times K. consoles him with promises of her eternal love and the joy that each of his returns will bring them. Sometimes—for both of them—words must have seemed to offer no hope! Trystan was fated endlessly to drift back to sea in the spume before being washed back onto the pebbles of what is clearly the Sussex shore, beneath the pier and both are unsure of their mental strength to withstand the sea's surge.

So, no more than a week after his return as they sat at their early meal of fruit and honey, Tristram told Yseult that he must leave her again. It must have seemed a particularly harsh blow, not only as it was so soon after his return but as he was to travel to his father—a man whom Yseult, with good reason, hated. No amount of logic or explanation seemed to satisfy Yseult and she left the table in tears. It was not until the afternoon that Tristram found her in the library and was able to discuss with her the best way to win over his father to the treaty he had—without permission—agreed. And it was not until much later that night that Yseult understood and accepted the needs of her man. Of course, Tristram was also hoping to persuade his father to accept Yseult!

In the early morning, Tristram sailed his boat away from Mljet; a few hours later he was tying her up at the wharf beneath his father's palace. As he trudged up the hill towards the royal gates, he must have been conscious of the enormity of his task (*tasks*, he reminded himself). He wondered how his father had received the news brought to him by the messenger from the south. He would soon find out!

In private audience, the King greets his son warmly, enfolding him in his arms before releasing him to his mother! Then there is silence as his son explains what has been agreed between him and Selim. He watches the play of emotions on his father's face as he speaks and, while there are momentary flashes of displeasure, Tristram is not disheartened by what he sees. To one side, taking no part in the discussions, his mother sits with a worried expression perpetually on her face.

After some hours of talk, his father claps his hands and calls in his ministers. He repeats much of what Tristram has said, pausing frequently to enquire if this or that will work, or if the country can afford what has been offered. Tristram slowly realises, that his father is adjusting his words—even his syntax and emphasis—to suggest his own agreement with the proposed terms of this new treaty so that his ministers are almost bound to accept it. In the end, as the shadows lengthen and candles are brought, there are only a couple of minor points to be ironed out. The King calls for food!

Alone with his parents after the meal, Tristram knows the time has come to talk about what has been in the forefront of his mind all day, even as the discussions have swung to and fro between the ministers and his father: Yseult. Even as he mentions her name, he sees his father's face darken and a tear slip down his mother's cheek. And the King cuts across his son's protestations of love—"I would speak before you, let me speak," he says. Quietly—and surprisingly—he recounts a story.

He explains that he has always known Yseult, and known who she is. Indeed, he, along with the Queen and her brother Guyan, had been present at her Name Day and that he was her godfather! It was Guyan, an uncle Tristram could scarcely remember as he died while serving as the King's first ambassador in the foreign court, who had brought about the privilege. Tristram cannot believe what he is hearing, nor understand his father's reluctance to accept his own god-daughter into his court.

But Tristram falls silent as the King explains further that he had been at the ceremony in the south, which took place shortly after the territories had come under his rule; his part in the naming ceremony was notional—an honour which was supposed to help cement that first treaty. But, he had said, that of itself was not the problem! The problem lay in what he had been told by her father—the country's first minister—the next day, as they were leaving. Her father had said that he had promised his baby daughter in a very favourable marriage—a marriage to his ruler's young son—Selim. He was so happy, the King said that I was left speechless.

The King continued that the very Treaty they are now negotiating would not be possible—indeed, war would be inevitable—if those in the south were ever to hear that Yseult was a part of his court. Her whereabouts is unknown, he explains, following her father's belated understanding of the enormity of what he had done and their subsequent flight.

He ends his lengthy explanation by reminding his son that he too had known love, and here he glanced fondly at his wife, and that Tristram was his only son—they, his mother and the King could only wish him everything that is good in his future life! And, he added with an uncharacteristic break in his voice, he should tell Yseult that he, the King, loved her as a daughter and has never stopped grieving for the way that their last meeting ended. So, although Tristram was his son and his heir, even an old and near-blind King can see how much he was in love with Yseult, and he urged them to flee—the island home could not stay safe for long now that Yseult was of age.

Tristram could see, and hear in his father's voice, the pain that this deep division—from the country of his birth, the country he would one day have ruled and from his parents—his loss to them—was causing his parents but felt powerless to do anything about it. He understood that he was no longer a part of his childhood destiny: that the wider world called him.

Tristram sees his mother is weeping openly now and goes to her.

In the days that follow Tristram is in a haze as he oversees the work of preparing the formal Treaty. His mind is in Mljet! He can think only of Yseult, and his need to return and protect her.

As editor, I have to note some inconsistencies and weakness in these lines and in the beginning of Canto iv. Lewis and I discussed this section at length as he was writing the poem but seemingly he could not understand my argument. My suggestion had been to bring forward the second reference to the daemons (lines 201-203):

The Daemons still frowned:
sensing a different division,
their power diminishing

I also urged him to make more of these difficulties that he faced during the voyage. Instead, Lewis' lines at the beginning of the Canto focus almost entirely on his *positive* view of the future. It is the task of this editor to fill in these gaps in Tristram's story.

Canto iv
Lines 185-192:
As to the watch…

And on his short voyage home, Tristram begins to understand his future. And then—it is all in those first three lines, that sudden slow-dawning realisation— he knew that his future can still begin with marriage! Everything seemed to point to it! To her! All—perhaps it was a sudden lull in the wind that made him grimace—*all* he realises that is left will be explaining to Yseult that although they have his father's blessing they can never return to his court. Worse! They have to flee Mljet! The rest of the short voyage is taken up with trying to understand how such an explanation can be made!

Tristram realises that she knows from her Uncle Iski that desperate lengths, even the death of her much-loved parents, have kept her home on Mljet secret and she knows that she was told never to leave, but she has no idea why! He has to explain everything—including the King's part in things; but, he thinks, I will swear my eternal love, my allegiance to her, first in the only way that I can! And as the island appears hazily on the horizon, his thoughts calm and for the rest of the short voyage he rehearses time and time again the words that he will use!

Both to ask Yseult's hand in marriage and to recount her almost tragic history to her.

Careful readers will have recognised that much of this is taken for granted or assumed by the lines of verse in 'Dark Ashes'. It is only with a complete understanding of the story so far, that the torment that Tristram must have been going through as he sailed away from his father, perhaps never to see his parents again, probably denying both his heritage and his rightful claim to the crown—can be understood.

The first line of Canto iv is noteworthy as being almost the only line of the entire poem where Lewis' draft indicates that he has changed his mind from the original and intended word to a more orthodox version. The first draft read:

As to the night watch a distant glim in the empty sea

while the final version expands 'glim' (a word he had used before in the short poem, 'Hope') as 'mast glint'—a far less satisfactory term that destroys some of the natural rhythm. Some other editor may have queried the word but I believe that the change was occasioned, at least in part, by an attempt to distance himself—his work—from his older life. 'Glim' is a far more ancient word (middle English, I think) and a word more likely to have come to Tristram's mind, redolent as it is with brightness or splendour. This, and the repetitious, comparisons of the first three lines wherein Tristram's desolation—his empty sea, empty horizon, and dark night—are relieved by the joy of the future: the glim, the island, Yseult's warm breath—is displayed so blatantly are what convince me of the veracity of the underlying story. However hard he may try, Lewis cannot escape his past!

As he stands watch after watch, Trystan—particularly in the lonely night watches—can only dream of K. And he is worried—scared—for their future while he "must forever navigate old horizons": K. left behind on the dock; K. pining; K. weeping—it is intolerable! But even as he watches the eternally empty horizon or counts the southern stars, K. seems to call to him—every wave, every cloud carries her image and her arms reach out to him and warm him. And, slowly at first like something appearing over the distant horizon, like the clouds which presage land not yet seen, he is aware—as softly as a breath of wind that raises pimples on the flesh of his arm—of the possibility of a new reality, and with it comes a new realisation, an understanding of how the pain of parting can be lessened! And his late understanding of their future brings him peace.

Line 193:
Their union had always been inevitable.

Grand passions do not always end happily with a wedding—indeed many writers would suggest that greater literature is the result when there is a tragic ending. One thinks, most obviously of Romeo and Juliet or of Trystan's mythological forebear: Tristan and his love for Isolde. But the narrative in 'Dark Ashes' could only result in marriage. K., appropriately echoing Catherine in *Wuthering Heights* has always felt at one with Trystan, that she *is* Trystan—he was always in her mind—"not as a pleasure, any more than I am always a pleasure to myself, but as my own being" when she offered him the line: "Your body travels with me, your blood flows in my veins."

So, any kind of real separation, anything other than marriage, was both impracticable and impossible to imagine. In the same way Yseult can no longer imagine life without Tristram by her side—when he is away she no longer has a life. She remembers when they first met how strongly he had affected her, how desperate she had been to keep him, how scared of losing him: there were two poems, dear to her heart, that she had searched out in her library and re-read when they were back on the island, and she remembers some lines from them now—the lines that meant most to her back then:

The face of all the world is changed, I think,

Since first I heard the footsteps of thy soul [110]

and

All thoughts, all passions, all delights,
Whatever stirs this mortal frame,
All are but ministers of Love,
    And feed his sacred flame. [111]

At the time she had somehow connected them in her mind with Christopher Marlowe's final line in 'The Passionate Shepherd to His Love': "Then live with me and be my love"! [112]

Lines 195-200:
And as again the land held him…

This time Yseult is waiting on the beach beside the jetty as Tristram brings *Bäckahästen* alongside and makes her fast. Her happiness and her joy at seeing him again confirm an almost ecstatic Tristram in his course while, at the same time, grieving him for the pain he knows his later story will bring.

Leaping lightly down from the jetty into her arms, he kisses her, and pulling her down beside him on the beach knows that if he does not begin now, his courage will fail him. But first he reverses his position so that he is kneeling in front of her while her face moves through several emotion as he struggles in the sand: puzzlement, understanding, hope, love, excitement—he takes her hand with the twisted band of gold with its jade stone still in place on her finger, kisses it, and with tears in his eyes asks her to be his own, to marry him and be his eternally. "I love you," he gasps, "I worship you"—there was never any doubt how Yseult would respond but the passion of her response nearly unmans him so that he cannot continue.

My love, he had whispered as he struggled to compose himself. But I have also, Tristram told Yseult, some news that will upset you … but, I promise you there is good to come as well! The treaty I have just seen signed by my father is

---

[110] Elizabeth Barrett Browning (1806-61) 'The Face of All the World' (Sonnet 7).
[111] Samuel Taylor Coleridge (1772-1834) 'Love'.
[112] Christopher Marlowe (1564-93) 'The Passionate Shepherd to His Love'.

with someone—Selim—to whom it seems you were promised in marriage as a baby—pulling back from him a little, she can only gasp, a hundred thoughts and memories rushing through her mind—and he continues, he knows that Selim now wishes to marry. Suddenly her uncle's dying words come to her and she understands what he had been straining to tell her and tears—for her uncle... and then for her father and mother run down her cheeks; Tristram feels powerless to comfort her; in some strange way—perhaps because of the more recent treaty—he almost feels complicit with Selim: guilty to be associated with him and seriously concerned that Yseult will never forgive him.

My father, Tristram continued, knows this because he was there at the time when your father and Selim's father, Suleiman, made the agreement—he remembers seeing Suleiman's tughra [113] (he said that it reminded him of a drawing of a prawn!) on the document that had been drawn up with your new name added after the ceremony. For he was there on your Name Day and my father is in fact your godfather—he loves you as the daughter he never had! He wants above all else for you to know that: his pain at the circumstances in which he met you again and the knowledge that every second you were in his court placed you in greater danger made him banish you—it was the quickest way to get you away! It was when *your* father came to realise the enormity of what he had done that he fled with you to Mljet. My father thinks you will not be safe here for long—he has given us his blessing, but he begs us to flee!

If Yseult's emotions had been in turmoil before, as the land around them somehow seemed to shine in a brighter light, now—in an instant—her senses were plunging into dark despair and she struggles to understand what she is being told. A whole new history! Her life was not what she thought! Her island! Her castle! Her people! Her new almost-husband! Whose father knew her! As a baby! Taking flight! Where? Her mind spins and Tristram holds her tight and whispers his love in her ear. She feels his strength and is comforted, but at the same time she is trembling for the future. For their future. She had thought that their island

---

[113] A tughra is a Turkish word used in calligraphy to describe the decorative monogram of a sultan; it is used on his seal or as a signature on all official documents and letters. All tughra have a fixed form—ironically, the two loops on the left—the Beyze—are said to symbolise the two seas that a sultan ruled (the outer larger loop signifying the Mediterranean and the inner, smaller loop signifying the Black Sea) so with his signature on the document dictating Yseult's future, Suleiman also foretold the life she would have hiding from her destiny: in a sea within a sea!

world—the only home she has ever known—was their personal heaven! Tristram takes her arm and leads her back through the sun dappled woods, across the inland lake and into the castle.

And as again the land held him—she shared his joy

The very land seemed to rejoice as Trystan re-joined K. in Ælle's [114] old kingdom. In their shared happiness the world seemed a wonderful place, and when beneath an old oak tree in Stanmer Park Trystan went down on one knee in front of her, K. almost wept with joy, although in truth, there had never been any doubt in her mind that the moment would come! Sometime! It seemed as if the world—indeed, time itself—belonged to them. Lewis' use of words borrowed from Wordsworth describe beautifully the quality of added light that intense joy seems to bring to the world:

… a time when meadow, grove, and stream,
The earth, and every common sight,
To me did seem
Apparelled in celestial light [115]

but we have to remember their source. At the height of the couple's joy, at the start of their life together, Lewis is reminding us of an uncertain future. But for now, all of Sussex, from the chalky downs to the stony beaches rejoiced with them.

Lewis has written some beautiful lines, which actually describe a later time in their life together—another summer—but I think they also capture rather wonderfully something of what Trystan and K. felt now:

Wonderful was that time in summer
of summary surrender that stilled my soul, awed
by the transcendent passion of love's lease;
wonderful was that time of trust

---

[114] Ælle was the King of Sussex from 477 to around 514, having landed with his three sons and won the lands in battle.
[115] William Wordsworth: 'Ode: Intimations of Immortality from Recollections of Early Childhood'.

of slow sweet lingering love, the joy
of each moment each owned: [116]

Lines 201-203:
The Daemons still frowned

I have already quoted these lines, noting that they might have better appeared a little earlier in the poem. Here, they remain a slightly bitter reminder of the dark days that the union may visit on those close to them. A daemon is a deity that divides but at this juncture they have to recognise that the division is between the couple and themselves. They have little or no further power over them.

Lines 205-210:
Lace dressed she came to him

In the little church—Crkva Sv Marije—in the shadow of the great castle when Tristram and Yseult first came together they were surrounded by a small band of well-wishers from the village who had come to know Tristram almost as well as they knew Yseult and respected him and loved him for his passions: his determination to understand their way of life and his wish to learn about fishing and beekeeping was almost as strong as his passion for their mistress. It would be a simple ceremony presided over by the village priest. Tristram—as tradition demanded—had stayed in the village, with old Srecko, the beekeeper. A neighbour, Stjepan, had brought in a jug of the local red wine to celebrate.

Later, as he was rowed across the lake and walked up the little rise to the church, Tristram looked up at the walls which rose above its little bell tower— itself scarcely higher than its roof—and wondered how long they would be able to depend on their protection. Already in the weeks since his return, he and Yseult had begun planning, although, for her part, Yseult could barely bring herself to consider life away from her home and her people. Srecko coughed quietly beside him and brought him back to the present, and they entered the little church.

Tears sprang to his eyes to see how the villagers had adorned it with garlands of flowers and branches of cedar and fragrant eucalyptus to celebrate their day. And as Yseult walked through the door, clad in a simple lacy shift and holding a

---

[116] From an unpublished poem—'The Summer of Love'— written by Lewis in 2018 and now in the editor's collection.

trailing bunch of her favourite flowers—magnolia, jasmine and hibiscus—his heart was in his throat at the wonder and vulnerability of their future together.

The service was simple and, consequently, short. As they walk back out into the sun amid a cheer and some thrown grain from the villagers, he watches her as their vows run through his mind. He sees perfection in her every move, in every ripple and wave in the thin material of her dress—he imagines her as the sea with those waves breaking gently on her shore, and hears in the gentle sound of those waves, in the rustle of leaves in the branches above a quiet ostinato that repeats again and again her melodic "I will". He imagines the wind catching the theme and perhaps improvising on it as in an Indian raga [117]:

I will, will will will, I I oh—I will oh, I will will. I will

until its echo reaches his father's ear. And he likes the idea of harmony, desire and joy that is implicit in the word, raga.

The village has laid on a wedding breakfast, a feast of everything they could provide: there is fish and octopus, a roasted goat on an angled wooden frame over the fire pit, skewered sosaties, an array of vegetables and fruit and yoghurt with honey and nuts. This is a celebration! And it can only end in dancing as the afternoon turns to evening—despite his lack of skill Tristram is dragged into the centre of a spinning circle of laughing village women which finally opens to allow Yseult to rescue him. In her arms he feels safe and he prays almost out loud—that she will remain safe in *his* arms forever. In the morning they must tell the villagers of their plans, but—for now—Tristram pulls Yseult into the shadows away from the fire and kisses her, before spiriting her away from the celebrations and back into the castle.

Many years later, Lewis and K. were married in a little village church in Sussex—Beddingham, on the edge of the Lewes Downs overlooked by Firle Beacon. I remember K. was late arriving and I had to steady Trystan—although the delay was unintentional as her car had been held up by the railway level crossing! But as the organ began, Trystan glanced over his shoulder and was

---

[117] A melodic framework for improvisation in Indian music, particularly Indian classical music, which while allowing extemporisation also has rules which control it. I was with Lewis when he first came across this term, explained by a jazz musician—with the aid of a paper exercise—at Ronny Scott's Jazz Club in London. The rules are complex, at least to Western ears, and I am not sure that Lewis has used them successfully here!

spellbound by what he saw—K., lit by the dusty late-summer sunlight coming through the high windows (a momentary half-memory of sunlight falling through some other window onto auburn hair disturbed him for less than a second)—K. was dressed in a lacy broderie anglaise dress of a very pale ivory colour and holding a simple bunch of the waxy-bloomed stephanotis interwoven with a few wild flowers. More flowers were twined in her long hair which fell simply over her shoulders to strike a contrast with the ivory dress.

Trystan felt that it was as if a Titian beauty—maybe Flora [118] he thought—or a Pre-Raphaelite maid such as Rossetti's Venus Verticordia [119] or Bocca Baciata [120] had stepped into the church! Maybe he was alarmed at the mixed symbolism that came to mind but he knew at least that the last image would stay with him through the day! And the night! Time seemed to stand still—or at least the service seemed to pass in a wonderful haze. All that Trystan is aware of is his bride—by his side at the altar, and at the register and amongst the gathering of the two families where they—the couple at the centre of events—are almost lost in a jockeying for position in photographs. But then, as they stand outside the church it is as if their union is eternal, their joy immeasurable! They are one! They are married! It seems as if nothing and no one can divide them.

Holding K.'s hand, Trystan looks up at the blue sky over the downs with its wisps of high cirrus cloud, at the trees gently waving their leaves in the light breeze, and hears the buzz of insects in the churchyard grasses—only the shush of the waves on the beach is missing, he thinks—but as the breeze touches the flowers in K.'s hair, he remembers how the wind has carried and is carrying their vows, immutable, unchanging, over land and sea, echo upon echo to the ends of the earth.

---

[118] Titian—Tiziano Vecelli (1490-1576) *Flora* c.1515: an idealised beautiful woman, holding a pink-shaded mantle and flowers and leaves—she is sometimes considered as a symbol of nuptial love.

[119] Dante Gabriel Rossetti (1828-1882) *Venus Verticordia*, 1868: perhaps not a timely thought for Trystan as "the changer of hearts" was supposed to have the power to change hearts from lust to chastity! Then again, they were in church!

[120] Dante Gabriel Rossetti (1828-82) *Bocca Baciata*, 1859: The title means the mouth that has been kissed, and is taken from an old Italian proverb 'The mouth that has been kissed does not lose its savour, indeed it renews itself just as the moon does.'

Lines 212-216:
They are alone!

The celebrations, or at least their part in them complete, the couple are alone. Alone in their own little world for a time. A *limited* time as in only a few weeks Trystan, this time accompanied by K., has to re-join his ship. Until then, the world—or at least a small hidden part of North Devon—was theirs alone. It was with a sense of melancholy that I joined the crowd waving them off, for I sensed that K. would now be Trystan's closest friend and ally. And I would miss him... but such is love and such is marriage, and I wished them well.

The lines that Lewis has used to cover the period of their honeymoon are both subtle and expressive. "Her arms held..." / "His arms warmed..."—they are equals: in love, in life. But I am also reminded of a later poem (unusually, written with empty lines between each line of text, which I always felt suggested the heightened breathless rhythm of passion), in which Lewis again used the sea metaphor, much as he does here to express both their mutual need and the fact that he saw K. as his strength and a means to keep him 'afloat'.

I think even then, Lewis was beginning to sense some possible failing or weakness in himself—perhaps perceiving a time when he might be seen to 'fail' in his career as he left the sea, but one that, I know, was eventually to surface (if I may be allowed to continue the metaphor) in periods where he simply could not write. Or, possibly, the idea that K. kept him afloat was, like any newly married couple, simply an uncertainty about their new life together.

Restless: my body is your ocean; my limbs the currents of the sea

You float on my waves—sink only a little

I hold your sacred vessel safe—we become one:

Unite in perfect harmony

Your body runs its course through my being

I feel you cleave my waves

I know you as we sink...

Black waters closing

And I know you as we rise

I hold you to float above the tide as we burst waves apart.

In the still of the calm you drift in my currents

Finding your port [121]

And while they took pleasure in their new found independent life, they also had a lot of work to do preparing K. for a life as an officer's wife on board his ship. There were new clothes to buy! There was her study library to furnish so that she could spend the large amounts of free time on board reading and advance her studies! There was so much to tell her that—perhaps like any honeymoon— the weeks rushed by until, suddenly it seemed, he was due to report on board.

So much planning! So much pouring over atlases and charts! So much to gather together ready for the voyage! Two days after their wedding, Tristram and Yseult had called the castle staff and the village elders together and announced— to a shocked and disbelieving silence, followed by a rush of questions—that they were leaving Mljet, never to return. Tristram had explained that Yseult's life was threatened and reminded them of the sudden death of her parents, but did not add too many details, and explained only that they would sail far: he gave no indication of which direction they would head, at least in part as he was unsure in his own mind where they would finally end up. He knows that if Selim's men ever arrive on Mljet they will extract any information that will point to their destination, and so his conversations with villagers one day mention heading north and on another west, and on yet another south as the direction they are planning to take. He emphasises that they have planned to take on stores at safe havens along the way, he talks of living in cold and another time in warm lands— anything to confuse!

Lines 218-223:
So few days joined and they...

---

[121] 'Ocean' Published in *Mostly Welsh* (2019). Talybont: Y Lolfa.

The repetitious emphasis on how little time they have serves only to add a sense of impending doom, but this is lightened by the fact that on this voyage, Yseult will be accompanying her husband! They will not be separated in the way that his previous sailings had parted them. As Tristram had in the past, they left the jetty quietly early one morning, thus avoiding an upsetting crowd of well-wishers that would have made departure difficult and upset Yseult more than she already was! She could not believe she was leaving her beloved island island—the literal centre of her universe—forever; that she would never see her castle, her bed chamber, her precious library ever again. And worse, that she was deserting her people, her faithful retainers, and leaving them to face a possible invasion! She did not understand how, in so short a time, her world had crashed to the ground while at the same time she was escaping the ruins. The joy of her marriage and of the prospect of life with Tristram could not but be shaded by her conscience. How could she be so happy?

Despite the hardships of the voyage to come, they revel in standing the night watches together and Yseult learns a little more about the stars and navigation, and sailing larger ships so that she can relieve Tristram during the day. When there is no land in sight, they steal time together in his little—and previously lonely—cabin. The cabin was little more than a closed off part of the hold, reached by a short ladder from the deck. It contained nothing more than a narrow bunk, some shelves on which Yseult had squeezed some poetry books between the charts, rahnāmags [122] and almanacs, and a trunk with their few clothes. Without a porthole and with little ventilation, It was dark and stuffy… and when the weather was poor, it was also damp! But Yseult loved it as their home for the duration of the voyage!

At first they sail north until they sight land and then they head west as far as they dare before turning again and heading south east for some days. This, for Tristram, is the most worrying time as they cannot avoid the relatively narrow area of water level with Selim's lands—he knows that they will not be in sight even from the heights of Lëkurësi Castle, but fears being seen by other ships. He knows that his *qārib*—even with no Zetan flag flying—would be instantly

---

[122] A rahnāmag is the old Persian equivalent of the modern day pilot books which list lights, ports and coastal landmarks to help in navigation. As regular sailors update them with sketches and new landmarks, these undoubtedly second-hand volumes found in Zeta would have been invaluable on a voyage into new waters, although it is doubtful that Tristram had information about the further parts of his voyage.

recognised after his time tied up to their stone jetty. But they escape the channel without being seen and turn to head south west.

Tristram begins to dare to think they may have escaped! His old charts show no land to the south but that they are running parallel to—but for the minute, out of sight of—the coast. He watches their supply of water and fresh food diminish and know that they will have to find a port where they can provision sooner than he had hoped. He wonders how far Selim's trade routes and influence reach, and wishes they had discussed that more thoroughly when he had been negotiating the treaty.

As Mljet is left far behind, Yseult's spirits lift at the thought of their future together. She busies herself when she is not conning the ship in making everything on board as organised and pleasing as possible. Although they had stowed away the volumes from her library she could not stand to be parted from, as well as anything they could find on medical and health matters, on farming (and the keeping of bees!), and on several other topics that Tristram had said could be useful, these were all wrapped in oilcloth and stowed out of easy reach so she had little to keep her busy other than Tristram and *Bäckahästen*. But she had kept back one or two small books of poems and when the sun shone and she had time, she would sit leaning against the mast with the sails taught above her head and Tristram visible every time she looked up, and read. She particularly liked these poems by Vasko Popa and read and re-read one in particular for the lines:

Out of each pain
Which we do not mention
A chestnut tree grows up
And remains mysterious behind us

Out of each hope
Which we cherish
A star arises
And moves unattainable in front of us [123]

… which seem particularly relevant to them at the moment!

---

[123] Vasko Popa (1943) 'Far within us'. *Vasko Popa: Selected Poems* (Penguin Modern European Poets) 1969.

K. has a small library in the cabin. And, once she has gained her sea legs some while after crossing the corkscrew swells of Biscay, when the sun shines she is glad that she has; for eight hours out of every day her husband is taken from her when he is on watch from midday until four o'clock and for four hours from midnight. She finds the hours trying at first but gradually adapts to the strange routine. They rise late, rarely in time for breakfast which doesn't matter as they have an early lunch before Trystan is due on the bridge.

Late afternoon and early evening are more sociable times but they usually retire early for a couple of hours in bed before the next watch. There seems to be a lot of time in bed! She often shares at least some of his night watch and occasionally the last hour of his afternoon watch with him, and once they are in the open sea she is taught to steer the huge ship and is presented with a Steering Certificate! Almost she feels that she is not finding enough time to study!

But when she is alone, she reads and makes notes, and writes and reads and reads. It would be so easy to forget her studies but she is determined not to waste this time she has been given. And so, Trystan's lonely watches and the long vigils by K., waiting for his letters, waiting for his return, become a thing of the past. Often in his letters, Trystan had written of how lonely he could feel in his big cabin—and even in the lounge amongst the other officers—but now the cabin has become a social centre where friends come to have coffee from the beautiful Wedgewood-blue percolator which had been their wedding present from me. Time passes—almost too fast—on this voyage.

Trystan tells her that the trip—across the Bay of Biscay, south round the bulge of Africa to Cape Town where they slow down while the pilot boat comes out from the harbour and travels beside them while—on the end of a rope she learns to call a heaving line—they swap a sack of mail to, with one from, home before picking up speed and, leaving the little launch behind to bob its way back into port, then rounding the Cape and heading across the Indian Ocean to Fremantle, and from there to Melbourne and Sydney—will be the same each time, with only the weather changing, but she knows that she will never tire of this great adventure with her sailor! Her only worry is that time is passing too fast and the time—after three voyages—when he will once again sail off without her is drawing closer—but, for now, her heaven is ship-shape!

Lines 225-241:
Above the day's depthless deep unbounded sea

K. is in awe at a vastness she had never imagined—or never thought to imagine—before she was a part of it. At the eternal sea and the vast skies which always seem to surround them until in some almost magical way the next port pops up before them to spoil the perfect line of the horizon. Trystan reminds her of a poem by the Welsh bard, Dewi Emrys which reflects on the illusory quality of the horizon—'Y Gorwel' is perhaps his most famous englyn, which in English may be rendered as:

Behold an illusion like a wheel's rim,
A magician's work surrounds us.
An ancient distant non-existent line,
An endless border it cannot define. [124]

He says the horizon she sees from two deck below his view from the bridge is not the same horizon that he sees and the horizon she has seen five minutes ago can never be seen again! He also reminds her that as they left the English Channel they had passed through a bank of fog when, for several hours, there had been no horizon and he shows her the radar which always sees everything around them—out to an electronic horizon some forty miles away.

When she is with him on the bridge, new worlds unfold. She sees a sky full of so many more stars than she has ever seen before, and Trystan shows her an instrument that measures the water beneath them and she realises she is floating miles above solid ground and miles beneath the sky—it is a strange feeling for someone who has never left the land before! Sometimes the infamous albatross

---

[124] I am not sure where Lewis first came across the works of Dewi Emrys as he did not speak or read Welsh but I know that he had used his years at sea—much as K. is doing at this point of the narrative—to educate himself by reading voraciously—novels, poems, works on history and philosophy, anything he could lay his hands on! Like me, Dewi Emrys was an editor but he was also a journalist and a religious minister as well as a poet who won the Chair at the 1948 Welsh National Eisteddfod. 'Y Gorwel'—the translation above is by David Llewelyn Williams (*The Cambrian News, Society Newsletter,* Welsh Society of Vancouver, Canada, July 2012 [p.7]). The englyn as originally written in Welsh is:

Wele rith fel ymyl rhod—o'n cwmpas,
Campwaith dewin hynod.
Hen linell bell nad yw'n bod,
Hen derfyn nad yw'n darfod.

drifts past the bridge (or perhaps it is another one) and on one magical occasion Trystan is able to point out a school of dolphin swimming alongside the ship, dipping in and out of the widening bow wave. Finally, one afternoon, Trystan calls her up to the bridge and point ahead—she can just make out land. Her first sight of Australia. Although she hates the thought, she begins to understand the breadth of the magical call which lures him back to sea.

Days pass and the taste of the sea, the eternal hum of the ship's engines that she had thought she would not be able to stand when they first left port, the wind, the storms, the magical skies sink into her soul and she feels at one with the ship, with its cargo and with its crew! Trystan keeps watch and navigates their way around the world, all the while amazed by his wonderful good fortune, delighting, he uses the more physical word revelling, in their love for each other!

I visited them when they were on leave after their first trip together and had an unusually long talk with K. in which she described her impressions. She had found it difficult at first, being so young as the only officer's wife on board; and had been frightened—in awe—of the saloon with its white-coated steward in attendance at every meal. But the ice had been broken as they joined their table for her first dinner. The other officers—much to her embarrassment—all stood until she was seated, but bending forward as he sat down, the third engineer had inadvertently allowed the tip of his tie to float slowly across his bowl of soup! After that, things were more relaxed!

She had been terribly seasick as they crossed Biscay and had taken to her cabin for so long that the captain had paid her a visit to encourage her to get up! She had only groaned—at that point she could scarcely believe that they would not stop somewhere to let her off! And then the weather improved, she recovered and began to settle into their routine—a routine governed by Trystan's watches and the weather, but one in which she read a lot—often while sunbathing on deck. And she began to understand the attraction of the life although, she said, she was often bored.

There had been another wife on board—the bosun's wife—and the two ladies got on well together—the more so when she found out that they both came from Sussex; and she made friends with many of the officers she met on deck or in the bar and gradually—although she said it took most of the outward-bound trip—she began to feel that she belonged. I think, from the way she spoke about it, the transition from university—almost from school—to an officer's wife was difficult, the more so as she did not really approve of the 'us-and-them' nature of the relationship between the officers and the crew. Trystan had explained to her the need and also that things were much more casual than they had been when he was first at sea… but the crew still lived in smaller cabins a couple of decks below them and that upset her.

Trystan had been wrong on one count: all voyages were not the same and the adventure of the first voyage was a little more intense than even he could have foreseen, and although it is not directly referenced in the poem I think the story adds both colour and gravitas to what otherwise might read like a pleasure cruise. He was actually reading a letter from me as the events unfolded, and this as well as his letter back to me with the story are in the appendix. Had K. seen Trystan grappling with a deranged stowaway teetering above the dark, plunging wake at the very stern of the ship some hours after they left Cape Town it is not likely that she would have let him out of her sight for the rest of the trip!

They had been lying in bed after his watch reading the first letters from the Cape Town bag when they had both heard a noise outside the window, two deck below. On investigating, Trystan had rushed to the 'phone and called the bridge, grabbed some clothes and, muttering something about a life raft inflating on deck, had left for the bridge. That was all K. knew until much later!

In short order, Trystan discovered that a stowaway who had been found on board shortly after they left the English Channel was now apparently trying to get a life raft into the water despite the fact that at the time the ship was heading east at about 25 knots, that the raft heard inflating outside his cabin was the third attempt, and that he was currently threatening an apprentice with a two-foot bread knife!

By the time Trystan caught up with the man, he was trying to scramble over the stern rail in the rather fanciful hope that he would be able to swim—in the dark and in quite choppy seas—to the life raft floating ever further astern. Aware both that it was certain death for the man and that the inevitable need to search for him would waste huge amounts of time—a sudden image of himself in a bouncing lifeboat trying to cope with the wind and the waves as he brought the boat back alongside under the hooks swinging wildly some thirty feet beneath the davits ready to lift them back on board flashed across his mind—Trystan grabbed at him.

By good fortune, although the man was standing outside the rails, when Trystan grabbed him, he was still leaning forward so that the bulk of their combined weight was inboard and, despite the still flailing knife, he had the advantage over the bigger man who was now held bent double over the rail. But there they stayed for about five minutes—hours it seemed while the stowaway threatened him with all kinds of revenge for thwarting his escape—as he was unable to pull him back onboard by himself.

Finally, someone in the lounge four decks above noticed the struggle and bosun was sent to help. Thinking it would be easier to control the madman if he was unconscious, Trystan told the bosun to hit the man, but was momentarily nonplussed by being asked how hard he should be hit! As they got the struggling man back over the rails, the apprentice arrived from the bridge with a set of handcuffs and the stowaway was secured to a stanchion. Which should have been the end of the story.

In the early hours, the stowaway escaped from the handcuffs, but he was not free for long—every member of the crew who was not on watch joined in the search and the job of locking and barricading him in a cabin—"You don't threaten one of our officers and get away with it!" seemed to be the watchword—and there he stayed until he was put ashore at Port Elizabeth. Ironically, given that he had originally said he wanted to get to Australia, the South African authorities decided that the easiest way to deal with him was to fly him on to Fremantle, where he arrived about four days ahead of the ship! No one ever discovered what had affected the affable stowaway so badly and had been the cause of his sudden need to leave the ship.

When Trystan got back to his cabin he did not go into details, so K. only discovered the details of his heroic adventure from other officers the next day! In a letter that I received from Fremantle and in subsequent discussions, I learned more about the incident. Trystan made light of the danger he had been in—both from the knife and from being pulled over the rail—but speculated wildly on the cause of the man's sudden madness while laughing at the fact that the bosun—traditionally the strong, tough, hard boss of the crew—had asked how hard to hit the man while they were in such an extreme situation.

It seemed that Eric had been well liked up to that point and the crew had accepted his story that he had only had sufficient money to fly his wife and child home to Australia, where he was planning to join them. No one knew if he had received a letter at Cape Town or whether it was the absence of a letter which triggered his manic need to get ashore, but all were agreed that he had no sense of the sea if he had thought he could get ashore by jumping after a life raft in the dark, and all were agreed that if he was seen in Fremantle, there would be trouble!

Lost to all she has known, Yseult was discovering a world that she had only read about—discovering how far it extended: a sea that seemed to have no end although Tristram assured her that they would see land again quite soon. Endless days when the sea stretched ahead of them were followed by mystic nights when the arc of the sky glowed with stars [125]. The magic of the sea, the very taste of it, the dampening in the mists they passed through, the fish beneath the bow, made up for the almost claustrophobic cloistering of their small cabin. She remembered and loved the phrase: "After the starry rain" [126]. If Tristram had not been there, she thought, if she was alone on the little boat, she would go mad!

Sailing south westwards, Tristram was aware that he had to spot a point of land with an island just offshore on his starboard bow before he turned on a north westerly course. Rather than miss the sighting completely, he began working his course ever more westward until he could just see the coast. He thought that the Isola di Capo Passero with its old fort could also be a place where they might land and find water and food for the next leg of the journey, so he doubled his lookout and had his whole crew watching the horizon! Remembering what she had been told about the horizon, some lines in the poem she had just read about the old monastery at Manasija, came back to her:

Blue and gold
Last ring of the horizon
Last apple of the sun

Oh Zograf
How far does your sight reach [127]

---

[125] I feel that it is unfortunate that Lewis has again made a specific reference to Australia—to Eingana's distant shores—at this point as for the reader, it interferes with the smooth transition from one life to the parallel, earlier one.

[126] Vasko Popa (1968) 'The starry snail'. *Vasko Popa: Selected Poems* (Penguin Modern European Poets) 1969.

[127] Vasko Popa (1965) 'Manasija'. *Vasko Popa: Selected Poems* (Penguin Modern European Poets) 1969. The Eastern Orthodox Monastery of Saint George the Zograf is on Mount Athos. The name derives from the belief that his icon miraculously painted itself on a prepared board. Zograf in Greek means "painter".

Eager to be the first to sight land, Yseult climbed to the highest point that she could and hoped her sight would reach far enough! She watched the hazy rim of the sea until finally spotting something, she called out and pointed over the starboard bow. Tristram, worried both that the fort may still be manned and whether the island was large enough to offer them food and water, approached cautiously until he was close enough to watch for activity. The fort seemed quiet and the island was an easy swim away from the mainland so he anchored to the south of the island.

It was clear as soon as they landed in the little rowing boat that the island offered nothing other than water so after refilling all of the ship's containers from the spring Tristram left Yseult on the *Bäckahästen* and rowed cautiously ashore to a small village on the mainland where it turned out he was able to buy provisions. As on Mljet, Tristram gave nothing away about their journey and did not mention Yseult at all! As soon as he had the rowing boat stowed again, he hoisted sail and they rounded the promontory and began the long westward journey hoping to see no land and no other ships until just before they had to turn north.

When he was planning the voyage, Tristram had sought a distant destination—distant from Selim for her safety—that he thought would please Yseult, knowing how troubled she was—and how sad—to be leaving her people on Mljet. He knew that she was as widely read as her library had allowed and that her uncle had educated her to the best of his ability but he thought that Yseult was hungry for more—to know more [128], to understand the books she read at a deeper level, and he remembered reading of a land where there was a place of learning in a country with a long literary and oral tradition—famous for both its music and its old writings. He hoped that both the country and the seat of learning would make them welcome.

Throughout the voyage Tristram had been troubled, as like Yseult, he felt a guilt for what he had left his friends, the people who depended on Yseult, to face. True the island may never be discovered but that seemed unlikely as he knew from his time with him that Selim was ready to marry and would be seeking out his bride. There were bound to be rumours of an auburn-haired beauty from an

---

[128] Those who read widely frequently feel the need to study and understand an author, or perhaps to follow an idea to its source. To this end I have devoted my life to scholarly research and writing, which in turn is why Trystan so often called on my help with a literary reference or a half-remembered poem.

offshore island who had been seen in his father's court. Despite the ever increasing length of the voyage, he could see no other way than to return to his father and persuade him to journey to Selim's palace—perhaps under the guise of ensuring the smooth workings of the new treaty—and to, and to... what? Every lonely night watch, he stares at the horizon looking for an answer.

Certainly, the King cannot confess that his son has run off with Selim's betrothed—the treaty is only just agreed. Could they pretend that Yseult had perished, perhaps from grief after her parent's death; was that believable? That she had married a sailor from the west who had called at the island—that at least sounded plausible, he thought wryly? Nothing seemed to make sense to Tristram. Finally, he thought it possible that, hearing from her late uncle about her destiny, she had fled the island and no one knew her whereabouts. But why should the King take that message to Selim? His duty was an ever-present shadow.

One night Yseult woke suddenly and came on deck to find Tristram half out of the boat astride the stern rail—the tiller untended and the sails slapping against the mast—the noise, she realised, that had awakened her. As she approached him Tristram had seemed to be fighting some unseen enemy and had been completely oblivious to her presence until she managed to grip his belt and pull him back a bit. She could not get him completely over the rail but at least she knew that most of his weight was inboard and that the crisis was past—she realised she had not drawn breath since she had first seen the danger in which her man had placed himself.

Pulling him to her, she saw that his eyes were fixed and staring at the horizon but she could tell he was not seeing the ocean over which they had sailed—and it was only as she spoke to him, repeating his name, comforting him by her very presence, by each touch, that he seemed to return to her, and was startled to see first his dangerous position and then the untended sails and tiller. He even started to tell her of the danger they had been in before he slowly began to understand that he had fallen asleep and that it was the nightmare daemons born of his anxieties over the fate of his friends on Mljet that had seemed to be bent on ending their journey.

As Yseult took the tiller and brought *Bäckahästen* back on course, Tristram began to tell her some of what he had been thinking—although without the suggestion of his return to Zeta—and she thought that she understood. And for the rest of the voyage, Yseult shared at least some hours of his night watches with him, fearful of the Moirai in the mist.

Lines 243-247:
But now his ship…

At each landfall, when they stopped for food or water, Yseult thought they might find a home but after each of the three landings there was always another departure. And then, just as Yseult's sea had led through a channel to a larger sea, so now the sea they crossed let them out into a further ocean [129]. Tristram turned northwards, promising Yseult that they would soon reach a destination. For all the length of the voyage, Tristram would have had it last longer: almost… almost he headed further west than necessary simply to keep Yseult by his side and to stave off the time when he would have to tell her that he was leaving again. He cannot bear the thought and his courage nearly fails him. He knows that they could land and make a home and forget what they have left behind—it would be so easy—but his conscience will not let him. The people of Mljet took him to their heart and welcomed him—he knows he must do his utmost to save them.

At last, the horizon gives up some low cloud on their starboard bow and then, shortly after that, a large land mass and Tristram calls Yseult to see the first glimpse of their new home. As they approach they can see mountains—a particularly high range to the north, the cloudy highlands of which must have risen up to over a thousand metres, shading to gentler—and much lower—slopes inland of the river mouth where they will make their landfall. As they pass over The Bar they are faced by two rivers and take the most northerly, passing to a mooring near a bridge behind the castle so as to tie up closer to the township. The land is green and lush with trees markedly different from those that Yseult knew on Mljet, and the weather seems cooler, but the land and people are welcoming and they are tied up to a small jetty in the river mouth beneath the remains of the castle which, while still a castle, seems quite different in style from those Tristram has known before.

Across the river, to the south, is a steep hill with curious earthworks circling its top, marked 'Dinas Faelor' on his chart. "Oriri" [130] breathes Tristram, lifting Yseult from her seat in the bow and handing her up onto the quay.

---

[129] The symbolism is unavoidable: A sea within a sea—a story within a story.

[130] Rise—Tristram would have been pouring over the chart as they approached the coast and—probably misremembering a name he had read on the map—subconsciously, he reverted to Latin.

Tristram has successfully navigated a journey far longer than any he had undertaken before and has brought them to this ancient seat of learning on Ceredig's shores. It is no mean feat as there had been a great storm a little way to the east as they came close to land and he heard that in a similar storm a few year previously many ships had been lost off the coast on some shallows known as the Goodwin Sands. But his sense of wellbeing is dimmed by the knowledge that in a few days or weeks, once they are settled in this new place, he must leave again. Until then, he will hold the knowledge of his departure to himself and they will enjoy the adventure in this new land.

When his ship once again takes onboard the river pilots and moves slowly up the Thames to Tilbury, slips through the locks and berths under the huge cranes, Trystan can scarcely believe that a year—three leavings and three homecomings—had passed. It is far too soon! To Trystan, it seems as if he has only just introduced K. to a new land, his second and sunlit land—to Eingana's shores—but now they are returned to his home port, an all too short leave and they will be parted. He cannot bear the thought. Often as they had sailed across the vast expanses of ocean he had wanted—been tempted on those long night watches—to vary the course by a few degrees simply to make the voyage last longer, but of course, he had never done so. Now, he was regretting it.

K. has always known that after a year she would have to return to her studies, that she could not sail the seas with Trystan forever, but that knowledge does not make it easier to bear. And his last few days rush past in a bustle of preparations, packing and unpacking for both of them. They have left Sussex for her University a few weeks before he must re-join his ship—but she dreads the separation, overhung as it is with the difficulties of re-establishing herself in academia and resuming her studies.

Despite all her reading during the year, she feels remote from books, literature and learning; unable to focus on lectures and seminars without the presence at the end of each day of her husband and lover. She feels that she had changed irrevocably from her previous study time and doubts that anyone will even recognise her!

Lines 249-259:
He knows she will struggle...

Trystan has already imagined, and imagined and imagined, what it would be like for K. returning to her old university department. All of her old friends would be a year ahead of her, leaving her feeling like an old hand amongst the youngsters around her... but an old hand who has forgotten what university life is like! He knows she has written nothing except letters and a few notes for the last twelve months and wonders whether she can turn her hand to essays and dissertations again. He remembers the awe he had felt when she had walked him around the vast old college library—as he had followed her, Trystan had thought that somewhere among the shelves must be hidden the stories of his lives, and he wonders whether—after a year with a mere shelf of books—she will be able to sit amongst those mighty shelves and work without giving in to despair. And he supposes she will be lonely! Over the last twelve months they had never been apart except for a few hours at a time and he knows that she will struggle.

They had spent much of Trystan's leave looking for somewhere to live near the University and, after a lot of searching, a friend had told them of a secluded farm cottage in the hills outside the town. They had arrived as the first lambs were shivering in fields still covered by the remains of some late snow—snow through which daffodils were poking in the hedgerows—and were welcomed to the farmhouse kitchen for tea and Welsh cakes even before being asked their business! An orphan lamb was warming itself in front of the range and the room was cosy after the cold and damp of the muddy farmyard.

The cottage itself—on the other, the East side, of the farmyard—turned out to be a little dilapidated and with a couple of the rooms that, by their tastes, at least, were in need of a coat of paint but K. was entranced and Trystan knew that they had found a home. It was their first house! Some two hundred years old and with walls almost two feet thick, the cottage had been the original farmhouse on the site and had been purchased with a small amount of land to extend the farm and provide a second dwelling when two brothers had taken over the main farm, which had been left to their as yet unborn sons.

When it was purchased, the roof had been lower and the two downstairs rooms had only a loft—a loft in which twelve children had been born and brought up, they were told by the farmer's wife with a twinkle in her eye—over them. Now, with the roof raised to provide three bedrooms and an extension on the back providing a kitchen and bathroom (where once had been an outhouse in which pigs had been salted!), it offered all that they could want and the deal was soon done! He is worried at the distance from the University but K. reassures him and within the week, they had moved all their few worldly goods in and started to make the place a home.

Slate-roofed, with whitewashed walls and cheerful red-painted doors and windows, it shone in the spring sunshine and Trystan is almost jealous of the fact that K. will live there when he leaves. It even has a little garden! Two days later on a wet and windy morning, as he leaves for his ship he feels that he is deserting her in a bleak wilderness with no easy transport, a hinterland from which there is no means of escape!

He hopes he is being melodramatic in seeing her weep for his embrace, pine for his arms—he knows she can be strong but—he smiles at the memory—she had said that the only text she needed was his body as they had lain together on their last night. He both hopes that she will and that she will not be lost without him. As he leaves her in their cottage, surrounded by a clutter of books, half emptied cases, and records (mostly Leonard Cohen):

> your eyes are soft with sorrow,
> Hey, that's no way to say goodbye. [131]

he hopes she will not be too depressed in the following days, that lectures, seminars, tutorials and the library will keep her busy. For himself he can only hope that his sanity will hold as leaving his wife in a wilderness does not sit easily with him and he finds that his focus is not entirely on his driving over the winding mountain road out of Wales as he heads back to his ship. In a few days he will sailing down the English Channel and lost to land for the best part of three weeks and he wonders what nepenthean [132] tasks might help his mindset for those weeks. They have promised each other to add to a letter every day but between those times he would rather that his mind was elsewhere.

Now the cabin they shared was once again his ascetic cell; but every inch, every chair, cupboard, shelf, book reminds him of K. He is not alone, he hears her singing

> Oh the sisters of mercy, they are not departed or gone.
> They were waiting for me when I thought that I just can't go on.

---

[131] Leonard Cohen, *Hey, That's No Way To Say Goodbye*.

[132] Nepenthean is derived from Greek: the suffix n- meaning not and penthos meaning grief or sorrow and is generally used to mean pleasurable—perhaps not quite what Lewis could hope for as much as painless—forgetfulness, often, although not in this case, brought about by opiates.

And they brought me their comfort and later they brought me this song.
Oh I hope you run into them, you who've been travelling so long. [133]

As he unpacks his cases, as he changes into his uniform, as he walks up to the bridge, as he watches the last containers swing over the deck, as he organises his first charts for departure, sets down the first courses he sees her. Eyes sparkling, long hair swinging over her shoulder. The soft 2B chart pencil snaps suddenly and he hurriedly erases the jagged line that had been scored south from Tilbury through Brighton while his mind was elsewhere. Later, ruefully he writes to K. joking about his current inability to draw a straight course line.

Still later as they pass through the shipping lanes entering the Channel and, a good way south of Brighton, head west he walks back from the front of the bridge to the chart table to plot their position and can still see her ghost etched on the chart. As usual, the shipping lanes are busy and he has no time to daydream but hurries back to the bridge-front windows and the radar, and adjust course by a degree to pass farther astern of a fishing boat. Shaking his head, he remembers once saying to K. that her body is the only sea he wants to navigate. Many years later he wrote:

Then I was a sailor
on her lovely coasts—
I learned to sail her seas
to map
    her harbours and constant tides [134]

Lewis seems attracted to the idea of love and passion, male and female as aspects of water, rivers and the sea and readers of his works will notice the symbolism frequently: "Restless: my body is your ocean; my limbs the currents of the sea" or "I drew lines on her skin / to chart / love's course in rolling waters" or "at my source / I was lost to your ocean" [135] or, as in 'Lost':

And then

---

[133] Leonard Cohen, *Sisters of Mercy*.

[134] From an unpublished poem—'The Navigator'— written by Lewis in 2018 and now in the editor's collection.

[135] 'Ocean' [in full, above] Published in *Mostly Welsh* (2019). Talybont: Y Lolfa.

at my source
I was lost to your ocean. [136]

Even within 'Dark Ashes', this kind of nautical imagery is used some six times. He is never far from the ocean. Given his years at sea, it is not surprising that the sea often provides the imagery he wants, but Lewis has a fine hand and the associations are beautifully used.

Yseult is entranced with her new land and she settles into some rooms in a town house overlooking the sea. There is not much room but at least they are on dry land at last! Each evening from outside their door they watch the sun set into the sea. Yseult, already coming to terms with the local poetic forms suggests the lines:

A green flash from the setting sun—and night
Now sea and sky are one
Dusk from the gold orb is spun
Thus this mystic day is done [137]

She says that although the rhymes are simple, the form demands a fixed amount of syllables which makes composition difficult: maybe it is easier in the local language. Tristram senses that she is working at becoming immersed in her studies and wonders if she has sensed something in him that hints at separation. Yseult does sense some nervous energy in her man but thinks that he is anxious to find a cottage of their own, that he is unused to living in a town and dislikes their crowded rooms.

So, they spend much of their time hunting the countryside just outside the town for a cottage and some land where they can settle. They also find Yseult a tutor who is willing to work with her and help her gain entrance to the *scholae*

---

[136] 'Lost' Published in *Mostly Welsh* (2019). Talybont: Y Lolfa.

[137] 'Sunset Englyn'—an unpublished poem by Lewis now in the editor's collection. A Welsh englyn is a straight one-rhymed verse consisting of four lines of ten, six, seven and seven syllables. The seventh, eighth or ninth syllable of the first line introduces the rhyme and this is repeated on the last syllable of the other three lines. The part of the first line after the rhyme must alliterate with the first part of the second line.

monasticae [138] which was rapidly growing in status: an institution and building unlike anything Yseult could have imagined, its towers more redolent of a castle than a place of learning but with a fine library that made her own library back on Mljet seem more like a bookshelf! A tear slipped down her cheek as she thought of her old home.

Tristram senses an optimism in Yseult as they walk around the library in the old building with the magister who has an evident love of books and scholarship and talks of his studies in terms that Tristram, at least, struggles to understand. Yseult is spellbound—entranced—to a degree that even Tristram had dared not imagine and his optimistic side hopes that this new life will be enough to distract her from his absence—something they have not yet talked about. His darker, less optimistic side—where "the sun shone black upon [his] soul" [139]—knew that she would struggle in his further absence.

When he is alone, Tristram broods on his departure and can only see a weeping Yseult—an Yseult who could find no distraction, let alone comfort, in her reading, knowing only one clear thought: her Tristram is gone, possibly—should the Moirai [140] decree it—never to return. He doubts that even his noble intent will find a place in her heart although he knows that she still worries about her people. Lewis' words at this point mix the academic with the nautical but his final lines of the first verse, "Alone, bereft, / she knows no shore" are graphically of the sea.

Tormented by his need to slay—if not literally, at least through mediation—the Ottoman dragon which threatens his father's peace as well as the people on the island of Mljet, Tristram at last confides his plans to an increasingly distraught Yseult. He is to travel back to Zeta… and already Yseult is protesting:

---

[138] Monastic schools—*scholae monasticae*—were, along with cathedral schools, the most important institutions of higher learning until the 12th century. The standard curriculum incorporated religious studies, but was extended to a much wider range of subjects as well. In some places—as here—monastic schools evolved into medieval universities, which eventually largely superseded them as centres of higher learning.

[139] 'Hope'. Published in *Mostly Welsh* (2019). Talybont: Y Lolfa.

[140] In Greek mythology, the Moirai—the Fates—governed all destiny. Even the gods' destinies were controlled by them: *"Because to the Moirai the might of Zeus must bow; and by the Immortals' purpose all these things had come to pass, or by Fate's ordinance"* (Greek epic poet, Kointos Smyrnaios/Quintus Smyrnaeus. The Fall of Troy Bk. xiii Ll. 559-).

it is a monstrously long voyage to be undertaken alone, and even ignoring the dangers of such a journey—and she well remembers the night watch daemons, to travel all that way and back again will take a time far longer than she can bear to be parted from him. But Tristram continues.

He knows that they are in agreement over the possible dangers to her people and over the guilt they both feel for having placed them in such danger, so something has to be done. And that has to mean his return. He tells Yseult that he will have to work hard to persuade his father but he is certain that when faced with the Mljet situation, the King will agree. His plan is two-fold: firstly the King should acknowledge Mljet as a part of Zeta and establish a small garrison at the southern end of the island. Secondly, he will petition his father to travel south to see Selim in Kalaja e Lëkurësit with the news and a proposition.

The King should explain that Mljet is now under his protection—something that had been planned for many years—and that in establishing his force on the island he had discovered that his lost god-daughter had been living there since her parents had fled Suleiman's court. Tragically—and here he could curse himself for the many delays in annexing the island, he had arrived on the island too late as Yseult had fled—he knows not where as the rumours on the island have her travelling in many different directions. The only thing of which he is sure, is that she fled on learning of the promise her parents made that betrothed her to Selim.

Tristram said his father would have to be especially careful and calming at this point as he wanted him to also give Selim to understand that Yseult had married and left the island with her new husband. Selim should renounce her, release her from her vow (what else could he do?) and thus himself be free to marry.

Tristram thinks that if his name is kept out of the discussions—the King could say that he had taken the unusual step of travelling south himself as he felt in some way responsible for his lost god-daughter—the plan may possibly succeed. Finally, the King will propose that Mljet should be governed by a court made up jointly—equally—of nobles from the Zetan court and some of Selim's ministers. There would be no need of a parliamentary presence on the island—it had managed well enough without until now and any disputes could be settled from the mainland. Her head spinning, Yseult works her way through the plan again and again, gradually being won over by its simplicity. Perhaps, one day we can return, she wonders. Gradually, over several days, Tristram wins her blessing for his plan and her agreement to his trip. There is work to be done.

As he eases his little craft away from the quay and out of the estuary, Tristram can barely stand to look back at Yseult who stand motionless beside the bollard from which she had lifted his last mooring rope. The weeks since their long discussion had been one furious turmoil of work: they had secured a cottage with a small but clean stream—the trickle of water was almost a 'nant' their new neighbour said—and a small amount of land, and Tristram had spent some days ensuring it was weatherproof and secure, and had bought furniture, some chickens and a small pony to take Yseult into town for her studies.

Once again, he had worked his way over *Bäckahästen* making her seaworthy, stocking her with a spare set of sails, cordage and some new charts he had come across in the port, and provisioning her with food enough to see him most of the way to Zeta. He knows he will have to stop for water along the way and will be able to top up his food supplies at the same time. And he had gone over and over the route—with its currents and prevailing winds—both on the charts and in his head so that should he be unable to leave the helm, navigation will not be a problem.

Now, as the tide takes him slowly further away into the world, he remembers how each night as they lay beneath the slates in their little cottage, their world had shrunk to hold only each second: then there was no past and no future, only the room, the sheet on which they lay, each other, and that moment.

Lewis captures this perfectly in the almost erotic lines in the third verse of his poem, 'Pastoral', where the two clever and rather beautiful spondees—redolent of both Hopkins and Dylan Thomas—in the penultimate line do so much to bring to mind that climactic gasp at the same time that they take from the line any sense of vulgarity:

But we are heedless
All save love is lost to us in the warm room beneath the slates
Nothing cared we that soft night
Save for the passion pressed close within our arms and love
The closer grasp the elated press and joy of the other held
The quiet journey up to the star high moon held gasp of harmony
Then tender peace amongst the soft night airs borne of the window gape [141]

---

[141] 'Pastoral'. Published in *Mostly Welsh* (2019). Talybont: Y Lolfa.

He remembers that last moment before sleep on that last night when, together, they had reached that breathless, urgent 'star-high' peak before falling back onto the rough sheets, his hand still resting on her hip, one of hers trapped beneath him. Before, his hands, his mouth had traced every contour of her land, felt every current in the salty sea that was her body; her hands had held him, encouraging, almost urgently willing him on—she is his ocean, his guiding star. Her soft lips had touched, and touched again and again, his body. He remembers the feel of her breasts, how she had gasped as his fingers touched her as if—once again—it was something new, her breath on his chest, how she had welcomed him. And the slow passion blazing, mounting, convulsing, rising, shattering their very beings with the joy of the moment. He gasps again! She has always been the centre of his world—his universe—now, that memory is the azimuth that will bring him back to her.

The pain in his left hand brings him back to the present and he realises just how hard he had been gripping the tiller. He turns, adjusts a sail and swings the tiller to round the headland; a last wave and she is gone. He stares blindly at the land as it eclipses his view. He is just in time to straighten his course and head a little west of south. The lonely days stretch ahead of him—he has to judge the wind and the currents, plot his course by the sun and the stars and by landfall and use his experience to assess the weather. His mind should be focused but at the moment, as his epic voyage begins, he can only see his world in Yseult.

Lines 261-268:
When will he... return?

Many days later, as he shields his eyes against cold rain and stares ahead, sailing under shortened sail in a wind that is a little stronger than he would have liked—but at least favourable—he wonders how long it will be before he see Yseult again. Even now, maybe half way though his outward voyage her image is fading and his body can scarcely remember the feel of hers against it. It is not surprising—he is permanently scorched by sun, lashed by rain, buffeted by winds; his body can barely remember any comfort! But he is making good progress; by his reckoning—or rather by his navigation—he is more than halfway to Zeta and the fresh water on board is getting low. He will need to find a landfall. All these daily worries help to take his mind off his wife—his lonely lover—but, still, always, he is counting the days until once again he holds her… not so much counting the days, he thinks sadly, as wondering how long: there are so many unknowns! Always in the grey mists he glimpses the white-robed Moirai who control his fate.

Tristram seems to spend all of his time calculating: distances, courses, wind speed, currents, stores left in the hold, water in the tanks—and it all comes down to time, days, time left until he is back with Yseult. Of course there are lesser periods of time he must also consider—time before Zeta, time in Zeta: how long will it take to persuade his father on the right course of action. He wonders if the King will expect him to help with putting the plan into place—maybe to travel to Mljet as the garrison is set up... he shudders at the thought. But begins calculating again.

Keeping busy seems to be the only way to stop worrying about the little cottage and its occupant—and then his mind swings off at a tangent and he is wondering about her work, the reading, the writing, the studying. He prays that she has become so completely immersed that time ceases to worry her, that—as he had always thought she would—she is enjoying her newfound knowledge. But his mind had not been entirely with her, on the horizon over the port bow he can see the beginnings of some hills—he breathes a sigh of relief as he recognises them and knows he will be able to find water and some fresh food. *And* that they mean the last leg of his voyage is nearly upon him.

From the English Channel, the huge ship travels south between the Canary Islands and down the West African coast, round the Cape and on to Fremantle, Sydney and Melbourne. Back at Fremantle for the second call of the trip, Trystan knows he is at last pointing his ship towards home, towards K. Throughout the voyage he has been planning their future together, but also struggling with his loyalties a little: there is no doubt in his mind that K. comes at the top of the list—she is really all he cares about—but he still feels some obligations to the company he sails with and is unsure how easily he will be able to leave them, although his initial three-year contract is coming to an end.

Every night watch when the mundane tasks are done, with a mug of coffee in his hand, he stares out towards the horizon, ever vigilant for that pinprick of light glimmering in the dark that would indicate he is not alone on this sea and that he must watch their courses carefully to make sure they pass well clear of each other. Ever vigilant with one half of his mind, but with the other planning a future! He thinks that it is ironical that he, navigator of the world's seas, is unsure of his course in life. Even as they leave the Australian coast behind and set course on a great circle route that will take them back to South Africa, even as his mind

148

runs over the dates when they will be off Cape Town, at Zeebrugge, at Tilbury, he wonders just when his domestic life—Hestia's [142] world, he thinks—will resume.

When will he walk through the red-painted door of their little cottage again—he remembers every detail of every room—the beams, the old range, the clumsy bookshelves—planks supported by bricks—he had constructed along one wall of the lounge, the open fire, the fifth stair that creaks when he steps on it, the bedrooms? The view from the window beside the range. And the cottage garden with its roses and honeysuckle! Despite his worries, his mind is made up and his resignation letter written long before they reach their home port.

In all the hundreds of words he has written and sent home, he has not once hinted at his plan—partly because he wants it to be a surprise and partly as he is unsure whether the company will want to retain his services for the last few weeks of his contract to take a ship round the UK coast or across to the continent… and indeed when he speaks to the personnel department they do mention the possibility, but send him on leave anyway. He wonders, once he is home, whether that ocean's pull will drag him away again. Only the fates know!

Canto v
Lines 274-280:
He will remember…

Lewis told me that the wonder of that homecoming remained with him for a very long time! Not only had he arrived home earlier than expected but, as they had hugged, K. had sensed something different, had pushed him back at arms' length and studied his face, had re-played in her mind his greeting and—suddenly—they were back in each other's arms as she realised that he was home for good, that she would never again have to bear his leaving for months at a time. Lewis said that he had never been so happy!

As he had walked through the door that summer's afternoon, the roses and honeysuckle had been abuzz with bees in the hot sun, K. had gasped in surprise

---

[142] The Greek goddess, Hestia—goddess of the hearth, governed domesticity, home and the family. She is celebrated in the twenty-fourth of the thirty-three hymns celebrating individual gods: "Hestia, you who tend the holy house of the lord Apollo…come now into this house, come, having one mind with Zeus the all-wise…draw near, and withal bestow grace upon my song." (Translation by Hugh G. Evelyn-White. Homeric Hymns. Cambridge, MA., Harvard University Press; London, William Heinemann Ltd. 1914.)

and pleasure as she looked up and, dropping his case, he had said 'I'm home!' before tossing the uniform cap he had been carrying back out the door, adding, almost under his breath, 'Shan't need that again!' And then they were hugging while his last words slowly percolated through her senses. And then more hugging! As the weeks passed, it became clear that the company had been kind to him and were not going to ask him to stand in for anyone: the sea had let him go! A life in the countryside lay before them!

When Tristram set sail from Zeta again, he was weary from the long weeks of work and planning with his father but buoyant with the thought of seeing Yseult again. His ship was once again provisioned and stored with as much water as his containers could hold and keep fresh; he had patched his old sails but stored them below decks, replacing them with the spare set he had purchased before the voyage and had his father's men careen the hull on the beach below the castle—he had done everything possible to ensure a fast voyage!

Persuading his father of the need and of the necessary course of action had not been difficult but they then had to persuade the court of the need to protect Mljet and prepare plans for the garrison, as well as for the King's journey south. The treaty which he had agreed previously was working well so they knew it would be a shock for Selim to see the King's Royal Standard at the masthead of an approaching ship and agreed that it would be sensible to negotiate in advance the idea of a state visit and—fortunately—Selim was delighted with the idea. And, he thought, the fact that he had been able to add his cypher to that of his father helped to distance him from the marriage and flight of Yseult.

As Tristram had set sail, so too had the King in his fine barque with his retinue in a fleet of smaller ships. Tristram dipped his flag as the King's ship crossed astern of him and then added sail for it was a beautiful day with a perfect sailing wind and he wanted to take every possible advantage of it. He prayed that the wind would be favourable for the whole voyage, but knew that it was unlikely. He is extraordinarily pleased with the way his visit had gone—everything was agreed as he had hoped and it looked as if the outcome would be favourable, although it was too soon to tell.

He had enjoyed spending these last days with his parents—he had seen far too little of his mother recently—and had also been able to purchase a number of items—tools for him and some furniture and linen for their cottage—not available in his new home town, as well as a small gold cross he found in the market that he knew would remind Yseult of Mljet, some gowns and fat books of poetry for her. The king had also given him a wooden box wrapped in oilcloth: 'a gift for your wife from a father who wished he had known her—who wished he had had the time to get to know her—better,' he had said. Adding that there was a letter to her contained within the box.

Many weeks later, *Bäckahästen* slides quietly up river to the quay and is made fast. Almost before he can lower and stow the last sail, Tristram is climbing the ladder and on the quay! He borrows a horse and heads along the track from town to home!

Summer has arrived while he has been away and as he crests the hill the little cottage among the trees looks lovely, garlanded by the honeysuckle climbing the wall and surrounded within the unusual stone wall by what is now a neatly tended garden. He ties the horse to a fence at a little distance from the door and creeps forward quietly. He will always remember the look of joy on Yseult's face as she saw him—in his mind bees buzzing in the honeysuckle and the warm honey of her lips as they embrace will always go together. She stands back from him and—almost scared to speak—asking for reassurance with her eyes. But she sees his smile and understands: his voyaging is over, the sea had let him go. Together, arm in arm, they walk up the hill to get the horse.

They never knew, but back in Zeta, history records that an accord was reached with Selim, who was at that time struggling to maintain his father's empire in its newly-won independent status. He was clearly angered by the disappearance of his wife-to-be but was wise enough to recognise that even as powerful a ruler as he—or indeed as Tristram's father—had small chance of locating her. He took little interest in Mljet as it lay so far north of his lands and allowed its rule to be overseen by Zeta. At the time he was busy overseeing the building of the Selimiye mosque in Adrianople, which may have distracted him a little from the old King's news.

Lines 281-300:
And now their life…

In both the present and the past, a bucolic haze descends over their lives, interrupted only by study. The men take to the countryside, and to the maintenance and upkeep of their property while the ladies study; together they cook food, paint walls and talk. Life is wonderful!

Once Tristram has unloaded his cargo and taken his boat to a permanent mooring on the other side of the river beneath Ship Wright's Row, he lets it be known around the port that it is for sale—not only has the sea let him go, but he is determined to let the sea go. His life now is in a much smaller world—a world unseen by, and unseeing of, the affairs in Zeta and Mljet! For him, it had been a huge step—although not a huge or difficult decision—to cut all his ties, irrevocably, with his family, with a kingdom he would have come to rule, with statesmanship, with wealth. But he is happy! Ecstatically so: he loves his new life in the country and willingly gives time to larger neighbouring farms during their harvests.

On his own small plot, apart from a growing band of chickens, he has a couple of goats and two horses to care for, as well as a garden in which he and Yseult grow all the vegetables they need, as well as some to exchange with the neighbours for hay or grain. He loves the fact that this little haven amongst the beech and larch trees has become the centre of their world; and—as the son of a king—that their world is within land named for another ancient king, Ceredig [143]. The poem's reference to the Elysian Fields—where 'men lead an easier life than anywhere else in the world' [144]—in the previous line is no coincidence as it reinforces both the epic nature of his own poem and the idea of rebirth, of another life. A fuller quotation from Book IV of *The Odyssey* is:

…the gods will take you to the Elysian plain, which is at the ends of the world. There fair-haired Rhadamanthus reigns, and men lead an easier life than anywhere else in the world, for in Elysium there falls not rain, nor hail, nor snow, but Oceanus breathes ever with a West wind that sings softly from the sea, and gives fresh life to all men. [144]

As the years pass and the west wind blows, they are blessed with three sons who toddle out amongst the chicken and the cats before—all too soon—learning to help on the land. Truly, they are blessed. And if there had ever been doubt, now he knows no one can tempt him back to sea. And as the early years pass too, he gains some book learning as Yseult always talks to him about her studies with the magister. Tristram toyed with the idea of following Yseult's example and joining her in her academic studies, but he knew that he did not have the necessary learning to sustain the long hours of writing and study. In another life he might do so, even continuing to make a career out of his studies, but now it

---

[143] Ceredig ap Cunedda (c.420-453).

[144] Homer, *The Odyssey* (VI.560-565). Translation by Samuel Butler.

was not to be. Instead, he continued to read in order to keep up with her and loved the words, the language and the way ideas can be painted with so few words arranged so carefully—he reads more and more poetry and is increasingly drawn to it.

With Trystan home, K.'s life got more complicated—more pleasurable, but certainly more complicated given that she had competing demands on her time. Not that he was demanding of her time, but she wanted to spend more time with him in the fields and in the garden, she envied him his new found freedom which contrasted so strongly with her need to study and write! Their new life was almost completely contained within their land: the little cottage backed onto what the remains of some cobbles suggested had once been the old farm yard, flanked to the west and north by old, stone-built sheds. The front of the house faced a small garden and beyond that, farm fields. To the east, the land dropped through another patch of garden full of nettles to an old gate that let them out onto what had at one time been a farm track and a path to the old well.

Walking south along the track, took them under some of the largest beech trees they had ever seen. A huge larch tree stood in one corner and seemed to be protecting them, while they were hidden from their neighbours by a hedge of elder, beech, hawthorn and an occasional blackthorn as well as by the cattle sheds. K. said that the trees were watching over them, that there was a mysterious female, almost witch-like feel to the hedge but Trystan was content to harvest the sloes and berries! Their garden was walled and the wall was capped by large pointed granite stones—the summer stones of Hafod [145] which made the wall stones even older than the two-hundred-year-old cottage and gave it a further feeling of standing guard.

Lewis often said how contented they had been: they were held by the land; they relaxed into it; as the poem says, it "held their hearts at ease". I have already quoted lines from 'Pastoral', but I think I may be excused from a second reference as its first verse describes their peace so perfectly:

In that happy heady grass-green Spring of my years

---

[145] The capping stones had been salvaged from the library roof of the nearby stately home, Hafod Uchtryd, when it had been demolished some time before this. The home had belonged to Thomas Johnes and features in Elizabeth Inglis-Jones' book, *Peacocks in Paradise* (1960), a classic account of the life of Thomas Johnes and of his estate. Llandysul: Gomer.

A time of lambent lamb slow lamb full days around a whited cottage
Lent us space and ease beneath the sun long sky
Golden glorious hours together in a single thought
With close chicken scrape and distant herd
When the swallows dipped to the fly buzz
When the kite climbed to a gliding speck
    And we knew peace
We knew our place in the low home mountains of the Bards
And uncaring of the wider world
Settled there amongst the poppies and the elder
Amongst the hedge rich blossom and the tall grass
In the farm heart—
Behind the red gate, shed-hidden, summer-walled
Beneath the beech trees
And down the warm, pale moon dusk
We lay beneath Owain's blessed heaven [146]

While Trystan's freedom attracted K., her work also drew him: initially there were long discussions over whatever she was reading, often repeated after he had caught up with the text or the poem, but these were followed by forays by Trystan into academia—sitting in on lectures or writing his own thoughts in parallel with K.'s essays. These were the early days of his writing where he tried out ideas and techniques and—in quite a short time—began to experiment with poetry. But these twenty lines of 'Dark Ashes' capture and even compress a number of years of their life together: Lewis farmed with his neighbour before following his instincts and embracing an academic life; K. studied, wrote, and taught; Trystan embraced the country ways—he even carved a traditional love-spoon with three caged balls in its handle for K. And always, they did everything together—they were rarely seen apart.

They were very much a part of the farm—not just because Trystan spent time working on it but because it embraced them. 'Pastoral' tells how they were introduced to horses and riding by the daughters of the farmer: "At dusk, there came to us young girls on horses / Bidding us ride" although the poem makes

---

[146] 'Pastoral'. Published in *Mostly Welsh* (2019). Talybont: Y Lolfa. It is worth noting the spondees in this verse—lamb-slow, lamb-full, sun-long—with their echoes of Dylan Thomas.

little of their poor horsemanship—I remember Lewis telling me how sore he had been on another occasion, after riding one of two horses some six or so miles as they were taken to the smithy to be shod! In a time of such unsurpassed happiness, unsurprisingly, it was also when their home was blessed by Arianrhod [147] and their three sons were born.

Safe within their lands, they prospered as the family grew. Trystan was not writing much at this time although he often said that K. was his muse and his inspiration, and it is certainly true that much of his later poetry has her at its heart. She may have been his muse but I do not know whether she encouraged him in the same way—or even to the same extent—as I was able to do, albeit remotely.

For some reason, despite my care for her in their early years together, and indeed my warm feelings for her, K. seemed not overly fond of me and I was rarely invited to their little piece of 'Ceredig's land'. But Trystan and I continued our correspondence and I saw many of his early attempts at versification: he was very tentative and unsure but it was obvious that he had the beginnings of a rare talent, and I encouraged him to keep writing.

Canto vi
Lines 304-311:
Through tens of years…

I saw several further drafts of the poem following Lewis' stay with me in Frascati—mostly I did not comment but my note returned following the final version was that the 'tens of years' following the arrival in Wales are glossed over rather abruptly (perhaps, in retrospect, a justified comment given that one or two critics later called the work 'disjointed'). Where elsewhere in the poem thoughts and passions are explored, here there is nothing. Lewis responded that he had used that—the passing of seasons, bitter Winter and softer Summer, until "in that Spring…"—to emphasise normality rudely interrupted by the unimaginable. Perhaps too, he did not wish to repeat in this poem a grief expressed so openly and comprehensively in his other writings.

As the seasons pass, as the years pass Tristram and Yseult become one with the land—with their new land: certainly their past kinships were never forgotten

---

[147] Arianrhod—her name has been translated as silver-wheel so that she is linked to the moon and represents the ever-turning wheel of the year, of time—was the Celtic Goddess of fertility, rebirth and the weaving of cosmic time and fate.

but the strength of their affinity, their attachment to their new home strengthened all the time. That their sons grew up as natives must have magnified that feeling intensely. The seasons were so different from their native lands—cooler, colder even, and more seasonally varied—this was one West where the Odyssey had its facts wrong, and they came to know both rain and snow, but each brought its own kind of peace, and they absorbed these new experiences and became stronger. The land gathered them in and held them.

No word reached them of Zeta and the lands they had once known so well. Tristram knew that his parents in old age must have handed over the country to be *res publica* [148] and hoped that they were content with the way this had worked out. He and his father had discussed this at length through many late-night sessions once he had established beyond any doubt that he could never return. They had even worked on the beginnings of a plan, and as they had worked through it, his father had come to see that in some ways at least it might be better for Zeta.

It had been far too early to look for the man who might make the new government work, but Tristram thought that his father had someone in mind. In Ceredigion, they often talked about Yseult's lovely castle hidden on the island within the island and wondered what had become of it but, like Tristram, Yseult had no expectations of ever being in her old homeland again. It was a fairy tale land that they described to their boys when they were young.

I know that Trystan and K. loved the country where they had settled: they once said that it was the best possible place to bring up their children—contrasting it with the rushing, often dirty life in big cities (although I always wondered whether perhaps their children came to regret the loss of the city excitement). The babies became boys and the boys became pupils in the school in the village. Over the years it became almost unthinkable for them to move: the cottage and their land became a part of them in a way that I never understood—they always say that a convert is the most zealous proselytiser and in the same way these 'incomers' were more wedded to the area, more attached to the land than many of their neighbours. They kept hens for their eggs, although as neither of them could bear to kill the young roosters the brood rapidly got out of control! When he could, Trystan worked with his neighbour on the harvest or to mend a

---

[148] Countries under *res publica* rule came to be republics: a form of government in which the country is not under the personal rule, is not the property of, a king or ruler but is governed by a head of state and his or her government.

fence, and often in the early evening he would stroll down to the lake and fish for a while, embracing the peace of the moment as much as any catch. In 'The Trout', Lewis captures something of the beauty of the moment:

The lake is still in the evening sun
A little breeze makes the longer grass sway on the bank
and a ripple disturbs the surface:
A mayfly lands
A swallow drinks and is gone before I see
With a rattle, a duck takes off from behind the island
Then it is still again
Beneath the reflections are fish
Sometimes—but not yet tonight—
A circle of ripples flows out from a rise [149]

He had been taught to fly fish by one of his neighbours but had never become an expert and rarely landed a trout, but as the poem goes on to say, it was not the catch but the rhythm of the cast, the peace and the tranquillity that he loved.

K. also took to country ways and crafts, and her patchwork quilts were admired by many. Living in the countryside was in many ways wonderful, but it also had moments that were less attractive. There was a summer evening when Trystan was out and K. sat in the fading light over her latest patchwork when she was disturbed by a slight scratching, scrabbling noise which she eventually located as coming from the wall where the chimney of the range entered the plaster. To her horror, she saw a tiny black hand emerge from the crack!

Moments later—when her heart had slowed again—the 'hand' became the little 'fingers' on the angle of the wing of a bat that then escaped the chimney space and began darting around the room! That only left her with the problem of persuading it out of the door, not in the least helped by the two cats! When Trystan returned, the horror of the moment—like something from the annals of Edgar Allan Poe—was not downplayed at all, and he could only comfort his wife—although they both enjoyed the humour of the moment too!

Walking outside in the dusk, they could still see the almost subliminal presence of the swooping bats, small speeding black shadows against the clear

---

[149] From the unpublished poem—'The Trout'— written by Lewis in 2018 and now in the editor's collection.

night sky in which the stars were beginning to show. It took both of them from horror to a rapt admiration of the almost mystic beauty of the moment before, arm in arm, they turned and climbed the stairs. This moment of appreciating their luck was just one of many they experienced over the years. As the poem says, the embrace of the land 'enclosed them'.

Although in the commentary I have frequently made connections to his other works, as any good editor should, this is only the second time within the poem, 'Dark Ashes', that Lewis himself is referencing another of his poems, speaking, albeit obliquely, of his own later connection with the place in 'Cottage Garden': "the only place they wished to know". Speaking of himself, later in his life, he had written:

This place is all I want or wish to know
And only where I wish to stay –
To tend, to minister, and bestow. [150]

Although it is not made specific in the poem, I know that K. became a teacher of literature who was adored by her pupils, while Lewis carved out a career for himself on the edge of academia as a consultant to libraries, initially in the University as a research officer but later on privately. I'm not sure how it started but I suspect that following his degree he baulked at the idea of working in a library, although that had been his aim when he selected the course, and sought out research work in the department. But I think his foray into academia must have been utterly unlike mine—he told me that, much as he had enjoyed his years of research, the department had been a strange place to work.

While I had lectured my students as a background to my writing, Lewis' only focus was on research and writing, and he very much enjoyed both. Looking back on his time, he often said that all those scholarly articles and research papers had honed his lexical skills, although I cannot think of poetry composition as being in any way similar to the articles by Lewis that I found during my research. But writing is writing, I suppose! He worked on the use of printed indexes using psycholinguistics and eye movement measurements before moving into the digital world as computers began to reach libraries; he learned to program and developed a suite of training software; he worked on a few reports dealing with library careers after students left university; and spent a long time researching

---

[150] 'Cottage Garden'. Published in *Mostly Welsh* (2019). Talybont: Y Lolfa.

the possibilities and problems surrounding the use of digital books in libraries—work which continued for some years as he set up his own research and consultancy company.

I think that they both enjoyed a number of close friendships with their colleagues, most notably K. with her head of department in school—a lovely woman who had been the first to encourage and support K. in her learning of Welsh; and Trystan with academic colleagues with whom he worked. Two that he had mentioned particularly come to mind—he researched and wrote with both of them—but the longest lasting friendship was with someone he told me used to be known as 'Fingers' for reasons he never divulged or possibly never knew—although he did say it had nothing to do with petty theft!

He was a larger man than Trystan, who looked up to him both literally and intellectually—a pianist and lover of music, he encouraged Trystan's own love of both jazz and classical music. I think they became very close over the years, often confiding their woes to each other—I was almost jealous—and he was a great support in Trystan's more difficult years. But poetry was never far from Trystan although few of his earlier poems remain. They were mostly appended to a letter, long since lost, or read to me during some long telephone call. But these were the early scribblings of the master!

Lines 312-317:
But in that Spring

I do not think that Trystan ever understood what happened: from their perfect world began a journey, which he would later capture in his version of Dante's *Inferno*, into hell. K. became ill and was diagnosed with cancer, and eventually with inoperable cancer. There was a period for which he never forgave himself during which he had never understood just how ill she was and indeed, he confessed to me, that even when they travelled to see a consultant he had taken work with him—he was working on a book and had pages of proofs to go through. Later he realised that he had been vaguely aware that other couples in the waiting room had seemed somehow disapproving of his focus, and when he was called in to join K. the shock of the diagnosis had been such that a nurse helped him to a chair and gave him water. In an early account he wrote:

As he spoke the shock hit, solid as a punch;
Left me breathless, faint, unmanned;

So obviously lost that chair and water came
And briefly the patient was I – not her. [151]

and in the poem he subtitled with a line from *The Inferno*, "E quindi uscimmo a riveder le stelle" [152] he once again relived the moment, but this time going on to recount their journey together through the hell of that final diagnosis until, at dusk, they left the hospital to drive home.

He spoke
And then it seemed
The mist and perhaps my mind swirled round

"But in that Spring" he seemed to see everything in shades of grey and white: every tree—previously loved for its form—and every field: his world was somehow diminished, no longer to be enjoyed. All he could do was care for K. and for the boys: work and writing were no longer in focus, and in Dark Ashes, in his second allusion to Wordsworth's 'Ode: Intimations of Immortality from Recollections of Early Childhood' he laments that things are not as they had been: "The things which I have seen I now can see no more" [153], or as it is expressed elsewhere, that "the gold [is] become dim and the finest colour changed" [154]. Only the fates saw the future; he could not bear that empty horizon.

That K. stayed with them all through that summer was some kind of miracle and a testament to the power of her will—on one visit she told me that she wanted more than almost anything else to give her boys—I think she meant all four of them—a chance to come to terms with what was happening, to make their peace with fate and to say their goodbyes. Lewis told me how at the same time that it had been a blessing, a time—again and again—to hold her for one last time, a time in which she too could say goodbye, I suppose, it had also been a terrible, black, destructive time in which there was no space in his mind except for her death: except for his loss. I know he felt guilty for seeing it as his loss rather than

---

[151] 'The Consultant'. Published in *Mostly Welsh* (2019). Talybont: Y Lolfa.

[152] Literally, "we emerged to see—once more—the stars" [*Inferno* 34.139]. From 'On hearing a Loved One's Fate'—an unpublished poem now in the editor's collection.

[153] William Wordsworth: 'Ode: Intimations of Immortality from Recollections of Early Childhood'.

[154] Lamentations iv, I. Tenebrae for Holy Saturday, 1st Nocturn, Lesson 2.

hers; for thinking of it as his loss rather than that of the boys—or even of her family. He told me that once, near the end, she had asked him to get into the hospital bed with her and hold her and that, just as he was reaching down to remove his shoes, her doctor came in with a sedative—and the moment never came again. His mind spiralled down. He coped, but only just.

At the end, twenty-nine years to the day after they had first met in London's Royal Albert Docks, it was just the four of them and K.'s immediate family. They supported Trystan and his sons wonderfully well—particularly his oldest of all friends, his wife's older sister. Although she must have been suffering herself, she stayed with him in Wales for a short while after the funeral to support him and his sons. At her sister's wish she also took on the role of joint guardian to their youngest son. I have included the letter bringing me the sad news of K.'s illness in the appendix.

I could not bring myself to attend her funeral and made some excuses about being abroad, but I heard that she was well eulogised, that a sister played while her brother-in-law sang Y Nefoedd—The Heavens—by T Osborne Roberts, and that her pupils read from one of her favourite poems by Gerard Manley Hopkins, the poet of her PhD studies—I think it was 'The Windhover' [155], a poem they had studied, whose "dapple-dawn-drawn Falcon" K. had always liked to link (she knew, incorrectly) with the red kites that drifted over their garden. There were so many Hopkins poems that they could have used. I hope that she had—I think she must have—sometime earlier introduced Trystan to:

NOT, I'll not, carrion comfort, Despair, not feast on thee ;
Not untwist—slack they may be—these last strands of man
In me ór, most weary, cry *I can no more.* I can;
Can something, hope, wish day come, not choose not to be. [156]

… or perhaps he knew it anyway—his companion studies during her doctoral research much surely have taken it in. It was fitting that her ashes were scattered quietly and alone by Lewis in the garden of the cottage where they had spent nearly all of their married lives, and where Lewis lived on when his sons had married and left home until he was forced to retreat to Sussex by his health. In the years that followed the death, he devoted himself to his art—he became a

---

[155] *The Poems of Gerard Manley Hopkins* (4th ed) Oxford: OUP, 1970. p.69.
[156] (Carrion Comfort) ibid. p.99.

keen collector and his little cottage eventually housed some fifty works; ironically, one of his favourite paintings—of fishing boats in Falmouth harbour—had originally been given to K. by her father in the year that they met. And of course his time was filled by his writing and his poetry. Some eighteen years later he finally destroyed the old love letters from his time at sea—"you in me in you"—and scattered their ashes over that same patch of ground:

But in the end
They were just ash
And I scattered them

Ashes to her ashes [157]

There is a brass plaque to her memory, which I found when I made my last trip there as a visitor after his death, hidden in the bushes above the new orchard. So I suppose it is not surprising that a garden—the garden—features in so many of Lewis' poems: apart from those already quoted from, 'Cottage Garden', 'Letters' and 'Time', there is 'Monument', 'Autumn', 'Winter from a Window', 'Lost Love', 'A Dream itself is but a Shadow', and 'On leaving a Hospital Room'. Perhaps my favourite garden poem is 'In the Veins of the Earth' in which the poet recounts how one day he dug up a tiny glass pendant:

Teased from the clod
    I find a tiny glass heart and this symbol
breaks mine, for here
      is cached my soul
      with the mortal dust of all I ever loved.
In this plot her ashes lie at peace these many years
      yet now it sends a sign: weathered, soil-scuffed
      But still its facets shine [158]

Lewis had been so much of my life that I succumbed to a temptation that had been testing me ever since Lewis moved back to Sussex and, after his death I

---

[157] 'Letters'—Published in *Mostly Welsh* (2019). Talybont: Y Lolfa.
[158] 'In the Veins of the Earth'—Published in *Mostly Welsh* (2019). Talybont: Y Lolfa.

bought the little property and moved in. It was there that I finished this book and I have great hopes that it will serve me as it served him in the last years of his life: as a peaceful hideaway to pursue my work, my writing. I had always loved its quiet solitude.

It was also there that, as I begun to decorate, I found—wedged in the mud foundation of a wall behind a loose skirting board in the living room and "teased from the clod" a small gold pleter cross [159] that immediately brought a lump to my throat as time swirled around me. The sun from the window had just caught a glimmer from the speck of gold in the sod—all that was showing of a cross with a plaited or braided interlace form that must have dropped behind the skirting board, or been swept under it by an over-zealous besom, long ago.

Originally, medieval pleter crosses were used in Zeta and would have been made from plaited wattle, so there was no doubt in my mind where this old gold token originated, but I could scarcely bring myself to follow the logic that was suggesting that Lewis and K. had come to live in the very cottage originally occupied by Tristram and Yseult... and that I was now its custodian. It was almost as if the cross, with its unending plaited pattern, represented the Ātman— the imperishable real self, forever remaining with each reincarnation of the worldly being. Robert Frost's line, "Nothing gold can stay" [160] (which in fact suggests such a natural cycle) flashed in front of my eyes. My mind whirled round and round the stories, lost and wondering at the magic of time's complex patterns.

When Yseult died so young, Tristram was bereft—his mind numb, his whole being robbed of purpose, of meaning. Had his sons not supported him he would never have managed her simple funeral, and had they not been there in the days that followed, he might have simply sailed into the night. As it was, he lived on in their cottage for many years to come and once the boys had left home, of course his only passion was his writing and his poetry, which he felt had come to take Yseult's place. He knew he was regarded with some compassion by his neighbours in the village—and probably mocked as an old grey-haired recluse by their children—but he could not escape his inbred depth of reserve and he never outlived his loss. As he was to write many, many years later:

---

[159] Hrvatski pleter. A stylised Croatian cross with origins possibly dating back as far as the baptistery of Duke Viseslav.

[160] Robert Frost 'Nothing Gold Can Stay'. *The Poetry of Robert Frost.* Edward Connery Lathem (ed.) New York: Holt, 1969.

It seems I cannot escape
my sadly muted mind [161]

The village probably wondered at his hermetic existence, saw his comings and goings as he passed through, and felt his loneliness as his sons moved away, but were powerless to help. He was happy enough living with his memories of that extraordinary life and with Yseult always in his mind—not a day passed but some thoughts of her slipped lightly across his thoughts—how could he not be content. Perhaps—we have no means of knowing, but it would be extraordinary had it not been so—he thought of Zeta and wondered how his country fared. Had he been a few years younger and had he still possessed *Bäckahästen* he might have considered returning to the palace, but he knew that all would have changed and there would have been no place for a prince who had left the country in her hour of need.

We shall never know whether he would have been able to sail past Mljet without stopping for water.

Had he done so, he would have discovered an island much changed. His father had found a natural leader in Srecko, the beekeeper, and ably supported by his wife, Tatjana he had governed the island and its growing population—for new villages of incomers had sprung up further south following the installation of the garrison—fairly but with a steady hand. The great castle had never had a new owner, but inspired by Yseult's love of learning, Srecko had turned the library and its adjacent rooms into a school for the growing number of young people living in the villages around the lake.

Eventually, other rooms began to find a use as offices and meeting rooms, and the old dining room was turned into a dormitory for use when bad weather prevented the school children from returning across the lake to their homes. Sometimes, too, Tatjana used the magnificent library to bring together the best students from Zeta and Mljet to discuss their future. But Yseult's chamber was never touched.

Lines 319-326:
From that first love...

---

[161] 'Sons Sans'—an unpublished poem written by Lewis in 2018 and now in the editor's collection.

In his concluding lines, Lewis simply pays tribute to the all-embracing and powerful love that had held their lives together, and in its power to sustain—his use of the word 'worshipping' reminding us of the passion in the early lines when his worship of K. was a "transcendent wonder"—I believe it still was:

In the ashes of the fire there is a memory of the flame

I think that it is very likely that Lewis was also referencing—why would he not—Hopkins

> ... blue-bleak embers, ah my dear,
> Fall, gall themselves, and gash gold-vermilion. [162]

in those greying ashes, those 'blue-bleak' embers of a dying fire which, falling from the grate, burst open to reveal their bright, still-burning heart—perhaps like both Hopkins' and Lewis' seemingly lifeless souls at the time of which each wrote—which, through suffering, come to expose true brilliance. In Hopkins' case, at least, the lines also are associated with Christ, who exposed the possibility of redemption through his death.

In all times, the skein which entangled and wove our hero's cloth was female love. Without it, his lives would have played out completely differently—he would have been a warrior king or a master mariner: all-powerful and very male oriented roles. The female influence, perhaps we may think, the *saving* or *balancing* female influence, might be said to have freed or energised his softer, female side—his anima [163]—with its aspects of desire, insight, virtue and wisdom. Without this transformative "force" to hold him, this development, his collective unconscious might never have found poetry and the world would be the poorer.

---

[162] Gerard Manley Hopkins. 'The Windhover' [final lines].

[163] In Carl Jung's theory, the anima makes up the totality of the unconscious feminine psychological qualities that a man possesses. Jung believed a male's sensitivity is often repressed, and so considered the anima significant. He believed the anima would manifest itself by appearing in dreams and would influence a person's attitudes and his interactions with the opposite sex. In ontological terms the anima—the yin to Lewis' male yang—offers balance and unity.

If his poem is a hymn of praise to anything, it is to female strength; not to Venus as the Roman goddess known for love, beauty, prosperity, and desire and fertility, perhaps best depicted by Cabanel in his painting, The Birth of Venus [164] but to *Venus Veneta* [165] (subsequently re-titled *Monna Vanna* and then *Belcolore)* *by* Dante Gabriel Rossetti: a Venus of strength with a hard penetrating gaze. Perhaps an image we may see as like his one-time lover's face, earlier described as: at once wilful and strong, and softly beautiful.

It took a while—some few years in fact—but eventually Lewis returned to his poetry, and his early poems from this period, many of them love poems to K., written in memory of K. are, I believe, some of the finest he has ever written. I could add so many extracts here, but have chosen verses from the three that are probably my favourite poems: a love poem, a lament and a memorial poem.

> There is no meaning
> > and no sense,
> > only clarity

> I loved you and my heart began—
> > past years unknown
> > past pulse forgot

> > Love created!
> > Our heart defined
> > our lips sang
> > our hands mapped
> > > love

> I loved you with my eyes   your eyes mirrored love
> I loved you with my mouth   you sang love

---

[164] French artist, Alexandre Cabanel's Venus was described by art historian Robert Rosenblum as hovering "somewhere between an ancient deity and a modern dream…the ambiguity of her eyes, that seem to be closed but that a close look reveals that she is awake…A nude who could be asleep or awake is specially formidable for a male viewer."

[165] A 1866 oil on canvas painting of Rossetti's main model, Alexa Wilding, with allusions to spring.

I loved you with my soul   you preached love

My being quickened:
My dust lived in your rain,
              grew in your sun
I clothed you with my passion

I loved you as I felt you ebb
        passion passing
        joy muting
        love defining.

And now

I love you

Still [166]

Lewis lamenting his loss is at his most enigmatic, perhaps nowhere more so than in the previously quoted 'Hen dŷ' or in the beautiful 'Lost love':

I am quiet now you are gone
now I am the sole sound in the night
darkness swallows my words:
…
I am quiet now you are gone
for you were the soft song of nightfall
…
I am quiet now you are gone
for I am the silence of our dreams
darkness surrounds my mind
only a whisper of my thought seems
to drift with the night owls through
the star chilled light streams

---

[166] 'Love' Published in *Mostly Welsh* (2019). Talybont: Y Lolfa. Here quoted in its entirety, as no part of it standing alone possesses the same integrity.

in the barren garden of my mind [167]

There are so many poems written *in memoriam* it is difficult to select one, but perhaps the most appropriate was written following the death of his near neighbour, whose great friendship with K.—whom she regarded, I think, as an additional daughter as well as a good friend—had led to her asking for some of K.'s ashes to be buried beside her. Lewis wrote the following poem principally for her family, but clearly it was also his final, private good bye to his wife:

At the Grave
As the rains came we followed
As the rains fell we listened
And walked towards the minister,
Passing by the dark grave wherein she lies,
To drop another daffodil, a final kiss from life,
On the pale box below.
And on, to cluster round beneath the trees
Circling the family, rooted by some strange harmony
Of communion: a drifting mass lost in loss.
On the hillside, as the first sods drop down,
They are united through twenty parting years
And peace comes to me in the silence
As the land heals its open wound. [168]

If anything should have become clear in my commentary it is the almost sacred love of a land that had taken in and made its own the families cast upon its shores. I have also written that Trystan never forgave himself for that lacuna— the inexplicable gap—in his empathy, his consideration, his caring for K. In this penultimate poem, these aspects of his being are both made explicit.

As I pass beyond my summer wall
Once more the land embraces my spirit
And its silence becomes my prayer
While I and heaven hear
The wind whispered psalm

---

[167] 'Lost Love' (extracts)—Published in *Mostly Welsh* (2019). Talybont: Y Lolfa.
[168] An unpublished poem written by Lewis in 2018 and now in the editor's collection.

As dusk caresses the treetops
That surround my field fane—
I walk slowly through its grassy nave
Lost in my old memories
And pause at the far gate:
The sun sinks low behind me
And my long shadow stretches out in penance [169]

Lewis finished 'Dark Ashes'—'Retrospective', as it was at the time—and it was published some nine or so months before his death in Sussex. I know that he was pleased with what was in effect his autobiography, his account of the lives he had lived, but—although it was quite well received by the public—most of the critics did not take to it. And so 'Dark Ashes' was born, phoenix-like, from its flames—if that odd reversal can be allowed!

And in writing those lines and thinking back over the process—Lewis' initial request, the debate about my drafts, the archive of his papers, his poems, his life—our life together—I recalled the envelope addressed to me with that simple boyhood symbol:

I had never opened it, indeed had forgotten all about it, and I retrieved it now from the coffee table shelf where it had lain since I cast it aside in my haste to

---

[169] 'Vespers'—an unpublished poem written by Lewis in 2018 and now in the editor's collection.

read Lewis' letter. I noticed what I had missed before, that the padded envelope also had the pencilled phrase 'A first gem from my archive!' on it and I opened it with some trepidation, wondering at this message from beyond the grave. As I broke the seal something dropped to the floor—it took me a moment to discover it in the cottage gloom, but then I found myself holding a ring of twisted gold with a rectangular jade stone! The shock was palpable!

It is almost impossible to describe the emotions that this small artefact raised in me. I slipped it onto my finger so that I might always have it with me as I finished my work… and it has never left my hand since then. Also in the envelope was a map—clearly some hundreds of years old—a hand-drawn map of an island. It was discoloured, creased and fragile as any treasure map should be, but I could see very clearly at the northern end of the landmass a small jetty beside a sandy beach, a track leading over a wooded hill and descending to a large lake containing a small island.

Tracing my finger past the island, I could see a crude drawing of a tower and close-by on the shore a small settlement; moving south down the lake I saw a narrow canal to the sea. I had found the island within an island; I had finally discovered Mljet! It would take some weeks of further work to amend my text so that it conformed more perfectly to the map, and to bring in from the notes and papers in the archive the further detail that lengthened the text of the old story considerably, but what a wonderful confirmation Lewis had sent me!

And so, reader, the task is done! In life, Lewis resisted my attempts to make his old story more visible, in death he validated my work; in Wales I was introduced to his history, in Italy he denied me, and back in Wales the story has finally seen the light of day. It gives me some sad satisfaction that this has happened through my commentary which as Nabokov suggested "represents an attempt to sort out [the] echoes" [170]. I had never expected the epic poem I first saw in Frascati to offer the detail now available in my commentary, but I was disappointed that 'Retrospective'/'Dark Ashes' hid our old story so thoroughly—that, in effect, Lewis denied the past we had shared as children. But "My work is finished. My poet is dead" [171].

I have tried to tread lightly over his lines while making clear the stories which underpin them but I, and the readers of this account, have also to remember

---

[170] Vladimir Nabokov (1973) *Pale Fire*. Notes on [non-existent] line 1000. Harmondsworth: Penguin. p.233.
[171] Ibid. p.236.

that—as I tried to suggest in the Introduction—a "story is an endless labyrinth of words, images and spirits, conjured up to show us the invisible truth about ourselves"[172].If I have a fault, it is that found in many an academic and scholarly writer approaching the end of a career: that of feeding into a text too many references, allusions and supporting facts. I must apologise to readers who find my footnotes are intrusive but I truly believe that they, and scholars of Lewis' work, will—if they can assimilate them as they read the commentary—be benefitted and will receive a fuller and more rounded understanding of 'Dark Ashes'.

It seems appropriate to leave the final words to Trystan Lewis:

End of a Galaxy

A blink
In the silent depth of night

As the last leaf of the beech tree
    As the silent tear of my love

End of Sanity

When the cold winds blew her soul from him
    he knew that death was a hollow laugh
    and love lay in her silent voice

In all the years he has stood naked
    on the shore:
        his morning
        his noon
        his night
        pressed cold against his flesh
           scourged by her dust

---

[172] Carlos Ruiz Zafon (2018) *The Labyrinth of the Spirit* (Volume 4 of The Cemetery of Forgotten Books). Translated by Lucia Graves. Weidenfeld & Nicolson).

End of the Wind

The last specks of sand touched him
as the sun lit his face
raised to the horizon

later   his epiphany
    came in the lonely
        stillness
    of the dark night

Three of eleven short poems from his sequence: ENDINGS (2018) [173]

---

[173] Published in *Mostly Welsh* (2019). Talybont: Y Lolfa.

Appendix

Early correspondence, referenced from the text, between Trystan Lewis, poet, and Chris Armstrong, friend and editor; as well as a letter from Trystan Lewis to his publishers

m.v. Otaio
Colon

Dear Christo,

Well, it has been a miserable beginning to my life at sea! I feel completely alone and lost in a wilderness of the seventy cadets on board with me—all of whom, including those who like me began the experience in the bustle of the Royal Albert Docks in London this trip, seem to know so much more than me, and to have so much more experience of life than me… but I suppose I am settling in! Although at the moment I am on light duties as I slipped on the wet deck during a morning PT session and grazed my leg, which has since picked up an infection (or from the deck, I suppose) that swelled and needed some sort of antibiotic after the doc lanced it—an experience made all the worse since in demonstrating the spray he would use to freeze the place, he manage to squirt it in my eye. I thought he had blinded me! Anyway…

We are at anchor for a few hours awaiting the convoy to go through the canal and this letter will be taken off when the canal pilot comes on board so I must make haste.

I think I told you in my letter from London before we sailed about arriving on board and finding a cabin etc. My cabin mates didn't return from leave for a couple of days so I had no one to tell me what was expected and the first inspection was both a surprise and a disaster that began when the First Officer ran his gloved (white gloves, I ask you!) hand along a shelf and found dust! So the first few days aboard passed in a confusion of odd jobs—polishing brass, carrying stores—wet sand (for a fire box) is very heavy!—cleaning and stuff… but I seemed to have a lot of time with nothing to do which was a bit worrying as I supposed that I should probably have been doing something somewhere. At the beginning, before it all settled down, no one seemed to be really responsible for us new boys and everything was very confusing!

Now we have had a couple of weeks at sea and begun regular work. I am in Starboard Watch C! Each watch (group of cadets) is either working on deck or in the accommodation, in the school room doing a correspondence course or on bridge watch. Haven't done that yet but I think we steer—learn to steer—or keep lookout on the forecastle head, or are on standby—the worst bit of being on standby is that you have to call the next watch—which means finding the right person in the right cabin and persuading them to wake up... or you and your watch don't get relieved! I wonder what steering a big ship like this is like! We have to get up at six-thirty if we are not on watch and work for an hour (or do the dangerous PT) before breakfast! Everything seems at once unknown and strange and somehow deeply familiar—very odd!

Everything is very formal and strict and there are inspections of our cabins twice a week, sometimes by the Captain, when we have to have brass polished, decks scrubbed (and no dust) and stand to attention as they enter. We haven't really had any rough weather yet—it's just been a bit choppy but I don't think I am going to be seasick!

Well, I had better stop now or I'll miss the chance of getting this off!

Missing your cheerful company

Yours
Trystan

Hi Chris,

Well, we have now crossed the Pacific (we went past Pitcairn Island—mutiny on the Bounty territory! and stopped to send Dead Eye Doc ashore in a lifeboat… meanwhile the locals, descendants of the original mutiny families, came out in longboats and sold us bananas, carvings and pieces of coral) and arrived in Wellington—well, we haven't as I write this but will have by the time it is posted! The weather improved and has been quite warm, but the first few days after the canal were stormy and I was on watch. No one told me that in really bad weather the lookout is kept from something called the 'Monkey Island' above the bridge—I tried to go forward and got shouted at from the bridge by the officer of the watch. I am sure I am getting a reputation for being the dumb, naive, innocent newcomer! But no one told me! Steering is quite difficult as when you turn the wheel the ship begins to swing very gradually at first and then faster—and you have to turn the wheel the other way to stop it. And you are expected to stay within one degree of the compass course.

Later—I had to turn to and serve lunch—we all take turns at that duty too.

I think I am settling in now—though a lot of it is still very strange and there still seem to be lots of things I don't know—but you will be glad to hear I am a bit happier now. I must have sounded quite depressed in my Panama letter! I suppose I am learning some things—we have to learn basic seamanship and I can splice a rope now (not very well). The correspondence course covers all sorts of things I knew nothing about—like navigation (I was expecting that), ship stability (lots of calculations supposed to keep the ship upright!) and ship construction (as if I'm going to build one!)… but there are two things that I really dread! We have to learn over thirty 'rules of the road' by heart and get tested on them and have to recite and pass a few more each week.

As you will remember from school, I was never very good at learning poems by heart and I don't seem to have improved. No idea why we have to know them by heart—they are all about which way to turn to avoid collisions and stuff. But even worse is signals! Learning the morse code isn't so bad and sending morse is OK because you start off with something you know—the letter—and remember the dots and dashes: A is dot-dash, B is dash-dot-dot-dot and so on, but when they are flashed at you as a jumble of random letters and numbers with hardly a gap between letters it is impossible. I don't think I will ever get the hang of it!

Just back from two hours in the school room—we have an extra officer on board who is the school master, but he is quite gruff and intimidating! And we did signals practice!

I think we will go from Wellington to Auckland, Port Chalmers, Timaru, Bluff and Picton before coming back via Panama again so I shall see quite a lot of NZ. We have to have permission to go ashore and—as a first tripper—I have to go ashore in uniform which is quite a pain. We are to have a formal dance in

Auckland and shall have to dress up in 'Whites' with a bow tie and a cummerbund… and dance I suppose! Me? Dance? I sort of hope I'm on gangway duty! Did I tell you that all that uniform I went to London with my parents to buy included white shirts with detached collars… of course I was nearly the only one to come on board with those and I had to get hold of some drip-dry white shirts before we left London! What a waste of money! You would have thought that my mum's cousin—currently the Captain of this very ship—would have let us know! The whole lot set my parents back over £100 too! (not just the shirts!)

When the weather is good they set up deck tennis courts over one of the hatches. It is played with a rope quoit but scored just like tennis and the Old Man is fearsome as he hurls it straight at the opponent's head! He only plays with other officers and occasionally one or two of the senior cadets; thank goodness! There are also cricket nets, but you know what I think of cricket!

I think we are supposed to arrive in Wellington about this time tomorrow (mid-afternoon) and I am not sure what happens then. I think we have to stand watch at the gangway among other things. I'll add a line or two before I go ashore to post this—you can imagine me walking into town in uniform!!

Well! we have arrived—and I was more help on 'stations' aft than I was when we left London! We have to get the heavy ropes and wire hawsers ashore and then tighten them up with a winch and make them fast to bollards. The ropes aren't so bad but the wires are greasy and often have sharp jags of broken strands sticking out so have to be handled a bit carefully. When I was winding one of the ropes around the bollards I had this extraordinary sense of having done so before, although in my mind the bollards were smaller—on a smaller ship. It was very odd. Oh I forgot, my leg is better! No wooden leg and parrot! No limp!

Your
Trystan

Dear Student!

How are things in Cambridge? I've never been there and would love to visit! Can I squeeze into your rooms for a couple of nights—I thought I might drive over and see you as things are pretty boring here at home and I still have a couple of weeks of leave left. I mean, I'm not just coming because I'm bored, I wanted to see you too!

How about it?

Or are you too busy writing essays… although the way I hear it most time at Uni is spent in the local hostelry—I'm sure you know a few nice watering holes—I'll even treat you to a steak somewhere! You probably haven't eaten anything but snacks since you last had your mum's home cooking!

I've been home a couple of week and been to the beach a few times, but the weather hasn't been up to much and there hasn't been much surf running. I'm missing your company like mad! Otherwise life at home is well, life at home. I've had to give slideshows of my pictures twice to my parents' friends!!! It's really embarrassing!

Give me a ring at home one evening—I could come down on Friday and be there in time for tea!

Let me know what you think—it would be great to see you again and catch up.

Tr.

Hi Chris,

It was wonderful to see you in Uni last weekend—sorry you couldn't spare more time but the essay on Trollop seemed to be going really well. I'm not sure I had heard of him before! And it was great to meet Yllka—the two of you seem to have so much in common (apart from the fact that you don't come from Albania!)—why have you never talked about her to me—kept her a secret! Is this really it? Are we talking love?

There was one thing we never got around to talking about although I wanted to, but there never seemed the right moment. I don't know whether it is because I am lonely on board ship or what, but I keep dreaming of being born again—whoops, I don't mean as in those dreadful school assemblies when their tame missionaries were wheeled in to talk to us—are you saved? have you been born again?—I mean as in rebirth and reincarnation and previous existences. Do you know what I mean?

I keep seeing myself—in the dreams—as a sailor on a sailing ship or as a married man with a lovely wife living in a tiny cottage, farming (farming??), or as some important man, I dunno, a politician or something trying to negotiate a treaty with someone in fancy dress! It's all nonsense but the thing is, I know the guy in the dreams is me and it's as if it was sometime in the past. It is so vivid and so clearly me that it has to be more than a dreamtime recollection of our childhood fable! I don't know much about religions—is it Buddhism or Hinduism?—that believe in reincarnation, nor do I really know how it works, I mean what is supposed to happen? I shall have to find a book on it if you don't have any ideas or wise thoughts! Do you think the new person—the reincarnation—even knows about his previous lives—I mean what he was in them? It would be funny if I had been a sailor before!

Sorry for that dense scribble! Let me know if you have any words of wisdom! I mean, it must mean something, right? You can't keep having the same dream otherwise, can you?

Your friend and confidant!
Tr

Dear Christo,

Sorry not to have been in touch since I got home on leave but I have been so busy! Whee… I don't know where to begin… but I am in love! IN LOVE!! I have met a wonderful, pretty, clever girl and she loves me and I love her and I met her on the first day I was on leave when she came to stay with my sister. It wasn't very fair on G. really, because she spent more time with me than with G! In fact my Dad had been to Brighton to collect her and picked me up from the ship on the way home—I think we knew we fancied each other by the end of the journey!

She was like a magnetic force that attracted my compass! (Sorry that sounded like a crude double entendre—it wasn't meant to be—I was just trying for a nautical reference!) You can probably tell I am excited—we have barely been apart until I came here to study and take my exams and now I go back to her home in Brighton—yes Brighton—each weekend instead of going home (parents not too happy!).

Do you remember when I was dating X, if you can call it that, I never once woke up thinking 'I love you' (I mean her, X, not you!) but now—every day dawns with that brilliant light and what sounds to me almost like a town crier bellowing our love. An overwhelming, dominating, all embracing joyous shout, of course!

Do you remember me telling you years ago that there was a family with a daughter I used to play with who lived at the end of our garden in Brighton when I was four—well this is her younger sister! Who I last saw in her pram! I'll send you a photo when I have some developed (no, not the pram!)

I should have asked, how is the job? What sort of things does the company publish? Are you writing at all? I feel *I* could be writing long poems about love—would you publish them? K. is lovely—did I say that? and her parents are really nice and quite happy to put me up each weekend when I sneak off from my studies at lunch time on a Friday. I get down to Brighton in time to meet her from school—she is in the sixth form—driving up in the MG makes everyone look out of the sixth form study windows!!

I can't tell you how much better I feel—I have never, ever felt so happy—I do hope you are also experiencing similar feelings. The only dark cloud on the horizon is my looming exams—including the dreaded signals—did you know I have to average 75% in all papers?—and the fact that it means going back to sea and leaving K. behind. I don't know how either of us will manage!

Whee!
Tr

Chris,

Forgive my last euphoric letter, which you probably didn't even finish! It was good to talk to you on the phone last night. As I said—I needed someone to talk to, really—and who else?!—as things are not <u>all</u> wonderful at the minute. I mean things with K. are more than wonderful but things at home—when I go back at all—are distinctly chilly. The parents spend most of my time there trying to persuade me of my foolishness—how they know better than I and hinting at all sorts of dark things in K.'s past—no idea what they think they know that I don't—as if K. and I have never talked—but they don't seem to understand the possibility of our really actually being in love. I suppose it is the old thing of her not being good enough for their son (how dare they!).

I am sure they are not acting 'malevolently'—when I tried to suggest that I drove K. on from Swansea to join her parents on holiday they were clearly acting in what they thought were my best interests, and to protect K. for whom they were temporarily responsible—in loco parenthis [sic] or whatever. But they think they know better, can control my life, and dictate to me! It's not right! I've been away from home for years now but they still seem to think I am their little boy as long as I am 'living under their roof'—well, I'm not really any longer!

And they were SO mean to K., the way they talked to her. I don't think she'll ever forgive them!

Ah, well, you helped me clear the air last night and I am off to Brighton tomorrow so the world has just got a LOT brighter! Cheers!

Love Trys

Dear Chris,

Quite exciting picking up a brand new ship from the builders in Strathclyde!

She is huge—looking particularly big when I joined her as she had no cargo on board and almost no fuel, fresh water or stores so was riding very high in the water with a very steep gangway to drag my cases up! Quite different in every way possible from the ships I have been on before, and green! She is over twice the length of my last ship and all her hatches are forward of the bridge and accommodation—and I have a very posh (and large) cabin with my own bathroom! All the cargo will be loaded in 'containers'—huge 20 x 8 x 8 foot boxes with doors at one end—and nearly as many go on deck above the hatches as go below decks—I am told I will only just be able to see the bow from the bridge over the tops of the containers!

There are all sorts of things to learn about this new ship—the Jervis Bay (she is one of six identical 'Bay Class' ships) apart from my way round it… and not only for us when it comes to manoeuvring and handling her, but for the builders. One of the (few) things I remember from my old ship construction correspondence course is that the strength of a ship comes from its 'box section'—on these containers ships, because the containers can only be dropped straight down into the holds, the holds' hatches go almost out to the sides of the ship so the box strength is all but destroyed—as one side of the box—the deck— is all but missing! But they have compensated by using extra thick, extra strong steel, BUT the builders have mounted hundreds of strain gauges all over the ship so we can take readings on the bridge every few hours and report back to them on how the ship is standing up to the strain of being at sea with cargo in it!! I am sure it is safe really! (I found a paper by the Naval Architect—an M Meek on 'The First O.C.L. Container Ships', which said it was the first time that designers found themselves without a basis ship [a model to work from]… "there was no adequate precedent in ocean-going ships of this size"—a comforting thought!)
[174]

Now we are in Tilbury on our maiden voyage, we are inaugurating UK-Australia container shipping—very exciting! Because we are named for a famous ship that was sunk by the German *Admiral Scheer* in 1940 as it saved the convoy, we were visited by her only survivor before we sailed!

I can't tell you how frustrating it is to have sailed from Scotland to London— back closer to K.—but to be unable to see her again. There is no time for time off before we sail. Did I tell you I love her?

---

[174] I was able to track down the paper Lewis refers to in the archives: M Meek (c.1964) The First O.C.L. Container Ships. London: The Royal Institution of Naval Architects. Paper No. 1.

Best wishes—I'll write from Oz or Cape Town or somewhere!

Trystan

Hi C,

I bet you are wondering what I am doing in a hotel at the end of the Reeperbahn! The company needed someone to look after one of the Bay Boats while it was in dry dock for its one-year guarantee 'service' and I have taken over for the last few weeks. I have to stay here in the hotel but walk over to the ship every other day—through the infamous 'red light' district—the Reeperbahn night clubs offer unbelievable shows even before you get to the actual red-light streets that run off it down to the river past a huge brewery. Then I go down a spiral staircase into a traffic tunnel (the cars come down in a lift)—which as you can imagine is full of exhaust fumes—under the river to the ship yard and the Jervis Bay, where I spend every other night!

I have had great fun exploring Hamburg. On one day I went into a huge park to walk to the planetarium for an amazing display. But almost more amazing was how tame the squirrels and birds were! I was walking back eating an ice cream and a squirrel ran up my leg looking for a taste! Since then I have had great fun feeding them—you can hold out your hand with some bread in it and birds will land on it—I feel like St Francis of Assisi! Why aren't they that tame at home? There is also a cinema that shows English films where I saw Vanishing Point last week!

The good news is that K. is coming over next week—you can imagine how frustrated we have both been being so close and yet so far away! I have a suite in the hotel with a huge double bed with a 'duvet' on it—no sheets or blankets, just this eiderdown thing to sleep under—and a huge lounge with a kitchen off it, so there will be plenty of room for her. I'm sure she will want to come on board with me when I spend the nights there but I dare not risk it! I don't have to do much except make fire rounds so I am getting through a huge amount of reading. The other night an alarm went off which I didn't recognise so I had to call the Chief Engineer in charge of repairs—he wasn't amused as I should have known it was the CO_2 alarm (he thought, but why would I?!) which goes off to make sure no one gets left in the engine room when they use CO_2 to douse a fire. It is triggered by opening the door to the 'cupboard' with the valves in it and one of the German shipyard workers had done just that so he could put his sandwiches somewhere safe!

I'll be back in the UK and on leave in a couple of weeks so hope to see you then. Do you want to have a look round the ship? After all, you have only seen her for a moment or two in the dark from the bottom of the gangway!

Cheers
Trystan

Dear Trystan and K.,

Well, this is the first letter to you as a married couple although you are on your second trip! Trys, I imagine you are a lot happier on board now than you were for the last couple of trips BW (before wedlock!)! How is K. enjoying life on board—I hope she has settled in OK and isn't getting too sea sick. I am addressing this to Cape Town so you should be reading this after only a couple of weeks away from home, I suppose—hope the trip is going well so far!

You have in the past told me all about your life on board—watches in the middle of the night (!), cargo, engineers, navigating with a sextant and so on, but not much about the social life. You do have a social life do you? And what does K. find to do all the time, with nothing but men to talk to?? I am imagining her sunbathing on deck, surrounded by frustrated sailors bringing her drinks!! You'll have to watch them! No, seriously, I am sure you are both having a wonderful time on your extended honeymoon, interrupted only a little by work!

My work continues to frustrate any hope I might have of a social life as well as any hope I might have of completing my book! You would think I could get through all the reading necessary during the day but there are so many interruptions and so much correspondence to complete that I frequently (read 'always') find myself bringing home chapters, drafts and proposals to read. And there are always deadlines!

I did manage to get to the opera the other day to see Mozart's Le Nozze di Figaro—really splendid—I am beginning to really enjoy opera—I remember you enjoyed going with a Radio Officer(?) to see Tannhäuser in Hobart a couple of years ago and how spellbound you said you were. You must keep it up! And how is the reading going? Do you have any time to read now? I know you said K. was taking a veritable library of books with her so I suppose you can dip into those—what poets does she have with her?

Well, I am writing this over a glass of wine and dinner before I go back to reading a terrible first chapter and proposal by someone no one has (or will, if I have my way!) ever heard of. Utter dribble! It's all to do with the Crusades and a search for some reliquary! Off to drop my plate in the sink and read a bit more before I damn it and add it to my growing heap of authors' rejections!

Ever yours
Chris

Chris,

I only got as far as the end of the first paragraph—the bit about the voyage going well—when I was interrupted—rudely interrupted! It was the middle of the night after I had come off watch and K. and I were lying in bed reading the letters—hers from her folks and my first was yours—that we had picked up an hour earlier at Cape Town.

I think K. heard the odd noise first. Our cabin window—the same one from which we spotted your car coming along the dock to the gangway—now looks out to sea, over a passageway alongside the accommodation two decks below so I am not used to hearing noises outside the window when we are at sea—and the odd whistling/hissing noise made no sense at all to me until I pressed my cheek against the glass and looked down to see one of our four life rafts inflating on deck! I rushed over to the phone to tell the bridge and grabbed some clothes, told K. what was happening and that I might have to help deflate the thing and left for the bridge… where the full story—or the story up to that point—we never did discover the full story—unfolded.

Weeks before we had discovered a stowaway on board as we crossed Biscay—the Captain's standing orders say that you never turn back but carry them forward to the next port—in this case, Fremantle. He was a nice enough chap—someone who had the need to get to Oz but couldn't afford the fare—so he was given a spare crew cabin. Anyway, the stowaway had decided he needed to leave us—don't ask, we never discovered why… and if the captain asks me again "Why do you think he did it"… The life raft that we had heard was his third attempt—he had pitched one into the sea from the port side and seen it bob astern so fast he gave up on it and had inflated the other port raft and been unable to get it over the rail.

What I hadn't been able to see from the cabin was that he was holding one of the cadets at knife point—actually not a point really as our bread knives, although about two feet long for some reason, have a rounded tip!—and trying to make him help get the life raft over the rail before he rushed to the stern to jump after it. As the officer of the watch could not leave the bridge, I ended up going down to see what was happening but only caught up with him as he was clambering over the stern rail! I had several thoughts running through my head at the time apart from the fact that I knew if he jumped, he was a dead man: I worried about the need to turn the ship and hunt for him in a choppy sea in the middle of a dark night and I knew that if we ever located him I would be the officer who had to take a boat to pick him up (and I didn't relish that task!) and of course, I was thinking of K. and the possibility of things going badly wrong and her being left alone!

But I grabbed him just as he was straightening, he was outside the rails facing me, standing on the edge of the deck ready to launch himself backwards into the churning wake. I had one arm round his neck and one trying to grasp his arm with the flailing knife and—because most of his weight bent over the rail was inboard he couldn't straighten up and jump... BUT I couldn't pull him inboard (I didn't really want to at first as I could see that I would lose control of him then). It was ages until someone arrived to help! The bosun arrived and we got him back on deck and handcuffed him to a pole. (I had told the bosun to hit the stowaway—I had in mind knocking him unconscious to make the task of getting him back over the rail easier—but the bosun asked, "How hard!" I almost laughed!) How little we really know of those we work with... well, I suppose that applied to both men! Anyway, that was the adventure that kept me from your letter! We put him off at Port Elizabeth and that was that!

I do remember enjoying Tannhäuser—I even remember the name of the Radio Officer, Sid Braithwaite—but haven't been to the opera since. All my 'artistic' energies are given over to reading now! It must be the influence of K. but I even tried writing a poem the other day—it was hard work... and terrible and I didn't even show it to K. I think it was just the joy of coming off watch and into the cabin and seeing her there waiting for me—I remembered the impression and some of the words that had floated across my mind and tried to get it all onto paper! Something—probably something better (or maybe not... I just remember a lot of fleeting thoughts about K.)—had floated across my mind when I was hanging onto that madman over the stern rail too! Perhaps that is where my determination and unusual strength came from—he was much bigger than me!

Well, it is time to have an early lunch and go on watch. K. has an early lunch with me as we miss breakfast most days after my interrupted night—NO—being on watch from midnight for four hours! K. says I answered the telephone call waking me up the other night and came back to bed telling her it was a turquoise owl on the phone!!? Fortunately she was awake enough to make sure I got back out of bed and went on watch!

All love as usual
Trys

P.S. It was something like this—I think it definitely needs working on! Or destroying!

Descending and
from the door
I see
the beauty of
my new horizon

A night watch of
looking out
for ships
now my love
waits to be seen

The Southern Ocean

is empty but
for us
navigating
the long grey swells

I close the cabin door
and we embrace:
the bed
a deep wide sea
on which to sail now

Ascending from
depths where
I knew
the beauty of
my new horizon.

Chris,

I hardly know how to write this letter—our lives are coming apart, shattered, destroyed—K. is ill! I mean seriously ill—she has cancer and may not survive. Oh God! I can hardly bring myself to write that—to think that—to think of her dying. She is being so brave and strong but I can see the pain she is in. I think she has been ill for a while without realising—or perhaps she did and just hid it from me—how bad things were but then I had to take her to a consultation in Shrewsbury—God! I was so innocent so un-knowing—when he said that she had cancer his nurse had to get me a chair and a glass of water—it was such a shock. She stayed at home at first but is in the ward now.

And now we know the worst and I have had to tell the boys—how do you do that? Tell kids that their Mum is not coming back from hospital? Answer: You discover in the worst possible way.

God! Sorry to dump this on you. But you have been such support to me in the past and you knew and loved my K. too. I don't even know what I am writing—I have just got back again from the hospital and it is past midnight. I was OK and then when I started writing…

I'll be in touch

T

Frascati, Rome

Jane Hillerby, Commissioning Editor
L A M Peter Publishing

Dear Jane,

I hope you are not too surprised to hear from me after such a long hiatus, nor to see that I am writing from Italy! But I bring you good tidings of great joy—I think! You will remember when last we spoke—what was it, about three months ago—that I had come to a full stop with 'Retrospective'—somehow I could not see what came next, or what had been next, I suppose, although I had had the story lines, the whole thing, mapped out perfectly in my head. Somehow at the end of the third canto our heroes were lost at sea. (Wrong phrase! I didn't mean they died at sea just that I lost sight of them!) The structure would not fit and the words were not the right words. I came to a dead end. I suppose it was all to do with the timeline, or at least with the unsung bits of it.

You will remember I have spoken of my good and life-long friend, Chris Armstrong—you will have heard of him as an English scholar, writer and academic. Seeing my plight, he invited me over here—he is teaching a semester in Rome—and it has been our long talks over the poem that helped me resolve things—and got me writing again! He did try to impose a reading on me that I had never intended but he also sorted out my problems with time: with all of the pasts and presents. So a small vote of thanks to him!

You will remember that the last lines you saw—the end of canto iii—had to do with having to return, Sisyphus like, time and again to sea, having time and again to desert his wife. Canto iv resolves this—or begins to do so—and our hero realises that his futures can be resolved with marriage to Y.

I hope to have the completed work with you shortly after I return to Wales in about a month's time. I hope that promise is not too ambitious—but at least you can relax in the knowledge that I am back on track.

Wishing you all the best.

Sincerely
Trystan Lewis

Addendum

Correspondence about the publication of Dark Ashes

Note from the Publishers.

As this version of Lewis' final manuscript edited by his long-term friend, Chris Armstrong, was going through our own editorial processes (the usual proof reading and marking up that takes place alongside cover design, the development of promotional material, publicity and so on) a series of letters were passed on to us which both echoed some of our own concerns about the editor's interpretations and seemed to threaten all the work that we—and he—had so far laboriously undertaken and, indeed, the very onward life of the book.

And then Lewis passed away. As it turned out, and we of course sought the advice of our own lawyers over this, there was in the end nothing to prevent publication. In the interests of literary scholarship and historical exactitude, the desk editor responsible for the project in consultation with the editorial team decided to append the correspondence to the book as a final section. The letters follow. We have chosen to insert them in full and unedited (other than for clarity); they appear in chronological order.

Christopher,

You have overstepped the mark as my editor! How dare you! It is not the editor's role to insert opinions or to add to the text—even in such a commentary as I asked you to provide. You seem not to have understood the very idea of a commentary—lest that IS the case, allow me to amplify—I was asking you to comment on and explain my poem, Dark Ashes. I was NOT asking you to write a veritable novella around it! And to do so and present it to my publishers without further reference to me—that is intolerable!

That they sent me a draft or proof copy is incredibly fortunate. You may well imagine that I have been through [it] with some care.

Please do me the courtesy of arranging a meeting ~~between them~~ between us and my publishers so that we may discuss how to proceed. As you know, I am far from in the best of health these days and would find a journey up to the city far too tiring so we shall have to arrange it here, at my house in Sussex.

I shall expect to hear from you VERY shortly!

I remain your good—if exasperated, friend

Trystan Lewis

My dear Trystan,

Let me begin by saying that I was both shocked and concerned to receive your letter. To suggest making major changes at this stage is not likely to go down well with your friendly publishers, to say the least. You must be aware of this. I believe that the final proof that I sent to the publishers in every way does justice to you and your fine poem—dare I say that my commentary enhances the original lines? And not only does it do justice to your writing, but it is exactly what you asked me to do. In case you do not have a file of our correspondence— I cannot believe that this would be the case, but nevertheless—I have copied out here the substance of what originally you wrote when asking me, begging me, if I remember, to undertake the task:

Dear Chris,

As I said when I telephoned you, I have a favour to ask of you—nothing as desperate as rescuing K. from the London docks!—but a favour none the less. You must know that my health is failing and that these days I rarely leave my home on the South Downs, valuing the peace of the rolling countryside and the view of the distant sea above companionship and travel; so when my publishers asked me to work on a new version of 'Retrospective' my first thought was to refuse. That was until I re-read the poem and was once again transported back to my early lives and loves. I DO believe that the poem deserves another outing! And what I believe would enhance its brevity are the stories behind it, but I have no longer the energy. I should like to see a commentary to the poem which opens up the histories which underpin my lines. Christo, having known me for most of my life I know that you will be able to unravel the often difficult themes and thinking lying behind the lines of the work I am now calling 'Dark Ashes'—but I leave to you the decisions on how you may explain my mind, or indeed my life. The histories behind my loves.

You will remember you went on to ask me to become your literary executor and archivist. Trystan, I know that there was further correspondence, but you never departed from this original brief. It was my very careful reading, my clear understanding, of what you wanted that persuaded me to take on the task all those months ago in a cold Welsh winter. That you seem to be suggesting scrapping my many hours—days and weeks—of work is unconscionable and unfair, and I cannot accept that this is what you want. I am writing separately to the publishers to assure them that the work should go ahead.

Sincerely, yours
Chris

Jane Hillerby, Commissioning Editor
L A M Peter Publishing Ltd

Dear Jane

I am enclosing two letters, which to date are the sum of a recent correspondence between me and Trystan Lewis. If necessary, I shall have to travel to Sussex to discuss this with him but I believe that, with sight of his original request to me, Lewis will be persuaded that my contributions to the volume should stand as you have them. For the moment I would suggest that you continue, indeed, continue working to the agreed publication date, unless you hear further from me. I would add that I wonder if Trystan is entirely fit to make editorial judgements at this stage given his failing health, and—I was going to say before I realised the irony—his age... which is also mine!

I will ensure that you are kept up to date with any further interference from Lewis.

With best wishes
Chris Armstrong (Editor)

Dear Chris,

It pains me beyond belief to hear of your intransigence. May I remind you that this is my poem and that the volume will appear under my name—something you may care to remember given that *that* is what will sell a work which will bring you much fame! I do have copies of all of our correspondence, of course, and did not need to be reminded of what I had asked you to undertake. I asked for a commentary and you have provided a work of fiction: a novella!

Your supposed commentary can only expose me to ridicule given the way that you have shared my past histories and the lives and loves within them. I hear from the publisher that you have instructed them to go to press, but I beg you to remember our friendship—the friendships, the love, the loves, we shared—and to reconsider. I suppose your beliefs—at least the Gnostic ones—allow some sort of self-determination of morality which, in turn, allows you to rationalise your selfish behaviour.

I am sorry to be writing this in pencil but I seem to have mislaid my beautiful fountain pen that you will remember was a present to me from yourself. My writing seems to be rather small too but I am afraid that this must be a consequence of my illness.

As ever, you have my love
Trystan

My dear Trystan,

I am at something of a loss. I have reread our early correspondence, your poem and my commentary, as well as your more recent letters, and can see no reason for your concerns. I have no hesitation—as I have said to the publishers—in recommending my commentary as a true and accurate account of what lay behind your lines. You mentioned in your first letter to me that you know that I will be able to unravel the story and that—crucially—you leave to me the decisions on how I may explain your thinking, or indeed your life. This is what I have done and I make no apologies for it. If your life is not as you would have had it appear when you view it now, I cannot help you further.

I am desperately sorry that our lifelong friendship has descended to this silly argument, but console myself that I have provided a lasting legacy to you—through 'Dark Ashes'—and thus to all of your works.

I remain your friend while understanding that you may no longer wish to acknowledge me as such!

I send you all good wishes
Chris

Jane Hillerby, Commissioning Editor
L A M Peter Publishing Ltd

Dear Jane,

You will have seen Trystan's latest letter to me asking me to reconsider both the decision to publish and indeed my whole text. You will understand that I am both puzzled and hurt by Trystan's requests as I have been mentor and advisor to him over the years and would consider myself his oldest and closest friend. Trystan seems to be living up to his Wagnerian namesake and betraying those closest to him!

I continue to hope that this can be resolved amicably and that our work—yours and mine—will see the light of day on the date you originally proposed. I plan to visit Sussex early next month to persuade Trystan that there is neither evil intent nor anything slanderous in what I have written. I do not know why he objects!

With best wishes
Chris Armstrong (Editor)

Dear Mr Armstrong,

I am sorry to have to write to you with the information that my father passed away yesterday. I believe that he was thinking of you at the time as there was a sheet of his favourite writing paper in front of him with simply the date and your name as the salutation. In his hand was his favourite pen which, as the strength left him, fell to the sheets so that his last mark in this life was a spreading Royal Blue cloud on the bedsheet. Somehow it seemed an appropriate way for a man of letters to go.

I know from a conversation with my father in the summer that you had some project together—he did not say what it was—and I hope that you will be able to complete it and that its publication will be his final legacy to the world of literature.

You may not remember but we met once when I was quite young—I think it was in Switzerland where my father was staying at some posh hotel for a conference on his work. You will not remember, but you gave me money for an ice cream that it had not occurred to my father to offer!

There will be a quiet family funeral in my father's village church, although I suspect that the old man would have wished something less spiritual—perhaps more in the way of a funeral pyre!

Yours sincerely,
L-
For the family

Lamby, Lamby and Smith
London
7 January 2019

Dear Mr Armstrong,

I represent the executors and estate of the late Trystan Lewis. I understand that you were both his friend and the editor in charge of his last publication, for which reason I am writing to you.

I believe that there was some small friction between you and Trystan Lewis over the details of the work you had edited for him. Having read the recent correspondence between you, it would be dishonest of me to say that I am entirely happy with the advice that I am offering but, taking full account of the last letter to you with explicit instructions from the deceased's son, I can see no reason for the estate to stand in the way of this latest book, and we are consequently sanctioning its publication.

I have sent a copy of this letter to Lewis' publishers.

I understand that you are named as literary executor. Please feel free to call on our services should there be any issues with royalties, documents, etc.

You may expect to hear from the estate in due course as a minor beneficiary of Trystan Lewis' will.

Your sincerely,
James Smith, Attorney at Law
cc: Jane Hillerby, L A M Peter Publishing Ltd

Dear Mr Armstrong,

Following our meeting at my father's funeral and the small altercation later in the day, you may be surprised to hear from me again. It still strikes me as a little unseemly for you to have stood and read *that* poem to the friends and colleagues gathered during the wake in Cedars Gardens, but I understand that you were my father's friend of many years standing and that emotions were running high. You were quite right in thinking that a few words from you in the church would have been appropriate and I can only offer my sincere apologies for not having considered you at the time. I am sure you will appreciate the stress that the family was under.

But I have more to do in this letter than offer my apologies for something that is in the past. The family—my brothers and I—has been going through my father's desk and office, and has uncovered a range of papers, letters, drafts, notes, manuscripts and so forth. Boxes of them! Now safely stored in my attic. We have also been able to access my father's computer, where there is also a wealth of material—much of it, I think, duplicating paper copies. I know that my father had asked you, as both friend and editor of his last work to take on the role of literary executor and archivist, so I hope you can find the time to visit and go through the papers. At the very least, they may inform your editorial thinking.

For the moment, you will find all the poems and verses that we found on the computer, gathered together on the disc which accompanies this letter. I am sure you will find good use for them in your work on Dark Ashes. I should also like to add that, when you wish to see paper originals or consult other of my father's notes and letters, I would welcome you to my home in Sussex, providing you are able to give me few days' notice.

Finally, I hope that you will now consider me your friend.

Yours sincerely,
L-

Dear Chris,

Following our editorial board meeting today, I am pleased to report that work on *Dark Ashes* is on schedule for completion and publication on the agreed date next month.

There has been ongoing discussion during the editorial stages as to attribution. While respecting your intention to have the work published in Trystan Lewis' name, we all feel very strongly that it would be very unusual for a scholarly work which critiques and explains a literary work to be published in any other name than that of the scholar who researched and wrote it. You are, of course, already well known as a literary critic and editor, and we are pleased to add you to our lists.

I hope that you understand our decision and are pleased with the outcome.

With best wishes

Jane Hillerby, Commissioning Editor
L A M Peter Publishing Ltd

Book II
Above Dark Seas

A Life in Voices

Imagine:

It is 1964. It is the end of winter. It is early evening. It is dark.

A darkness lit by the inadequate lights on the warehouse walls and beneath the cranes. A darkness that casts long shadows. A darkness broken by the dim headlights of the little tractors towing their little trailers. Darkness. A darkness that is also damp with a drizzle that makes the concrete shine and leaves puddles between the gleaming wet tracks on which the cranes travel. Opposite the warehouse is the black wall of a ship's side lit obliquely by the light clusters hung over its rails, which do little to help the work of the men below. In the gloom is a bustle of movement. Activity. All around is noise: the whine of machinery, the rumble of the tractors, shouts, curses, the bump of cargo pallets, the clank of chains, occasionally the ringing bell of a moving crane.

The scene is repeated—with some variations—beside each ship lined up along the quay.

The scene is repeated—with minor variations—in ports around the world.

The scene is repeated—with little variations—for the next seven or eight years… before it is overtaken by the advance of big boxes across the quays and the cleaner, more ordered, computerised scenes of container transport.

It is a scene that will become surprisingly familiar to our ten young voices; a scene—with all its variations—that one of them will ultimately leave behind.

But for now…

Darkness. Rain. Noise.

This is our background.

Somewhere below decks on board a large black cargo ship moored somewhere in this scene, somewhere in these London docks, an officer in navy blue uniform, complete with cap, walks into the long, low-ceilinged room which is mess room for seventy of the ship's crew: seventy novices in their first few years at sea, seventy aspiring officers, seventy cadets, and strides up to its sole occupant sitting at a table mid-way down the room, who quickly places his coffee cup back in the small pool of cold milky coffee in the saucer and stands up almost to attention although he is off duty and not in uniform, pushing back his chair to make room. If he is surprised at the visit, he hides it well. He has only been back from his leave and on board for a matter of hours.

This will be his last trip on the ship and he is the senior cadet: he is tall—as tall as the officer—and well-built but running a little too fat: he is the Cadet Captain—Captain Trot—and likes to exercise his (limited) power... a bit pompous perhaps, but as on the last trip—for the next trip his responsibility will be the smooth running of this deck and the welfare of the seventy apprentices. Over the next few days 47 other cadets will return from leave and join the dozen already on board; will settle down into the old routines; will miss their homes (briefly) and their girlfriends (less briefly); will make the mess room untidy and noisy; and will begin running their parts of the ship again. And ten new cadets will join them.

This is the motor vessel, Otaio, on her thirteenth voyage—like all the other company vessels running under a Māori name: she has six hatches—three holds aft, and three forward, of the bridge and accommodation superstructure—and carries general cargo outwards and mostly frozen and chilled cargo homeward bound, and she is both home and workplace to the seventy cadets she carries as crew in her specially designed accommodation. The junior cadets act as seamen but as they grow more senior they begin to understudy the officers navigating on the bridge watches or those running the engine room.

They have each left one home and for each, the Otaio is now another—one where they live most of their lives. They soon come to know her well, to trust her and to love her: she is their new locus, the new centre of their little world in that much larger world they will discover, even their surrogate mother (although her master, the Captain, will never be regarded as a father figure!) and in some indefinable way she guides them and guards them from their new life's pitfalls.

The First Officer—the Mate—he who has just interrupted the Cadet Captain Trot's coffee—is currently in charge until the Captain returns from leave:

All right, Trot—there you are—ten new cadets coming tomorrow—get them settled in; make sure they know what's what—start them on some easy light duties—they'll be a bit lost to start with, especially the ones who have just left home and not been to pre-sea school. God! Half a dozen softies straight from their mother's tits—we'll waken them up I suppose. We'll have to! Make sure they all have cabin mates who will keep them on the straight and narrow!! You're the Cadet Captain—they have to look up to you and know they can come to you if they are lost! Make sure you tell the Watch Captains the same when they get back! We've got six days before we sail and the rest of the lads will be back in a couple of days.

Captain Trot

Yessir!

Chief Officer

Good. Come up and see me tomorrow when they have all arrived. I don't expect any will turn up before lunchtime—they're coming from all over. The nearest comes from Colchester!

[the Mate leaves the mess room—
There is a slight pause—

Captain Trot (muttering)

Back from leave a day early to do the bloody mate's paperwork and play nursemaid to a load of trippers. Bloody hell.

[He looks at the list that he's been given and amuses himself
thinking up nicknames as he finishes the rapidly cooling
cup of instant coffee he had made himself after the
scratch dinner served up to the few cadets on board.
He returns to his cabin with the list and compares it with
a plan on his cabin bulkhead:

Let's see which bunks in which cabins are free... Hmmm... Christ! What's his name—Trystan Lewis? Lewis... He can be Louis... cabin 15 with Neddie and Brian;

With a name like that we'll have to call him Ding—cabin 12;

Hah—Blake... he can start off as Sexton: cabin 20.

That's an unusual name, I bet they end up calling him something like Eppi or Peppi...—that's it, Pepsi... and he can go with Jim and Tom in cabin 21. God, this is boring—who is on gangway duty tonight? I might go ashore for a bevy. Erm…

Ah! I give up: Woody can go in cabin 30;

Chris what? so far as I care he *can* go west… Westy… he can go … w-cabin 10;

Richard what? Baldy? No! Bet he's a Dick with a name like that, cabin 24!

Fritz can go next door to him where Tony used to be and this Dave character can go with them as well, and finally,

Bill Ch…—he's short! I'm going to call him Plum! Whoops! Cabin, dum, dum dum, cabin 9.

Right! I'm off ashore. If the mate's got any more chores he can whistle!

Smithy! Don't lean on the rail while you are on gangway duty. Stand up straight! I'm going ashore for a while. If any cadets arrive take their names to give me when I get back. If one of the new trippers arrives—they shouldn't, they're due tomorrow—show him to his cabin and settle him in. Get Kiwi to help—he's a friendly face on board! Here's a list of their cabins!

These, then, are the ten principals in our play—the ten whose lives will interweave with and flow on, around and over—be guided by—the final player: the voice of the sea, the voice of all ships—Otaio. This will be how it begins for our ten—for all of them their future is unknown, even unimaginable. A new stage of their lives is opening and we shall watch their entrances and exits, and the parts they play: we shall see one man in his time play many parts…

Imagine:

This is how it begins…

It is early Spring, it is afternoon: dismal dock drizzle hazes everything beneath each yellow damp lampglow and dulls the docker din and the winch whine as cargo is loaded. A smell that is a mixture of the salt sea, old oil, steam, old and filthy dock water, smoke from the barge tugs, sweat and stale beer is held down against the ground by the wet mist. A line of huge ships can be seen fading into the distant haze along the damp grey dock, in the drizzle grey, dusk grey, smoke grey dither above the loading labour. A tug whistles.

Unknown pallets swing overhead and the boy ducks unnecessarily as his father points him at the gangway of the nearest ship. The black bulk is high in the water towering over his anxiety, the square opening just below the busy deck, the opening that will swallow his innocence, the ship's unknown, unwelcoming maw waits at its top. Further astern unseeing portholes glimmer a suggestion of warmth but his only focus is the upright figure waiting at the gangway's top. The senior cadet, Captain Trot stands an unwelcoming guard welcoming new cadets; stands at the ship's gun port door more terrifying than any cannon; Cerberus at the mouth of a future which is the death of all he has known—of his childhood. He is here at the beginning and at an end.

This is how it began…

They have travelled by train, by underground and finally by taxi to get here: his mother and his father guiding him for the last time—guiding him through a geography he does not yet know. All of his life, they have guided him, directed him, helped him, pushed him, and now their time is at an end. Neither the boy nor they have recognised this change. Today they will leave him and travel back by taxi, underground and train to the little South Wales port where he grew up.

They will be silent on the journey, nervous for their son, wondering at his new world, and at his ability to join it. At his ability to be a part of it. But for now, they stand on the dock side with their only son, beside the huge sheds, beside the huge ship, beneath huge cranes and amongst the huge noisy rush and bustle of the Royal Albert Docks; like him wondering at the transition too suddenly forced on them: the parting, the futile advice, the small figure with the too-large cases struggling upwards. Onwards. Away.

This is where they are. This is now…

The men are working; the foremen, the winch men and crane drivers, the lifters and pushers, the shouters and swearers, the big and the small, the surly dockers and the smiling, cheerful dockers. Little tractors pull trailers with a variety of cargo to sit beneath the swinging crane hook, waiting; elsewhere the men rush around guiding, pushing, catching, lifting, heaving pallets and nets into the place where another hook will swing down from the ship. Every docker seems to know what to do. And the boy feels envious—not of their industry, but of their absolute certainty. Of their unity. Their rowdy shared male labour is completely alien to him and makes him even more nervous of his future. And his ability to cope with it. He makes his goodbyes. His mother kisses him awkwardly and—equally awkward—his father shakes his hand and mutters something about 'being good'.

The boy squares his shoulders, at least mentally, and can be seen, with little conviction and still less enthusiasm, to trudge the last few feet to the gangway.

Unaided he drags his two cases up the steep incline of the gangway and gives his name. He vanishes from sight. He is shown to a cabin with three bunks that he seems to have to himself—for the moment at least. And left. Left to what? To unpack, you idiot—the voices in his head are constantly questioning what he is doing—the few words that Captain Trot had said had scarcely been heard, had helped little and had left him uncertain about… about everything … does he have duties? Jobs he should be doing? Is there food sometime? Where else can he go on this confusing ship? But mostly, just, who will tell him?

Captain Trot… _Cadet_ Captain Trot… back on the lookout by the gangway for the rest of the first-trip-at-sea apprentices—the new shell shocked, shocked from their cosy homes, ship shocked, work shocked, soon to be sea shocked innocents—stares across the dock dreaming gloomily of his own first trip to sea and wondering how the latest offering will ever survive.

Otaio

I sensed his arrival and his nervousness on the quay. I knew that his parents offered little comfort there—_could_ offer little comfort. His mind was swamped by his next few steps… by the unknown that—he understood—was unknown to them too. He is not the first innocent to leave home under my care! I have been in service for a few years and sailed a dozen voyages with my crews of cadets—Captain Trot was just one to have been here before this nervous lad: lots of first trips into the unknown—lots of boys sailing away from home—excited boys, nervous boys, scared boys, confident boys. They grow up fast! Boys no more…

Captain Trot

I had been to pre-sea school so things weren't so strange for me. Definitely wasn't as innocent and shy as this one!

Voices from the past—Roy first—can be heard

Do you remember me—I joined two trips before you.

Jamie

I was much earlier—trip 2, I think. The first few trips were strange—the ship trying to find its routine for us.

Pete

I hated it—left after a couple of trips! I'd just met Meg and she had gone on into the sixth form…

Meg

Ah! School was no fun after you left! I couldn't study for dreaming…

Mrs Beynon

Oh but we had trouble with Megan after Pete left—couldn't get her to focus. Never knew a girl get it so bad. What did he have to run away to sea for? And then he came back and she had another reason to skip classes!

Meg

I never did! AND I got my 'A's before I went to work in Pete's old man's factory as secretary! He'd invented jiffy bags with padding made from macerated newsprint. He made a fortune!

Jamie

I'm Junior Third now and I tell you getting my ticket was a lot easier for me than for some. Some I met from other companies had spent their apprenticeship being used by the mate as an extra seaman and got no help from the officers with their correspondence course!

Phil

Those cabins were a bit small for three weren't they? No room to move—I had quite a big bedroom at home in the farmhouse—that silly design with the L-shaped cabin with a second square cabin within its two sides—although I suppose it did mean each cabin got a porthole… even if one was down a narrow bit with nothing in it except the desk.

Mike

Yeah—we shared a cabin. *And* that nurse in Auckland!

Jinny

Hey—don't be like that—it was two different trips! And you were both as useless as each other—always the fun of the chase and then a lot of clumsy fumbling! Your parties—what did you call them, 'jags'—were infamous amongst the nurses at the hospital… we knew we would be starting in the lounge with some dancing to records and then sneaking out somewhere for a kiss and we would probably end up missing the food. Which one of you took me up to the crow's nest before discovering there was no room up there to…

Phil

That was me! But we had some fun, didn't we?

Mike

Well, it was forbidden to take a girl back to the cabin—although plenty did… although with three to a cabin you might find the door locked when you got there! And you might run into the schoolie doing his rounds! But *that*! That was mad!

Matt

We had some really bad weather my first trip—barely got out of the Channel—half of us new boys were sick! The waves were breaking over the bridge! But we didn't do any deck work for a week!

Tim

I felt lost for the first few days after joining! No one seemed to take charge and it was all odd jobs—a bit of brass polishing, loading stores, cleaning… and then there were all the shore trips to get our Seaman's Cards and Discharge Books…

Fred

… and then the group photo! All of us trippers with rigid caps sticking out over our ears. I could hear Mam laughing when she saw it—she always said the uniform made me look daft!

Mam

We were proud of you, love! But that cap…

Tim

Yeah, my parents were so proud they made me wear it down the avenue to wear in the leather shoes—*they said*—but they just wanted the neighbours to see me! Mind you—I'd never had leather soled shoes before.

The voices from earlier trip fade away with Dannie …

You should have seen my photo on the Seaman's Card—I looked like a baby convict!

… and Phil

Ah… but the joy you felt as your first voyage ended!

Otaio

I think the boy was hiding from his future. At the beginning of the voyage there are others: new cadets have arrived and some old hands are already on board. But he has to take the first step—to venture out of his cabin. Eventually he has to—nature has her own way of forcing introductions—and he has to get rid of his cases and hang up his oilskins in a locker.

Bren

Do you think he'll be alright, John? He looked so small and lonely on the gangway. Unsure! I don't think he really wanted to do this!

John

It's natural—he's never been away from home before… and you spoil him, pamper…

Bren

No! Not pamper!

John

Well… he's always been looked after—that's all I meant. It's time he started finding his own feet—he won't be the only one! Remember the war forced us to grow up fast—this'll be like that… the making of him—he'll come home in a few months full of tales of foreign ports! Louis will be OK once he settles in!

Bren

What did you mean, 'If you can't be good, be careful'? I didn't understand…

John

Hah! Father's advice!… Look! Here's a taxi…

Otaio

And so they left! I do not know, but I imagine it was not an entirely comfortable journey home—the mother upset and struggling with the idea of her first child leaving home, with the idea that he would be unable to cope, with the idea that they had not prepared him well! And the father frustrated at the little help he had been to his son, worried that he had left him both socially and sexually naive, that he should have said more, at his inability to comfort his wife, at others in the carriage watching.

John

Bren! Bren—don't cry… he'll be fine! It'll all be strange for all the new lads at first—they'll all be in the same boat [he grins, despite himself].

Bren

John!

John

Well, you know what I mean. He was bound to be nervous and unsure as he went on board—it was a big step for him, a step into the unknown—but didn't the joining letter say there were nine others joining for their first trip today? They'll get to know each other quite quickly and then it'll be them against the rest!

Bren

Against! Do you think the new ones get bullied? I was just thinking that cadet at the top of the gangway was there to meet him. I thought how nice of him! He looked nice.

John

Not 'against' like that! I just meant they would form a natural group—all in the same

Bren

Don't say it again!

You're probably right. But it doesn't stop me worrying … and missing him! The house will seem empty without him!

John

Look! We're in Cardiff already—only another hour! We'll get a taxi at the station to get home quickly! You'll see… everything will be fine tomorrow. And they're not sailing for a few days—he'll probably 'phone home—there's bound to be something he needs!

Otaio

By the time they had travelled that far, Louis had probably discovered and eaten dinner in the mess. But he had explored a bit earlier. He found the mess first but no food was being served yet; he walks through the accommodation—back towards my stern down the starboard side and finds a schoolroom and then carries on across the aft end of the cadets' accommodation where there is a lounge and he introduces himself rather shyly to someone who is also on his first trip and then back towards his cabin past a smaller lounge come library—he pauses to see what there is to read—and the engineer cadets' schoolroom. Things are falling into place.

Woody

Do you remember me, Louis? I was sitting there, alone in the lounge when you crept in. You looked as lost as I felt. As desolate.

Louis

Yes, Yes I remember. I remember. *You* looked as if you belonged. Then Kiwi came in and I had a chat with him and the padre from the Seaman's Mission who was doing the rounds!

Kiwi

Second time he's been on board since we docked in London—I suppose the company encourages him to visit with all us youngsters on board!

Plum

We all felt strange—although Fritz and Pepsi, Dave, Dicky and Ding had some preparation—they had been to pre-sea schools—Pangbourne or... They had been away from home before.

Sexy

At least you all arrived with your gear—my trunk got put in the sheds. It nearly got loaded as cargo! I only found it the next day.

Westy

We were all innocents. And none of us knew who else was new. None of us knew what came next!

Ding

Some of us moved into cabins with old hands—we were lucky, we learned a few things. I don't think we thought to pass them on, though!

Louis

Even when I was told things, I didn't know what they meant! What did it mean being in Starboard Watch C? What were stations?

Dicky

You could have asked! You were always quiet!

Louis

Lost in confusion!!

Fritz

But we got down to things, didn't we? Settled in? Work began at any rate.

Captain Trot

Attention!! Captain's Inspection!

Louis

That was my first confusion! No warning and no idea what I was supposed to do as the First Officer knocked and came into my cabin on the second evening…

Fritz

GROTCO! That's what he came to be… but at this stage he was the feared boss: Get Rid Of The Chief Officer!!

Captain Barny

Settling in alright? Good, good.

Louis

And then they were gone. Next cabin. Repeat.

Repeat… Ah!

Repeat! That was life: repeats of repeats! Washing decks, cleaning cabins, polishing brass, bridge watches, school, correspondence course, washing decks, cleaning cabins, polishing brass, PT…

Datey

Ah, but you lot were slow at learning Morse!

Sexy

PT! Do you remember Paddy—cross little Irishman of a PTI in charge of keeping the accommodation cleaned as well as PT!

Louis

I remember slipping over in some sort of PT relay race on deck and grazing my leg. It became infected and I had to have time in bed with a hot poultice and antibiotics before the doc got around to lancing it! That would have been OK if he hadn't demonstrated the spray anaesthetic and squirted it in my eye. I thought he had blinded me! And he thought I was some sort of sissy for shouting when he thought he had only squirted the anaesthetic on my arm! I had a few more days on bed rest—which gave me time to catch up with some letter writing! And my infamous diary everybody joked about!

I think I managed to sound reasonably happy in my letter home—I hope I did—but in my letter to my best school friend, Chris, I think I sounded as depressed as I had in my letter to him from London before we sailed—talked about everyone else knowing more than I did in the new and unknown world of the ship! I was on light duties until after we got through the canal. It was only when I got back on my feet that I began to settle in. Sort of!

Chris

Your letter from London scared me a bit! I don't think I've ever heard you so down! And your letter from Colon wasn't much better! What with your bad leg—that sounded like you might have had quite bad blood poisoning—and your escapades on board! I was never sure that you were cut out for the life at sea... did you really see yourself as a Captain?? Certainly didn't sound as if you were a real sailor in your letters!!

Strange that it was always you who kept the sea travel going in that endless adventure story we wrote together when we were younger! I think we ended up sailing around the coast of Croatia and Montenegro didn't we?

Louis

I had forgotten those stories, Christo! They were real *Boy's Own* or *Eagle* adventure stories weren't they? I suppose reality was alright really! It got better! But I felt like a fish out of water for a long time. I think the other cadets sensed it too—I was always the odd one out, I think!

And, actually, I was lonely! And when I slept, I dreamt—not happy dreams of home but dark dreams that plunged me into a terrible abyss of fear. And when I woke it was as if I was in shock. Utterly alone and scared to sleep again, scared to waken to another day. I was lost. I watched the others live but life washed over me. I had no idea how to find myself.

I needed to be alone but hated the loneliness—sometimes I got up and walked on deck in the dark... in the silence with just the noise of the wind and the waves, alone between the stars and the dark maelstrom that was swallowing me—that silent well of my loneliness and inadequacy. I think I spent a long time not talking much—not engaging. Really, I needed *not* to be alone and to become a part of this new family. Time passed—I survived—I sank into the depths and rose again! Gradually the sun came out!

Otaio

I watched over those early dark days, knowing that he would discover his new self eventually. But I worried for him. For his inability to become a part of me. For his inability to enjoy this new companionship. This new life.

Chris

Things got more serious back home too… but not like that! You went away to sea and the sixth form wasn't great—I had to work really hard—it wasn't like O Levels… but you remember that—you did a term in the Sixth while you waited for your ship. At least you were doing something different… but I suppose at least I was still living at home for a couple more years—Dad was still off down the docks all the time surveying ships and Mum kept me in books with extra pocket money and a library ticket! Literature was always my thing… and it got me to Cambridge eventually! I was a bit older than you when I left home… perhaps a bit more ready for it! Although it was still strange at first.

Louis

I don't think I was ready for change—my folks hadn't really prepared me for it—we never really talked about what it would be like… but that was them, I suppose. They didn't really do feelings! And I was young!

Chris

I think at least up until 'O' Levels, we just lived for the day… not much forward thinking or planning needed! And your folks didn't really push you into focussing on your future, did they? Even after you had told me you were going to sea you never talked much about it! I had no idea what you would be doing on board until I got your letters!

Hutch

Chris kept us all up to date with your adventures—those of us in the Sixth, at any rate. I think we were all quite jealous that you had escaped—were seeing the world… I've no idea what our boyish minds made of that phrase… we were all innocents! But you had got away from that school—we had two more years of assemblies, hymns, choruses, missionaries' talks, being 'saved'…

John

Yes, but school changed after you left—it all got more serious! We had to work where we had cruised through the fifth form! Do you remember when Mrs Rose gave the two of us bad marks for discipline in maths and felt she had to explain why to us. And you said we only ever talked after we had done the set work and had had no wish to disturb anyone else—you barrack room lawyer, you—she almost apologised!

Mrs Rose

I don't think I did! And who is 'she'—the cat's mother?! But you were very polite and deferential when you explained—I didn't see you as a barrack-room lawyer—I suppose forecastle lawyer would be more apt, sea lawyer they say in the States—and I had understood why you were talking—you two always finished first but I don't think it occurred to you that you were disturbing the others. And me!

Paul

My folks moved away after O-Levels so I went to a different sixth form in Hull and we lost touch. I was sad about that—we'd been good friends for a couple of years! But I often thought of you on a swaying deck with waves breaking all around and a sextant to your eye... or something like that!!

Louis

You were a bit ahead of yourself there! I didn't even see a sextant for about eighteen months—you should have seen me with a wooden leg (no parrot) hauling on ropes or scrubbing decks! And as for seeing the world—I missed out on the first bit of my education as I couldn't go ashore!

Fritz

You missed the nightclubs in Colon! That *was* an education! We had our eyes opened there!

Louis

I was supposed to spend my time off learning the Rules of the Road at Sea. We had to learn them by heart for goodness sake! I think there were 31 of them weren't there?!

Westy

I would never have believed what those women did if I hadn't seen them myself!

Plum

And the heat of the canal as we made our way slowly through the locks! Good God! It was humid! Sweaty! It was good to drop the pilots at the other end and get under way to blow some air around the ship!

Louis

And that was when I did my first bridge watch.

Otaio

For the cadets, my days are divided into four: an hour before breakfast, morning, afternoon and early evening—the first of which will be either PT, seamanship lessons—knots, splicing and so on, or deck scrubbing. Then watches are assigned to school, working below decks or on deck, or to one of the three bridge watches, where, as juniors, they either keep lookout, learn to steer or are on standby.

Bosun

You lot go down to Lampie and get some chipping hammers—then starboard side of number 2 hatch

Bill Gray

I'll take Louis and Plum to rig the safety lines

Lampie

Hello Tarny—you all chipping the deck? You'll need these and some scrapers. How many of you are there—is that enough?

Otaio

Down at my very stern was the paint locker: and the stores ... down a little hatchway in the deck. This was where Lampie ruled! He called everybody Tarny—Jim Collins was the kindest old boy—he limped a bit and seemed to be about 70—but always looked after whichever cadet he was given for the week as his helper. It was a cushy job helping him!

Louis

We rigged the rough weather safety lines for'd of the bridge in the morning, tightening them with bottle screws, and I did my first bridge watch in the afternoon. I remember it well!

Jim Mac

Och! Ye'd remember the night watch better! You relieved me as lookout twenty minutes late!

Louis

You're lucky I got there at all! Nobody told me…

Jim Mac

Just because you had helped rig the safety lines to hang on to! Didn't it seem odd that the door onto the foredeck was dogged tight?

Louis

Yes, yes. I know.

Jim Mac

But still you…

Louis

I was so worried about not doing what I was supposed to… and I knew lookout was kept on the fo'c'stle… so…

Jim Mac

But the waves were breaking over the foredeck…

Louis

Yes, yes. I was really scared—if it was like that at the aft end of number 2 hatch… And then the beam of the Aldus lamp from the bridge hit me and a megaphone told me to get the hell up to the bridge! I think the officer of the watch thought I was a simpleton!

Jim Mac

Well…

Otaio

The fo'c'stle—lookout duty right in my bow could be a peaceful hour or two on warm starry nights. Lookouts were supposed to see lights of other ships before the officer on the bridge—although he had the advantage of height and his horizon would be further away than theirs. Lookouts rang one bell for a light on the starboard bow, two to port and three for dead ahead, and they had to repeat the time signals that the helmsman rang on the bridge. Sometimes on calm nights they could lean over and see dolphins playing beneath my bow… or phosphorescence on the bow wave…

Ding

Sometimes I used to take my guitar up there with me—at least it kept me awake!

Westy

I remember your twelve-string guitar! We used to sing along to it sometimes—the Clancy Brothers—The Shoals of Herring—The Irish Rover— There's Whisky in the Jar…

Ding

And a bit of Dylan!

Otaio

Come, it's night time, creep up to the bridge—the officer is pacing around and one of the senior cadets is talking to him in low tones about navigation or his correspondence course while the third junior cadet of the watch is at the helm—steering at my wheel. There is an autopilot at the front of the bridge but the cadets steered anyway. And they had to keep within a degree of the set course even when the sea was fighting them to push us off course! Spin the wheel against the turn, wait to feel my yaw steady and then spin the wheel the opposite way to stop sliding back past the course and zigzag all the way to New Zealand! Like most ships, I can play games! And, every half hour, sound the bell... from one bell half an hour into the watch to eight bells at the end!

And in all the cabins alongside number 4 and number 5 hatches, all the cadets who were not on watch slept like babies! Coughed and scratched, grumbled and grunted in their sleep. The cabins warmed as the night wore on and the air smelled of teenage testosterone, of sweat, of dirty socks. They dreamed of home, of girlfriends left behind, of girlfriends they were heading back to, of girlfriends not yet found; they dreamed of time ashore, they dreamed of their next leave, they dreamed of their last leave; they dreamed of girls. No cabin was entirely still, entirely quiet. But they slept, and snored and grunted...

And in their dreams the voices of the cadets who had gone before them whisper and call out to them.

First Cadet

My cabin! My bunk!

Second Cadet

Mine too before you. Snug we were there, in Auckland with pretty Kitty

First Cadet

I remember Wellington!

Third Cadet

She was my first! I had never...

First Cadet

Whatever they say, I bet none of them had before they joined! I was innocent as new dew.

Fourth Cadet

I bet you soon learned! God! But the bunk boards rattled! Anybody walking past would hear the fun.

Fifth Cadet

My girl was as tall as me and beautiful… lovely, long blond hair—her breasts were so soft, I…

First Cadet

Polish the brass! It's rounds this morning. Tidy the life jackets on top of your lockers and straighten the caps perched on top! Tidy up!

Sixth Cadet

Rounds are tomorrow! Now is the time for…

Fourth Cadet

Too true! I wonder if Susie is still nursing in Timaru—you're going there. I'd like to see her again. I'd like to…

First Cadet

How can you sleep when you don't know the first eight Rules of the Road—you've got a test tomorrow… How can you…

Fourth Cadet

Every vessel shall at all times proceed at a safe speed so that she can take proper and effective action … Rule of the Road for Jags… Every cadet shall at all times proceed at a safe speed so that he can take proper and effective action…

First Cadet

Dream on bunk mate!

Otaio

…but I say, they slept, snored and grunted and slept and dreamed until roused by a call—perhaps they were the next watch and would be woken quietly by the standby of the watch before, or perhaps they were not on watch and were woken by him by mistake, or perhaps—the lucky ones: they could sleep through until the morning call for PT or washing decks or seamanship lessons.

Woody

Seamanship classes before breakfast—under the forecastle in Bill's locker bouncing up and down as the waves pitched the ship around trying to splice a wire hawser or a bit of boat-lacing or a mooring rope! We learned to whip ropes too!

Fritz

Wasn't it you who fainted? Bill thought you were sleeping and shouted at you and you just slumped…

Dicky

And then back for a wash before breakfast, picking up flying fish from the deck sometimes! But we ate well—full cooked breakfasts, three-course lunches and dinners served to the rest of us by the week's mess peggies…

Mess Peggy

The soup is… something you can't do: split pea… and then there's fish and chips and sponge pud!

Westy

That was Barry, wasn't it? Always the same joke! But the mess peggies got to eat their food afterwards and had even bigger portions! And at smoko sometimes we got tabs—I suppose we would call them tray bakes now! We ate well enough!

Louis

I used to quite like washing the plates in the little kitchen behind the serving hatch! Big breakfast after we finished!

Woody

And then back out to whatever duties we had. On deck or in the accommodation or with Mr Barton or—later trips—Datey in the school room. Two hours of work on our correspondence course which covered everything from ship construction to ship stability, navigation…

Fritz

And we always ended up with half an hour of signals—usually Morse, reading from the little pinprick of light at the front of the school room as Datey sent from the Morse key on his desk. One of you sat with his back to the light while the other read the seventy-five-letter blocks of random numbers and letters out. Louis loved that!

Louis

I knew the Morse code OK—A dot dash, B dash dot dot dot and so on—but couldn't ever recognise the characters from the flashing quickly enough!

Otaio

And all this while in their little South Wales port, in their little semi-detached house, in their little safe world his parents knew nothing of his life, of his trials, tribulations, little failures. Of his dark times. Milk bottles clinked on the doorstep. His sister went to school in the Convent and came home to her studies before tea. The baker came—a large white and a Hovis, please. Groceries were delivered. His mother shopped, cleaned and cooked—washing in the twin-tub on Monday—cooked again … lunches, or baked … then buttered and sliced the bread thinly to eat with home-made jam, with paste or sandwich spread for tea.

His father came home from the bank, pecked his wife on the cheek and sat down at the head of a table no longer pulled out from the wall to allow a fourth place and helped himself to some bread-and-butter before peeling and quartering an apple with his penknife. Sometimes, he read *The Telegraph*. Life went on. The same life. Quieter. There was cake for tea.

John

It was certainly quieter without his pop music—his tape recorder in his bedroom or on the radio down here! And even on the TV… what's it called Top of the Pops? Can't get away from it! And it's always so loud. I think he's deaf.

Bren

I miss the music—I quite liked it! Most of it! Oh, John—do you think he's alright? He sounded quite down in his letter from London asking me to send some drip dry shirts instead of those silly collar-detached ones. Still, it was nice to have a letter! I wonder when we'll hear again.

John

It was only his second day! He'll be fine! Stop fussing.

Otaio

And in his cabin below the bridge, Captain Barny wondered about his cousin's son. Had he been right to encourage him to come to sea... encourage his cousin, really, he thought ruefully—he had never been sure about the boy's wish! And now here the lad was on his ship! Of course, he had had a private meeting in his cabin once they were at sea to tell him there would be no favours, no special treatment—they had both known it, of course, but the meeting had to be seen to happen. He wasn't hearing wonderful reports but it was early days yet. He hoped! Captain Barny thought he had better keep a weather eye on the lad from afar. His mother would probably expect it! He would write a letter from New Zealand.

Bren

It was good of him to write... I'm not sure I took much comfort from the letter though—it sounded as if Louis was taking a while to learn the ropes—to settle in. And he is not much good at learning things by heart either! Oh dear, I worry about him!

John

Don't! Some boys take longer to find themselves than others. He'll be alright! We weren't strict enough with him at school—he always gave up on learning things by heart... but seemed to get away with it! I sometimes wonder about that school—whether we made the right choice!

Bren

Well, at least his sister is doing OK—she'll go into the sixth form! She's even left the tea table already to do more work! But she misses having him around too, you know. We must make an effort! Louis was OK in the prep school—his marks only went down when he started in the grammar school. He's not stupid—I just think the teaching didn't inspire him, didn't make him *want* to learn more! The teachers didn't... Oh, I don't know! Try some of this jam—I quite like it—I might make some more if I can get any more fruit.

226

The blue tits had been at the milk bottle tops again today—when I see the milkman to pay him I'll ask if he can put a slate on top of the bottles when he leaves them.

John

Hmm! Yes. Did you see this in the paper—Johnson's got some civil rights act signed into law—no segregation... that'll go down well, I don't think. I see trouble coming—good thing Louis doesn't sail to the States!

Bren

How would I have seen the paper—you had it? That's another thing—we should have made him more worldly wise, more aware of world affairs. He could get into trouble in another country. Oh, dear. What have we...

John

Nothing! New Zealand and Australia are quiet peaceful countries. They're never in the news! He'll be fine. I keep saying...

Bren

Yes, I know—but saying it doesn't make it so! Do you think I ought to ask my cousin, no! I can't... perhaps he will anyway. He did write!

Otaio

Twice a week cabins were inspected. Mid-week was the First Officer's inspection and at the end of the week it might be the Captain accompanying one of the other officers, sometimes the doctor—he had precious little else to do. Decks had to have been scrubbed, brass polished, not a speck of dust had to show up on the Mate's white gloves when he ran them along some un-thought-of surface, everything had to be tidy. In fine weather cadets were expected to be out of the accommodation; if it was stormy they had to snap to attention as the officers entered their cabin.

Fritz

It was all a farce really—pretending to be the Royal Navy. Of course Barny was RNR—and flew the blue ensign in port—but the regime was all down to GROTCO!

Woody

And the grand old tradition of church parade for officers and crew—and especially cadets—on Sunday mornings always took place—on deck in fine weather or in the anteroom otherwise—when we all had to be in clean shirts, number one uniforms, clean shoes, pressed trousers, cap on straight...

Ding

Oh, hear us when we cry to Thee,
For those in peril on the sea!

Pepsi

Well that was right! Real peril if you weren't turned out smartly for the Captain's inspection parade before the service!

Plum

A prayer for the ship...

Captain Barny

...Bless our endeavours and our labours and look after us on these your seas...

Woody

... and one for our families at home

Captain Barny

...Oh, Lord, look after our loved ones; keep them safe while we are away from them...

Dave

A Bible reading—might be one of the other officers or one of the senior cadets had to do that

Dicky

Then wise and uplifting words from the old man while we all tried to stand still 'at ease'

Westy

A blessing—huh!—and we were dismissed.

Louis

It was the payoff for Saturday evening. Lying around on deck under the stars watching the mast sway lazily beneath them and a rubbish film projected onto the small canvas screen rigged up during the afternoon. I think the first time we had the film on deck it was an old short called Twinkling Fingers about a couple of pianists, a 'carry on' film or something—might have been "Watch Your Stern"—probably was! And then another short about that racing driver, what was his name? Fangio!

Sexy

Rubbish film it might have been but it was the highlight of the week! Start again with boat drill on Monday, like as not!

Fritz

At least we got a bit of a weekend if we weren't on watch! There was deck tennis to play... deck hockey... And life at sea wasn't so bad—hard work, but...

Ding

Depended what jobs you were given! soogee-ing or Teepol-ing the paintwork to get rid of the salt and the rust smears, chipping rust off decks, painting rails and the decks we had just chipped and oiled, painting derricks... painting anything—winches, winch houses, the funnel, the accommodation block... we had to keep the ship looking smart!

Louis

I'm a bit deaf and I'm sure it was the noise of the chipping hammers did it. No ear protectors back then! And do you remember covering your hands with Vaseline and using cotton waste dipped in the white paint to paint the rails? And then washing the paint off our hands and arms with paraffin! Lampie's ever-ready bucket of paraffin!

Plum

Do you remember when we were chipping the foredeck and the Mate came down to see progress and one the seniors on the chipping machine, *apparently* completely unaware of his presence, changed the angle he was working at and sprayed rust-red dust all over his whites. He was furious!

Louis

But the Mate couldn't say anything—with all that noise nobody would have heard him arrive and with those goggles we had and his head down over the machine he wouldn't have been seen either! That's what Bones said anyway! There was so much noise when we were chipping—you couldn't talk. It was just two hours to be lost in your own mind—you start off trying to remember the latest Rule you had been trying to learn and then your mind glides to the easier shores of some book... and ah! we are in "the watery part of the world"—will we see the white whale as the oil smooth sea slips past our noisy work—what great beasts—leviathans—lie beneath us?

"Call me Ishmael," he said as he stepped aboard. Could he have known, could he have guessed, what lay in store... well, no more than we! What might I have said as I came dragging my cases to the top of the gangway? "Call me Trystan!" I don't think so! Now I think our very own Starbuck will have his revenge as the voyage wears on—no one could have guessed how soon.

Sexy

Greasing the rigging and the derrick's guys and wires... and the mooring lines. Yeah, that was fun. Not!

Westy

And holy-stoning the wooden decks—usually before breakfast... real work began later.

Woody

Unless there was a boat drill or a fire drill. In fine weather we would have to turn the boats out on their davits while wearing those bulky lifejackets. Or fire drill...

Louis

The first fire drill we did, I was wearing the breathing apparatus and we had to rescue one of the senior cadets—was it Bones or Lammy—Lammy, I think—and he made it really difficult by going completely limp! I think we banged his head on the bulkhead as we went round one corner! Serve him right!

Pepsi

And always we had to keep our cabins clean and tidy! GROTCO was always on top of us! Do you remember the case of the dirty towel? That was his revenge!

Dave

Oh yes! He took in all our towels because someone had handed in a dirty, torn towel at linen change. How many days without towels was it? Bastard! He made old Trot assemble us in the lounge and lecture us until somebody confessed! Surprised he didn't turn the water off!

Otaio

And then we got to the coast—New Zealand—and life changed again! We crossed the international date line and moved suddenly from Thursday 9th April into Saturday 11th and—just as suddenly—the coast came into view. We arrived at Wellington as one of the company passenger ships—the Rangitoto—left, and had to anchor until a berth was free the next day. The mail came on board at the anchorage with the pilot and Louis had eight letters from home! On anchor watch that night, one of the senior cadets showed him how to use the compass to take bearings and make sure we were not dragging the anchor and drifting. As if I would!

Imagine!

Land of the Long White Cloud. Land of the Māori. An unknown land. A land seen from the horizon appearing from beneath cloud. A land seen from an anchorage. And then a land seen from the security of the ship moored to a wharf outside of the town. A land that is alien. Unknown.

This is his welcome:

It is early morning. It is fine with a blustery wind. The anchor is raised. The ship swings. Flags get tangled around stays and have to be cleared. They open hatches ready for the cargo to be unloaded. The ship noses through small waves in the green-blue sea and is nudged against the wharf by tugs. They are in New Zealand! Almost before the gangway is down wharfies are swarming on board and stashing their sandwiches and rain gear in winch houses and behind the winches.

Strange accents—and occasionally words in a strange language—can be heard. Men take charge of derricks, winches, hatches: of the deck! Below them on the wharf other men are waiting impatiently for the first cargo to land. This is what the last weeks have been all about… but none of this activity—this final delivery of cargo—has anything to do with him! The quiet organisation of life at sea is rudely interrupted. He can only keep out of the way!

Imagine!

He has never been out of Britain before and suddenly he and the other cadets have weeks ahead of them in New Zealand. For some of them—those who missed the nightclubs of Colon—it will be their first chance to set foot on dry land anywhere for about six weeks. The routines they have struggled to get used to at sea are about to change: for the more junior cadets gangway watches—the tedium of standing smartly at the top of the gangway for hours, relieved only by the hourly fire rounds—replace bridge watches.

They discover that as trippers, they have to go ashore in uniform and that they have to report out on shore parades on the hour—and woe betide them if they are not smartly turned out—and report back in when they come back on board. Around these realities life goes on much as usual working on deck— although there is some variety as painting over the side can be done in port… balanced over the water alone in a Bosun's Chair or with one of the other cadets on a 'stage' held away from the ship's side by a couple of transverse stretchers.

They have to learn quickly how to secure ropes to their planks so that they can raise and lower them… without dropping themselves in the sea! On one occasion when they were painting under the flare of the bow where he had kept lookout so many times, bowsed in against the side by a rope, they had climbed up the hawse pipe on the anchor chain at smoko!

Imagine!

They will travel from Wellington to Auckland, Port Chalmers, Timaru, Bluff and finally Picton, stopping some days in each port. Long enough in each for them to have a chance of going ashore. And as they arrive in each port, hatches have to be opened—maybe down to the lower hold, and derricks topped ready for use, ready to be swung out and set up for the wharfies.

Imagine going ashore in uniform and walking around Wellington, or around a small town like Port Chalmers where the wharf leads directly onto the short main street! Even in the country's second city, Auckland, Queens Wharf leads straight onto Queen Street—one of the main streets of the town. Imagine the novelty of these towns with their pavements covered over by the shop-front canopies, towns where all the cars seem to be half a dozen years out of date! Imagine the strangeness of it all!

Imagine having to wear dress uniform with black bow ties and cummerbunds for the dances that are sometimes organised if they are in port long enough. An afternoon spent decorating and preparing the anteroom—coloured bulbs, tables for food, LPs and a record player if a local group couldn't be found—the accommodation suddenly quiet as everyone gets dressed up, and then groups of girls arrive by taxi and are ferried down by the Gangway Quartermaster (who will miss all the fun). Everyone to be ashore by 23:00!

Imagine watching the unloading of a huge variety of cargo—a few cars, crates of CKD (Cars Knocked Down—unassembled), steel in all shapes and sizes, cables, machinery, pallets of bricks, salt, whisky, Royal Mail from one of the chilled rooms that could be locked, chemicals, fertiliser…

And then loading frozen lamb carcasses brought on board in slings of about forty at a time—odd to see these sliding down wooden chutes from the warehouses or out to the sides of the holds from the central area under the hatch where they had been landed, frozen so hard that they might as well have been wood as they were picked up and dropped into the cargo nets, boxes of frozen lamb joints, or chilled butter and cheese…

Imagine!

Their first jag! The afternoon off for all cadets to prepare the anteroom and the trippers' nervous anticipation of receiving the girls—nurses usually—on board. Every cadet had to appear in dress whites—a short white jacket, navy trousers, cummerbund and bow tie. For the first dance, the shy Louis was glad that he was on gangway duty! He may not have understood his father's final words, but his parents' influence on his behaviour and—despite his comprehensive school—his lack of close encounters with girls left its mark on his behaviour. Louis wrote to Chris that they were "to have a formal dance in

Auckland and shall have to dress up in 'Whites' with a bow tie and a cummerbund... and dance I suppose! Me? Dance? I sort of hope I'm on gangway duty!"

Otaio

The last port before we set sail for home again was Picton—just across the sound from Wellington. We had covered a reasonable amount of New Zealand and been on the coast for more than six weeks altogether so my lads are getting restless and thinking of home. They have had fun on the coast, had some good trips ashore, bought souvenirs, discovered New Zealand beer, met New Zealand girls...

I think some embraced the new experiences more than others. Some had to make a larger leap of faith.

Ned

Hey Louis, here's my camera—come onto the wharf and take a couple of shots of the finish of the inter-watch whaler race—we're going to have the finish line near the end of the Ferry Wharf.

Louis

OK! I was only reading! Should have been learning the last couple of Rules really, so any excuse! When are you starting?

Ned

Now! Paddy and Tom Sawyer are going to tow us out to the start with the crash boat now. You've got a couple of minutes—we don't row that fast!

Otaio

This was their last half day before sailing—some of the seniors had gone ashore but most were on board reading, sleeping, washing underwear, socks, shirts, or writing letters to girlfriends and family! A few were even doing their correspondence course! Captain Trot has permission to stay ashore for the night with family friends. The whaler race has been won by Port Watch—much to Louis' disgust and the afternoon is winding down towards dinner. From the alleyway outside Louis' cabin come some gleeful shouts and a lot of banging and scraping...

Louis

What the hell's going on out there?

Ned

Don't ask! Its Lammy and Bones working on their revenge on old Trot after he stopped them going ashore to meet their latest girls yesterday because their cabin was such a dump. Keep your head down!

Bones

Come on Terry, push! Lammy'll have the hose ready by now.

Terry

It's heavy and it's nearly as wide as the alleyway. What's the rush? I'm trying not to scrape the deck or the paint!

Bones

The mate or Paddy might come down!

Lammy

Come on you two—I've got the hose through the porthole and the end of the old mooring rope too!

Ned

Oh, my God! That's what they're planning! They're going to put a forty-gallon drum in his cabin and fill it up with water from a hose through the porthole! Sounds like they are going to coil a rope on his bunk for good measure! Bet they get the drum so he can't open the door when he gets back!

Louis

How the…

Ned

Oh Lammy'll get out through the porthole and up onto deck… slight risk of getting caught but he'll be OK… until Trot gets back! He'll guess who it was!

Captain Trot

[walking through the accommodation,
banging his fists on the walls, shouting

OK—everybody in the Anteroom! Now! Turn to! Turn to! Now! Everyone! Anteroom, everybody! Out of your cabins! Turn to!

[Ten minutes later...

Captain Trot

You're all here with me and the Second Officer because—as some of you may know—while I was away I was locked out of my cabin by some wag filling an oil drum with water right behind the door! So instead of a last evening off or a last evening ashore—some of you may have wondered why you weren't allowed ashore when you reported out—we are going to have a two-hour debate! We'll cover all sorts of things but nobody gets to leave! I think two hours will be long enough for some of my *friends* to sort out my cabin!

Cookey

A good prank but I don't want to hear of anything like it again. Aside from anything else accessing or getting out of the cabin via the porthole is incredibly dangerous—we could have lost one of you into the harbour... and that would be difficult to explain! The Cadet Captain has persuaded me to take charge of this evening without referring it to the Mate—so consider yourselves lucky! Right. To start with I want a debate about who has the hardest time on board the deckies or the engineer cadets. Brian—start us off—what do you think?

Westy

I'd forgotten that evening! I wonder why! I reported out at 18:30 and was refused and sent back down—I think it was Pepsi, Fritz, Plum and me going ashore! We were all crammed into the Anteroom for two hours while Bones, Terry and Lammy sorted out that cabin and scrubbed it out before joining us for the second hour of the debate! God, it was boring!

Plum

Yeah—I fancied a last beer ashore and a game of snooker down the Mission! Peps said he was going to beat me this time!

Fritz

That was it—we sailed the next day… or should have done, there was no shore leave, but in the end we didn't leave until the day after—rain delayed loading and a consignment of cargo didn't arrive! So we sailed late on Friday afternoon about 26 hours after we should have left! Still stations were quick and we were back down for tea!

Woody

Back to the humdrum routine of life at sea for five weeks! Boring!

Sexy

Heading for home and some leave, though… I wonder how long we will get! Bet we don't pay off until we get to London though—we've got cargo for Hull first, haven't we?

Ding

Yes—I saw it being loaded! Not much of it though so probably only a day there. With luck! We get two leave parties don't we, so only half of us will go on leave on arrival in London! Tough on the others!

Ned

The second leave party may get a chance for weekend leave—some of them might, at any rate! Depends on whether you live close enough!

Sexy

I should be OK! Aren't we going to dry dock after we unload—might get quite a long spell of leave.

[There is a slight thump and shudder and the noise of the engines dies and picks up again but quieter than before.
For the next hour or two we proceed on one engine!
The helmsman counteracting the uneven thrust from
a single screw with two turns of port wheel!

Dave

Here we go again! More delays! No more excitement until Pitcairn—I suppose we're calling in their again—I wonder who will be on duty for the crash boat to take the Doc ashore—who will be Doctor's mate!

Dicky

It'll probably be the same lot as last time! Be nice to have some fresh fruit though. It WOULD be nice if they sent some water out too—I'm getting fed up with the shortage—everybody trying to fit showers and dhobi into the short time it's on! What's the problem?

Louis

Didn't someone say a tank had got contaminated so we only have half as much as we should have? It was certainly a bit salty to drink the day before they announced the rationing. And the dried milk wouldn't mix up properly!

Dave

You said it would be me in the crash boat again didn't you! It's not much fun anyway—you don't get ashore unless you are the Doc's mate—that was Floyd this time… and the Doc wasn't ashore for long—you probably took longer getting those two slings of dunnage over the side than he did ashore! I saw the boats floating them back in through the surf to the beach as we came back. Did somebody buy me some bananas?

Westy

Yeah—and oranges! Enough to see you through to the canal!

Otaio

And so life on board goes on—cadets on watch, cadets working on deck with the Bosun, cadets working in the accommodation with Paddy, cadets in school with Datey. More steering, more painting, more scrubbing and polishing, more correspondence course. And signals. The Mate got over his flu a couple of days after they left the coast and returned to his normal pleasant self! The Bosun, Bill and Lampie had all got used to the trippers and had begun to treat them as grown-ups. Paddy… well, he was just Paddy…

Woody

We seemed to get to the canal very soon! And went through without having to anchor and wait. Although we had to wait for a couple of hours before we got to the last lock as rain was making visibility so bad. We had the usual posh salads for the canal—the entree was crayfish and the main course was turkey…

Louis

That's right! Never found out why we always had salad for the canal transits! Probably find the pilots demanded it! Or maybe it was the old man—so he could eat easily on the bridge! Whatever—it seemed to give Paddy indigestion—he was in a foul mood the next day! I was mess peggy and Bones had only just laid up the tables when he came in, lifted a corner of one table cloth and claimed there were crumbs on the table. He went right through the mess pulling the cloths off each table and sending the crockery all over the place. We had to clear it all up and lay up again!

Sexy

And a couple of days later we were in Aruba! Oranjestad, not Curaçao as usual as we had some apples to unload… so no swimming in the sea pool across the bay. And we had to shift from a berth to the oil terminal after just a few hours! Looked a nice little port…

Westy

Wouldn't have minded a run ashore! The Third Mate went ashore. There were some nice looking women wandering around selling fruit! Not apples! Obviously!

Ding

The old doc was busy this trip—apart from Louis and his leg, he had two trips ashore to tend Pitcairn mutineers and a couple of days out of Aruba we had a call from the Coptic for medical help… and I was crash boat crew!

Louis

Don't remind me about my leg! I was on watch but Ned took over the wheel—as a more experienced helmsman—as we came up to the Coptic. We kept station with them about three cables away with them about two points forward of the starboard beam while the crash boat took the doc over…

Ding

…and waited for about an hour while he tended to the wounded seaman. It was best part of two hours before we were back on board and under way again!

Louis

Yeah—I had to take over from Ned again for the last half hour of my time on the wheel! While I was standing by I was sent to get a sample of the seaweed in a bucket! There was masses of it floating around us—Sargassum Weed, Cookey said, we were in the Wide Sargasso Sea. No idea what he did with it!

Fritz

And then it wasn't much longer until we were approaching the Channel… but a bit before that Louis said he saw a whale surfacing several times quite close to the ship but didn't have time to get a photo… so we'll never know! The next day the Old Man held a meeting in the anteroom instead of the Sunday service and told us what was happening for our leave and who would be the Cadet Captain and the Execs. next trip.

Westy

Two leave parties, the first paying off when we got to London—no surprise there… apart from the fact that we are having a whole month off! Tough on those—not me—in the second leave party who will have to wait another month before they get to knock off. They'll have to take the ship round to Falmouth for dry dock.

Sexy

I was first leave party, too! But first we were in Hull—the ship swarming with trainee customs officers all determined to find some smuggled tobacco or drink! They went over the ship with a fine tooth comb but I heard that some of the greasers had created a pipe in the engine room from deck to deckhead out of those round tobacco tins and painted it and covered it in grease so it looked as if it had been there forever… that never got found!

Louis

We were only in Hull for about 36 hours but I managed to get in touch with an old school friends whose parents had moved to Hull and he and his Dad came down to the ship, had a look round and took me out for a look round Hull and a cup of coffee. It was good to catch up with Paul again!

Woody

And then before we knew it we were taking on river pilots and moving slowly up the Thames! For some of you the anticipation of paying off and going on leave was almost too much! All I had to look forward to was London and Falmouth! Over the years we would come to discover that getting into the London docks always takes forever... this time we didn't have to anchor, but even once the pilots were on it is a slow journey up river and then stations last ages as you manoeuvre through the locks, drift slowly up the dock nudged and pulled by tugs, and find your berth.

Louis

We topped the derricks on the aft hatches as we went up river! We had the company inspection later in the morning and then a pep talk from one of the managers before pay off in the mess after lunch. Still couldn't go though as the guy with the travel chits had got stuck the wrong side of a lock! Finally shared a taxi with the second electrician and an engineer and headed off to Paddington Station.

Otaio

It's always a strange time when the lads... or some of the lads... leave! Unlike the officers and seamen they don't get replacements or stand-ins—they just go... and behind them life goes on as if nothing had happened—cargo comes out of the hatches and is swung ashore and vanishes into the warehouses—the wharfies take over in port! The cadets' accommodation seemed quiet with half of them away!

Louis

It *is* strange—you spend so long looking forward to getting off the ship, going on leave and then a few days after you get home, you want to be off again, doing something! A couple of lazy days getting up late and not doing much apart from recounting tales about the whole trip time and time again and then it was time to hit the beaches! Catch up with school friends! Play tennis! Life was good! But so many evenings were taken up showing photos to my parents' friends!

And it turned out that as I was home I could join my parent's holiday in North Wales—touring around mid and north Wales in my father's little A40 car! I remember on the way home through mid-Wales we were to call at an old ruined abbey—Strata Florida. We never made it! Half way up the lane to the abbey we were met by an advancing flood from an overflowing river and had to back up quickly!

And then suddenly a month had gone by and I had to find my way to Falmouth.

That month in Falmouth was great! The ship was already out of dry dock and tied up alongside the outer wharf and there wasn't much work to do—gangway quartermaster of course and a bit of work round deck and in the accommodation keeping it all clean and tidy—but there was plenty of time to explore the town and its surroundings. I even got home for a couple of weekends! Sometimes, one of the officers would take some of us out in the crash boat fishing.

We found a couple of good pubs quite close to the dock—no surprise there! And there was a fantastic ships' store-cum-marine antique shop-cum-chandlery called The Bosun's Locker that I often visited just for the experience! I don't remember ever buying anything there! Although I did buy a couple of leisure shirts on one trip into town—a posh maroon one with a satin lining to the yoke and a green check lumberjack's shirt that I got ribbed about on board!

Once when I telephoned home, I heard that a family who had been our neighbours when I was a toddler were holidaying just along the coast and had invited me to call in one evening. Rang their landlady to pass a message with the ship's phone number and had a phone call back the next day.

Pepsi
[looking over his shoulder as he wrote in his diary,
"Phone call from Mrs M.—
arrangements for tomorrow!"
What's this? Affair with a married woman, Louis!

Louis

I knocked off at lunch time the next day and got changed and walked westwards along the cliff path until I got to the road into Maenporth and saw the house sign "Blue Seas" where, walking down the drive past the main house, I reached a bungalow at the bottom of the garden overlooking the sea and spent a pleasant evening with the family. I used to play with the oldest daughter when our gardens had backed onto each other and I was three and she was five! It was a little strange meeting her again, along with a sister who must have been twelve, and a younger brother and sister.

Mrs M.

Come in, come in! You'll remember Marianne of course, this is Kathy… Nicholas… and Elizabeth! I'm so pleased you could take some time off—we were planning a swim this afternoon at Kennack Sands near the Lizard—do you have to be back by any special time or can you stay to supper?

Louis

That would be great—the last swim I had was in the harbour by the ship—not great! So long as I am back by about ten, it will be fine—thanks. Are you sure that's OK?

Mr M.

Of course—I can run you back—it must take best part of an hour to walk!

Marianne

Did you bring a swimming costume? We've been to Kennack before—it's a lovely sandy beach but not many waves because it is on the East coast of the Lizard. Water's clear though!

Louis

Great!…

Although she said little to me that afternoon, that sister—Katherine—must have noticed me… but little did I know how important she—and indeed Blue Seas, and the whole family—would become in my life a few years later! We had a very pleasant afternoon with a visit to The Lizard after the swim and some time on the beach; then we went back to Blue Seas for a snack supper before Mr M.

drove me back to the ship. If I remember rightly, Mr and Mrs M. came down and visited the ship one evening a few days later—Marianne came as well, but not the rest of the family.

Otaio

It all repeats, one trip after another! It all gets more familiar, more normal, more run of the mill... the sun shines and they work on deck if they are not on watch—painting, chipping, cleaning, maintaining my decks, masts, Sampson posts and derricks, winches, winch houses: varnishing, greasing—regular old salts now who knock off for a cup of tea and a smoke mid-morning sitting on the floor under the darts board at the end of the mess because they are still in their dirty "shit-gear"—their working clothes splashed with paint and grease despite their weekly wash...

Woody

Do you ever get the feeling we've been here before! This same bit of sea on the way to the Suez Canal, for instance?

Louis

I remember one trip we called in at Genoa and Piraeus before we went through the canal—was that our second trip?

Pepsi

Yes, I think it was. Or the next one!

Louis

Then it must have been the first time we were in the Med! Anyway! That's right, we had been to Antwerp and Rotterdam! And then on to Genoa. It was a little bit foggy as we headed for Greece. I was on deck as we went round the tip of Sicily and I saw this unusual little sailing vessel heading west in one of the patches of fog—not thick fog, more of a mist or a haze and it didn't seem to be worrying them, almost as if—for them—it wasn't there—they had full sail on and the wind was favourable for them—they passed down the port side quite fast and disappeared. Odd!

Fritz

Come on guys—smoko is over… stop dreaming, Louis! Back to painting or GROTCO will be down on us again…

> *[They leave the mess grumbling and head*
> *for the aft end of the bridge deck where they had been painting*
> *the vents beneath the funnel*

Otaio

That was a good trip for the cadets—the company laid on a coach trip east along the coast to Santa Margherita Ligure and Portofino—a pretty little fishing town beneath the sixteenth century and curiously named Castello Brown—while they were in Genoa, and another to the Acropolis while they were in Piraeus.

Louis

I remember lots of huge yachts in Santa Margherita and a wonderful ice cream in Portofino! The sea was only a few inches lower than the pavement that separated it from the fronts of some of the colourful houses! All very picturesque.

Fritz

Do you remember we bought some very rough cheap Chianti in one of those straw-covered bottles and shared it one smoko while we were in Genoa… don't think GROTCO would have approved of that! Still… one bottle between eight or ten of us—we didn't get much each! We must have had a few days there!

Sexy

I remember wandering around the Acropolis with you, Louis—I think I took a photo of you with your camera! And we walked past a government building or palace with the Greek Royal Guard in dress uniform—with those pom-poms on their shoes and that weird high-stepping march—on guard outside… more photos! God! I got drunk in Piraeus one afternoon—you got me back to the ship, Louis!

Louis

And then it was through the Suez Canal, Aden for bunkers and across the Indian Ocean to Oz! Got to Fremantle exactly two weeks after we left Aden!

245

Woody

It was a short stay in Fremantle—about 24 hours I think—and then on to Melbourne, Sydney and Brisbane before we headed off to NZ!

Louis

That's right—a long stay in Timaru and then onto Napier… where we had Christmas before carrying on round the world to head home via Panama at the end of December! I remember getting a letter from Chris in Napier—he was at university by then—and suddenly he had a girlfriend!

Chris

I found the love of my life while I was at Cambridge—although she returned to her native Albania without me—but I don't think Louis ever experienced a similar love—even when he was on leave! Actually, I'm not sure he ever really had any girlfriends. I know he told me after his third trip to sea that he had plucked up the courage to ask one of the girls he had worked with at the local nurseries on school weekends out for a walk when he took the family dog out, and after that they had gone together to the cinema and out for meals when he was on leave. But they were never close—I think she was just a 'companion' and she had other boyfriends.

Louis

Chris is right! I did ask one of the girls out but what followed did nothing to end my innocence and although we went out together several times to see films at the cinema and even for an occasional meal, I knew that she had a 'real' boyfriend and that while I was welcome to put my arm round her shoulders as we watched the film, nothing further was on offer! I think I probably kept the relationship going out of desperation—on leave, I was lonely… especially after you went to university. My parents were desperate for it to be a real relationship—they made me bring her back to coffee after the cinema one evening—I knew she didn't really want to, sensing an attempt to make our relationship something more than it was—but she was a good sport and came anyway.

Bren

I wonder what happened to her. I liked her! Louis went out with her for a few leaves before he met…

John

Well we set that up, didn't we… although the idea never occurred to us at the time! But you're right I liked her too.

Bren

Yes! I thought you did!

Louis

It was her sister who sold me my first car!

Chris

They only wanted to see you settled and happy! I don't suppose you talked to them about girls or about her! And they wouldn't have talked to you about relationships! Maybe I should have… but while our own relationship was so close in some ways, it made it difficult to talk about sex!

Louis

Well, you didn't in those days, did you?

Westy

We had some rough weather soon after we left the coast—it had obviously been expected as we put the storm covers over the for'd winch house windows and the bridge-front windows aft of number 2 hatch before we left! In the end it wasn't so bad and didn't slow us down much.

Louis

The next trip was a similar pattern—we discharged in Oz (Melbourne) and then loaded in NZ! We left London in mid-February, spent a month on the coast finishing in Opua, New Plymouth, Timaru and Picton—two whole weeks there, and then home via Pitcairn, Suez and Curaçao! Back on leave at the beginning of June… home for my birthday!

Otaio

By now the ten were settled in and further batches of new boys had joined—Louis was no longer a junior or a tripper! And he was beginning to feel at home on board after the best part of a year! And so it all starts again—they go home on leave, they come back from leave, there is another company photograph of everyone in uniform in front of number 3 lifeboat and another trip begins!

They did five or six trips with me in all before being sent off in ones and twos to join one of the other company ships for a final voyage before they went ashore to do their Board of Trade exams.

Floyd

Do you remember that the two of us failed our seamanship exam in Liverpool and had to retake it a week later? We did our lifeboat exam OK in the morning and then I went in first and then you followed me—we both failed and then he seemed to soften up and everyone else was in there for about half the time we had been... and passed! A few days later we had to report to the Shipping Federation and spent a whole morning revising with their instructor in a room equipped with a model hatch with derricks, a working model of a steam winch, a steering wheel, and so on. We both took the exam in the afternoon and passed with no trouble!

Louis

That was a relief! But it turned into a good day out... with minor celebrations when we got back on board! But the real laugh was the First Aid exam on the Aussie coast, which consisted of a lecture about the need to act quickly in an emergency followed by some role play where I was injured and bleeding from an artery—the rest were asked what to do and—to a man—they hesitated!! The doc said something about the need to act quickly before I bled to death and passed us all!

Floyd

Typical! Sounds like the same doc we had the trip before!

Westy

We were all wondering how you would do! When we did the Efficient Deck Hand after you two had been in, we were scarcely asked anything difficult—couldn't work out why you had been in so long and failed!

Ding

The next trip was the one when we stopped half way through the canal for the north-bound convoy and had a chance for a swim. And then a bit later the steering gear jammed and we bounced off both banks before we stopped… then we had to stop again while a diver was sent for to check for damage!

Louis

I remember that—it was difficult getting back on board after the swim—I climbed up the mooring rope but my hand slipped out of Jim's at the top and I fell back into the water and then—like the others—I was winched up standing on a cargo hook—Fritz… you sent me right up in the air before letting me back down to the deck! And I was on watch… but not on the wheel, thank God, when we hit the bank later! Captain Barny was not amused! He had to use the engines to get us back on course without much room to play with!

Sexy

I remember Fritz messing around on the winch!…

Fritz

…Sorry, Louis—couldn't resist!…

Sexy

… but that was the long trip, wasn't it—we were on the coast from the middle of August until November!—two and a half months!! I don't think there was a port we missed out apart from Darwin! And we did Melbourne, Sydney and Brisbane twice for good measure!

Westy

Plus Townsville, Cairns, Adelaide and Fremantle to end up. But we earned some money on the coast cleaning up the empty holds and sorting out the dunnage!

Ding

That was a sign we were more senior now! That and the change to our activities on watch—now we were understudying the officer of the watch and navigating. It depended which watch you were on but you would probably have to take the noon sight or do stars at dawn or sunset.

Westy

Or if we were on the coast it would be fixing our position by bearings and using the radar… it finally began to feel as if we were doing what we signed up for—especially as we got to eat in the saloon with whichever officer we were working with!

Dave

And while we were in Melbourne the second time we had a company coach trip to Mount Dandenong and a wild life park where we could walk in amongst the kangaroo and koala bears!

Louis

I was on watch in the Indian Ocean after we left Fremantle and standing on the bridge wing with a huge albatross floating level with me. It was just like in 'The Ancient Mariner' which we studied at school, where the "Albatross did follow, / And every day, for food or play, / Came to the mariner's hollo"—the wandering albatross often follows ships in the southern seas—perhaps simply to pick at their leavings but more likely in order to take advantage of thermals and wind drift. This one fixed me with its beady orange eye and just stayed there as if he was attached to the ship by a wire!

Pepsi

Bloody hell, Louis! What's with the poetry? Give over!

Louis

I remember on the way home—can't remember whose birthday it was—we held a party in the port alleyway because the cabins were so hot and we sailed close to a thunder storm when one of the flashes of lightning lit up a ship on the horizon—it looked as if it had hit the ship—it would have made a great photo if someone had had a camera ready! Not sure how we came to notice it—we were sitting on the deck drinking beer—it was always tins of Tuborg or McEwans, that was the only choice—and singing to Ding's guitar at the time! Some of us must have been on watch, I suppose, but the rest of us had a good time! We always had parties on a Saturday so we could sleep it off on Sunday if necessary…

Plum

… not much chance to sleep it off as there was always the church service and one watch would have to get up and hose down the decks!

Otaio

So they grew into their lives! They grew up and became the men they had dreamed of being! Although between times spent playing at being an officer life went on as usual in the accommodation, in school and on deck! Paddy ruled the mess peggies below decks, Datey ran school sessions and the Bosun, Bill and Lampie ran the deck work! All ten had changed cabins at some point and some of them would become Execs for their final trip and rule the roost over a new bunch of trippers! And when they had time off they sun bathed, read, wrote letters home, played cribbage or table tennis or darts, ate copious amounts of food, saved up beer rations for cabin parties when someone had a birthday … or slept. Slept and dreamt. Dreamt and slept!

Fritz

We called in at Piraeus and Valetta on the way home and paid off in London for Christmas at home! Re-joined in Liverpool in mid-January.

Louis

Yeah, we had a good long leave… I think it was after that trip that I bought my first car! I loved that little MG Midget, with its fibre-glass hard top that I could use when the weather was poor! And it was fast—I remember driving around the Cowbridge bypass once—which led downhill to a right-hand bend before it started back uphill out of the valley—and I was doing about a ton at the bottom of the hill and only just made it round the bend! I think it was the next leave that I drove over to Cambridge to see my best friend, Chris, who had just started his degree.

It was great to see him again and to catch up with his news and fill him in on my news since I had last seen him about six months earlier. I met his girlfriend, who was reading English too… but he was in the middle of an essay—on Trollop, I think—that was due to be handed in so I was only able to stay one night. But we chatted into the small hours! He was very much the scholar in his gown! But my spare time at sea had allowed me to get in some serious reading and I felt I was quite well read in my own way—although I had never read any

Trollop and had got into a lot of Russian authors such as Sholokhov, Tolstoy, Pushkin and Dostoevsky that Chris didn't really know.

But we talked a lot about literary criticism and the need to study the authors I liked in more detail. It would not be an exaggeration to suggest that Chris' advice greatly enhanced both my reading and my literary skills... and altered the selection of books I took away with me! I began to read more poetry.

Otaio

Call me Otaio! It is an echo from the past! In some years—never mind how long precisely—as I sail about the watery part of the world—I am become the voice of all ships! There is nothing surprising in this. I speak for the sea.

Sexy and Louis joined the Haparangi for a voyage before they went ashore for their ticket leave. They joined in Liverpool...

Sexy

We were ABs! It was during a seaman's strike and the company used us to get the ship up to Glasgow to load whiskey. Once we there we turned back into cadets!

Louis

And were given the job of making sure the whiskey was stowed without loss! Some chance! The wharfies had the measure of us—they all came on board with bottles of lemonade and expected to be able to dilute it with whiskey! If we complained too much and got in their way they simply knocked a case on the hatch coming as they swung it inboard so that it fell off the pallet and when it smashed the cardboard case acted as a perfect sieve to make sure they didn't get glass in their drinks!

Sexy

Do you remember that waitress we met in a cafe in Sauchiehall Street—I fancied her and she fancied you?

Louis

God! Yes! I remember. We waited for her to knock off and the three of us spent some time together... but I found the whole behind-the-bus-stop thing embarrassing!

Once we left Glasgow things settled down—we had a great Chief Officer who treated us as junior officers and made sure we learned a lot practising navigation and cargo work. He also made sure we got included with the deck officers when he had drinks in his cabin! It was a good trip!

Sexy

… and he made sure we had fun on the coast—he sent us off with the Chief Steward to a brewery when he went to order supplies… and to an abattoir, as well!

Louis

Somehow he got us to Waitangi—did he come with us or was it one of the third officers, I can't remember—to see the Māori Treaty House—I had to write up the visit for the house magazine—my first attempt at publishing!

Sexy

Then we came back to London and paid off and went our separate ways for some leave followed by some time at College preparing for our Second Mate's Ticket—you went to Cardiff, I was in London… and both of us, I guess, spent weekends at home!

Otaio

Louis' famous expertise in signals came back to haunt him and while—after a month or two at college—he passed the written exams and orals with little trouble, he failed signals. Fortunately you could hold onto your passes for six months while you completed the rest of the exam. Eventually Louis became an officer and went back to sea after that long shore leave.

Louis

I also passed a radar course in a little hut out on one arm of the harbour entrance—a week chiefly remembered now for the excellent salad and egg sandwiches that the Merchant Navy Hotel provided and which we ate on a bench in the sun behind the hut! Everybody who took their ticket in Cardiff stayed at the 'Merch' by the station and we walked through the city, past the museum and the law courts to the College every day. There was a favourite pub that had a grey parrot on the bar conveniently situated on the way back for an early evening drink! It's strange what you remember! I can clearly see everyone in the hotel TV lounge watching Lulu sing 'The Boat that I Row'!

Imagine:

Passing written examinations in ship construction, ship stability, and navigation at the 75% pass rate required, followed by an oral exam—again passed—and the whole thing blighted by Morse code! You could re-take the signals exam every two weeks... and Louis did! Until he passed!

Imagine!

Suddenly finding yourself heading back to sea as a Junior Third Officer! No matter how much he had prepared for it, the responsibility of being in charge of the ship for eight hours a day suddenly seemed a little awesome! As it turned out, he wasn't left alone on watch to start with as—being the fourth and junior officer—he was on the four-to-eight watch with the First Officer. It was only when he had settled in that he kept part of the watch alone.

After a couple of trips as Junior Third, Louis graduated to the eight-to-twelve watch as Third Officer and did three or four more trips—including a short one to South Africa and back—on the Piako, the Huntingdon, the Tongariro and the Northumberland. One trip they tied up in Auckland behind one of the company's passenger ships which was under the command of his uncle and he wandered over to pay his respects...

Captain Barny

Well hello, come in! Good of you to pop across now we are both tied up one behind the other in port—I've got the use of a car, come over tomorrow afternoon if you want to and I'll take you up the coast to some hot springs. Bring a costume!

Do you want a coffee?

Did you have a look round as you came on board—the passenger ships are a bit different from yours! All sweeping staircases, mirrors, grand saloons like on the Queens... well, the passenger decks are. The crew live a bit more like you!

Louis

Your cabin is a bit bigger than our Captain's cabin—but I suppose you entertain?

Captain Barny

Oh, yes! It's expected! Look, you only just caught me! I've got to go ashore in a moment to meet the Agents—come over about two tomorrow—can you get off then?

[The following afternoon...

Captain Barny

It always takes longer to get here than I expect! I try and fit in a jaunt up here most trips—it's nice to get away from the ship every now and then! Joan found these thermal baths when she sailed with me about ten years ago. Ahh! That's good—watch it! The water's bloody hot if you're not used to it!

How are you doing now you're not a cadet any longer? Life got a bit better?!

Louis

Yes, I'm OK now. Third Officer—almost time for my next ticket leave! But you're right—that first trip wasn't good. I joined with nine other trippers: half of them had been at pre-sea schools… of the others one had been a scout leader and was well used to being away from home and the rest were all much more confident than I was! I was the smallest and the least assured! My parents had done very little—nothing really—to prepare me for a new life—a life away from the security, safety, cosseted comfort and care of home.

They had not pushed me into finding out about life on board—what would be expected of me, that sort of thing. I think I knew there would be a correspondence course to do but had forgotten so it sort of came as a shock that there was more school work! And I knew nothing of girls! Even you hadn't offered any advice! Not even the suggestion that drip dry shirts would be better than collar-detached ones that the uniform list described! You know my parents—they followed Monneries' list to the unthinking letter!

Captain Barny

I was probably over anxious that you shouldn't be seen to know more than anyone else!

Well! It all worked out in the end! Here we are in New Zealand! What do your parents think of your life?

Louis

I suppose they are quite pleased to be proud of me! I go home and tell them tales of the sea, tales of foreign ports, of cargo, of storms. They are hungry to hear what I do and what life at sea is like... but I suppose they have no real concept of what it is like being away for months at a time... or perhaps they do—they went through the war... that must have been even worse, I suppose. But they don't seem to think of me being away time and time again.

Captain Barny

You think too much! Get yourself a woman! Let's get changed and get back!

Otaio

And so life as a Deck Officer went on!

What did he remember of those trips? Different ships, different captains—some good, some more difficult, different colleagues, different friends, different ports, different cargoes!

Louis

The cargoes were mostly the same one trip we loaded apples in Tasmania, another butter, cheese and lamb in New Zealand... and once we loaded great twenty-foot baulks of timber in Bunbury in Western Australia. They used to grease them so they would slide into position in the holds—you wouldn't have wanted to get in the way of one those when the wharfies got it moving!

Bob

I bet you remember Bunbury for another reason too! You nearly rolled the hire car when you didn't see that bend coming... we stopped astride the railway line and had to be hauled off before the train came through! Amazingly the garage got us back on the road and we carried on—I think I drove after that—into the vast wooded area that our cargo had come from and some of us climbed the Gloucester Tree in Manjimup—the highest tree for miles with a lookout platform at the top to watch out for forest fires!

Louis

Yes... that could have been nasty! We had that big automatic Ford and I don't think I felt the speed... and the road was dead straight for miles and then—

without warning—turned ninety degree sharp right into the town! But we got away with it—somebody was looking out for us!

We bunkered at Durban on the way home that trip—I remember going ashore with some of the engineers and getting drunk! Another trip we went to Cape Town! And another trip we had a weekend in Bluff with no cargo work being done and the Second Mate organised a trip to Queenstown and taught me to ski! I think that was the trip that the Captain took us through the Galapagos on the way out and cruised slowly into a bay to take soundings so as to improve the charts.

I sailed with some good Second Mates—Ric who took me skiing, and Peter on another trip, both made sure I helped with the cargo planning in preparation for my time as Second Officer. As it turned out I went to OCL where the whole thing was computerised!

Ric

That was a good skiing trip—I had my New Zealand girlfriend—soon to be my wife, Christine, with me and there were a couple of the engineers came with us, but they weren't interested in skiing. You learned quite quickly on the nursery slopes, I remember… but I probably shouldn't have taken you up on the ski lift and left you to follow me down! Still you survived!

Dave

We did two trips together and became good friends, didn't we? And you followed me into Container Fleets and we did another trip together! I think I tempted you to change companies… not the least by promising to leave a string of oil drums behind me so you could find your way on the first trip you were Second Officer and in charge of navigating your way to Oz!

Louis

I remember that conversation—cheeky bugger!! And when we got back into London, I went to the OCL offices and did one of those weird psychological tests where you had to pattern match and stuff… and they gave me a job after I got my ticket. But first there was some leave—it was summer again—and then back to college and more Board of Trade examinations!

Otaio

They paid off after a couple of days in port. He did not know it—and probably wouldn't have guessed it—but that arrival in London signified a whole new stage in his life. Everything changed for him in a moment!

Louis

I remember that final trip before my ticket leave very well! Particularly the last hour of it when my father and sister came to pick me up and brought with them someone I had last seen on a beach in Falmouth… studiously ignoring me! Now, some four years later, she had grown into a lovely girl and there was an instant attraction—a spark that passed between us… particularly as I discovered that she was to holiday with my family for a couple of weeks! By the time we had driven to South Wales, the spark was buzzing with anticipation!

Imagine:

It seems extraordinary that the young sailor can have been entirely innocent, but that is certainly how Louis would have described himself when he left home to join his first ship… and some years later, too. Looking at his story, we can see the strictly religious upbringing foisted on him in which although love, let alone sex, was never discussed he was somehow aware that love before marriage would constitute a dreadful and unforgiveable sin.

His father's awkward parting words (unexplained) to him as he boarded his first ship, "If you can't be good, be careful" did little to help. So, while in his early time at sea opportunity must have presented itself, he was shy of women and did not find it easy to form even innocent friendships with girls…

Imagine!

The effect of being suddenly and unexpectedly thrown into close contact with a lovely girl who was in awe of him, who wanted to know him…
Imagine!

Louis

There were times when I had to leave her behind, as I sailed away again. Agonising, horrid goodbyes. Followed by the torture of separation. She looked to me for help but there is little that I can offer beyond the assurances of eternal love, the promises to return soon… she cried out in the agony of parting.

It could not go on!

I remembered the scene that has been repeated so often—all those ports, all that cargo loaded—that too familiar scene with all its variations, and I finally recognised my ultimate destiny is to leave it all. To start anew!

And now, with the sea behind me?

Now I wonder, as I so often have before, why we keep these things in our heads—an endless archive of our dreams, of our lives—which, from time to time, we review, subconsciously deciding what memories to keep and which to repress. With each retelling, the volumes are rearranged, some falling off the shelves, others coming to prominence: perhaps there are even histories we may have never viewed before that find their way to the front. In the recounting of all these conversations, all these memories, I know that I have drawn a line under my life at sea … and, I think, under my life as a single man! Will I revisit those lives? Will those lives ever revisit me?

I do not know!

And with those questions… and without needing any answers… I realise that this is the point when I can finally say that I have grown into my life!

Imagine:

This is how it ends…

The warm summer night is lit by a pale moon that shines gently through the open window of the little room under the slates. In their bed, they hold each other close: he is dreaming of the rough seas off Cape Town and the stowaway whose life he had saved; she is dreaming too—and stirs in her sleep beneath his out-flung arm. A breeze from the hay fields stirs a few leaves on the beech tree and the curtains.

Outside that window of their little Welsh cottage on a little Welsh hill farm; outside their minds, are the tree-bound stubble fields and the dew damp barley heads bowed before the harvest cut; outside their hearing soft on the wind a distant lowing or a far lamb bleat is lost beneath the dipping moon and the hunting owl's flight call over the hedge rustle or the grass whisper of a field mouse or vole. But the lovers are heedless … are at peace with the sunborn fieldbound world outside their dreams and their loveheld closeheld life. Again, a breeze stirs the Welsh air and the Welsh spirit that now holds them safe—landlocked amongst their studies.

…or begins.

Book III
A Letter from the Dark

Introduction

I suppose it is not very often that a scholar is asked to act as a literary executor.

I have been a publisher, an academic, a minor biographer and an author of any number of scholarly works, but never before have I been an executor of any kind and I realised, if I'm honest, that I scarcely knew what the role involved. It was not something I wanted to turn down—of course I didn't—so I set myself to discover something about the task. A literary executor, I discover, is someone who will look after the deceased writer's literary estate. Well, yes.

In other words, as the Merriam-Webster Dictionary puts it: "a person entrusted with the management of the papers and unpublished works of a deceased author. In other words, a literary executor specifically handles all your literary property, including overseeing your copyrights, contracts with publishers, outstanding royalties, etc." Of course, I knew I could do that; I had publishing experience from both sides of the page, as it were, and I knew about royalties. More to the point, as the poet's life-long friend, I was already pretty intimate with the works involved.

And as a scholar, I knew that I would revel in discovering the early drafts, notebooks and correspondence that lay behind them. In truth, I was already seeing some publications of my own further down the line! But I realised that it would not be simply a case of cataloguing his papers and of arranging their safe storage in some university library vault—of writing up their provenance and histories, I would be managing his posthumous reputation… so not only was it an honour but a huge responsibility. All these thoughts and the poor man wasn't even dead yet!

So I was never going to turn the task down. Obviously. Especially when you consider that I was at that time already working for the poet on a commentary for some future publication of his. And he was an old, old friend! In truth, I was a little shocked that he should even be thinking along such lines—we were the same age—but, literary and academic pride, as well as my personal need to publish something of note, something worthy, pushed that thought aside and of course I wrote back to him by return accepting the role.

Sadly, it was not long after that exchange of correspondence that he died. I hadn't even completed my first editorial task for him, let alone begun commenting on the new poem he had sent me when suddenly there was no one to whom I could comment. It felt as if one side of my world had been ripped away—was missing, and if I turned too fast, it might all be lost to me. I should be tumbling through space unanchored. Lost to the literary world. I could not believe he was gone. He WAS a loss to our little world.

Of course, I went to the funeral and made a fool of myself. I could not accept that there was anyone else grieving for the passing of a great poet... it was just him and me. The absence of him and me. His sons and the family were there, of course, but they were mourning the loss of a father, a loved one, a relative; I...I was mourning the loss of a poet—of a great poet. Perhaps somewhere at the far back of my mind I felt a sense of importance as his (unacknowledged and, if we are honest, unrecognised) literary executor, editor and friend. My God! So many years of friendship, of debate, of love. So many years together! All reduced to clerical research. And to this...loss!

It was probably that moment of despair, as much as anything, that made me so determined to do his memory justice in my work, in my writings. He should not go unremembered! Already there was my work on 'Dark Ashes', which was nearing completion. That would be a first requiem! There would be more! So, eventually, some weeks later—after the will had been read... and I had presented my 'credentials'—the letter signifying my role—to his sons, I began. It was clear that they did not understand the full extent of my responsibilities, nor the fact that, in due course, the entire archive would be stored and catalogued in a university library, most probably the university of which their father was an alumnus, or possibly my own university.

Initially, the work was tedious—I went through the computer disks and their backups listing files and contents first and then moved on to the far more interesting ephemera: the notebooks and letters, the diaries, the printed out drafts of poems with his editorial scribblings on them, and—most valuably, to go with the Excel file of titles, several paper files of all his poems in the order that they had been written... what a gift for an executor and editor! I was several days into the work by now and longed for the time when we could arrange to have the whole lot shipped off to their new home, where my work would be considerably more comfortable than in this dusty loft.

So, it was while I was sorting through that huge accumulation of papers, letters, notebooks and proofs that together made up the physical, and rather dusty archive of my good friend Trystan Lewis that I came across a small leather-bound notebook with my own name inscribed in his elegant hand on the fly leaf. Some readers may know the name Trystan Lewis as he is, or rather was, the poet who wrote the famous 'Elegies of Time', as well as several collections of poems—*Mostly Welsh,* is perhaps the best known.

I had never seen the notebook before and having recorded it in my master spreadsheet—the ever-growing catalogue to the archive—I put it aside to look at more closely later. Lewis passed away quite recently while I was working on a task he had set me—a commentary to one of his longer poems—and it was as a part of the request to me to undertake that task that had made him suggest that I should also act as his literary executor—although I thought it had been clear to me when he made that suggestion he thought it wasn't something that would trouble me for some time to come.

The text which filled every page of the book to bursting was handwritten in the favourite royal blue ink with which Trystan always filled the fountain pen I had given him so many years ago. At a first glance, the text appeared to be an extended letter to me and, it was obvious from the gradual failing of his once careful penmanship (it always amazed me that someone who wrote so much—obviously he typed his manuscripts on a word processor but in his lifetime he filled over a hundred notebooks with his jottings and wrote thousands of letters—someone whose focus was on the word rather than the script could over so many years maintain such a perfect hand) that it must have been written in his last days.

I felt a lump in my throat and I have to confess that I had tears in my eyes for my old friend as I skimmed through the first pages—we had known each other since childhood and for the most part had stayed close during our adult lives but there had been some discord—a minor disagreement that flared into something more—during the last months. The last months before his unexpected death which had left the friction unresolved... or more accurately, for me, still festering. Even his funeral had caused me angst beyond any brought about by his loss.

I felt that I could not read—certainly could not concentrate—on my friend's last words squatting in his son's attic—we had yet to agree on a permanent home for his archive—so I ended my work for the day early, put the book in my briefcase and headed for home. I suppose I should have consulted with his son about its removal but I had recorded it and it was addressed to me so I did not feel any guilt in that omission. In any event I was the archivist!

Driving back to my temporary home in Sussex—I had closed up the cottage in Wales and decamped to lodgings nearer to Lewis's archive so that I could work through his papers and notebooks recording, dating, copying and evaluating everything I found—driving, my mind went back over our long history together. We had grown up as boys in Swansea in South Wales before going our separate ways—Lewis to sea and I moving into publishing after my degree in Cambridge before both of us became writers! I following a mostly scholarly career with many articles and publications to my name while Lewis became a poet—a fact that hardly needs to be recounted here!

One of Lewis's early poems was obliquely autobiographical and some while after he had first published it in his *Mostly Welsh* collection he decided to republish it and asked me to put a scholarly imprimatur on it by writing a commentary to accompany it. Obviously, I was both touched and proud to have been asked and accepted willingly. (It was in his letter to me confirming what he wanted that Lewis also asked me to become his archivist. Looking back now, I do wonder if he knew even then that he was not long for this world.) Much of this will become clear in the reading of Lewis's long letter to me that follows, but I feel that I have to explain our disagreement.

When I sent my final draft of the commentary to Lewis it was the first time he had seen my interpretation of the poem and for some reason I only partly understood he hated what I had done! We had always been so close—shared so much—thought in the same way—his angry outburst shocked me, and I am ashamed to say, its harsh words entrenched my views and made me the more determined to have my commentary published as it stood. Lewis's letter to me—I have copied a part of the first paragraph below—was so outraged that it should have stopped me in my tracks while I reconsidered my text, but it did not!

You have overstepped the mark as my editor! How dare you! It is not the editor's role to insert opinions or to add to the text—even in such a commentary as I asked you to provide. You seem not to have understood the very idea of a commentary—lest that IS the case, allow me to amplify—I was asking you to comment on and explain my poem, 'Dark Ashes'. I was NOT asking you to write a veritable novella around it!

I knew that what I had written was an accurate portrayal of the poem's story. If Lewis was in denial about his own writing, so be it—but we had lived our lives together, sharing thoughts, families and histories and I had used my own careful and scholarly research to ensure accuracy so there was no doubt in my mind that I had 'done a good job' and had produced an accurate portrayal of his lives. The only possible objection that I could allow Lewis was that some of my interpretation had not been—or he did not accept that it had been—explicit in the poem's verses.

All this ran through my head as I drove home. And it was still running through my brain as I made and ate a meagre dinner. I suppose I was troubled that we had parted on bad terms and finding this letter from beyond the grave unsettled me. There was nothing for it—I had to see what Lewis' thoughts had left me. I poured myself a generous single malt—Loughraig is my favourite and I had treated myself to a bottle in my digs—settled in the more comfortable of the two tired armchairs and began to read.

Several hours later I put down the book and smiled—a little tearfully—at my reflection in the mirror on the back of the door. We were friends again! From wherever he was, Trystan had not just forgiven me, had not just accepted my text... had understood and substantiated both my gloss on his life and, in so doing, he had accepted his past. I hope... I am sure that it meant he was at peace when he died. I feel sure that Trystan had intended to mail the book to me rather than leave it for me to find but time got the better of him. A shame, as had it reached me in time, I would have travelled—rushed—down to Sussex to renew and confirm our friendship.

What follows is a reproduction of the text of the leather notebook, complete and unedited. This is exactly what my friend wrote.

The Leather Notebook

I scarcely know how to begin…

Dear Chris,

My doctors tell me that I am approaching—rather faster and sooner than I had hoped—my last days. Other than the vague and unworried suggestion to you in an earlier letter, I have not shared that news with anyone until now—somehow it is a deeply personal thing, this intrusion into my life, this rude and almost abrupt—shocking—discovery of mortality, and I am somewhat at a loss as to how to deal with it. Indeed, the worst, the harshest, truth is that I do not have to—whatever plans I may make, they will be as nothing, come to nothing so far as I am concerned, because I shall not be around to ensure, even to see that they are happening!

My death is not something I have ever contemplated and even when I became ill a month ago, I did not ever consider that it was a subject for review! We are I suppose all far too careless of our lives, as if we expect them to just go on rolling out endlessly in front of us! We know we are getting older, of course, and that is frustrating… our ears, our eyes, our joints remind us… but the stopping of that getting-older process in the only way it can (and will) be stopped is just not comprehensible. We see the world only through our own eyes—I might hazard a guess at your view of my life, or of my son's impression of my past and future, but in my mind I am still thinking of my me, a me with things to do… of all my tomorrows! And—worst of all—I cannot begin to envisage the world that is now around me the moment or the week or the month after my death.

Of course, logic—cold, cruel logic—says that I shall not see it, hear it, sense it or be a part of it… but somehow my mind does not seem capable of seeing a world without me! Life and death conjoined. Like Damien Hirst with his physical impossibility of death in the mind of someone living, I am finding it hard to grasp this simultaneous manifestation of my life and my death.

Not imaging the world without me! That sounds terribly vain! I don't mean it to be! I don't mean that I cannot understand the world *managing* without me— you or my sons managing without me—or without my verses—they will carry forward, at least partly I suppose, thanks to you—it is more chillingly logical than that. If I have died how can I feature in the scenes I am trying and failing to imagine? Even as an observer! Now… now, I can think about tomorrow—or the day after—and visualise myself sitting at my desk or by the fire writing this letter, or drinking tea in the kitchen with my son. I can look in my diary for next week's meetings. But my future—I almost need to write 'my future future…' is getting murkier, more indistinct.

I suppose part of the trouble, the real trouble, is that I cannot imagine you after the event. I hope you will not mourn, be sad, despite our long and close friendship—but curiously *that* is not quite what I mean. I mean that I cannot see you as you move through your world, the world that was our world, I cannot think of you on Wednesday, or on Saturday when you may be… what? I don't know. This week I can make a reasoned guess at you—see you writing or typing, scratching your head, straightening your glasses, thinking, working. But when I have gone, what then? I am saddened by the thought that nothing that you will then do can or will delight me. Or trouble me… which brings me to the crux of the matter.

You will notice that I have stepped back from the habit that began in our childhood and have stopped addressing you as Christo—in my mind, I am seeing this reversion to your real name as a more intimate and a closer, more friendly thing to do… and I want to be friendly and close to you—more so than ever— now, in these last days. The more particularly as I want to lay the ghost of our squabble—an argument for which I take all the blame and that I wish in my deepest imaginings and from the depths of my heart had never happened. Can you ever forgive me? I may, I suppose, excuse it—at least to myself—by suggesting that it may have sprung from my need to hide from my past, my inability to accept it, my distrust of it. Perhaps—I hope—you will understand that. I am sorry for making your life so difficult for you!

What a sad excuse for a writer I am—it seems that I cannot, as I have just said—said at length, for Pete's sake—accept either my past or my future! I have spent all my sorry life trying to describe, explore, write, rhyme the worlds around me quite often in terms of their past or their future possibilities and yet… here I am unable to accept my past or imagine a future! So maybe you and Valentinus are right in that Gnostic assessment: there *are* three kinds of people—the spiritual, psychical and material; but I have not in all my life moved beyond the material: you were wrong to suppose that I had. I have no spiritual understanding!

Perhaps old men—or men in their last days, at any rate—get maudlin. I want to dwell on and in the past here—OUR past—in those days that Dylan Thomas described as a time "when I was young and easy under the apple boughs"—I want to, damn it, I want to reminisce! We had a splendid span between us and I need to relive at least some of it with you. I want to hold you to me… or perhaps, I should be honest and say I want to hold life to me. I am not ready—another echo of Dylan here that I know I do not have to spell out for you—I still have so much to do, to contribute. I am "too proud to die". Is anyone ever ready?

Also, yes, also I want to explore my past (I know, I know… 'now' of all times, when there is so little time!) to try and make sense of the past you uncovered and that hitherto I have refused to accept. I need to play the detective! As Socrates is supposed to have said when contemplating his own death, "The unexamined life is not worth living"! I think he was talking of daily—hourly?—introspection: the Socratic debate rather than an almost-too-late review… it's certainly a bit late for this poet to *learn* anything from his past!

So—perhaps I need to beg your patience, but I hope you will enjoy the journey as much as I and that no further apology will be necessary. Would that we could do this in front of my log fire with a glass or two of wine, together. But I fear the delay that such an arrangement would necessitate! I feel the draught from the grave! I hear the rattle of old Death's bones as he approaches! (Even if I cannot imagine his arrival! Or, more to the point, his later—perhaps momentarily later—departure!)

I am working on this letter—well, not working at it—I mean I am sitting and writing as the thoughts come into my head every hour of the day and night—I don't sleep much these days—that I can manage. You may sense, even hear, the chill urgency in the scrape of my nib, in the scrape of my poor draughtsmanship—my handwriting seems to be deteriorating by the page. There is so much that I want to say! Perhaps I should have resorted to the word processor, but I am comfy here by the fire and the office is distant, upstairs.

So, I have confessed that there is a second reason for this long letter, a reason beyond the repairs to our friendship and the joyful reliving of our times together. Through the writing I am searching my past—searching *for* my past. You will remember that I sent you—along with 'Prometheus Redux'—a map that I had come across amongst some old family papers. I passed it on to you because it seemed in some almost mysterious way to be linked with what I, at that time— up until that moment—was thinking of as the fable you were writing. It was a salutary find that brought me up short and made me think again: discover a revision of my history—histories. Indeed, it and the ring seemed to suggest that you had remembered more of my past than I.

I seem to have blotted it out completely although we must have discussed it! Sometime in the distant past! The not-quite-as-distant past! Perhaps when we were young and innocent... and my mind was untrammelled with more recent, more accepted chronologies. So you will see that in rehearsing all of our time together I am hoping to illuminate my past and discover once again the lost links.

It is so strange! Other than some vague conversations with you around the time I went to sea I have no memory—is that the right word—no recollection of ever having a past life. I cannot find anything familiar in your text—no matter how hard I try and focus on a place or an event, there is just nothing there. Indeed the conversation I am thinking about was only brought about by one of those feelings of déjà vu that everyone has. And of course we got all theoretical and it became about life as an endless cycle, with transmigration or reincarnation or whatever—the idea that some part of a living being, be it the soul or the mind or the consciousness, starts a new life in a different physical body or form after each death … you were more into theology than I and enjoyed the debate, I remember … rather than the specifics of a, of my past life. So this letter will be very much a journey, an exploration of that past which you seem to know better than I! So bear with me! Travel with me!

I am hoping that in scratching away with my pen, rambling to you in this letter, my subconscious may just start me on a path of discovery, writing what my conscious mind has pushed away or buried for so long. I wonder why—I really have no idea, cannot even begin to guess or analyse why—I have so repressed what—according to you—seems an entirely innocent past from so many years ago that it can hardly affect my 'present self'—certainly not to the extent that guilt or horror or whatever might make me bury it deep in some Freudian well!

Of course, we met at the end of summer and at the start of term—how ironically appropriate is that as our first sentence… now! Somehow, amongst the shouting, laughing, thrusting throng of us in the playground we were drawn to

271

each other, almost magnetically—mystically—I remember… and physically too, as the crowd from Year 3 let loose from class for the first time to explore the playground pushed and flowed through the classroom door and pressed us together! I think we both felt the same, almost sexual, charge.

We had both been called on to speak in class, to introduce ourselves to the other boys and girls, and—while I can only speak for myself, I do recall you saying something similar later in the day—we had both recognised in the other a kindred spirit. A reader. A dreamer… an explorer! Perhaps—I think I did—after your too brief and too breathless autobiography, I adjusted my words to mirror your enthusiasms. Where you spoke of reading, I said that I buried myself in a book—oddly you never mentioned poetry… I of course had to go that one step further and was then caught out when the teacher asked my favourite verse; when you said that you dreamed up stories in your head, I think I spoke of capturing my dreams on paper. We both spoke of the sea—you more so than I; of travel… and of myths and fairy tales!

So, in that minute in which our young bodies were squeezed into an embrace, we were not so much embarrassed as elated. Without that moment, that electric frisson, we may never have found the courage to become what we did—and indeed what we remained for most of our lives, effectively if not literally—inseparable friends exploring worlds—worlds within worlds—together. We became almost immediately inseparable: were two halves of a whole: left-right, black-white, the yin and the yang: I suppose I was the creative yang to your quieter but ultimately more controlling yin.

I remember that released from the door-squeeze, cork-like we popped into the playground, looked around almost in distaste amongst the noise and bustle and both—as unconscious mirror images—propped ourselves against the classroom wall to enjoy the sun and find out what it was that had attracted each to the other. I remember when we were called back in to class, the teacher—Mrs Gough, I think it was—said rather pointedly that we had been sent out to exercise and she had expected us to go further than the step! If we were the odd—oddly isolated, oddly self-contained and oddly self-sufficient, at any rate—children of the class, we were unusual children in an unusual school!

Both the preparatory and the grammar school a quarter of a mile down the road were appendages to a religious college that trained missionaries, and whatever else we may have been or hoped to be, it was neither an altar boy nor a proselytiser on some distant mosquito coast! Of course, at that moment, future plans—plans beyond meeting up at the weekend—were very far from our thoughts!

And so, our lives began! Most obviously, school was the hub of our friendship—the place where we spent more time together than with anyone else. I remember other names of course: Duncan who lost his father in a car accident and for whom for some inexplicable reason on his return to school our class was organised to collect for and buy a riding crop, Richard who was always getting into fights, Cheryl with the bright ginger hair, Johnny—curly blond haired Johnny with a sister already in the grammar school—who (before you swapped with him) had sat next to me, and who like Neil and Simon was a border, the pretty and petite Jan with whom—along with Simon and sometimes Neil—we made sure to walk the few hundred yards to her aunt's bungalow as we left school, the shy Shontoo, who joined late in the term—or maybe the next term— and I seem to think was the great grand-daughter of the famous Indian poet, Rabindranath Tagore, and 'Dogger' whose car-driving toy I briefly coveted. Do you remember it—I borrowed it one weekend. But they were simply images painted onto our prep school back cloth! We were the principals!

What else do I remember of those early days of our friendship? We had similar tastes in so many things—we both enjoyed gardening in the little plots at the edge of the playground, although perhaps my interest was greater than yours! All I remember taking home were radishes but we must have grown more! Neither of us was very keen on ball games and I can remember staying on the edge of any games like that—rounders, I remember, was a favourite with the teachers—no one ever explained the rules, we were just expected to know that sort of thing, I think, as a natural consequence of being a child! It was the same with rugby when we got to the grammar school!

But most of our break times were spent planning the next weekend or talking. I do not remember what we talked about at first but as our games focussed on adventures and stories we gradually began making up stories—mostly the writing took place at home and the planning took place in the playground. We must have seemed very stand-offish to the others—I think we were entirely self-contained and almost unaware of the play around us! Of course it turned out that you lived just down the road from me—ridiculous that it took meeting at school to find that out, but my parents didn't really let me go out to play in the street— although, once they had discovered a school friend only a few houses away meeting up at weekends to carry the adventures forward was easy!

We both lived in a quiet avenue on the hill that lead from Swansea Bay to the Gower… I would cycle down on my old bike and we would both cycle around in the road for a bit before retreating to your bedroom to play with some board or pen-and-paper game—Battleships was a favourite—or to start fanaticising about… I remember I had found a stash of wartime American Green Lantern, Superman and Wonder Woman comics that my father must have brought back from the States during the war and—to some extent—these must have influenced our earlier games of make believe… although I don't think we really got into the whole super heroes thing! Just too weird!

My mother was encouraging me to read—I was already well versed with the Secret Seven and the Famous Five and had begun on Biggles even before we came to Swansea and had even read an Agatha Christie novel, but she would read Rider Haggard—*King Solomon's Mines*, *She* and its sequel, *Ayesha*—to me while she ironed. I was never sure how she did both at the same time without burning herself or the clothes but I do remember sitting at the dining room table spellbound behind the smoothly warm piles of sheets and towels, imagining sailing on some quest to Africa or the Orient—magic place names—on the high seas.

I remember that I imagined us mostly alone at the helm and sails of some small vessel or alone hacking a passage through dense jungle in search of some treasure or secret place. Initially I was very much influenced by the 'ironing board stories' I think! When she took me into town shopping we would go to Boot's library where my mother suggested new titles that we could explore together. Later on when I was in the grammar school, I bought some of Rider Haggard's titles in the shop's Olive Classics series so I could re-read the stories for myself. I think I bought about a dozen titles altogether—I even struggled through *Pilgrim's Progress*—although that might have been a present from my aunt!

I don't remember how we came up with the idea of writing our stories down—ultimately writing books, or perhaps booklets would be a better word—but I am sure it came from a need to extend, and so the need to document the complications and intricacies of—the make-believe stories we invented. I also remember that it was around this time that my mother told me that her brother—my second name is his—had created a weekly newspaper during the war with a friend across the road… I have recently donated a small stack of them to the Imperial War Museum and they are mentioned in one of its publications, *Young*

Voices: British Children Remember the Second World War. It's difficult after all this time to remember the trigger, but I suppose all these things came together to push us in that direction.

The first story we made up—as opposed to a game of pretence—the first that we wrote down, I think had to do with smuggling Jan out of her aunt's house after it had been taken over by enemy agents—this was the time of those war-story comics—the War Picture Library, I think, so some of our first stories started with that unfortunate influence. She featured as our heroine in several early stories; of course once we were in the grammar school there were other heroines to choose! But of course our childish attempts at writing were just explorations where we discovered our voices and the huge pleasure of writing, of communicating.

It may sound as if we spent all our young lives in some kind of whirlwind of creativity—not so! That imaginative world was a constant backdrop to all the other fun we had! We would come back to it several times a day when we had a good story running, and then somehow, in between homework and all the other day-to-day activities—the chores and eternal tidying of bedrooms at home, school and homework, and hobbies such as my stamp collecting (both parents collected stamps so that hobby was inevitable; I still remember the orange *Stanley Gibbons Stamp Catalogue* and the Bridgwater Stamp Club that sent out monthly lists of stamps for sale so that I spent much of my pocket money), we would manage to write the best bits up as little stories.

I suppose the half-hour walk to and from school gave us plenty of time each day to take the current story forward, to extend the plot. On fine days you will remember that we would walk home—I don't think we were meant to—through the local rhododendron gardens, their little paths leading from the main drive, under the huge trunks with their peeling bark, we could not but help shuffle through the huge furry-backed leaves on the way to the middle gate opposite our road. And one path led past a tiny folly—a small round turret with a castellated top reached by a spiral stairway that ran once around its outside—which had to be climbed.

When it was built, it probably gave a view over the bay, but the plants had grown so tall now that it served no useful purpose. Other than to feed our imagination, of course. Naturally school itself took up most of our time—somehow we ended up in the same class throughout our time at school so we were almost never parted!

I wonder what you remember of school, the teachers and the teaching! When we moved up to the secondary school—conveniently nearer home and nearer to the village and the beach—we were suddenly in a larger—both in geography and population—space and, I know that I at least, found the move difficult and my work suffered. The remote figure of the headmaster—a Dr Priddy—was never seen other than at morning prayers and our education was left to a ragbag of other teachers. Looking back on it—and you will remember the poem, of course—I never felt that any of the teachers inspired me to learn:

I was taught in Wales
In Swansea's English Grammar
But little learned of little taught
And left in search of glamour

I have often wonder if some of them were trained teachers at all! I am so envious of some of my friends who had inspirational schooling with teachers that led them to extend their thinking and to read beyond the curriculum. I don't believe I ever did more than the minimum required of me! I wasn't lazy—it just never occurred to me and no one ever suggested reading around the subject. I liked Miss Sherwood—she was strict—but she made Latin interesting, and Miss Rose who taught us Maths—somehow I was quite good at that, often finishing class exercises first and getting the sums and the workings right!

Of course, I was banned from choir lessons after a few weeks and sent outside—along with Mickey Williams—to lose myself around the school until those who could sing had finished the lesson! Miss Fitzherbert taught us French and the irascible Don Pavey who tried to control the class and teach us geography. Who was it that unspooled a reel of cotton passing it from one person to another in the geography room in between the table legs to trip him up as he paced around in his usual way? Who else do I remember?

Miss Rush in the art room, several woodwork teachers—they seemed to come and go, and who could blame them—Mr Roche who taught science was quite good, I think I learned a lot from him! I really think the most interesting times were in the little printing press with Mr Crane after school!

I suppose it was because we were so self-contained—the two of us—that we never really got to know the others in our class well. I remember the names—Prosser, Mellalieu, Saliot, Rice, Jones (several times), Edwards, Clark, Hodder,

Abba… Do you remember John Abba? I was friends with him briefly just before he left—I think his father was an army chaplain or something—he was unhealthily interested in guns and arms and had somehow acquired a couple of side arms and a few old Lee Enfield rifles, complete with bayonets and for a few weeks that all seemed quite interesting!

Interesting enough that—to my parents' evident surprise—I once took home one of the smaller guns and showed it to them! They would have been even more worried if they had known that halfway home, I had been unable to resist taking it out of my shoulder bag to look at! Can you imagine! I think, somehow, the military atmosphere was very familiar to me and handling the bayonets seemed quite natural, although somehow they were shorter and straighter than I had expected.

I don't remember—and you didn't manage to shed any light on it—whether I had that sort of training in some sort of military unit or in the nautical academy before I was sent abroad by my father. And there was the rebel of the class, who was always getting into trouble. I remembered him into a poem too!

Old School
The way the pink-flecked skin peeled from the flesh
and the taste of the drink from between the nodals
on a stem of Japanese Knotweed in the playground
was far more real—and left a lasting impression

the time stolen in the lab before the master arrived
stretching glass rods in a Bunsen's flame—
they are better remembered
than any lesson

the summer English class under the large tree,
reading Dickens or Shakespeare in the heat
did not make in me a love of literature
but of the dappled sun.

The girls we scarcely knew who sat on the other side
of the room and had their own playground—
some of their faces have stayed in my mind—
are all trapped in the clockwork school photo rolled up

in a drawer somewhere

and the boys whose time I shared between classes
on the playing field or the waste ground that was our space—
it is all remembered—like my leather satchel,
the grey fountain pen, the initials in the old oak desks
and Kenneth Watkins' finger

shortened one night when he tried to improve on a firework.

And around all that, our life went on! We swam, we fished, we did all the other things—or most of them—that other boys of our age did: we made plastic models of fighter planes, I collected stamps, we fished off the pier, we dug bait in the bay when the tide was out, and when it was in we swam again. There was just one breakwater—when the tide came in over the miles of muddy sand where the lugworms lived—just the one that somehow had a small pool beside it that was deep enough for a proper swim.

The water would be brownish and warm from its long shallow flow over the sands and the small pool was only about chest deep before the sea became shallow again but it was ideal for a quick swim... often under the eyes of the passengers passing on the electric tram that ran all-round the bay to the pier. I worked in the local nursery—either in the work room wiring flowers for wreaths or in the gardens with the two workers. I remember them so well—one was a retired miner who had won on the pools and didn't need to work—he had a cyst on the back of his hand which fascinated me; and the other older man was a professional gardener who taught me everything from how to saw wood with a two-man saw to how to plant shrubs!

He was a dour old man that most of us kids were in awe of, almost scared of, but he took me under his wing and I liked him well enough. He always came to work in an old blue suit, complete with waistcoat worn over a collarless shirt, and a flat cap. If it was raining he would string an old hessian sack over his shoulders. He lived in a cottage at the far end of the nurseries, which in their heyday ran along behind the whole length of the village—he took me there once at the end of a Saturday morning when we were working at that end to meet his wife.

What I remember most about the visit was that he cleaned his spade and fork on a sack and took them into the cottage to hang up to dry on the wall over the fire! In my mind now, it seems as if that was in their sitting room! I wrote a poem about him too! I took you to the nurseries a couple of time. I think I had a hope that you would like the place and come to work there too, but it was one thing— I think the only thing—that we differed on! So, yes, around all that, we floated through life on the edge of our families.

And in those long hot childhood summers, we spent a lot of time on beaches—although it usually required parents to get us to the better swimming and surfing beaches that were further from home. We loved swimming and surfing—some of the bays often had decent waves for a body board or at high tide we would swim from the rocks. I preferred the sand and the surf, but there was something very familiar—as if I had spent years swimming off rocks—about high tides.

Strangely, *my* rocks—the rocks in my memory—led me into much warmer water! And always, I seemed to be swimming beneath the walls of a castle... and then I would look up and it was just the rocky shore and the cliffs! When we were a little older, we would sometimes cycle out onto the peninsula to the better bays—with no surfboards we learned to body surf without them! Looking back now at our early teens, it is surprising that girls did not feature more... somehow they did not—I think we were so self-absorbed that we didn't notice their lack! And I was a bit shy. And again, in my mind, I felt I had always been that way, I knew that I would have to be much older before I fell in love!

Of course, you will remember we talked about girls—mostly the girls at school that had caught our eye, but who remained segregated and seemingly aloof on the other side of the classroom and in their own playground. I wonder what we talked about! Did we fantasise about asking them out? Did we dare to think of a kiss? It could have led to our first quarrel for I think we both liked the same girl! I wonder if you remember her! We probably just lay there, soaking up the sun after half an hour or so surfing with unformed, and certainly unrealised, ideas about being on a beach beside her—well beside two of her, I suppose— while we dried off and our salt-caked hair dried in a tangle until one of us leapt up shaking sand and dried salt crystals over the other and raced for the waves again.

I think Pobbles Bay by the golf club was our favourite beach but the bus would also take us to Heatherslade with its narrow bramble- and gorse-edged path down from the cliff tops, a good beach if the tide was out; and then there was the little cove near the stony beach of Pwll-Du which we christened with a Norwegian name, Soltun, which it turned out should have been Solstrand (for sunny beach) but we never changed the name—swimming off the rocks if the tide was in or on a private sandy beach if it was out!

We used the more popular beaches sometimes if we wanted company or were playing tennis at Langland, and there was always the warm muddy water behind the breakwater of the town bay if we were in a hurry! I remember taking my sister there once—I suppose she would have been seven or eight—and when I gave the word to cross the main road coming home she ran straight across instead of stopping on the island as I had intended. I never knew how she got away with it! I probably shouted at her afterwards!

We talked about, shared, everything; you can probably still remember our rambling conversations about nothing in particular—you must do, certainly better than I! But of course I knew of your love of literature and your wish to go to Cambridge and work in publishing, and you knew of my interest in the sea. I do not really remember where the idea of *going* to sea—as a career—came from and looking back on my life then, I wonder why I didn't end up in horticulture!

Of course, the sea was in the family blood: in my mother's family tree, the oldest member she had traced had gone down on a man o' war—the Sterling Castle—on the Goodwin Sands in the great storm of 1703, more recently uncles and second cousins had been at sea, my father had been at sea in the war—and one of the cousins was still Commodore of a shipping company's fleet. And, then your father got wind of my interest and sometimes took me down to the docks with him to look at ships he was surveying—I had been under a ship before I had been on one!

And if the huge vessels in our dry docks were alien to me, something in the salt and tar atmosphere of the port, the cleaning of ship's hulls, the ropes and bollards, the cranes, the wharves and cargoes, the bustle and confusion of departure, the jetty at the harbour mouth with its flashing beacon, the heady feeling of leaving a secure berth and sailing into the unknown as I watched a ship unmoor, take tugs and manoeuvre out into the bay letting go the tug lines, the whole maritime mystery made life at sea seem somehow my destiny: pre-ordained! Familiar! I could almost see myself as a part of that naval history—not simply a minor continuance of it but within it, already a part of it, under sail on my own ship. No wonder I ended up at sea!

And so I left to plunge into my life as a Merchant Navy cadet and then officer while you went on for a couple more years at school before going to Cambridge... so the school can't have been all that bad I suppose! But our parting was almost as harsh as the sudden ripping from home comforts—the bosom of my family—into the unfamiliarity of my first time away from home and the cadet ship! Looking back on it from this vast distance, I remember how home sick I was and how unfamiliar the whole environment was—although being at sea was also strangely familiar. I am sure I wrote to you at the time—of course I did, it was one of the letters you included in your magnificent edition of 'Dark Ashes'—of the feeling of déjà vu. It was very odd! Looking back to that time now I can almost bring back that feeling... but no more now than then can I discover the source of that feeling!

So there I was. For ten whole years! Of course, we got together whenever we could when I was on leave—especially the longer shore leaves when I was taking my Board of Trade exams that turned me from cadet to deck officer, and you probably have a whole file of our correspondence from overseas—somewhere, your letters to me still exist. As you know, the first few trips were not easy... but I settled in well enough in the end although I never felt entirely 'one of the crowd'... I was shy and couldn't bring myself to take part in the casual liaisons overseas. I'm sure everyone thought I was a little reserved—or maybe they just recognised my shyness!

Of course, here I am looking back on it from half a century later... it probably wasn't as bad as I imagined! I know I often went ashore with one of the other lads that joined with me—Roger—and we joined the same ship together when we left the training ship and became good friends. Always, too, I moved at the same time in an invisible personal world where some past recollections would always be floating around me. Almost every task I did was somehow familiar!

Some places! I remember once—probably the first trip we went out through the Suez Canal—feeling that I really seemed to know or have some close affinity with the Mediterranean, and then somewhere south of Sicily I thought I saw this unusual little sailing vessel heading west in a patch of fog that seemed to be moving with it. It was very strange... but incredibly real. I was working on deck alone so I never knew if anyone else saw it pass along our port side. What if that was me nearly meeting my past life? That past life you have drawn out so well from my poem—was that the lovers fleeing their island? Is such a think possible? Do you remember me telling you that story when we next met?

I did five trips on the Otaio slowly graduating from the mundane life of a deck hand—painting, cleaning, greasing, deck scrubbing and keeping lookout or steering the ship on watch—to under-studying the bridge officer, using charts and maintaining our course, using a sextant to take sights and find our position, taking shore bearings with the compass—all those tasks that would be my future life! All those tasks that were so familiar!

And then there was an unremarkable time—some years—when I simply lived the life that had seemed my destiny: I became a deck officer in the merchant navy and for every twenty-four hours at sea, eight of them were in my charge. I kept watches, navigated, plotted courses, wound chronometers, corrected charts and pilot books, checked cargo as it was loaded or unloaded... all those varied but mundane jobs that were involved in getting a ship from home ports to the Australian and New Zealand coasts and back again!

But you have heard me talk about that time before! You will remember that I was in an odd frame of mind then... I suppose I was both content with my life and discontented, enjoying the travel and the work but miserable at my inability to find companionship. Lonely. Perhaps, even when you were around! Until I found female companionship!

Our affair began with two summer weeks—the first weeks of a long leave—followed by another hot week in Cornwall, and by the time that had passed the rest was inevitable! After a couple of days, the rest of the world did not stand much chance! I think—actually, I am completely certain—it was as I knelt beside her on a Gower beach that we knew our future.

I remember saying to her—something that almost brought our fairy tale crashing down—that it was strange how all my meetings with women involved sand. I spoke the words and had no idea where they came from—what they even meant! She was my first! The only way out was to describe a recurrent dream—which viewed from this distant vantage point—I can see must have been linked with the island on the map. The story seemed to calm her jealousy. Hah! had she only known! Even writing 'Dark Ashes' I remember the dream with a struggle! When there is something you have never remembered before—an island, a lake, a castle... I don't know, the mind plays tricks on us! I thought I was writing of a courtship interrupted by my travelling back from Brighton to Cardiff every Monday for my studies towards my Master's Ticket, but now I understand it was a very long time ago:

Life spun:
to the west the profane skills of the sea held him;
at each easting his very being was uplifted by her:
  she was his guru
  his sun.

But after that nearly disastrous first sentence—and my seemingly absurd explanation—our declarations of love cemented our future. There was no going back now! You will remember how very much against the union were my parents—it meant that my life became very difficult for several years—even after we were married, as K. wanted nothing to do with them. So we had a difficult two years! Idyllic and wonderful… but difficult. You were a godsend—someone remote from the tension to whom I could talk—and you supported me! Gloriously! Do you remember rescuing K. from Tilbury? That was a 'Cruel Parting after Such Passion'!

My God, I owed love to you for that! She told me afterwards how kind you had been on the long drive back to her aunt's house. Do you remember meeting me for a pint one evening when I was at my lowest—about to sail away for two months, to leave her for two months, when I could see no future knowing how she struggled in my absence! After all those years at sea I knew how other wives suffered when their husbands left—much easier, as I said in a poem once, to leave than be left behind. I worried for K. It may have been the drink—I don't think so—but I returned to my ship happier and more resolved to make things work. And I knew you would look out for K. It was still two lonely months but now I could look beyond them. Always.

I think that was the trip when I was sailing with a new Master—a Master whose reputation went before him—and before we had even left port, wanting to discuss our courses, he came down to my cabin, walking straight in and then straight into the bathroom to find me sitting naked in the bath under the running shower wearing a dirty oilskin coat! At least it stopped him in his tracks and silenced him for a moment—until he realised I was simply scrubbing the oil off it. But I could see an edited version of the story going round the fleet—in days if not in minutes! I would be the second mate so drunk, he… I would be the second mate who showered in oilskins. Surprisingly, I got away with it, and went on to get on pretty well with that Captain who had such a fiery reputation!

And then we were married—sorry my old friend, not you and I (not even, that Captain and I!) but my only love and I. It may have always seemed inevitable to you, I may have been dreaming about it for all of my last trip, but I had some hurdles to overcome at home. And when I had left my last ship I hadn't supposed that dream could ever work! Then one afternoon we went for a drive and a walk in Stanmer Park in Brighton and I found myself suggesting marriage—it was a very poor sort of proposal—it just popped out as a sort of logical conclusion! But I was forgiven for that!

K. was at the end of her first year at University and could take a year off, which would mean she could come to sea with me, and so why didn't we! We fixed it all up in that single leave—K. spoke to her university, I spoke to my personnel office, the banns were read, arrangements made, invitations sent, the wedding, the reception, a honeymoon in Devon... and then straight back to sea together! And we were lucky; unusually, the company let K. do three trips running as she would be back at University and unable to do trips for the following two years.

Also inevitable—and probably foreseen by you—was my departure from the sea! After a year during which we had scarcely been apart, sailing away was even harder and I spent every spare moment—every moment when I was not focussed on navigation or cargo—dreaming of leaving the sea: dreaming, uncertain of the future, determined, planning, and finally writing a letter of resignation. But I never breathed a word to K.—never even hinted.

I don't remember, but she probably didn't know that my initial contract had only been for three years... or indeed, that the three years were nearly complete. We were never entirely certain which day we would be able to go on leave after our replacement arrived, so it was a complete surprise when I arrived home one sunny afternoon. And it didn't take long for the momentous news to escape my lips!

She held him close and at arm's length, examined his smile
Understood his passion:
    he would never leave; the sea had let him go.

And we were so happy in Wales! We never moved from that little cottage that we had loved from the moment we first saw it. It was a decision we both agreed: that it was the place to bring up our children. And in the fullness of time, of course, we did! Although looking back on it all, I wonder if they would have liked the excitement of the city more! Of course, you know all this, I'm just rambling and reminiscing! But the history that you uncovered that suggests my earlier self had lived somewhere in mid-Wales too is so strange—I wonder if that is what made me feel so at home there! It probably is. What a romantic idea!

I would be there still but for my health… and I am unbelievably sad to think that I shall never see my little cottage again: my little garden walled with those pointed stones from the roof of the old mansion of Hafod (see several poems! I think the one I liked most was 'Uchtryd's Summer Place'—although that does not mention the stones.) Again those thoughts with which I began: the incomprehensibility of death in the mind of someone living! All those places I love—all those corners of my garden, my beech trees, all those mountains and valleys, 'Llyfnant', for instance—I see them in my mind as if I would pass their way again; I don't see them as a fading memory. I suppose that at least is something to be thankful for! But I still mourn my past. And as I wrote that last sentence I suddenly realised—it was my transformative moment—my Damascene moment—the revelation that in a hundred years, or two hundred, a new me would pass that way and this same spirit will pass to him. This same love.

And so, peace.

And so, my sons were born—over a spread of eight years, which meant that my youngest was still quite young when his mother—my beloved K. left us. Oh those years were difficult. My hair turned white. But I am so proud—she would be proud—of them all! They survived, although in some ways that is the least of it! Survival… what I should say is that they have moved on: never forgetting, not that, they just progressed, triumphed in life. And—in turn—I have grand children to be proud of. Life somehow goes on.

And since the youngest left home all those years ago—right up until a few months ago—I lived in my little cottage alone—I suppose I am seen as a lonely soul, a poet, a writer, a recluse, but I have been happy in my way. Perhaps I dwelt too much in the past—*you* might say I didn't dig deep enough!

And now I find myself returned from that lovely Welsh writer's retreat, my cottage in the mountains, to the ancestral home in Sussex to be near—in my last days and hours—those sons… and here I sit in front of a log fire, looking out over the English Channel when the darkness and the weather allow.

And so we get to the point in my narrative—our reminiscence—when I asked you to work on 'Dark Ashes' and then, some months later when I knew I was ill, on 'Prometheus Redux'. So I was still writing but at the same time I was researching—as well as I was able—in my family archive. You will remember that with Redux poem I sent you a package of a map and a ring that I had found... and which you did not open for some weeks or months. But I was still trying to get to the bottom of the history you had unravelled. I was digging! Although I suppose you did not—could not have—know that.

There was a writing slope in my possession for as long as I can remember which got damaged in one of those little floods that the cottage was prone to in the early days. You remember the spring that—after heavy rain—somehow rose under an internal wall and flowed across the lounge, under a wall and out the garden door? A problem, I suppose, that houses without foundations may be prone to! That flood! I only discovered the damage a year later as I had supposed the box was on too high a shelf to have got damp—I was so disgusted at my lack of care that it was put in the loft and forgotten until a few months ago when—in a fit of craftsmanship—I took it down and repaired the veneer and, inevitably found the map and ring that had lain in its hidden drawer all these years.

You can imagine perhaps, my shock and subsequent struggle to remember its history. To remember anything! I could not believe that I had found this so soon after you had uncovered for me the history to which it belonged! So soon after you had described the ring. And the island. It had been passed down to me through the family of course, and I had never thought much about it nor realised its age. It has a cipher of initials on the lid and I had thought it was empty until, a rattle as I turned it over, and I discovered the little drawer under the pen tray. How I searched my mind—and all the family papers—for a clue!

I hope you are still reading this letter, because it is about to get even more interesting. Here is my last gift to you. For which you may thank the eagle eyes of my son who spotted only yesterday the fact that the base inside is half an inch higher than the base outside! It took me some time to find a way into this second secret compartment. And then... Ah! And then. This deserves a new paragraph! A new page!

Perhaps I should begin with the cipher on the lid as it is about to become important!

I had not paid it much heed until we found the second compartment... and a very old oilcloth-wrapped parcel bound with a light cord with sealing wax on the knot. There was a handwritten note fading beside the knot: "To be opened when you are together again". Inside—amazingly still intact—was a letter headed with that same cipher! It has suddenly come to me that as your text dealt with a story within a story and an island within an island... now we have a letter within a letter! As nearly as I can tell—my language skills are famously poor—the letter beneath the cipher topped with its royal crown might be rendered in English as:

My Dearest Daughter. My dear, lovely Yseult
My wife and I weep every day knowing how little we saw of you, how we were never able to get to know you, and that we will never see you again! But we are happy knowing the love you share with our son.
And I am so pleased to have this one last chance to speak to you—our last meeting still grieves me more than I can say. At least my son has explained to you the reasons, not the least of which was my certain knowledge that if I acknowledged you, if there was even a whisper of who you were, spies would have carried that news to the husband to whom you were promised....
You will never know—I hope—how painful that day was—how my wife broke down weeping as soon as the court had cleared—for, after T. stormed out in your wake, the noblemen left quietly and the servants withdrew to offer us some privacy. And I was little able to comfort her—she understood, of course, why I had acted as I did, but I thought she would never forgive me. She did of course—she was a wonderful consort.
I know T. will have told you of my part in your very early life and I hope you will have understood my actions and forgiven me. All those years ago

just before you were born I had spent some months in discussions with Kanunî Sultan Suleiman in order to bring peace to our countries. They were hard, difficult months—too long spent in Saranda and too little time at home with my wife although—blessedly, she and T.'s older brother were with me at the signing—and it was with great relief that I signed my name to a treaty a couple of days after you—daughter to the Sultan's first minister—were born.

Your father was a great favourite with the old Sultan and his most senior advisor so when Suleiman suggested that his young son should be betrothed to you—the baby daughter he had just met—your father was both proud and pleased. To be honest, it would have been impossible for him to refuse but I saw the pleasure he felt at the honour. Your father and I had become good friends during the negotiations so it was not surprising—particularly in the light of his daughter's importance to the court—that he asked me to take part in your naming ceremony.

While I was privately appalled at the political wedding planned for such a tiny baby, there was little I could say. Your father must have guessed something of my unease—perhaps it was even what caused him to flee the country to save you so soon afterwards—you must have been about two years old, I think; it was certainly what brought him north to my territories. And thank the gods that he brought his friend and aide, your Uncle Iski with him. I knew it was ill advised to return and beg the Sultan to release him from his bond but I could never have guessed how severe his punishment would be. I think you were only four years old when he travelled away from Mljet leaving you in the care of your uncle. Only four when he and your mother were executed by the Sultan. Word did not reach me immediately—when it did perhaps I should have sailed South but what good would war have done? It was better to keep you safe so I could not reveal what I knew. Can you ever forgive me?

My dear daughter, live in peace and prosper in your new home. I so long to hear that you are happy, that you have children... your news, but I know it can never be. My son—your brave husband—must not make this long and perilous journey again. There are too many hazards both at sea and here. You both have a new life in your new country. I wish you love, happiness and prosperity. My wife and I—your parents—pray for you.

It was signed with a scrawl that could have begun with an M but ended with a distinct and separate flourish of an 'R'. Suddenly, I was trying to remember Zetan kings. The initials from the cipher. Names flashed before my eyes and echoed in my ears... Miloš, the hero who had something to do with an Ottoman sultan; Hrvoje, a patronym meaning simply from the country of my birth (how did, how could I be even thinking that?) and Bunić one of the great noble families with several poets numbered in its family tree—where have I heard them before? Where did this knowledge come from? Why do they suddenly mean something to me now? What has awakened these deeply buried memories? Why had I repressed this knowledge for so long? I need more time, but alas, you are my time, old friend!

A word of caution here—the letter is understandably fragile. If you know a conservator who could stabilise it, I should be forever... I should be even more in your debt, my friend. For now it is safe in the box.

And I am so desperately sad! The joy of discovery and of validating your work is at once and irremediably dashed with the thought that Yseult can never have read the letter that would have meant so much to her. It is so sad. For both of them. That oilcloth-wrapped box that travelled all the way from Zeta with the prince after his last meeting with his father had not fulfilled its role—had simply been a gift from the king to his daughter-in-law. Its heartfelt expressions of paternal love undiscovered. So sad!

Also in the box—in the open part—a couple of things I must have seen before but not heeded: an old pamphlet on bee keeping, and what I now realise is an old diary or ship's log—they are both amongst my papers so you will find them and no doubt the latter will verify and provide some timings for your story of at least one of the long sea journeys. Now, I am excited, my mind already in research mode—would there be port papers in the National Library of Wales? Or deeds for the cottage?

Chris—you have much to go through in my archive of papers and my various computer drives... but my sons have the family archive—that until now has been in my care—to make some sense of. It has become apparent that my literary and family archives are inextricably linked! Perhaps—I hope they do—they will call on you for help. They should do I suppose as—as we can see and they should— there is an overlap between my, and my family's, papers and my literary archive. (I appear to have fallen into a 'preaching to the converted' mode!) Perhaps you should interrogate the boys—have you found anything from...? to do with...? I know I do not need to teach you research skills, old friend! But keep an eye on the lads.

Ah, but I am tired! It is late into the night and the fire is reduced to glowing logs. Out of the window I can see the periodic sweep of the lighthouse across the low sky hazed by the Channel fog. Not enough for its horn to disturb me, thank goodness. I still remember vividly on my first trip to sea—as watch standby—taking tea and toast up to the bridge. As junior cadets we were not supposed to go up through the officers' accommodation but had to go outside and just as I was climbing the last steps to the bridge wing, the foghorn sounded. That close, it was like a physical blow—I had never heard anything so loud—or sudden, and am amazed that I didn't drop the tray of mugs! I don't remember, perhaps I did!

So how should I end? Before I end? Before my end?

My last words to you are of love, of course. And I want to repeat my apology for making your life so difficult as you worked on 'Dark Ashes'. After all we have shared it was unforgiveable... although I hope you have—or will. I am so happy that you overcame everything, that you persevered, that you made sense of my silly poem, that you made sense of me!

AND I am happy to have been able—just—to share these pieces of the puzzle. I wonder what you will do with them!

And so to the last lines—the lines that as a child we ended our Christmas thank-you letters with—With love from... But you know that! Au revoir, old friend! Until our future selves look at each other, scratch our heads and say, "Don't I know you from somewhere?"

I wonder where we shall be. And who will record our new lives!

I w—

As I read my friend's last words, I confess that I wept. I imagined him sitting there, perhaps a little chilled, his book—this book—in his lap, as it was in mine now—and his hand dropped beside it, as he thought of his next suggestion that would tie us still closer together. As if he needed to cement our love any closer! I too remember the good times we shared, remembering how many years our friendship has covered and all the times we had together—the discussions, the arguments, the fun! How could I not? From those early days of our childhood... so many years, so much love.

I know I shall miss my old friend, the poet.

Envoi

So, we are here, at the end of everything.

Our souls have come together and we are united again. My lives have been laid bare and I rise from this world, from my personal vale of Hinnom. For this is the time of Janus:

There is no one to feel his tears, there is no one
to see his footprints.
There is no life here now.

Void of movement, time does not pass. It is
as though he sleeps…

                                        …and wakes.
And waking, sees the ocean flowing past
his feet: suddenly, he knows a future beyond the moment,
and feels his past drop below the horizon on which
he stands…

from: The Fourth Elegy of Time

Alone at the resolution of my lives, alone in an empty cottage, shriven of my past, I celebrate our anabasis: our journey away from the sea, our expedition into my interior selves. Like the throbbing of a single string, a second melody has finally risen over the first for me to hear. It is sufficient. Unto my night.

Now, all that is left of me is this "hard corpus of a permanent ghost"—if I may borrow Kamel Daoud's description of a manuscript.

This is how it ends.

Like a bird on a wire.

"And through the chant a second melody / Rose like the throbbing of a single string:" comes from Longfellow's The Sicilian's Tale; King Robert of Sicily